PENGUIN BOOKS

The Daisy Chain

Alexandra Campbell has written two other novels, *The Office Party* and *The Ex-Girlfriend*, both published by Penguin, as well as two books on interiors co-written with Liz Bauwens, *Spaces for Living* and *Country in the City*. She lives in South London with her husband, David, and twins, Freddie and Rosalind.

ALEXANDRA CAMPBELL

THE DAISY CHAIN

PENGUIN BOOKS

PENGUIN BOOKS

Published by the Penguin Group
Penguin Books Ltd, 80 Strand, London WC2R 0RL, England
Penguin Putnam Inc., 375 Hudson Street, New York, New York 10014, USA
Penguin Books Australia Ltd, Ringwood, Victoria, Australia
Penguin Books Canada Ltd, 10 Alcorn Avenue, Toronto, Ontario, Canada M4V 3B2
Penguin Books India (P) Ltd, 11 Community Centre, Panchsheel Park, New Delhi – 110 017, India
Penguin Books (NZ) Ltd, Cnr Rosedale and Airborne Roads, Albany, Auckland, New Zealand
Penguin Books (South Africa) (Pty) Ltd, 24 Sturdee Avenue, Rosebank 2196 South Africa

Penguin Books Ltd, Registered Offices: 80 Strand, London WC2R 0RL, England

www.penguin.com

First published 2001

3

Set in Monotype Garamond
Printed in England by Clays Ltd, St Ives plc

To David, Freddie and Rosalind
and
Hilary, Richard and Hannah Talbot

Prologue

As I stepped out of the sunlight and into the cool stone shadows of the church, I saw Stephen and Max together at the altar, silhouetted in the speckled light of the stained-glass window. Max placed his hand on Stephen's shoulder, and, as their heads bent together briefly, I had a split second of clarity and panic. I wondered if I was marrying the wrong one.

Max and Stephen always set each other off, as dark and light, elusive and strong, introspective and straightforward, leader and follower, and I never really knew either of them properly until it was almost too late.

I

I met Max and Stephen on the same night, at the history department Friday Disco, in a place known as Hell's Basement, a dark, sweaty cellar with strobe lights and pounding rock music. Max bought drinks for the friends I was with. He had black, shoulder-length hair and a powerful face with dark eyes that swept restlessly over the tiny cavern, looking for something. Not my type. Too intense, I thought. He handed me a flat, warm cider that tasted of bathwater, and we circled each other warily, exchanging all the old questions that everyone asks to propel themselves through the first few weeks of university life.

'I'm at the Art College too,' I told him, on hearing that he was in my department, feeling that politeness obliged me to add: 'Where do you come from?'

It was the first time I saw that crooked, ironic smile. 'Nowhere. Almost anywhere.'

I refused to be impressed. Everyone was trying to out-cool everyone else at that stage, and anyway my eyes, like every other girl's in Hell's Basement, were already straying towards the tall, blond man standing like a Viking on his right. I turned, fractionally, away from Max and towards him. If Max couldn't be bothered to answer sensibly, that was his problem. Arrogant creep.

'I'm Stephen Everett,' shouted the blond Viking. 'Dance?'

'Excuse me,' I yelled at Max as Mud's 'Tiger Feet' stomped into its final, deafening crescendo. 'See you around.'

If I'd known about Max and Stephen then, I might have been a little more careful.

Max slapped his tray down next to mine in the Art College canteen a few days later.

'Oh, hi.' It took me a few moments to remember who he was.

'I'm sorry if I was rude.' He launched straight into the conversation as if there hadn't been a gap of several days since our first meeting.

I must have looked insufficiently surprised because he added, 'My father was Polish, and got out at the beginning of the War. He fought alongside the British, but never went back because the Russians took our land. Eventually he married my mother, who is Hungarian, after her family escaped from the Communists, too, in the early 1950s. I was born in England, which makes me British, but my mother has since married another Hungarian and now lives in the United States. It's very complicated to explain, so I simply try to shorten it. Like my name. We used to be called Galinski, but my father changed it to Galliard.'

'Oh.' I wasn't quite sure what to reply to this. We were all having to adjust to meeting people whose backgrounds seemed exotically different to our own, but everyone else I'd met seemed to come from places like

Manchester or Southend, or, if they were smart, Wiltshire and Hampshire. I came from Birchington, in Kent, a quiet 1950s seaside resort where very little happened. 'So do you live with your father or your mother?'

'My father's dead. He died of a heart attack when I was four. Most of his family were killed in the War, and he lost touch with the rest. If there are any Polish cousins or aunts or uncles left, I wouldn't know how to find them. I don't even speak Polish, and I live here.'

'Here?' I couldn't conceive of a student living 'here'. Everyone had somewhere else where they returned, like homing pigeons, for a square meal, clean laundry and a sense of reassurance.

I saw a flash of vulnerability in his eyes. 'Come and see.'

Over the next few months I discovered that Max Galliard was considered one of the most talented of our year group. He was tipped for brilliance, predicted as Britain's answer to Warhol or a male Frink. He gazed moodily out of black-and-white photographs with his abundant curling dark hair and the face of a Renaissance angel, illustrating articles called 'New Talent'.

Only I seemed to see a vulnerable boy, hardly out of school, his family dead or scattered around the world, alone in a grand but almost empty room.

But I couldn't help being impressed – even slightly overawed by Max – which was extremely bad for him, me and our relationship. I don't think it was his wealth; I never gave money a thought except when my grant ran out and I had to search through my pockets, on the floor and under the bed for lost pennies. Everyone had the same amount of money, you see, at universities in those days – when grants covered everything – although it was clear that Max had slightly more. All I knew about money was what my father had taught me, and, because he worked in a bank, he believed it was important. It was, of course, but not as important as love. Like every other little girl I knew, I was brought up to believe that if you found True Love, then everything else would fall into place. Prince Charming, after all, always has a castle.

Max's castle was a high-ceilinged room with elaborate cornicework, dusty floor-length windows overlooking a wrought iron balcony, and a crumbling marble fireplace. It was almost completely empty, except for a Victorian terrarium he used as a giant hookah, several bean bags and a massive waterbed. He hung his own dark, experimental paintings on the walls. He occasionally had black moods, when he would lie on the bed all day, smoking and staring at the ceiling.

Perhaps it was his easy familiarity with love and passion that overwhelmed me. Used to the fumbling and grunting of adolescent boys, the choking tang of their sweaty feet, the incoherent, almost gnomic utterances, and their total lack of connection with their own bodies let alone mine, Max was a revelation to me. We fitted together as if we had been made for each other, although I did sometimes wonder whether this proficiency might be due to a great deal of practice with the many other girls who hovered on the edge of my consciousness. This was the Seventies, after all: post-Free Love and pre-AIDS. Sleeping around was considered smart – indeed virtually compulsory – rather than unhygienic, and anyone who complained about it was deemed over-possessive and uncool.

We danced warily around each other for a few weeks at first, not exactly dating but acknowledging a mutual interest.

When we first slept together, I thought it would be a one-night stand. I left, first thing in the morning, in a hurry, feeling the beginnings of a sore throat and afraid of getting involved. In his black leather jacket and with his dark, brooding stubble he seemed cool to the point of remote, although the sight of his face lingered in my mind all day. I almost thought he'd looked slightly hurt that I'd left so quickly.

But the following day I woke up feeling as if I had swallowed razor blades and found that I could barely lift myself off my pillows. The sore throat, which had sent tendrils of pain all over my body the day before, had completely taken me over. I drifted off to sleep again until a fierce rapping at the door stirred me into consciousness.

The door opened before I could make my voice work. I tried to get up, but when I saw the now-familiar black leather jacket and torn jeans, my heart crashed so suddenly against my chest that I virtually passed out again.

'Christ!' said Max. 'You look terrible.'

'Thanks,' I murmured, thinking that that was it. No more Max. I was too weak to care properly, and drifted into unconsciousness again.

At some point I was aware that he was back again, with someone else who, judging by the thermometer he put in my mouth and the painful requests he made for me to say 'aah', must have been a doctor.

'She needs looking after,' I heard him say, through a fog.

'Don't worry,' I thought I heard Max say. 'I can do that.'

I tried to mumble something to stave off this potential romantic disaster. He'd never fancy me again if he saw me being sick, which was almost definitely what was about to happen.

The wave of nausea passed, and there was more mumbling, after which I was aware of Max gently dressing me. 'Only a short journey to my place,' he said, half-carrying me. 'Not long. Then you can sleep.'

And I did. Occasionally I woke up and saw him, sitting against a wall at the other end of his huge room, sketching, or sometimes I mumbled something about water, and he'd bring me a glass and help me drink. Then I'd drift off again.

He told me that it was five days later when I eventually sat up, weak but feeling like myself again.

'Oh,' I said, too weak to work it all out. I could only vaguely remember getting there.

He grinned. 'How does toast sound?'

'Heaven,' I admitted.

It was another three weeks before I went back to the student hostel, and in that time Max and I created a secret, private world that was all our own. He went out to lectures and occasionally even to parties or pubs, but he never left me alone long, and spent most of his free time in the bed with me, with piles of books.

'Austen or Eliot?' he asked one day, proffering a selection of battered paperbacks. 'George, that is, not T. S.'

I grimaced. 'We did those at school.'

'Did?' He scoffed. 'You don't *do* books, you read them. Anyway, here's one you won't have *done*.' He threw me Khalil Gibran's *The Prophet*, along with Jack Kerouac's *On the Road*. 'These have changed people's lives.'

I scored a point by telling him that we had actually done *On the Road* at my school, but wrapped myself round *The Prophet*, suggesting that he bring some of my books back from my room next time he was passing. I was determined that this wasn't going to be a teacher–pupil relationship. We swapped books, read in silence together and read bits aloud to each other, made love and made toast. In the evenings, he'd buy cheap wine from the 'offie' and we'd drink it all, although the flu made it go to my head.

When I got better, I knew instinctively that I had to create some distance if this relationship was going to last. Max's restlessness and intellectual curiosity would always triumph over the kindness that I'd so unexpectedly discovered. In those weeks a pattern was set where our relationship belonged to us alone, and not to the outside world, so we both carried on with largely separate lives outside it.

I found Max fascinating, endlessly compelling, but, deep down, I always knew how much he wanted out of life. In his search to taste all that the world had to offer, I thought he would be off and I began to steel my heart against the day. I was careful – painfully careful – never

9

to make any assumptions in our relationship. As we learnt to cook together and browsed in junk shops, or went to art galleries, or walked through the woods with the autumn reds and golds tumbling down around us, I could hardly imagine where he ended and I began, but then I would return to my quiet, empty hostel bedroom for a few nights and feel afraid of my dependence on him. I'd exchange cups of coffee and pleasantries with other girls, but only made superficial friends because my emotional focus was on Max. I don't think it was the same for him – I didn't dare question him about what he had done when he wasn't with me, but we often bumped into people on the street who I'd never met before but who he clearly knew quite well. We made love every night we spent together, but we didn't spend every night together. I pretended that I was busy and happy on our nights apart, but they seemed unutterably cold, long and dark.

When Max was out in a crowd, he was often at the centre of it, laughing, or making other people laugh. Somebody once said he created a party atmosphere just by walking in the door. But at home he flung his public personality off, along with the black leather jacket which he'd toss carelessly over a chair. The man I got to know behind closed doors was thoughtful, surprisingly careful – he never liked me walking alone late at night, for example – and gentle.

I took Max home that Christmas. He didn't want to go to the States for some reason. 'I usually go to Stephen's,' he'd explained, 'but I think things are a bit tricky there this year.'

My father rustled his newspaper in interest when he heard his name. 'There was a Polish banking family with a name like that, wasn't there?' he asked Max. He knew a lot about banks and money, although at his level he never saw very much of the latter.

'Yes.' Max hated questions about his background.

My father put down his paper. 'I thought everyone died. In the War.'

'Yes,' said Max, again. 'Everyone except my father.' And then, because he didn't want to be pitied, 'I never knew any of them, of course. I was born here. Much later. I'm English.' There was a certain defiance in the last sentence.

'Of course.' My father looked thoughtful. But I could see that he thought Max was too rich, too clever and too foreign for me.

Max and I battled out through the north-easterly gales to walk along the wind-whipped strip of concrete we called the promenade, past the shuttered, peeling beach huts that had once been painted so brightly but were now faded to the tones of birds' eggs and candy floss. A dark green sea thundered against the breakwaters, occasionally throwing up spumes of spray twenty feet high in the air. When Max kissed me I could taste the salt on his lips, and his fingers smoothed wet tendrils of hair away from my cheeks.

I shivered against him. 'There's a café up on the cliff. We always used to buy ice creams there when we were little. Let's get some coffee.'

'You're so lucky.' He hugged me to him as the wind buffeted us again, and the seagulls swooped and screeched over the dunes. 'You've got all these memories. This is your home.'

'You must have memories too.' I never let Max get away with being too much of mysterious outsider, because now and again I suspected he played it as a card.

'If you hardly ever go to the same place twice, you don't have memories, just a muddle of impressions. Hotels all over the world, blending into one great blur. I felt like a piece of luggage half the time. Great big houses full of servants, or rented flats, depending on which stepfather my mother was married to at the time. Stephen's house. Stephen's house is lovely,' he added, 'and his mother can be wonderful, but she's got her own problems. It's not exactly what you'd call a happy home. Not like yours.'

He kissed me again, more thoroughly this time. 'Yours feels like you: warm and loving and safe.'

Not exactly the qualities the average teenage girl really aspires to, but if Max loved me for them, I supposed they were a good thing. Although I couldn't help feeling that if someone beautiful and brilliant and dangerous came along, then warm, loving and safe might get forgotten.

And I'd never really thought about my home. A solid, just slightly dreary 1930s cottage close to the sea, with its upright Fifties armchairs in tones of pale sludge green and mustard yellow that had been so fashionable when my parents bought the house. At that stage I couldn't wait to leave it behind. I felt a twinge of disloyalty because Birchington-on-Sea had given me a very happy, if uneventful, childhood, but I wanted adventure;

although, until I met Max, the most exciting thing I'd done was think about amending my name, perhaps to Suzanne, or Susannah, or Suze, or even – very trendy, this one – Zan. Anything but responsible, sensible Susan.

But the way he soaked it all up, from my mother's shepherd's pies – she was a good, plain English cook – to my father's jovial, if cautious, overtures with his favourite sherry, made me realize how desperately Max wanted to belong. To somewhere. Particularly to England rather than to the restless, rootless international world he'd been brought up in, where most people spoke five languages but none of them perfectly. Perhaps that's why we found each other in the first place – because neither of us really felt we belonged to the privileged, golden university world into which we found ourselves dropped. It was only later I discovered that no one else had thought they belonged there either.

At that point Stephen belonged to the part of Max's life that went on without me. He was reading architecture in London and the night when we'd all met had been one of only a handful of weekends when he'd come down to see his old schoolfriend. He'd danced with me a few times, then with a couple of other girls, after which he'd gone back to London. Max went up to see him every so often, but I always stayed behind. It was obviously a very old, strong friendship and Max clearly didn't want me involved in it. He had a tendency to compartmentalize his life, the way men do, and, at that time, I belonged in one compartment and Stephen in another.

But occasionally the three of us would spend an evening together. Unlike Max, Stephen seemed to know exactly where he came from and where he was going. He intended to become a brilliant architect. Max was completely intense in anything he did: he'd take out his Rizla cigarette papers and spend nearly fifteen minutes carefully smoothing and damping each piece to make an enormous, crooked joint. But, in spite of his obvious talents and the sudden, artistic passions that would totally engross him for a few months while he worked on a piece, he seemed dangerously directionless as far as the bigger picture of life itself was concerned.

As Max and I completed the three years of our degree, the future began to yawn ahead of me like an insuperable chasm. After the exams there was another month of term, to be spent hanging round and making plans. Everyone edgily began to talk about what they were going to do next. In my heart of hearts I expected Max to pack up the contents of the big, high-ceilinged room, tell me we'd had a great time together and wish me well for the future.

But instead he took me to an expensive restaurant a mile away from the Art College – one which students could rarely afford.

We settled ourselves on wooden chairs, and Max restlessly picked the wax off an encrusted wine bottle that Luigi used as a candlestick. I waited for him to tell me that I had meant so much to him, and that he would always remember me with love and affection. I waited to be told, in the gentlest and tenderest of words, that we were finished. Fishermen's nets with Chianti bottles entangled in them drooped over our heads, and there was a deep gloom in the other empty corners of the restaurant. Luigi hovered over us with a giant pepper grinder.

When he finally stopped fussing, Max spoke.

'The last three years have been incredible,' he said, with such finality in his voice that I almost ran out of the door there and then. 'And they wouldn't have been the same without you.'

All I heard at the time were the words 'without you'. He would regret it, of course, but in future he would be without me.

'I had a job offer today.'

My heart began, bit by frozen bit, to break up into tiny pieces.

'From a television company in London. A traineeship. It's a fantastic opportunity. They had over a hundred applications.'

I smiled, stretching my lips across my teeth painfully. 'Congratulations.'

'Will you come with me?'

I was so busy with the narrative inside my head that I hardly heard him. 'What?'

'My brown-eyed girl . . .' he tangled his fingers round the dark corkscrew curls I struggled to control, and sighed at the impossibility of what he was going to say next. 'I love you. I love you so much.'

He had never said the word 'love' before. Perhaps he'd thought I would use it in evidence against him.

'Do you mean properly together, Max?' I still couldn't quite believe it. 'Or just for now?'

'Properly together. You and me.' His eyes creased up in a smile, but behind them he looked almost anxious. 'If you want.'

But the city gradually tore us apart. Max got a permanent job in television and went out to parties, and, after getting trapped too often with people who glazed over when I turned out to be unimportant, I stopped trailing along. The Galliard millions – if they were millions, I never really knew – began to matter. I was struggling to make ends meet as a junior in a graphic design department of an incredibly trendy, fringe magazine which came to be known as a hothouse for talent but, at that stage, had trouble even paying the minuscule wages they offered their staff. He had a frog-eyed sports car, a smart job, and a flat in South Kensington where I lived with him rent-free. But he couldn't understand why I didn't keep the fridge stocked up with fruit juice and the best butter, or why there wasn't always a decent selection of beers and wines in the store cupboard. I hated having to tell him that I couldn't afford them, because he'd simply open his wallet and peel off some notes, pressing them into my hand as if I was selling something. And out in restaurants with the huge gangs of glittering, glamorous people he'd discovered, I could never pay my share, so he had to stump up for us both. I'd sit there, for hour after hour, hoping no one was going to order brandies, then gazing in despair at a bill of which my share approximately equalled what I had to spend in a week.

Max would push his credit card over. 'That's for two of us,' he'd say. Even so, I dreaded invitations to go abroad with him, or away for the weekend. If it didn't involve paying for tickets – completely out of my reach, so he always bought them automatically – there was the question of smart clothes and presents for the hostess. None of this had ever happened at Art College because students were expected to be scruffy, and no one gave those sort of parties anyway.

Relationships survive on give and take. Max gave money, and I took it. I gave Max the love he needed and he took it. I began to feel bought.

It slowly became easier and more fun to share a bag of chips with Stephen, who'd drop round to see Max, only to find that Max was never in. Occasionally we nipped round the corner to the pub, and talked about the meaning of life over halves of lager. We split the bill because Stephen's architecture degree took longer than the frivolous degrees that Max and I had been awarded. Sometimes I bought a round and he bought the next one. Or he brought a bottle and I whipped up some scrambled eggs. Max would come home and be funny about the parties he'd been to. We'd laugh with him, and Stephen and I would agree, tinged with jealousy, that it had sounded like hell.

But Max went out alone increasingly often, coming back later and later, and when he eventually turned up he always seemed to have grown further away from me. I thought I detected the smell of perfume on him, and he thought I was being ridiculous when I said so. He no longer told me he loved me, and I no longer dared say it to him, because it felt like just another sentence. The kind of sentence that imprisons people.

Max was too busy to read books curled up in bed with me, and when he reached for me in the night, urgently, without asking me what I wanted or how I felt, I could have been anyone. I felt as if we'd both been trapped in two separate lives and two different bodies, and that there was no longer a connection between us.

One night, finally, he didn't come back at all, and I knew that it was over. No love can survive waiting all night, not on top of so many other lonely hours.

I packed my suitcases, and picked out my favourite things as fairly as I could bear to, waiting only to say goodbye properly. My heart, I decided, was not for sale. Not at that price. Not at any price, for that matter.

'It's not what you think.' His eyes were bruised with tiredness, even darker than I'd ever seen them.

I shrugged. 'You've never been one for clichés, Max, don't start now. Please.' It was almost a relief to end it, to stop having to wait up for the sound of his key in the door. To stop hoping that one day the relationship would burn again. I would walk away, my head held high, not cling on embarrassingly. He put out his hand. 'Don't go. Please, don't go.'

'I'm not staying, Max. We don't have a life together any more.'

As I closed the door, I couldn't help feeling that it was me who had somehow deserted and betrayed Max. That if I really loved him, I'd have stayed. That just shows you how clever he was. He'd spent the night out.

I felt guilty. Well, I decided, I wasn't going to be a victim in this relationship.

But, as I walked away from Max that cold, wet morning, I had to suppress the thought that Sensible Susan had won.

Of course, I went to Stephen. I hardly knew anyone else well enough, because everyone we knew in London counted as Max's friends. Only Stephen now belonged to me as well. He dried my tears, and took me out to a bistro. He poured red wine down my throat and persuaded me that love didn't have to be quite so lonely. Finding Stephen, after the restlessness of Max, was like going home.

Unlike Max, Stephen belonged, comfortably and confidently, in his world. His family lived in a crumbling rectory, surrounded by portraits of the past. His father, a dominating, intolerant man, was almost obscenely proud of the fact that there'd been Everetts in their county – it was one of the shires – since William the Conqueror. Whenever I joined Stephen for a drink at the architecture department bar, I could see that he was one of a tribe – of clean-limbed, clear-skinned, straight-teethed blond or brown-haired giants that dominated the room. He knew them all, rowed with them, played endless different ball games at different times of year with them and drank with them. They were kind and honest and open and nice, and Stephen was the kindest and nicest – and most talented – of all.

Suddenly being without Max's money was very frightening, but I knew I could do it because Stephen did.

And when he suggested we split the rent of the basement flat, it seemed to make perfect sense. I was equal at last, free to love and be loved.

Three months later, on a rainy Saturday afternoon, Max rang the doorbell, unexpectedly, and asked me to marry him.

I laughed. I couldn't think how else to respond. It's much easier to make a joke of things. 'Have you been drinking, Max?'

'No.' He stood there, with his great dark eyes, under an expensive umbrella, with water streaming down over its sides. He must have been the only person I knew in those days who actually bothered with an umbrella.

'Well, whatever you're on, I think you should adjust the dosage.' I was shocked to feel myself trembling. I refused to let Max get away with turning my life upside down again.

'Must you be flippant about everything?'

'Well, yes I must, so you can get very irritated by me, and then leave me alone.' I was horrified to find myself talking as if I was contemplating this mad idea of his seriously. I knew I couldn't face all that pain again, and besides, there was Stephen. I knew he was special. There had been none of those invisible barriers between us that had made Max sometimes seem distant, even in bed. Stephen spelt strength and safety; and he was watching the rugby only a few yards away on the other side of a wall. Stephen called me Suzy – 'sweet little Suzy' – and it felt like my name now. As Stephen and Suzy, I'd found the identity I'd been looking for. For the first time in my life I felt like a couple, rather than two people caught up in a whirlwind together.

Stephen and I had a thoroughly normal relationship – we argued, made up, took each other for granted sometimes and made joint friends. All those everyday things I'd never really done with Max. Max and I had never argued, for example, because I just let him be Max. Looking back on it, I realized I'd been afraid to make either demands or plans. Stephen and I made plans. He would be a great architect, while I painted.

And I didn't have to wait up for Stephen at night, and smell the scent of other women on him when he finally got back. I couldn't do that again.

I gave another, slightly shaky, laugh. 'Max. Be sensible. Come on. You know perfectly well that we couldn't possibly marry each other.'

'Well.' Max shook the umbrella at the rain as if he could command it to stop.

'I thought . . .' He looked ashen, with a faint shadow of dark stubble across his chin. I resisted the temptation to touch him and to feel its sandpaper roughness beneath my fingers.

'You didn't think,' I said, anger suddenly flaring up. There'd been so much fury bubbling away inside me for all these months. 'You didn't think about Stephen. Or me. Or any of that.'

I saw a flash of anger in response. 'No,' he spoke very evenly as if keeping himself under control. 'I can honestly say that I was not thinking about Stephen when I came here. Does he really matter to you?'

'Yes,' I said, determined to hurt Max as much as

he'd hurt me. 'We're in love.' It sounded trite, even to me.

But Max merely turned away to climb the narrow side steps that were made for servants to slip in and out of the house unseen by their masters. He looked back, one last time. For a brief moment our eyes met and I felt a tug of disloyalty as my body responded to his dark, intense gaze with a wild, yet oddly familiar, spurt of raw desire, and I could see that he felt it too. But I moved to close the peeling basement door. 'Really, Max,' I said. 'No.'

'In that case,' he sounded very calm – almost wooden – and the roar of a truck virtually obliterated his next words, so that I never really believed he'd said them, 'I shall marry Anne.'

I was trembling when I closed the door, and suddenly, for no reason at all, rushed to the loo to be violently sick.

But, because I thought Max had been joking – at least that's what I wanted to think – I told Stephen about his visit that Saturday afternoon when he asked me who'd been at the door. His eyes went china-blue with anger.

'I've been like a brother to Max,' he said. 'And this is what he does. You can't trust him for one moment. You really can't.'

I realized I'd made a mistake, and tried to insist that it was just a prank, but everything I said seemed to make it worse. We had a blazing row, which I never knew how to handle because I'd never had these sorts of arguments at home when I was growing up.

After blaming me for leading Max on, and blaming Max for taking advantage of me, Stephen slammed the door and stayed away for a few hours. When he came back, he sank silently into the sofa and watched the football.

I soon forgot about the row because I discovered that I was pregnant.

No wonder I'd been sick, I told myself. It had been nothing to do with Max's visit at all.

When I look back on those days it seems extraordinary to think that we had three options: marriage, abortion and adoption. The last two seemed quite impossible to me. In the Seventies, it was still a scandal, a complete, impossible, life-changing scandal to bring up a child on your own. I came back from the doctor's surgery, my legs trembling and a tight knot of panic at the core of my being. 'I don't want to trap you.'

'You're not trapping me.' If there was a glimpse of desperation in his eyes, it had gone almost before I could see it. 'I won't let you down.'

As a proposal it showed more commitment than Max's spur-of-the-moment rainy day suggestion.

'I want us to make a go of it,' he said, looking frightened. We were both frightened. As I hurled myself, relieved, into his arms, he murmured: 'I don't quite know how we're going to afford it, but I'll think of something.'

When I wrote to my godmother and told her that I was getting married she alarmed me by offering to lend me her necklace.

I was slightly worried that I would be weighed down

by a great big, old-fashioned piece of jewellery that would be quite out of keeping with my simple cream cotton kaftan and the circle of flowers in my hair. But it was exquisite – as simple and fresh as a child's daisy chain, sparkling with drops of morning dew. On my wedding morning, I clicked the clasp closed at the back of my neck, and I realized that real gems add a lustre to the skin that paste cannot match. Feeling childish, I counted the diamond daisies round my neck. He loves me, he loves me not, he loves me, he loves me not. There were five, strung along a silver chain. He loves me. As I looked at myself in the mirror, my eyes shone above the glittering stones, and I believed it would work. I would never have done it if I hadn't believed that, not even for the baby.

Standing at the church door, I remembered that moment and touched the necklace once more for luck. Panic over, I inhaled a deep breath of cool, incense-scented air, and walked slowly up the aisle as the organ music reached a triumphal roll. I married my best friend. And to prove that he had forgiven him ('may the best man win and all that'), he insisted that Max be at his side.

Like the diamonds around my neck, I vowed that this would last for ever.

But perhaps I should also have remembered that a daisy chain can easily break.

Love stories always end with a wedding, or a baby, and it was my wedding to Stephen that ended the love story with Max. After that, relationships are about real life, which is what I knew Stephen and I would have together.

I never thought about those endless weekends curled up with Max in his giant bed, aware of each other's warmth even when we were completely wrapped up in a book or listening to a piece of music, or of the lazy, casual way Max would stretch out a hand to draw me closer, or to pour another mug of rough, red wine. For years afterwards, whenever the sharp, raspberry-jam-and-vinegar flavour of cheap wine evoked all those memories for me, I would place the glass down carefully and walk away, claiming to prefer a glass of water.

2

Twenty-five years later, I bought the November issue of *How?* magazine, and with clumsy fingers flicked apprehensively through to the 'At Home With The Designers' feature, hoping that there wouldn't be anything in it to upset Stephen. He'd got where he had by getting the detail right, and he hadn't been entirely happy about doing 'publicity'.

But he'd been advised that it would be good for the practice. It would reassure people that the architect who'd won the Crown Project – a very-high-profile glass tower on the banks of the Thames – was in touch with real life. 'There's been a lot of controversy about a classical architect getting this, what with modernism being so much more ... well, now. People are talking about another Poundbury,' explained Zara, the Public Relations Person hired to see them through the avalanche of not wholly flattering press that had cascaded over Stephen's head. 'We need people to call him *the* Stephen Everett. It's all about Lifestyle these days,' she'd added.

So there'd been a three-line whip for the photo-shoot, with the girls shrieking and demanding trips to the hairdresser's and new clothes, and Stephen spending the whole weekend lining up shoes in descending order of size.

Three months later, my home was spread out in front

of me in Patel's Newsagents, looking utterly familiar and completely strange at the same time. I touched the glossy pages, seeing what we'd achieved in twenty-five years set out beautifully, all the pain and struggle swept away, with only triumph and tidiness allowed to show. It all seemed so much more than it was in reality, and perhaps, also, in a funny way, rather less.

The article was written proof that we had a perfect life. There was Stephen at his drawing board, turning towards the camera with one of his crumpled, self-deprecating smiles, looking absurdly handsome in cream chinos, a collarless shirt and his now ash-blond hair cut into a short assertive chunk. 'Above: Stephen Everett believes that the time has come to rediscover classical values in architecture,' said the caption. 'Left: his wife, Suzy, and two daughters, Jess, 19, and Polly, 24.' The girls and I had crowded on to the sofa, Jess grinning, her long legs draped across the side of the sofa, and her long dark hair streaming out behind her thrown-back head, while Polly, as always, was neat, blonde and pretty, like a china doll, wedged up as close to me as she could. I'd buried myself in the middle of them, because I hated having my photo taken. There always seemed to be too much of me, and I was too pale, with the curly dark hair now faded to metallic tones of weathered steel. Too tall, my mother had worried, back in the days when tallness in a woman was virtually a disfigurement. Now, with one of my daughters taller than me, I hardly gave it a thought, but the habit of not liking photographs had stuck.

The magazine had sent a stylist to arrange each picture, who claimed to be called Marzipan, and who had instantly locked in head-to-head combat with Zara of the PR company.

Zara had narrowed her eyes at the jumble of floral, beaded, striped and tapestried cushions in worn but joyous shades of pink and red that piled up over the sofa and chairs. For years, I'd never had enough money to buy more than one of anything at a time, so any concept of matching had had to be abandoned from the first day I started to scour charity shops or jumble sales. I love different shapes and textures: the patina of polished wood, the way different colours spark off each other when they crowd together. My finds piled up so that they could contrast with each other – an antique beaded handbag, a beautifully calm pottery bowl made by an old lady potter in Brittany, a mad Spanish donkey with a gleam of mischief in his eye, even a couple of dear little watercolours found in an old curiosity shop near Stonehill. The walls were equally crowded: framed pieces of work from the children's art classes next to Stephen's family portraits, and a collection of Thirties glass neck-laces wound round a small metal chandelier I'd bought at a cheap chain store.

'Heavens,' Zara had been taken aback. 'It's like a kasbah. Very pretty, of course,' she'd added, suddenly conscious that I was the client's wife. 'But not quite what people will expect from an architect.' She'd begun picking things off the mantelpiece carefully.

'Suzy's a magpie.' Stephen spoke with mild irritation. He just hated me spending money, even in tiny amounts.

Marzipan had narrowed her eyes, tilting her head to one side. 'It looks good. Leave it.'

Zara'd given her a crocodile smile. 'Not quite the image, I'm afraid.'

I'd left them to it. Zara won and Marzipan had gone into a sulk, although she'd brightened at the bathroom because I'd glued thousands of shells to the walls along the skirting boards and around the mirrors. 'She won't be able to pick those off,' she'd muttered.

I read on. The article said, 'However hectic his schedule is, Stephen always makes time for a family Sunday lunch.' This captioned us both, grinning self-consciously over a joint of congealing beef. What it didn't add was that this happened only about once a month, and that otherwise we mainly talked on the phone, or in passing on the stairs, or as I sat propped up in bed sleepily while he paced up and down, hanging up each item of clothing neatly as he explained that classical architecture didn't mean sticking pillars on to modern boxes. I never worried about his absences. Stephen's passion was entirely for his work.

After re-reading the article twice – and smiling at the tiny inset photograph of Truffle, our cat, who had arranged herself, with feline awareness of her own per-fection, on top of a pile of neatly ironed clothes – I decided that the whole thing was probably all right, although in some way not what I had expected. I had the feeling that somewhere along the way, something had been lost.

It was time to drive back to the staff room of the school where I worked as an art teacher, and show everyone our perfect life, then to get ready to go away for the weekend.

*

Stephen and I purred up the endlessly winding A12 to Stonehill in our new car. Well, not exactly brand-new, but at least recently acquired, and an altogether racier model than the capacious, dependable, battered wagons that had seen us through the last two decades. It smelt ostentatiously of leather, and had hardly any miles on the clock. We were going to visit Max and Anne. We always visited Max and Anne. They rarely, if ever, visited us. I'm not sure why, except that they have Stonehill, and we have a perfectly ordinary house in an inconveniently unfashionable part of South London.

And when I say 'always', that didn't mean we saw Max and Anne very often. Stephen stayed in touch with Max, of course, because he was his oldest friend, but I always found Anne quite difficult. I suppose that was not surprising.

Max had married Anne three months after our wedding. So he hadn't been joking. Not about that, anyway.

When we got the invitation – a stiff slab of white card with heavily engraved writing, so unlike the piece of ordinary printed paper that we'd had to use for our wedding – I wondered what would have happened if I had said yes to him. What would have happened to Anne?

He'd have run us both together, I suspected. I was well out of it.

I first met her at her wedding to Max, which is an unfair time to make a judgement about anyone. After that we went up to stay with them regularly, at least once a year, but I never felt I got to know her any better than when I first saw her walking, veiled, up the aisle on her father's arm. That was the right word for her: veiled. She was like a distant princess. She was the girl who has everything, moving gracefully, and with slow, confident steps towards her prince.

At that point, marriage still felt brand new to Stephen and me. He worried a lot about money, but I'd trusted, deep down, that it would be all right in the end, and had allowed myself to enjoy the gradual swelling of my belly and the joyous beginnings of the first few kicks. I felt that the baby protected me against the pain of Max's wedding, and was glad that I was so obviously pregnant and so definitely Stephen's.

But as soon as we drove up to Suffolk and saw Stonehill for the first time, I knew that something had stirred up an old anger in Stephen.

'Max is marrying her for all this, you know,' he said, in a tight voice. 'He's so materialistic.'

Anne was the heir to this enchanting red-brick Elizabethan manor whose tall geometric chimneys towered up ahead of us like the turrets of a fairy-tale castle. Max later told me it had been built at the height of Anne's family's fortunes and had replaced a much humbler manor house. We stopped the car and parked outside the moat, and we stood there, just looking. I had never seen anything like it, although Stephen was muttering about the cost of keeping it up.

'I know Max is rich, but he's made a big mistake here. The Smiths poured their entire fortune into a place like this and they still had to sell up in the end.'

We walked round the moat, and he tutted at the way the walls of the house dropped straight down to the water. 'Terrible problems with damp. Terrible. And the whole place is an absolute wreck.'

It looked magical to me. I touched his arm. 'As the best man, shouldn't you be looking after Max?' The wedding would take place in the little church near the end of the drive, and Max had spent the night in Stonehill's West Wing. I wondered if Stephen should have joined him, but presumably if Max had wanted him, Max would have asked.

Stephen shook my hand off his arm impatiently. 'In a minute. You go on to the church. I'll see you there.'

So I teetered down the drive on my own, and bumped straight into Max by the church.

For one moment I thought his face lit up, but then it shut down again. I didn't dare kiss his cheek. We only kissed socially now, when other people were around. If we suddenly found ourselves alone together, we stepped back and muttered 'Hello'. There was an invisible glass wall between us. Occasionally I thought I saw a flash of hurt in his eyes, but I reminded myself that he had been the one to betray me first.

'Well, good luck,' I said, twisting awkwardly and wishing someone else was around to rescue me. I tried to think of something encouraging to say. 'Marriage is very nice, you know.'

His face split into a smile, and he looked amused. 'Really? I'm glad to hear it. Nice will do me nicely.'

I blushed, embarrassed, and Stephen came running up behind me. They started joshing each other the way men do, seizing each other's non-existent beer bellies, and criticizing each other's haircuts, waistcoats and the state of the polish on their respective shoes, with shouts of laughter and rueful grins.

I relaxed. I could safely leave it to them, and began thinking about Anne. After all, she probably hadn't known about me, so the split hadn't been her fault. She wasn't the enemy, I told myself. My heart was not convinced.

The reception was full of people I distantly remembered from my time with Max, most of whom either ignored me or looked puzzled, as if trying to place me from somewhere. At one point I found myself cornered by a small, smartly dressed girl in a huge hat, who looked like a mushroom with very sharp teeth. 'I introduced them, you know, at my party,' she squealed. 'It was so romantic.' The teeth made small chopping movements, like a baby shark's, as she prattled on, and I tried to remember if I'd ever met her, or been invited to her party with Max. But no, by the end of our relationship, I'd dreaded it all so much, I'd hardly bothered even looking at the invitations.

'Anne asked to borrow my telephone because her mother was ill,' gushed the mushroom. 'Apparently she'd promised to call home every evening to check up, and that very night she was told that her mother was actually dying. Really suddenly. It was during the rail strike, do you remember, at the end of last year? Anne simply had no way of getting home to see her. So Max, who'd just arrived as Anne was leaving, overheard her and simply said, "Don't worry, I'll drive you there." It must have taken him all night. I mean, it was a good four hours all the way up here in those days. Straight up and then straight back down again, she said. He can't have got back before dawn. So romantic,' she repeated. 'It was obviously the beginning of everything. It was love at first sight, like a fairy tale.'

I fought down a queasy, pregnancy lurch that welled up from deep down inside me. That must have been the night that I'd waited for him, imagining him in some nightclub or someone else's bed. That had been during the rail strike. I wondered, for one second, if it would have made any difference if he'd explained, and then remembered that it was all too late, and that it hadn't been about one night anyway. 'Goodness.' I peered past the massive brim, hoping to spot Stephen. I didn't want to be here, watching Max marry Anne.

After our weddings, we all settled down to our respective life patterns.

Stephen and I agreed that I would teach art so that the children's school terms and my work would fit round each other. Lower childcare costs, you see. After all, I was the one who wanted children. And Stephen was obviously the one who would be able to earn the most. It didn't really even require discussion.

And Max and Anne were installed, permanently, as our oldest — although not, of course, our closest — friends.

Most of the time, we saw each other at weddings or were invited up for big celebrations, or, from time to time, we were summoned for a family weekend because our children were virtually the same age and got on well.

Max and Anne's Jamie had been born just four months after Polly – a real honeymoon baby – and Harriet was eight months older than Jess. Jamie was like Anne, tall for his age, cool, polite and distant, although the girls adored him and said that he was very funny. Harriet had always been a cuddly little tomboy, with mud all over her face and an irrepressible grin.

But with Jess spending the year in Japan as part of her Oriental studies degree, and Polly living with three other girls in Clapham and cooking in a friend's restaurant, this weekend was one of the few when we would be together as friends, not parents with children the same age. In fact, I wasn't quite sure why we were going, except that you get into those 'we must see you soon' conversations and sometimes it seems rude not to get a diary out and pencil something in.

And I was slightly nervous. Children, even almost adult ones, are a very good barrier between you and the rest of the world.

As we pulled away from the ring road round Ipswich, the advertisements on the radio began squawking at us. The artificially cheerful voice of the voice-over artist urged us to 'get away for a short break'.

We had never really had any time together alone. We'd almost always been parents. It was time, I thought, to be a person rather than a wife.

'Don't you think it would be good if we had a break? Just us. We've never done that.' I looked hopefully at Stephen. 'Somewhere cheap and easy to get to. Everyone says Latvia is lovely at the moment. A bit like Prague before it got crowded. What about a long weekend?'

He shook his head. 'Not with the Crown Project.' I felt a glow of pride. Stephen, at least, had won one of the glittering prizes that had been promised to us all by further education. And I was by his side, even if I hadn't won any of my own.

His next remark dashed me. 'And, besides, we can't afford it.'

I sat up, a worm of fear wriggling inside me the way it always did when Stephen talked about money. 'Surely now that the children are gone we can afford things?' I tried to keep the worry out of my voice. It did seem a bit odd that we were still so broke, although I suppose this car had cost a bit. 'What about the Crown Project? It's the most prestigious piece of architectural work this decade, according to the *Guardian*.'

He frowned as a Porsche shot past us, doing at least 120mph.

'Prestige doesn't necessarily mean money. You know that.' Stephen sounded reasonable and balanced, as he always did.

'I don't quite see why—' Money had really been the cause of any problems that we'd had in our marriage, and I'd hoped that that would now all be over. With his new-found success, we could finally relax. Not bicker at each other about trivial things, not feel terrified at the thought of the boiler packing up or the car needing a new clutch. . . . 'I don't quite see why,' I repeated, 'architects don't seem to earn very much.'

'Oh, Suzy, for goodness' sake. You know about the lean times when no one's building anything. They last for years. And you know about reinvesting in the practice. You know we never get those telephone-number-sized City bonuses that the bankers get.'

There was a pause and he added: 'And you know that my kind of architecture hasn't been exactly fashionable until now.'

Stephen, you see, believed in his principles. It was just slightly sad that until now the only people who shared them had wanted swimming-pool pavilions in Barbados rather than houses in Britain. And when he was asked to compress his principles into designs that would fit on to a housing estate, he'd fume, although he often took the job. 'Just to feed you lot,' he'd grumble. 'If I was on my own, I'd rather starve.' So you see, it wasn't just me who'd had to compromise. We'd both had to put away some dreams, folding them neatly in acid-free tissue and heaving them into the attic along with my wedding dress.

It made me feel guilty. I felt permanently guilty about money and Stephen. I used to think that being grown-up meant being married, with children, probably a house, almost definitely a career or a job. But now I thought being a grown-up meant being able to do money.

'Anyway, you shouldn't complain.' Stephen had reached the end of the disciplinary lecture and was on to the moral-building bit of the conversation, so I didn't want to interject that I wasn't. 'You should count our blessings. Once we've sorted out the overdraft, then perhaps things will be easier.'

The Overdraft was like some malevolent household god which had to be appeased with regular sacrifices. We'd had an overdraft – of course – of frightening proportions when we first married. Everybody does. As I'd trundled babies to the park with other mothers, we'd discussed how broke we all were, but as everyone got more successful and moved to bigger houses, people stopped talking about money, and started talking about the things that money can buy. Overdrafts became furtive, like secret drinking.

But it seemed that the more you earn, the bigger overdraft you're allowed to have. Being the daughter of someone who worked in a bank, overdrafts had originally had a raffish, Bohemian image to me. My father would tut over the daring, exciting antics of bank customers who went to Spain on holiday or bought dilapidated houses to rescue *in spite* of their overdrafts. These people had sounded like enchanting free spirits to me, but I'd been taught to respect and fear money and couldn't imagine myself one of them. It would be too frightening.

And it was. The Overdraft was in charge, and had to be consulted before making any major decision. It constantly threatened to engulf us in a terrifying slide into debt unless we behaved.

Still, I told myself, we'd really done very well to get to where we had. Two utterly adorable children safely brought up into quite reasonable adults as far as I could see. A Victorian terraced house in an only slightly seedy neighbourhood. A smart, newish car. A pension scheme (Stephen's, of course). And my necklace. My godmother had left it to me in her will, and although I often forgot about it completely, it was still my last resort.

So we were lucky. Some people would even consider us wealthy.

Not, of course, Max and Anne, I thought, as we reached the gates of Stonehill.

'New gates.' Stephen noticed such things. 'Max must be doing well.'

There was always a faint undercurrent of envy when Stephen made these comments. It rankled with him – only slightly, of course, but it still rankled – that Max, the outsider, now had all this.

I got out of the car, my legs stiff with sitting in the same position for two and a half hours, and fiddled with an electronic box, pressing buzzers until eventually a fuzzy voice answered at the other end, and instructed me to get back into the car and wait for the gates to heave themselves slowly apart as if opened by a ghost. It was typical of Max to install gates that were so impressively massive and metallic that they would have looked more at home barring the way to Hyde Park. You couldn't help wondering who he was trying to keep out.

But, as Stephen always confirmed, disapprovingly, as we drove up to the house, Max had spent a fortune transforming Stonehill. I remembered visiting the first summer after Anne's father died, when Polly was only nine, the girls crammed into the back of our dismally unreliable second-hand car, and me trying to explain to them that the drive, a triumphal 'S' flanked with tall, slender poplar trees, standing like sentinels, was not a road but Max and Anne's garden path. On either side were patchwork fields of emerald green, gold and even, as it was mid-summer, a few squares of astonishing blue flax. With the green of the poplars punctuating the gently rolling landscape on either side of us, it epitomized the tranquillity of the real English countryside.

But when we had crossed the little bridge to the courtyard, and cricked our necks in an effort to take in the full forbidding magnificence of the house, home to the Dewarson family for almost a thousand years, even the girls had been appalled by the smell of decay. The hunt, Max had told us, used to send their dogs into the outhouses and even through the old Jacobean kitchen to flush out foxes. One part had been rebuilt by a Victorian Dewarson, with big square-paned windows, panelled walls and solidly high ceilings. Most centuries, however, including most of the twentieth, had simply passed by Stonehill's gates without leaving any impression. The house had seemed dark and dangerous, and Polly and Jess had each gripped my hand anxiously.

Now, fifteen years on, as the leaves drifted down in a dignified cascade of gold, orange and chestnut, Stonehill appeared ahead of us glowing with prosperity, its stone windows ablaze with light, the formal gardens rescued from wilderness, and the woody scent of log fires curling from the tall chimneys through the autumn air. It had once been twice the size, encompassing the island courtyard on three sides, but half had burned down several centuries ago. Max had planted a deliciously English walled garden where the old buildings had been, and restored an *allée* of pleached limes to stretch majestically out from the front door to a seat overlooking the moat. Surrounding the moat there were more gardens: lawns, a wild garden, a bluebell wood, a pet cemetery, a rose walk, a parterre, and, of course, a vegetable garden.

Max, lord of all he surveyed, was waiting for us at the porch, as he always did, breathing in the cold, slightly salty air, as if it was nectar, anticipating the sight of people's faces as they came upon Stonehill. However many times you'd been there, it was always a shock to find it just there and just so, and there was always something new to notice, some extra detail that Max had perfected.

And there he was, striding forward to greet us as we got out of the car, grappling with Stephen in clumsy masculine affection. Stephen was his best friend, and Max, in a way, clung to him as proof that he could have something as normal, English and as *long-standing*, as a friend from prep school, someone who'd been with him from the beginning. 'Do you know,' he said, smiling, to Stephen, 'we've been friends now for thirty-eight years. *Thirty-eight years.*' He loved the way the strands of time bound you to people. That was what Anne had, that was, I suspected, part of what he loved in her. The Max I'd known had not been materialistic, but he'd craved a home, and a history less dark than the one he'd inherited.

Inside, Stonehill was no longer gloomy and dangerous, but airy and sunny, almost glossy-magazine perfect. Max and Anne had restored it, tearing away generations of making do: ripping out ugly tiled 1930s fireplaces to discover wide brick inglenooks and bread ovens behind them. Max had peeled off linoleum and wrenched up plasterboard floors, polishing the stone pammet tiles underneath, or allowing broad, pale floorboards to be their own uneven selves. He and Anne had stripped the house back to its bones, retrieving its beauty by taking away fussiness – such as the old, chokingly dusty, velvet curtains – and opening up partitions that had been closed for centuries. They'd steamed off old, stained wallpaper to find timber beams criss-crossing the walls, and they left them exposed, painting the plaster between them with distemper rather than modern paints, so that the walls could 'breathe'. They were proud of the house's scars, such as the burn marks left by tallow candles on the wall beams ('studs' Max called them). All this had become very fashionable, of course, but Max was doing it before anyone else. It was almost, but not quite, a stately home, hidden away in the folds of what some people called 'the Bermuda Triangle of Suffolk'. 'Once you go there,' Max had joked, on one of his occasional jaunts back to London, 'you're never seen again.'

Max was, of course, seen again, but not as often as he had been. When he married Anne, he left London, leaving behind the world of film and television, and took a job at the family brewery. He couldn't, after all, have commuted from a small Suffolk town to Soho. And he wanted his life with Anne to succeed. He valued what she valued. Not the money Stonehill represented, but the sense of history, of belonging to the land. At least, that's what I thought when I was thinking kindly of Max.

And why not think kindly of Max, when you were about to enjoy his hospitality, which was always so generous?

'Suzy.' He folded me in a big bear hug. As I disappeared into the clean smell of his starched cotton shirt and felt the scratchiness of his tweed jacket, now authentically worn and patched with leather, against my face, it still seemed odd that my own personal code of honour forbade me to hug him back. I patted him lightly with my hands, sensing the way he had grown more solid and powerfully muscled over the years, the awareness of the contact making me pull out of the embrace. Now I was determined to stay on my feet, not be swept off them by Max's exuberance. Eventually he came up for air and seized Stephen by the arm again.

Anne, tall and elegant, with white hair streaming out behind her in the wind, strode out from the stable block, crossing the moat, and leaving behind an elegant square of loose boxes with a clock tower, which had been built by one of her Georgian ancestors. Its ancient brick walls supported hundreds of rambler roses, which tumbled down throughout the summer in a cascade of pink pom-poms.

'Hi.' Anne waved at us as she scraped off her welling-tons by the side door. She never used the front door. Since getting to know Max and Anne, I'd realized that people in big houses never did. Front doors were for those who didn't have a large selection of side and back doors.

Anne was tall and rangy – taller than Max, in fact – and completely without any kind of artifice. When I first met her she seemed gawky, with long, thick dark hair, a gaunt face, overlarge features and huge feet. Now the hair was still thick and long, but it had gone strikingly white quite early on, and she had never dyed it. Over the years, the sharp cheekbones and strong jaw softened into something that could be called conventionally handsome, and she had amazing ice-blue eyes and clear country skin. Every now and then, when Anne turned against the right light, she looked stunning.

But although I would never have expected Anne to become a great friend, not considering how we started out, I still found it strange that she was such a cipher to me. Did everyone have a friend who was such an unknown quantity, or was Anne set apart because she was Anne Galliard of Stonehill? Perhaps being the only child of older parents, growing up in an extraordinary house, had made her remote.

Yet she was unvaryingly pleasant – almost the perfect, computer-generated hostess, gliding upstairs to hang a huge fluffy white towel in every bathroom, see to a log fire or arrange a little posy of flowers on each bedside table. It was so unlike our mismatched duvet covers, scrappy family bathroom with bits of toothpaste hardening on the tiles and uncomfortable sofa beds, that I felt like a child in comparison.

Anne never complained, asked questions or cracked a joke.

Perhaps she was just one of those brisk, horsey women who were very practical and down-to-earth. That was what I usually told myself when I found her slightly . . . dismissive.

'Snowball's got a hot leg again,' she shouted to Max, virtually ignoring us. 'Mandy's going to call Fortescue if it's not better in the morning.'

Anne had four horses, which meant sixteen legs that could go wrong in some way. I always found it very difficult to work out whether horsey conversations were simply reruns of earlier ones about the same horse, or whether it was a different horse with the same problem. I came to the conclusion that it didn't really matter which horse it was because the conversation would be the same. Fortescue was the vet. Mandy was the groom. I knew they'd both come in separately during breakfast tomorrow to have exactly the same conversation about the symptoms, that Anne would rehash the details of how she'd felt the leg heat up and cool down, and they'd then go over the details one last time, this time all together. Other horsey people would drop in during the morning, and the leg would be debated over coffee or, later on, sherry. Everyone always seemed to enjoy it all so much that they'd run it through just one more time before departing, while I re-read every Sunday supplement.

Stephen always went out with Max, accompanying him as he checked on fences, organized the drainage of soggy bits, irrigated dry areas, ordered things to be cut back, or have them fertilized to make them grow, but as soon as they strode back in, rubbing their hands and talking about a drink, those who were interested in horses' legs melted away. It always reminded me of the birds in our garden when next-door's cats came creeping along the back wall.

Amidst this country-house splendour, there were still a few traces of the old Max; in the ancient greenhouse by the sunniest wall he grew a few marijuana plants among the tomatoes, occasionally lighting up a home-grown joint instead of a cigar after a dinner party. His children, Jamie and Harriet, decreed this 'sad', but Max merely retorted that he thought it was a lot sadder to drink so much lager that you threw up or passed out. 'Each generation to its own poison,' he'd assert. Max was almost the perfect English gentleman, but there was still a part that remained an incorrigible old hippy.

'You need a drink,' bellowed Anne as she hung up her waxed jacket on one of a long row of pegs by the back door. 'Or a cup of tea.' Stonehill was so big that everyone always had to talk at the tops of their voices.

We accepted the tea, and assured her that we'd really had a very good journey now that the Wanstead underpass or bypass or whatever it was called had opened. 'Door to door in two and a half hours.'

Anne's face darkened slightly, as she envisioned the quiet, winding lanes and rosy-pink Suffolk longhouses being colonized by invaders from the city. She said nothing in reply, and merely told us that we were in Bluebell as usual. All the bedrooms had names that related to some part of the gardens, and there was a famous bluebell wood at the back of the house, dating back to the time when Anne's ancestor had first been granted the land by Edward the Confessor for some kind of support.

Bluebell always fired me with enthusiasm to go mad with wallpaper in our bedroom at home, because it had panels of antique blue toile de Jouy between the dark beams that traversed the walls at unpredictable angles, a faded blue toile de Jouy wingback chair and a matching bedspread. There was a huge, dark mahogany wardrobe, divided inside with trays and drawers and compartments that slid soundlessly out and back again with a soft click.

As usual, Stephen said, 'We ought to have one of these.'

Not for the first time, I pointed out that if we had one of those in our bedroom you wouldn't be able to get it in the door.

I just lay back on the big carved bed and stared at the mottled ceiling with its spidery lines that reminded me of the wrinkles of a grand old lady, thinking about the luxury of having the outhouses, wine and coal cellars, linen rooms, toolsheds, sculleries, coatrooms, cheese stores, walk-in larders and dressing rooms that were so abundant at Stonehill. It must have been the suburban housewife in me. I never felt jealous – well, hardly ever – of the drawing room, or the morning room, which was in the bit that had been rebuilt in Victorian times and was usually draped in dust sheets, or especially the formal dining room, which was called the Great Hall and was like eating in a very cold church. But I did envy them their storage space. Houses in cities were always so shuffled up together, as if they'd all been asked to tuck in their elbows to fit in just one more. We had cupboards 'cleverly' squeezed into odd corners, where things tumbled out on your head if you didn't open them carefully.

Stephen leant on the stone window seat and opened the window to hear the last of the evening's birdsong. One of the unique things about Stonehill was the utter depth of the silence. There was no faint buzz of traffic in the background, just the sound of a few quarrelling birds and the occasional drone of farm machinery. All you could see on either side were the trees and fields, gently sloping with the curve of the earth, and the stone tower of a Norman church in the far distance. 'Smell the fresh air.' He breathed in deeply. 'We must move out of the city soon.'

'Must we?' This was another rerun of a familiar conversation. I began to feel more sympathy for the horsey lot and their interminable debates on fetlocks. Perhaps conversations weren't really supposed to achieve anything. Saying the same thing over and over again was just a reassuring way to pass the time. I thought Stonehill was wonderful, but it was a world which I visited, not one where I belonged.

I knew that Stephen really wanted to live in The Old Rectory again, where he grew up. We had seen it advertised in *Country Life* the other day, looking so groomed and polished, almost as if it was in another country, and costing several million pounds. We couldn't believe it. And, naturally, we couldn't afford it. So that made Stephen, or a part of him, feel a failure, although in anyone's eyes he was a raging success now. Perhaps I was lucky not having roots I wanted to get back to. I never hankered after Birchington-on-Sea. Or perhaps it was the difference between men and women. Men wanted to return upstream like salmon to their spawning grounds. Women would make the ocean their home if that was where they found themselves.

But I wouldn't have dreamt of saying that. Not when he'd closed the curtains, and turned round to look at me in that way that he had. I tensed up, just slightly. After twenty-five years, sex had become a tiny bit of a chore, but I knew it was important. To Stephen, anyway.

'So. We're alone at last. No need to lock the door.'

After years of locking the door against unexpected interruptions, the sound of a key turning was a necessary part of foreplay, as far as I was concerned.

'I don't think I could do it without the door locked. It would be like having it off in the street.'

He smiled affectionately, all the tension of an intense week at work gone from his face, as his finger began to trace the shape of my collarbones. He unbuttoned my shirt slowly enough to make me feel a sense of anticipation. Perhaps, after all, this time it would be all right.

And, as if something had shifted in my brain when we climbed Stonehill's big, solid stairs with our suitcases, it was. It was difficult to concentrate on what it might have been, as Stephen's hand pulled the shirt out of my jeans and opened it, returning up to circle a nipple lazily, tracing slowly and gently over to the other breast. He delicately drew my body until its outlines began to melt and spread.

It was time to let go. I watched the jeans slip to the floor, as we slid into each other's arms with an easy familiarity. There's a great deal of pleasure in a dance where each partner knows the steps.

Stephen fell asleep afterwards because he's always so tired. I spent ages soaking in a vast, claw-footed bath with tea-coloured stain marks trickling down from the taps and a huge brass pillar instead of a plug. After giving Stephen a nudge so that he could get up in time for dinner, I went on downstairs alone to find Max in front of a roaring log fire with a bottle of champagne on ice next to the decanters of whisky and gin.

'A toast. To the next stage in all our lives.' I was

touched. We clinked glasses, and, suddenly, although it was just the two of us, toasting each other, I felt at ease with him for the first time for twenty-five years. All that old business between Max and me was long over. Max was a friend. He'd even been a good friend over the years – he'd lent Stephen money once or twice when things had been particularly difficult, for example – and it wasn't disloyal to Stephen to enjoy his company. There was no longer any need to look anxiously towards the door in the hope that someone else might come in and fill the awkward, accusatory gaps in the conversation. I felt my shoulders drop in relief.

'Vanessa and Barry will be here soon.'

I was pleased to hear that. We'd first met Vanessa, who'd been at school with Anne, in the mid-Eighties. She'd stood in front of the fireplace at Stonehill, her slight blonde frame glittering with logos; she was wearing flat Gucci loafers with little chains on them, shrinking her down to her five foot one, thick black opaque tights, a tiny, tight black skirt, a Hermes scarf, and dangling a small Chanel handbag from her shoulders. There was more Chanel clipped on to her ears, and a big black velvet bow in her hair. I'd recognized a type, but found it hard to reconcile it with the paunchy, balding man by her side, a good few years older than she was.

'This is my husband, Barry.' She'd introduced him in light, laughing, cut-glass tones.

'Pleased ter meet yer.' He had a flat, London voice, and a nice smile behind crooked teeth.

Until I got to know them better, I'd assumed that their union was a straight swap. Class for money. Youth for age. But I was beginning to think that they were possibly one of the best-matched couples I'd ever met. People say that money doesn't make you happy, but it made Barry and Vanessa very happy indeed. He lived for making it, and she adored spending it.

There had been brief difficulties in the early 1990s, when the dip in Barry's property business had coincided with a move towards minimalism on the logo front, but Barry quickly re-established himself converting lofts and Vanessa got to grips with the New Spending, which turned out to be very much like the Old Spending although less frilly for the first few years. Barry had briefly protested, so she had quickly worked out that in order to fulfil the contradictory demands of staying fashionable and keeping your fifty-something husband happy, you had to have two houses. The modernist haven in London and the rose-strewn temple to chintz in East Anglia. The spending opportunities had multiplied in a most satisfactory way, and they were now Max and Anne's 'neighbours'.

'So.' Max looked at me through a tulip of cut glass. 'Are you going to work full-time now that the girls are gone? Or give it all up to become a painter? A member of the Royal Academy? Design your own range of fabrics? You could, you know. You always had the talent.' His eyes challenged me. To be something more than a part-time art teacher at a brutish comprehensive where most of my pupils aspired to nothing more uplifting than graffiti.

'Oh,' I replied casually, as if I'd hardly given it thought. I didn't want to say that we'd decided, on the whole, that we'd give the finances another year or so before making any big changes. My life would be on hold – only temporarily, of course – before taking any risks. And being an art teacher is quite an enjoyable career, really; although, to be honest, if you only went into it in the first place because you wanted to minimize childcare costs, it does get a bit wearing after twenty years.

'I've rather missed the boat, you see.' I smiled firmly and took a slug of drink myself.

He looked surprised. 'What I've always admired about you is your get up and go.'

'Well, it's got up and gone.' I grinned at him. Jokes were the only way to keep Max at bay. He always expected much more of me than I was able to give. Or, perhaps it might be more accurate to say, than I wanted to give. Max was so ambitious that he couldn't conceive of anyone being happy with my life.

But, I reminded myself, I had a happy life. A good husband, a family, a job, a home. Money, now, at last. All those things that everybody wanted. Having Max, from his pinnacle of wealth, belittling any of it was definitely not welcome. How dare he sit in his lovely house, surrounded by all his beautiful things, soothed by acres of peaceful Suffolk fields, and pass judgement on my clattering, chaotic, cluttered life? For a moment, the anger, suppressed so long ago, flared up, and I squashed it firmly by reminding myself that I'd had the sense to marry the best man in the end.

Stephen and I had talked about my working full-time when Jess left. Underpinning it, but not discussed, was the fact that, even without children, someone needed to be at home to collect the dry cleaning, do the weekly shop and prevent the pile of clutter on the kitchen table from colonizing every corner in the house. Stephen had always worked very long hours, and running the house was my department. One hundred per cent.

'You could go to evening classes and take up your art again,' Stephen had said, and a knife of bitterness had suddenly, painfully, twisted deep in my heart. Evening classes. Selling my daubs at a local exhibition for fifty pounds. I couldn't face picking up a paintbrush, only to find out that the work wasn't as good as the paintings I'd done at sixteen. And as for design, I hadn't a clue about the technical processes involved these days.

Why, then, did I hear a little voice whispering in my ear: 'Is this it, then? Is this all?'

I suppressed it. It was a greedy, ugly voice, and I didn't want to hear it. I reproved Max for conjuring it up: 'Not everyone, Max, wants to be rich and famous.'

'Just as well,' he replied, with an edge in his voice. 'Considering that none of us is.'

'Well,' I laughed, 'Stephen's getting quite famous, and you're rich.'

He swirled the ice round in the glass and looked into it. 'I only wish we were.' I'd heard this from him before. Lots of rich people simply didn't think they were rich, like all the beautiful women who didn't think they were beautiful, and worried that their chins stuck out too much. And even if things were a bit tight, there was always a Rembrandt to be found in the attic, or a field that was suddenly suitable for planning permission. People like Max never went broke.

'Really, though.' He sighed. 'The competition from wine and foreign beers is really hitting the brewery in the big cities, and we've always been beaten by Adnams on our own patch. Anne's father – ' he looked up as if to make sure she wasn't coming into the room ' – never invested in anything, except his pigs.' I thought of the smell of rot and stagnant water that had characterized the early years at Stonehill, and contrasted it with the scent of beeswax, country roses and lavender that drifted through the house now. 'It wasn't just Stonehill that was going to rack and ruin when we took over,' he continued. 'The company was in much the same state, and it's cost a lot of money to pull it round.'

'Darlings!' With a tinkle of her jewellery, Vanessa, her petite form encased in golden suede trousers and a creamy cashmere top, launched herself into the room, followed by Barry and Stephen. Vanessa always had men trailing behind her. She could scarcely have been a more unlikely 'old schoolfriend' of Anne's, I thought, as she wrapped herself enthusiastically round Max.

'Dearest, you're looking very *well*.' I got two air kisses and a hug.

'Is that code for fat, Vanessa?'

'Absolutely not.' She scrutinized me. 'I must say those Celtic gypsy looks do wear very well. When I was your age, I was planning my first face lift.'

I told Vanessa she was being absurd. She and Anne were only four years older than me, and, as far as I knew, she'd only had one 'tidying up' around the eyes. But Vanessa was a beauty, a chiselled, English rose, with curves that still brought building sites to a stop, and she intended to keep it that way as long as possible.

She simpered happily at the expected compliment and turned to Stephen. 'And you're getting so famous! I'm dropping your name all over the place.'

This was entirely likely. Vanessa was a strange combination of a crashing snob and an exceptionally warm-hearted person. Basically, she loved people, but she liked to feel that they were important. Most of the time her friends were, but when she accidentally met someone she liked who wasn't famous or rich – like us – her way of dealing with it was to talk them up so that it was okay to be seen associating with them. She'd been introducing Stephen as 'you know, the well-known architect' for years, and I'd always enjoyed the bemused looks on people's faces, as they tried to work out who he was. She'd been a bit more challenged to turn me into a great success, but had finally settled on 'terribly artistic'.

Vanessa bubbled away at me and Anne while the men murmured together with the odd shout of laughter. I noticed Anne's face soften as Vanessa related the impossible tribulations she'd endured having a Japanese garden installed in the London house. Anne's life was so busy that she didn't have time for frivolity, so Vanessa must have provided an essential occasional dose of sheer escapism. Perhaps that was the secret of their apparently unlikely friendship.

'Really, Vanessa. Ten thousand pounds on some white gravel and three odd-shaped stones.' Anne shook her head on being told that Vanessa'd got a special discount from the garden designer. 'Really. You are the absolute end.' But she couldn't help laughing.

'But think of the weeding,' explained Vanessa with evangelical fervour. 'Or rather not having to weed. Or fertilize. Or mulch. You simply must have a Japanese garden here.' She waggled a finger vivaciously at Anne. 'All I have to do with this garden is contemplate it.'

With the half-critical words 'I've never met anyone less contemplative in my life', Anne slipped away. She was one of those hostesses who are so busy that you never get a chance to talk to them, and if you offer help they politely refuse it and chase you into some large, comfortable empty room with orders to relax.

When she came back, it was to command everyone into the Great Hall to eat.

This had been favourably compared to the one built by Henry VIII at Eltham Palace, and it had, for a few generations in the eighteenth and nineteenth centuries, actually been used as the family chapel. Anne's father, however, who had been famously eccentric, had kept his pigs in it. Max and Anne had rescued it just in time, and now its magnificent oak buttresses and hanging tapestries were restored to their former grandeur, and, finally, after centuries of different uses, it was once again a dining hall. Max had had it painted crimson, which was stunning, but did make me feel as if I were in some huge cavernous stomach, like Jonah when he was swallowed by the whale. The long, dark wooden refectory table looked like a piece of doll's house furniture in the middle of it, and as for being able to heat such a vast space, well, not even Max had managed to find an industrial boiler big enough.

Anne's electrically heated hostess trolley, a ludicrously twee piece of kit from the 1960s, was always trundled through the stone-flagged rooms in order to keep the food and the plates warm.

I remember, as if I had taken a snapshot of the scene, the six of us sitting on those great gloomy Victorian Gothic dining chairs with faded velvet seats, and chattering, laughing occasionally or making the odd thoughtful remark. Three couples who had been friends for years, spending a Saturday night together. Successful, comfortable couples, at ease with each other and life. I had no idea, then, that it could all fall apart so easily. Nothing, as I discovered later, was exactly what it seemed.

Vanessa took advantage of a quiet moment to invite us all to the Designer Baby Ball.

'It's always such fun, and such good value. Only a hundred and fifty pounds a head. I mean that's hardly what you'd spend in a restaurant.'

'Hardly,' echoed Stephen, winking at me.

Barry frowned. Money was what sex used to be, something you lied about to your partner and glossed over in public, while everyone made jokes about never having enough of it. From the way he was looking round the table, I got the impression that Vanessa had slipped up in some way. Perhaps Barry hadn't been told the cost of the Designer Baby Ball until now. Still, he usually enjoyed Vanessa's extravagance.

'When is it?' Stephen sounded politely interested, but I knew he was stalling.

'It's our third ball that week,' interrupted Barry when he heard the date. 'You promised we wouldn't be going out too often this winter.' He turned to me. 'All these late nights Vanessa insists on give me indigestion.'

Vanessa avoided Barry's eye as she burbled away at Stephen, informing him that there was going to be an auction of celebrities' knickers to raise money for intensive-care units for premature babies.

'Max and Anne are coming, aren't you?'

'Of course,' Max loved parties.

'The farrier's due around then,' murmured Anne with a warning look.

'The farrier can come any time.' Max dismissed him.

'Oh, do say you can all make it. It'll be a gas.' I had the sneaking suspicion that Vanessa'd promised to fill a whole table, and was short of numbers.

I caught Stephen's eye. Written across his face, as plain as if he'd said it out loud was 'Too expensive.'

A volcano of frustration erupted inside me. I did know that this life at Stonehill was borrowed grandeur and that on Monday morning I'd be pounding round the supermarket aisles like everyone else. Blowing three hundred-plus pounds in a single evening was madness for us to even contemplate. But I was sick, sick, sick of being told that everything cost too much.

I turned to Vanessa with my sweetest smile, and said that would be lovely, thank you. Of course, we'd be there.

And I turned to Max and suggested that he and Anne stay the night after the ball. We had fallen rather too much into the role of poor relations, always accepting their hospitality and so very rarely repaying it with any of our own because we knew Anne hated the city, and our house didn't seem big enough compared to Stonehill.

'We're very close to the centre,' I added – it was true, we lived in an area more usually associated with inner-city deprivation than charity balls. 'A taxi for us all would be easy.'

Max looked pleased.

'We'd love to.'

I didn't dare look at Stephen. Vanessa and Barry, too, definitely weren't on speakers. But why the already chilly temperature of the Great Hall had dropped to freezing between Max and Anne, I couldn't imagine, except for her famous dislike of spending any time at all in town, let alone staying overnight. But we all agreed that the Designer Baby Ball was going to be such fun.

'That's settled then.' Vanessa dug happily into her pheasant casserole. 'I'll send you the tickets on Monday.'

Someone else's house is a safe place for a row. It's far enough away from your own life to stop it getting too serious.

Max and Anne never seemed to argue. In fact, they seemed to slot together without even needing to communicate. I never heard any of those tetchy exchanges that pass between other couples, about details that have been muddled or messages that weren't passed on.

Max got up early on Sunday morning, and went to church, followed by some meeting with the vicar and the churchwardens. This new sanctity surprised me until Stephen pointed out that it was all part of being Lord of the Manor. 'You know what Max is like for old customs. He'll be reviving *droit de seigneur* amongst the village maidens next.'

I giggled at the thought of Max ravishing a stream of buxom village girls.

'He'd love that. But he's pretty faithful to Anne, wouldn't you think?'

Stephen looked across the garden to the stables, where Anne was having the predictable debate over fetlocks, with the latest stream of people with muddy cars who kept driving up to join in. 'Let's just say he'd never do anything to endanger his comfortable existence at Stonehill.' He took my elbow. 'What about a walk? Round the lake and over the fields.'

I felt slightly nervous. Stephen sometimes really loses his temper about money, but he was always utterly charming when other people were around. His bad temper seemed saved almost entirely for me. But that's probably what all marriages are like.

We walked in silence for a bit.

'Don't you think,' he finally spoke, 'that we should discuss any major expenditure before just bowling ahead?'

I sighed. This ball was now Major Expenditure. Guilt made me angry. 'It's just a party. Just one evening. Not an investment in a Timeshare in the Algarve.'

He drew a deep, disapproving breath, so I continued: 'After all, we never usually do anything like go to a ball. I just thought it would be fun with Max and Anne and Barry and Vanessa.'

'We're different from Max and Anne, or Vanessa and Barry.'

'No we're not,' I replied crossly. 'They just have more money, that's all.'

'Don't be obtuse. You know perfectly well that's what I meant.'

'I'm sick of everything having to come down to how much we've got.'

'Really, Suzy.' He spoke as if to a wayward child. 'But you know it does. That's life. I don't know what's got into you.'

'Weren't we the same age once?' I dug my hands into my coat pockets and shrugged my shoulders up around my ears.

He sighed. 'For God's sake. I don't like always having to be the one that moans about money, you know.'

This brought us temporarily to a standstill, because otherwise I'd have had to say 'Why do it then?' And he'd have had to say 'Because I'm the one that earns most of it. It's basically my money.'

So I circumvented this part of the argument by going straight to: 'Perhaps I should get a better-paid job.'

I didn't add 'and do something with my life'. That wasn't what we were talking about.

We looked at each other and the prospect of a seismic shift in our relationship opened up in front of me.

'Is that what you want?' Stephen sounded ominously reasonable, but suddenly seemed rather a long way away.

'Not necessarily.' I wished I didn't sound quite so like a sulky teenager.

'Well, then.' He began to walk slightly faster, so that I had to hop a bit to keep up. 'Look, Suzy, we've been over this already. If you want a career, now's the time to go for it. Although, of course, it really is already too late. But don't kid yourself that it's going to be easy, or that you'll become a high-powered, well-paid superwoman overnight. Forty-something is quite late to be starting out. But if you want to do that, I'll support you in any way I can. I'm there to pick up the pieces if it all goes wrong.'

I kicked a few autumn leaves with my toe. 'Actually, I don't agree with you anyway,' I heard myself say. 'Life isn't about how much money you've got. I think we've got enough to enjoy ourselves. If we concentrate on the important things.' I kept my fingers crossed, because no one could place charity balls high on the list of things that really improve the quality of life, and I still hadn't really justified my desire to go, even to myself.

Just as I thought he was about to get really cross with me, he ended the conversation with a weary 'Look, we're committed, so let's just make the best of it. But, please, Suzy, no more three-hundred-pound evenings out. We do still have some university fees to complete.' I was so relieved that I hugged him, and gave him a socking great kiss to say I was sorry. I felt his body solid in my arms, hard and unyielding.

'Shall I wear the necklace?'

He started to say something but Max came striding towards us just as we were crossing the moat. Stephen took his hands out of his pockets, put his arm around my shoulders, holding me closely, as if I might escape.

'Of course, darling.' He kissed me back, as I saw his eyes slide towards Max.

My heart lifted. Wearing the necklace always transported me away from dreary, domestic reality.

Yes, we would go to the ball. I hugged him again in gratitude.

'I was looking for you two lovebirds,' said Max, waving a photocopied sheet of paper from the Parish Church Council in a distracted way. 'It's time for a drink, wouldn't you say?'

3

Perhaps I should explain the necklace, now that it was mine and no longer borrowed.

When I was born my parents lived in a rented cottage owned by a terrifying old lady in her early seventies, who lived in the large, gloomy, red-brick Victorian villa next door. She was called Theodora, and when she discovered that both my father and my mother played bridge, she commandeered their company two nights a week. As my mother's bump grew, Theodora let it be known, in a rather gracious way, that she would be prepared to be a godmother, and by the time I was born, my parents had penetrated her stately loneliness enough to feel that it would be hurtful to turn the offer down.

Accordingly I was christened Susan Theodora, and I received a fiver every Christmas along with a card written in a spidery hand. Sometimes, in my days of experimenting with my name, I considered using the Theodora, but although Max used to call me Theo as a joke, I couldn't really imagine carrying it off. Looking back, I would have liked to have known Theodora better. I hardly thought about her, except for the sudden surprise letter offering to lend me the necklace for my wedding.

When Henry Everett, Stephen's father, saw it round my neck, he gave me his first – and only – grunt of approval. In every other way he regarded me as an entirely unworthy daughter-in-law.

I didn't like him much either. The first time Stephen took me back to The Old Rectory, my immediate impression was one of crumbling elegance. With its huge Georgian windows, high ceilings and rambling generosity it was one of the loveliest houses I'd ever seen, but as soon as you walked into the black-and-white flagged hall, you knew that the cold, clammy feeling was not just the lack of central heating. It was tension.

We'd all sat down to a tough leg of lamb.

'Well,' gushed Stephen's mother, a ravaged beauty, 'isn't this lovely? So exciting to have a wedding.'

'I suppose we must make the best of it,' said Stephen's father, who gazed at either my breasts or my waistline throughout. 'This lamb is like shoe-leather, Daphne.' He then subjected me to a cross-examination about my background. None of my replies appeared to please him. Stephen occasionally interjected to defend me, but his mother put a pleading hand on his arm, and I shook my head, frowning. Stephen's mother was clearly terrified of his father and I was nervous of causing a row on my first introduction to my new in-laws.

Later I discovered that his father's study was the only room in the house where a fire was ever lit, unless they were entertaining formally. He would spend all day in there, only to emerge at mealtimes, shouting at Daphne, Stephen's mother, because she hadn't brought in enough logs, or complaining because the food wasn't ready exactly on time. Daphne responded to this by wringing her hands, apologizing and darting into the pantry for a regular swig of sherry.

'Dad's a bastard,' apologized Stephen as we drove away. 'I'm sorry. You shouldn't have had to go through that.'

But at the wedding, Henry spotted the necklace. 'I daresay they're not real, eh?'

I raised my head. 'As a matter of fact, they are.' I had no intention of saying that I'd borrowed them.

'Mm. Good girl.' I would have liked to slap his face, but he was Stephen's father, and Stephen, beneath his veneer of defiance, was desperate for his approval.

Whenever I picked up one of our wedding photographs to look at it more carefully, the necklace filled me with hope. It symbolized a day of borrowed magic and dreams come true, while the dazzle of the stones suggested a glittering life ahead. I always put the photograph down feeling stronger, suddenly convinced that everything would work out in the end.

When Theodora died, aged ninety-eight and still playing bridge, she left me the necklace. I was utterly amazed. It was the most valuable thing my family had ever owned, and didn't somehow fit into the life of mortgages, nappies and sleepless nights that Stephen and I now believed would be ours for evermore. I was determined not to sell it. Things were just improving – Stephen now had good work and the practice was getting better known, and we'd been able to afford to buy a little house. But The Overdraft still waggled its imperious finger over anything we wanted to do. The thought of simply feeding the necklace to it, letting it swallow, burp, and then return a few years later, probably even bigger and more aggressive, to make our lives just as much of a misery, seemed awful. I didn't want to do it.

My father did not want to see my only inheritance swallowed up in house renovation or debts from Stephen's practice. He wanted me to have something that was clearly mine. 'Every woman needs a little independence,' he counselled me. 'You're not going to be able to earn very much in the next few years – perhaps not ever.' I knew he was disappointed that my education, the privilege we'd all worked so hard to win, was being swallowed up in domesticity. 'You need something to fall back on.' The 'you' he spoke of was me, rather than us. So I managed, in the face of some opposition from Stephen, to hang on to the necklace.

We couldn't afford to insure it, but my father paid for its storage at a bank. I suspect he thought that it was the only way I'd manage to keep control of it.

Imprisoning something so beautiful inside a dark, cold bank vault seemed cruel to me, and I stroked its velvet pouch lovingly as we handed it over.

Since then we'd taken it out a few times, just for very special parties: a dinner dance Max and Anne had given to mark their tenth wedding anniversary when they took over Stonehill, the lavish opening of one of Stephen's buildings by Royalty and Polly's twenty-first birthday party. I came to think of the necklace as marking milestones in our lives, symbolizing the end of a particular era and the beginning of a new one.

Max and Anne taking over Stonehill completely had been the first time – although not the last – that a huge gap in wealth had suddenly opened up between us and friends. It had been the beginnings of a certain desperation in Stephen's eyes, a fear that he'd be left behind. And it was about more than the difference between Stonehill and our little terraced home in South London.

Stephen's mother died a few years after we married. She basically drank herself to death, although the way Stephen's father kept her chronically short of money can't have helped. He used her drinking as an excuse for being mean. He drove the car – he didn't trust her at the wheel of a smart car, he said – while she rode a bicycle or used a battered wreck to collect the boys from school. He had smart suits and dinners at his club. She dressed from the charity shops and drank alone. Stephen longed to slip her some extra – even though we were desperately hard-up ourselves – but he didn't dare, because he knew she'd just drink it away. 'Dad's just trying to help her by keeping money away from her,' he'd said, looking worried. 'I know he feels that if she has anything to spare, it'll just make everything worse.'

But Henry remarried two months after Daphne's death. Jean, a hard-faced woman, made it clear that Stephen and his brother, Nigel, were not welcome at The Old Rectory. When Henry himself died two years later, Stephen's childhood home, the paintings and the fine furniture were left entirely to Jean, including most of Daphne's own personal possessions. Henry Everett died without a word to either son, and Stephen was left with nothing to remind him of his mother or his childhood. I hated his father for what he did to Stephen.

From time to time, Stephen would raise the subject of selling the necklace. I almost thought he saw it as a threat. The only time I ever really wanted to sell was when I found I was pregnant again. Stephen and I talked about it. The thought of a third child frightened us both. The time. The exhaustion. The physical drain on my body – it already creaked and groaned from the first two pregnancies, which had both left me with chronic back problems. There was no room in the house. We couldn't afford it. I'd have to stop work again, and what would happen to the mortgage? I thought of my first sight of Polly's delicate, crumpled little hands with their tiny, perfect pink nails and suggested selling the necklace. Stephen laughed in a terse, grim way at my naïveté. It would be a drop in the ocean compared to bringing up a child. How would we manage financially without making the two children we already had go without? And we'd be dividing our love and attention three ways too. How could we do that?

Stephen had taken my hand. 'I know this' – he couldn't bring himself to say the word 'baby' – 'er, is all much closer to you than it is to me. I think you should make the final decision. You'd never forgive me otherwise. And I'll support whatever you do.'

Horrified at what we were doing, yet even more terrified of the consequences of not doing it, we decided on an abortion. I too pushed away the word 'baby' with all its related associations of softness, vulnerability and soapy, milky scents, and thought, when I allowed myself to think at all, in ugly, impersonal words, such as 'foetus', words which have no colours or sounds or smells. Even

69

so, I was ready to say 'Forget about the money, we'll manage somehow', up until the last minute, until the night I found Polly crying herself to sleep. Eventually we discovered she'd been systematically bullied every single day at the local school – a particularly bad one because of the catchment area we were in. 'I can't bear any more, Mummy. I want to die.' Stephen and I looked at each other.

'Let's send her to St Catherine's,' said Stephen of a fee-paying school nearby, his face white with anger. 'We'll find the money somehow.'

No, there was no room in our lives for a third mouth. Every night after the abortion I would wake at three o'clock, my pillow drenched with sweat and tears. I'd creep quietly out of bed to sit in the window of our sitting room, my head leaning against the cold glass, watching the silence, the occasional car swishing through the wet roads, and a ragged fox nosing around the dustbins in the hope of a discarded takeaway. The luminous yellow light from the streetlamps made it like watching a film from another era. I waited for the redemption of dawn, for some signal that I had done the right thing, but it was the middle of winter, and I was usually driven back to bed by tiredness and cold before the sky changed from dark fluorescent green to a wintry stone grey. I always tiptoed into the room that Polly and Jess shared, watching them sleeping in rosy innocence, the brightly coloured bedclothes rising and falling evenly as they breathed, wedging a teddy in more tightly here, pulling a sheet up more closely there. If anything should happen to these little girls, I thought, my heart freezing at the idea, I simply couldn't bear it. I was amazed that anyone, much less a loving parent, could put a price on a child. Then, aching in my bones and my mind, I'd crawl back under the bedclothes for a last, precious hour of sleep. Stephen would turn over, murmur something sympathetic and draw me towards him. I hadn't known what the sense of loss would be like until it was too late to go back. But this lasted only a few months, and eventually the summer came and I started to sleep again. Stephen and I never spoke of it after that, but for a while afterwards we were brisk with each other: quick to flare up and slow to reach out.

When I thought of the necklace during those apparently endless hours between the dark and the dawn, it seemed like a friend who had tried to help. I resolved that, having not sold it for the baby who was never born, I would never sell it now, unless things got really desperate. In my heart of hearts, I sometimes admitted that if I ever wanted to leave Stephen – not that I did, of course – then it would keep me and the girls going while we sorted ourselves out. Funnily enough, knowing it was there as a last resort, a little pocket of financial freedom, actually made our marriage better. He used to shout at me over the children's heads, and I'd think to myself: 'If he goes any further, we're off. The girls and I. With the necklace.'

And Stephen would see some glint of determination in my eye, and walk off for a few hours of quiet sulking, after which we would both behave as if nothing had happened. But all of this was no worse than what most couples went through. If I'd had to describe it, I would have said ours was a good enough marriage.

4

Returning from the weekend at Stonehill, we parked outside our house, one of an identical row in a slowly gentrifying terraced street. I felt the last of Stonehill's grandeur fall away from me with a certain sigh of relief. It was beautiful, but it wasn't mine. This house, with its comforting red brick and generous bay window draped in wisteria and ivy, was home. We belonged here. Every corner held a memory. I knew all the twists and turns of the roads through years of school runs, the man at the corner shop was an old enough friend to give me credit if I'd forgotten my purse, and I was even familiar with the crime statistics, because I was on the Neighbourhood Watch Committee. It was mainly car crime and graffiti round here, or kids getting in through open windows to nick the video. Occasionally there was a purse snatch, or, slightly further away, on one of the estates, something more exciting happened. Although these incidents occurred only a few hundred yards away, they seemed very remote and usually involved some private dispute over drugs or sex.

'It's freezing in here,' grumbled Stephen, as he unlocked the front door. He turned the thermostat up fractionally – sometimes he behaved as if turning up the central heating was about as extravagant as buying a yacht – and I let the friendly, human movements of the house settle around me with satisfaction.

The house had started to feel too big and empty when Jess finally went off for a whole year, but now, in comparison with Stonehill, it seemed to have shrunk over the weekend, and fitted me nicely. Fitted us both nicely, perhaps I should say, except that Stephen tripped over a coffee table in the dark sitting room, and barked his shins.

Still hopping, he switched on the light beside the sofa.

'If we redecorated,' I said, as the blaze from the bulb suddenly illuminated the difference between Stonehill's polished, comfortable antiquity and the kind of shabbiness that creeps up on you unawares, 'we could wire up this room so that the lamps can be turned on by the door.'

Stephen rubbed his leg. 'You don't get your money back on redecoration.'

'I wasn't thinking of getting my money back.' I could feel my temper rising. 'I'd just like it to look nice.'

'It does look nice,' said Stephen, going upstairs with his bag.

After the weekend away, we skated quickly through to mid-November. The first half of term, though, had seemed endless. I had struggled through the usual cold-bath immersion that signalled the beginning of each school year, feeling bereft that there were no children at home as well, to marshal with timetables and new coats and pencil cases. Even after half-term, whenever I passed Jess's room, unnaturally neat, with a pre-historic Blur poster peeling off the wall, and a row of battered teddies on the bed, or Polly's narrow little single cell, with its faded roses, something caught in my throat and I closed the door softly. Instead I tried to fill my days with my pupils. They seemed more sullen and graceless than usual this year, and it was getting increasingly hard to believe that I could offer them anything that would make the slightest difference to their deprived, television-filled lives. Their idea of a good portrait was one that looked like a photograph. I tried a joke on them one morning, and they just stared back, dulled into submission. They couldn't recognize humour unless it was accompanied by canned laughter.

I got the necklace out of the bank on the day of the party and walked briskly home with it, my senses temporarily heightened to the possibility of someone trying to snatch my bag. I slipped it deep down into my coat pocket, and walked with my head held high, proclaiming a street-wise city dweller who knew exactly where she was going. As I entered the house, I turned round, apparently casually, and checked that no one had followed me. Just like they do in films.

Once I closed the front door, I rested my head against its comforting wooden solidity. Homey. The phrase from the children's old chasing game came back to me. 'Home', or 'homey' as they called it, was where you were safe, where no one could touch you. The worst part of the chasing games, I seemed to remember, had not been the chasing itself but the arguments about where 'homey' was. Polly, ever cautious, had wanted huge, extendable homeys easily within reach, while Jess, always wanting a challenge, insisted that it should be somewhere small and difficult to find, a little patch of territory to defend. But they agreed that once you were home, nothing and no one could touch you.

The hall seemed quiet and empty, and my footsteps echoed on the wooden floors with the faintest, irregular echo from upstairs slotting in behind them like an out-of-time metronome. A double click, like someone tinkering with a latch. I stopped and listened, but could only hear the thumping of my heart. There is no one else here, I told myself. No one.

But I heard a different noise: a stealthy sneak of a creak, light and furtive. The Neighbourhood Watch leaflets always stressed that you should call the police if you were concerned, but I didn't think a few clicks really merited concern. There was just a fractional tightening in my chest that told me to be careful.

A small, dark shape slipped apologetically round the top of the stairs and twined itself against a banister.

'For God's sake, Truffle.' I was crosser with myself than with the cat. 'What on earth have you been doing?'

Once I'd retrieved the marble that Truffle had been tormenting – the clicks had been the sound of it hitting the skirting board – I slipped the necklace case into the breadbin because Stephen suggested that I always keep it somewhere unexpected as a security measure, and turned on the radio in the kitchen to fill up the room. It announced that there had been an unprecedented rise in crime. A police spokesman came on air to say that the figures were not, in fact, as bad as they seemed, it was just the effect of crimes being counted differently.

I switched the radio off. In spite of the reputed seediness of our neighbourhood, crime meant very little to me. I was used to walking over crunchy little heaps of diamond-sized glass where car windows had been smashed, or seeing the graffiti scrawled colourfully across garage doors, but these had just become hazards of life, like traffic jams and queuing. It was people like Max and Anne, who really had possessions, to whom burglary seemed more of a reality. They had spent an enormous amount on fitting sensors behind pictures and under floorboards, and rigging the stable yard up with security lights so that if you went out for a breath of fresh air after dark, you were blinded with a battery of searchlights more appropriate to an escaping prisoner of war. We just had a burglar alarm we hardly ever switched on.

When Stephen came home that night, everything, surprisingly, was ready. The beds were made, with clean sheets, there was plenty of bath water available, and I had hung up the dress, carefully removing all the shop tags.

'You're looking good,' said Stephen, as I handed the necklace to him. 'Is that a new dress?'

'Not really.' I laughed, suppressing a very small amount of guilt. It had been in the sale, but even that could potentially trigger off a row if he was worrying about money.

'The price of antique jewellery's doing well at the moment,' Stephen remarked, as he clicked the clasp of the necklace behind my neck. 'I think it's time to sell.'

My hand flew protectively up to my throat, covering up the glittering gems. 'Why?'

He pulled his dinner jacket out of the cupboard. 'The current jewellery boom just isn't going to last.' He pulled his trousers on, sighing with satisfaction as they did up without straining. Stephen had not put on the weight that some of his friends had. 'And I think we should move. To somewhere bigger. Really clear out everything we've got. The necklace would probably pay the moving fees.'

'But we don't need anywhere bigger.' I was astonished. This house was our achievement, our bricks-and-mortar evidence that we were a family. When we moved in, I'd thought it was for ever. If we went somewhere else, where would our memories be? And as for selling the necklace to pay moving fees – it was worse than just feeding it to an overdraft.

'We need to move somewhere more valuable while we can still afford it.' Stephen was beginning to sound dangerously patient. 'House prices are going to go on going up. It's our last chance to move out.' He fiddled with the bow tie, and checked the effect. He was still a very attractive man.

'Move out? Where?'

He readjusted his cufflinks. 'Surely you don't want to live here for the rest of your life?'

'Why not? It's where we belong.'

He looked surprised. 'No, it's not. It just happens to be where we live at the moment.'

'It's our home.' I felt horribly as if I was going to cry.

He turned away to straighten the curtain. 'You can make a home anywhere.'

'I don't want to sell. The necklace or our house. You

said we couldn't even afford tonight, and now you want us to – ' I struggled to find the words ' – I don't know what . . . buy some fantastically expensive house.'

He looked at me with exaggerated patience. 'It's an investment, Suzy. In our future. Tonight's just money down the drain. Surely you can see that.'

'So we'll bust a gut to move to a new house we don't really need, and spend the next few years being almost as short of money as we used to be, just so that we've got more of an investment? Is that right?'

Stephen picked up his hairbrush. 'Well, obviously things would be a bit tight to start with, but we can have fun without spending too much.'

'Yes, we can,' I replied grimly, turning away from him. 'And that's why I'm sick of doing everything for the future. When the children were growing up, I could understand it. Now it makes me think of Alice in Wonderland – we only ever have jam tomorrow.'

'Hardly.' Stephen pointed out that we were, in fact, having quite a bit of extremely expensive jam tonight. 'But, I'm sorry, darling.' He moved across the room to kiss me. 'I shouldn't have sprung it on you like that. Of course, if you don't want to, we won't. But think about it.' He turned my face up towards him. 'Will you promise me that? Just to think about it.'

Feeling unreasonable, I agreed to.

But as I rushed downstairs to answer the door, I caught sight of myself in the mirror, and once again the glittering stones made all the difference. My worries melted away, and my heart lifted. I caught a brief glimpse of a beautiful dark-haired woman, and hardly recognized the sparkling being as myself.

'You look lovely,' said Max.

I kissed him and laughed. 'You old flatterer.' But I could see that, tonight, it just might be true.

Anne looked magnificent in a simple long black dress with her thick hair tied back in a chignon. 'Goodness,' she murmured, as she came in the door, 'I'd forgotten how dreadful the traffic is in London. I don't know how you stand it.'

I found myself simultaneously apologizing for the entire traffic system of the Mile End Road and proffering drinks while we waited for the taxi. I thought everyone looked good – Max conveyed an impression of power in his dinner jacket. He still wore his hair over his collar, his only remaining rebellion against the conventions of the society he'd made his home. Stephen, following me downstairs with a shout of welcome to the others, looked extraordinarily handsome in formal clothes, I thought, very strong and in control.

5

We arrived at the red-carpeted ballroom entrance of the Grand Park Hotel as people swept in, eyeing each other to see if they were famous. Max paid off the taxi with his usual generous flourish, before Stephen could find his wallet. Max waved his protestations away, and we sailed in, led by Anne, to find Vanessa and Barry somewhere under the majestic chandeliers of the ante-room where 'drinks' were being served.

We found them almost immediately in the middle of a spat, as usual. Arguing was meat and drink to Vanessa and Barry. Barry broke off to hug me, then Anne, while Vanessa smothered the men in squeaky little kisses. In an off-the-shoulder wisp of white silk that curved and fluttered down to an exquisite pair of jewelled shoes, and diamond clips sparkling at her ears, she looked like a princess.

'Honestly, I can't tell you how stuffy Barry's being.' She pouted.

We all looked at him. He shrugged. 'I just think this evening is more about lining the organizers' pockets than about premature babies. None of the ticket price is going to charity, just the auction.'

'The auction will fetch thousands,' protested Vanessa, 'and organizing something like this is a lot of work. I think the person who pulls it together should have their expenses covered.'

Barry pulled out his pocket calculator. 'One hundred and fifty times – ' his eyes scoured the room ' – say, two hundred. I don't need a calculator for that.' I did, so I was glad he added: 'Thirty thousand pounds.'

'Barry!' Vanessa frowned at him as he continued counting.

'Say, twenty-five pounds a head for the food, such and such for the flowers . . .'

'Carnations,' she hissed at me, 'I can't imagine what their florist was thinking of.'

'The cost, I expect,' interjected Barry. 'I reckon this evening is netting him about fifteen grand. How's that for "expenses"?'

'For goodness' sake, darling,' murmured Vanessa. 'That's just the way it works. You know that.'

'Surely he can't actually be taking money that ought to go to charity?' I queried.

'People can do anything when they're in the pursuit of a lot of money,' said Barry. He should know, as he made his fortune building smaller and smaller houses and charging larger and larger sums for them. His company won awards for rather dubious achievements, such as 'Most Creative Use of Landfill Sites' or 'Compact Kitchen of the Year'. Still, there was something very honest about him underneath it all. I'd trust Barry in a fire, as my father used to say.

'I suppose I'm being poncey about my integrity,' he admitted, ruefully, helping himself to another passing glass of champagne. 'Anyway, let's try to drink as much of his profits as we can as a revenge, shall we?' He grinned wickedly, first at Vanessa, who pretended to be cross with him, then at me, and I settled down to enjoy myself.

The room buzzed with Rich Talk. I could hear a group behind us discussing the relative pros and cons of IVF over buying Brazilian babies. 'They're very cheap,' I thought I heard one man saying. 'If this next round of treatment doesn't work, let me know, and I'll get my man to send you some.'

The talk soon swung round to holidays, as one of the guests revealed that he'd just come back from the Cayman Islands. 'Visiting the bank manager, ha ha.'

'Really?' A banker called Nigel came into the conversation for the first time. 'I have to say that I always swear by the Swiss for my money. All that efficiency is just what you need when it comes to banking. And it makes it worth having a chalet for skiing.'

I caught Anne's eye, briefly. Her money, I knew, was all in Stonehill, tied up there as inextricably as the ivy that climbed up the pointed wooden porch that surrounded the heavy oak front door. It had a rope circle of weathered bronze instead of a handle, which clanged against the worn wood with a dull ring when you let go of it. And if anyone had asked her whether she banked in Switzerland or the Cayman Islands, she would have politely flinched from discussing anything as vulgar as actual amounts, although she might have murmured something about Stonehill.

'Ah, Stonehill,' they would have sighed. 'So beautiful.' Its very name was like a whisper of envy. These people with their homes all over the world – I could hear someone behind me saying that their place in Tobago was much smaller than the 'cottage' in Cornwall, but that somehow you didn't need seven bedrooms in hot climates – didn't have the sense that their bones would be interred with the bricks of any of their houses. Anne had roots, gnarled and deeply woven into the curving green landscape.

'Daddy always made sure all my trust funds were in Jersey,' squeaked Nigel's wife, Emma, who was tiny and neat, like a bird in chiffon. 'Keep it British, but don't pay tax, that's what he always said.' She turned to Stephen. 'Where do you keep your money?'

'Oh, here and there,' said Stephen.

I suppressed a giggle, along with the words 'in a saucer on my dressing table'. I looked at Emma's delicate hands, just turning translucent in her mid-forties, and manicured to pale, pretty points.

Even Anne started to look slightly desperate, although as well as Stonehill they also owned an indeterminate proportion of the village, also called Stonehill, and all the surrounding fields. As Anne had once said, 'We could ride all day and never leave our land.'

Max had raised his eyebrows. 'Only if we rode round in ever diminishing circles, dearest.' Anne's face had darkened, and I remembered someone saying that they'd slowly had to sell off parcels of land, and the odd cottage. The income from farming continued to dwindle every year. When her father died he'd actually sold quite a bit by then already, and death duties took more.

Someone told me that Anne and Max had been quite shocked by how little was left: 'Only about eight hundred acres, apparently.' Eight hundred acres sounds an awful lot if your garden is eighty foot and shaped like a railway carriage, so I hadn't thought any more about it.

It had never occurred to me to desire all this wealth, but I did long to be free from the gnawing anxiety that underpinned the lack of it. Now, however, with Stephen getting so famous – I could see him being swept off to be introduced with murmurs of 'you know, the Crown Project', and with the girls grown up, I had the sensation of being within reach of a safe shore. I could see an end to worrying, and the chance, at last, to have some fun. I really didn't want to take another huge risk, buying some eye-wateringly expensive property we didn't need just before some unforeseen downswing in the market. It would just be saddling ourselves with more complex responsibilities. Surely Stephen would see that. I touched the necklace again, briefly, for luck.

As Vanessa ushered us to our named places, I was surprised to be sat next to Max. I'd somehow expected to have to sing for my supper with one of the Nigels or Ruperts, and had been mentally priming my small talk. And I'd thought he'd have wanted to sit next to the celebrity on our table: Molly John, widely lauded as the 'most intellectual rock-star wife on the scene'. She wrote books which were famous for their 'insight and sensitivity' while her husband Jonathan smashed up guitars in hotel rooms. I wondered what the knickers she would have donated might be like: pure white silk, I imagined, to emphasize her lack of interest in anything frivolous.

'I'm sorry,' I turned to Max. 'It's awfully boring for you to have to sit next to me when you're staying with us. You ought to be next to someone wildly exciting.'

Max threw back his head and laughed, and Molly John shot him a sharp look. She'd been explaining the finer points of structuralism to the supermarket lord, and it was a serious business, judging by his intent expression and nodding head.

'Really, Suzy, you are absurd. There isn't anyone wildly exciting, as you put it,' he grinned, and added a tease: 'Not more exciting than you.'

I raised my eyebrows in mock disapproval.

He poured me some wine. 'So, have you read any good books lately?'

In anyone else I would instantly assume that this was small talk, but a vision of Max's beautiful empty room, his huge bed, and the piles of books we'd read together lying on the floor beside it swam instantly into my mind.

'I read a great one last week.' I rummaged through my memory. '*The Tortilla Curtain*.'

'A girly book?' he queried, and I remembered our arguments about whether books were for men or women. He'd said that there were good books and bad books, and I'd said that there were girls' books and boys' books, and that men would let a book get away with anything provided there was enough murder and gore in it.

'Not girly at all,' I reassured him. 'Written by a man.

But I did read the perfect boys' book recently as well. You'd have loved it,' I couldn't resist teasing him in turn. 'Every time I worked out who a character was someone came up behind him in a cinema and strangled him with piano wire. Or threw him off the top of a ten-storey building. I must lend it to you.'

'You must.' He took up the challenge. 'And I shall find out that it is a wonderfully written piece of post-modernist irony to be ranked amongst the great novels of the twenty-first century. You women – ' he was definitely flirting ' – take everything so literally.'

'There's something very literal about reading about the tops of people's heads being blown off like a boiled egg,' I agreed.

He knew I was winding him up, and we settled into a good ding-dong about books, forgetting that we ought to be talking to the people on either side of us.

'I'd forgotten how much I enjoyed these conversations,' he said, suddenly.

'Doesn't Anne read?' I wished I could have bitten the words back as soon as I said them. I didn't want to sound critical of Anne.

He gave a short laugh. 'No time.'

I let that one go. We had both agreed, over those mugs of rough, red wine so many years ago, that if you really wanted to read you got on with it, even if it was only for ten minutes before your eyelids closed at night. Max was as busy as Anne, but he clearly found time for books.

'So when do you read?' Was I being too personal?

'When Anne thinks I'm doing paperwork.'

I almost felt as if he'd told me he was having an illicit affair.

'And in bed at night, of course,' he added. 'What about you?'

'Oh, bed, too.'

The man on the other side of me, who'd been abandoned by his other neighbour, craned his head round in curiosity and leant towards us expectantly.

'We were just talking about what we do in bed,' Max included him in the conversation. 'How about you?'

I annoyed myself by going bright pink. Max was such a schoolboy sometimes.

'Ha, ha. Er, um,' spluttered the man, who obviously didn't want to be considered uncool. He caught Nigel's eye across the table. 'Nige!' he bellowed. 'Bought any good companies recently?'

'Well, as a matter of fact . . .' Nigel shouted back, and our shoulders sagged in relief.

'Saw him off,' muttered Max. 'Now what were we saying?'

On his other side I could hear a hissed argument between a husband and wife across the table as to whose chauffeur should be kept on duty for the evening. 'There's absolutely no point in Martin bringing me up from Staggers if he's just going to go straight back again,' said the wife, with a logic that was beyond me. Eventually they agreed that they would travel in the car with his chauffeur, but that her chauffeur would follow behind 'just in case'.

Max and I exchanged glances and tried not to laugh. I felt warm and happy.

When our separate neighbours eventually claimed our attention, I sat back to listen to a long diatribe on how clever Nigel was, and wondered about Max.

Occasionally I risked a glance at his surprisingly powerful frame, the way he poured out the excellent wine and leant back in satisfaction, and I remembered the intensely ambitious, poetic boy who'd burned with a desire to make his mark in the world. However much he loved Stonehill, I couldn't quite believe that this was what he'd had in mind.

'Of course, Max is a great businessman as well,' boomed my neighbour. 'He's really put Grand Oldest Brew on the social map.'

Grand Oldest Brew tasted pleasantly brackeny, like clean pond water, and Max had managed to get it into at least two smart clubs in the West End. Everywhere else, however, hip European lagers and New World wines were eating into the money that kept Stonehill's stables stocked with fine, intelligent horses and its gardens lavishly stocked with glorious blossom.

6

Although the Designer Baby Ball had begun in a starched, competitive atmosphere, with an immaculately groomed minor Royal Personage touring a few selected people, the atmosphere loosened up once the celebrity knicker auction got going. Each pair of knickers had clearly been purchased by the celebrity with their image in mind rather than rifled from their top drawer, and had obviously never been worn. It deteriorated into a riot of jokes, good-natured booing and badinage. My bet was right: Molly John had donated a pair of extremely expensive plain white silk ones – quite the nicest of the lot, in fact. Jonathan John had come up with a pair of Sixties-style Union Jack trunks. They smiled at each other as the bidding reached record levels for their items. Molly's was eventually purchased for three thousand pounds by a hot-looking middle-aged man who presented them back to her with a flourish, accompanied by stand-up cheering from the rest of the room. She kissed him demurely on both cheeks, and Max ordered another round of champagne for everyone. Stephen took my hand, laughing. I relaxed. He was finally beginning to accept that we could afford, sometimes, to enjoy ourselves. The shadows of his childhood, and of our early married days, were fading at last.

When the band struck up, Stephen got up from the

table and came round to me, leading me out to the floor.

'You were right,' he murmured into my ear, drawing me close to his dinner-jacketed chest. 'It's good to have an evening where we can forget ourselves. And I've met some very useful people.' He touched my cheek gently. 'You're looking good.'

I hugged him back. 'Sorry about the extravagance.' I felt grateful that I had a husband who could look at me through the gauze and Vaseline of twenty-plus years to see the girl he'd originally fallen in love with. 'But I don't want to sell the necklace.' I hadn't meant to bring this up during a happy evening. 'I'm thinking of the girls. I'd like to pass it on to them.'

He stroked my hair, as we revolved slowly. Everyone else was leaping around, shouting and probably putting their middle-aged backs out. 'I'm thinking of the girls too,' he murmured. 'I'd like to give them as much as we possibly can. And this is the best way. Go all out for the best property we can possibly afford.'

It was no time to make a final decision, but I couldn't help myself. 'No,' I repeated. 'Really. I'm sorry.'

Stephen's face darkened momentarily, and he shrugged. 'It's your necklace.' We revolved, slightly stiffly for a bit, until he added: 'But would you consider moving, anyway?'

Well, what can you say? I owed it to Stephen to try. And anyway, once we looked at what we could afford, I was sure he'd prefer to stay where we were. And we could redecorate instead, perhaps.

And perhaps I should be braver. The dancers around me, shuffling and twirling in their glittery Versace dresses, were not afraid of overdrafts. They simply restructured them when they got out of hand. Perhaps there was too much of the small-town bank clerk's daughter about me. I resolved to be braver, and gave Stephen the slightly forced, but wide, smile I summoned up for parents' meetings. 'Of course, darling.'

He kissed the tip of my nose as the music ended. 'Good girl.' He looked back at our table. 'Anne's on her own. I'd better ask her to dance if you don't mind.'

I bumped into Max after he left. He indicated the dance floor. 'Shall we?'

It was a slow number, and he drew me into his arms just as the last notes were dying away. We waited, slightly tense.

A vibrant salsa exploded from the band, and we both smiled, moved apart and let the beat take us with it.

Yes, it was time to have some fun, after all those years of scrimping, saving and worrying. I felt my body move in a way that I thought I'd forgotten long ago as I laughed and danced with Max.

It was two o'clock by the time we got home, drunk and elated to be up so late.

Afterwards, I tried to remember those last few minutes before we went upstairs, when we were making so much noise. Who was last in? Who shut the door? But all I could remember was Max singing 'Some Enchanted Evening', and Anne leaning back against the graffiti-covered wall opposite, laughing. I think Stephen was trying to kiss me, but I pushed him away. It was too embarrassing in front of Max and Anne, although they were far too drunk to notice. Perhaps — it was a last, desperate straw of a thought, this one — we didn't shut the door at all? Of course, we did. We must have done.

I remember sitting down on the bottom of the stairs, kicking my shoes off and laughing in that way that makes your sides hurt. I can't remember what was so funny, and it all seems pretty silly looking back on it. Since then, I've often wondered if there was someone quietly studying us in the shadows, or perhaps keeping an eye on us from a car. Slipping into the house behind us and concealing himself somewhere in the darkness. We wouldn't have noticed. My memory of the evening now has dark shapes around the edges, as if we had been in a wood full of hidden watchers. But I have to believe what I was told. That nobody had planned anything. It was all just chance.

7

I can't sleep properly when I go to bed late. I twist restlessly, opening my eyes to see the clock flashing unbelievably slowly, feeling my throat grate with thirst and my eyelids so dry that they don't close properly. Usually I slip into the blissful depths of real rest around seven just as the alarm goes off. Stephen lay toppled across the bed, snoring, apparently unconscious.

I was woken by a soft click, and lay there for a few moments, trying to make sense of the darkness. Years of instant alertness to two successive sets of teething, to Polly's asthmatic cough, to a sudden wail and 'Mum, I've been sick' fought against the desire to go on sleeping. Someone must have opened the door by mistake and shut it again quietly so as not to wake me up. Or Truffle was up to her tricks again. Perhaps I wouldn't put the light on, because that would wake Stephen, but I ought to check if Max or Anne needed anything.

Everything seemed familiar when I opened the bedroom door, but the darkness of the corridor flickered as the door to Jess's room swung slightly in the breeze. Perhaps I had been woken by the wind. I closed it, and was about to go back to bed again, when some tiny inner voice pointed out that I had heard a door shut, not open.

I don't know why I moved so quietly, edging down the stairs, moving as if there was someone out in the shadows waiting for me. All I knew was that some shapes and sounds just didn't make sense, and I was dimly aware of my brain rearranging things into their more usual order, before getting confused and reshuffling it all again. I waited halfway down the stairs, my heart fluttering in sharp, staccato beats. Too much wine, probably.

The front door was open. I was about to go downstairs to shut it, but I suddenly saw the flicker of a torchlight, from somewhere above me on the stairs. I froze.

There was a creak, as if weight had been shifted from one foot to another.

I was paralysed for what seemed like a minute but could only have been a few seconds. There was the quick rumble of footsteps and a hand seized my arm. For a moment, time stopped, like a freeze-frame on film. I had chosen wrongly. I should have done something else. Then the hand pushed me, roughly, and I felt the thrust of a foot against my back as someone clattered down the stairs. My shoulder crunched apparently painlessly against the bannister, and I curled up in a ball like a hedgehog, against danger.

Then I screamed, the noise ricocheting up the house and echoing down again like a fairground rollercoaster, as a shape, outlined against the streetlamp, ran quickly through the door. I can't remember anything else. It was not much to go on.

Had I heard anything, the police asked me later, such as the sound of voices or a car driving away? I couldn't remember.

Anne was the first to appear on the landing above, moving downstairs. 'Better check the house,' she said, in her low, authoritative voice. 'There might be someone else.'

I felt my knees begin to tremble. 'Surely not?' I looked around but no longer trusted my senses, and besides I didn't know what to look for.

She shrugged and tied the knot of the dressing gown tightly round her waist. Doors upstairs opened. Stephen, bleary and with traces of anger, Max anxiously asking me if I was all right.

'We must call the police,' I headed towards the kitchen.

'The police?' asked Anne, and finally I saw fear in her face, as if she'd only just realized what had happened. 'The police? Is that really necessary?'

But it was she who took the telephone out of my shaking hands and dialled 999, giving the address calmly, as if giving directions to a party. 'There might be someone else here in the house,' she said, 'but we don't think so. Everyone's up now.'

I switched on every single light to banish the demons, and the uniformed police checked each rumpled, chaotic room, striding up the stairs two at a time as their walkie-talkies crackled with terse comments. I flapped about, finding out that a milk bottle full of ten pence pieces was missing, saying that I was sure, absolutely sure, that a couple of the knives in the knife block in the kitchen were probably somewhere safe, but I just couldn't think where now. My handbag was gone and the television was unplugged, and 'ready to go', said PC 267, who was wearing a short-sleeved cotton shirt in the middle of a cool night in November, and Max didn't think he could find his mobile, but then remembered he'd left it at Stonehill after all. Otherwise nothing had been disturbed. 'He probably didn't even get right upstairs,' said the policewoman kindly, adding, 'Which one of you smokes?'

She had found a cigarette stub at the top of the house. On the floor, beside a knife that had been taken from the kitchen and placed at an angle pointing towards Polly's bedroom. 'Did you leave this there?'

'No.' I shook my head, sickened at the thought that the knife might have been intended for one of us.

'We don't smoke,' added Stephen. I clung to thinking about details, such as the cut of her trousers, and the walkie-talkie clipped on to her belt, as Stephen murmured reassurances about 'just a prowler'.

The police asked us how we thought he got in. Everyone looked at each other.

'I didn't double-lock the door,' I knew I sounded shaky, 'because I wasn't last in.'

Had anyone else double-locked the door? I thought Stephen had done it. He said he'd left it to me. Max and Anne didn't bother to comment, as it wasn't their house.

Everyone looked at the catch and agreed that, without double-locking, it wouldn't be that difficult to break in, although the policewoman pointed out that there were no signs of force or lock-picking. None of the windows was open, except our own. It was possible that he'd climbed up the house, they said, and slipped in that way. I thought of a big, dark, faceless man quietly walking through our bedroom, past our sprawled, snoring bodies. I felt a lurch of fear swing giddily down to the soles of my feet, leaving me icy cold all over. I wondered how long he'd watched us sleeping, whether he'd thought of violence.

After another brief inspection, the policewoman confirmed that they still didn't know how the intruder had got in. PC 267 asked me if he'd spoken. 'I don't know,' I said. 'I can't remember.' They exchanged glances.

'Did he hurt you?'

I couldn't feel any pain and shrugged. 'No, nothing.' I wondered, desperately, how I was to make my home safe again if I didn't know how it had been breached in the first place. Did someone have some keys? Was it someone we knew? I flinched away from that thought. Of course, not. Still, we'd better change all the locks in the morning. PC 267 began to take a brief description, asking us if he was black or white.

'White,' I said. 'When I realized there was someone in the house, I thought I should have stopped him in some way. What should I have done?'

He shook his head. 'Just got out of the way, like you did. He was probably on drugs, almost certainly prepared to use a knife. You want those kind of maniacs out of the house, not trapped in it. You did the right thing.'

'I thought he was black,' murmured Anne. 'I saw him too, but just from the top of the stairs.' We looked at each other, and the pen hovered over the notebook, poised.

I tried to remember why I thought he was white. 'He had gloves,' I dredged this up from the few seconds I'd seen beyond the door. 'Black leather gloves.' I could only remember parts of him, irregular chunks cut out of a nameless, faceless shape.

'Approximate age?' The pen hovered again.

'Young.' Anne sounded very sure, just as I said, more hesitantly, 'Middle aged?'

PC267 wrote 'young/middle aged???' He turned to me, quite gently, and asked why I'd thought so.

'I don't know,' I admitted. 'It was just an impression.'

'Build?'

'Quite heavy, really, but not too tall,' I said, feeling increasingly unsure of my ground. Anne muttered that she thought he'd been quite a big man. 'But I wasn't at a very good angle to tell by.'

'I'm afraid,' she added, 'that you're not getting a very satisfactory description from us. It was all over so quickly, you see.'

As suddenly as it began, the police were off to another call. I wanted to keep them there, for them to ask more questions. I wanted them to stand between me and the dark shapes that I now sensed in the shadows, shapes that were hidden and waiting for us to sleep so that they could come back.

'I'm so sorry about all this.' I didn't know why I felt I had to apologize to Anne.

'Don't worry,' she said, setting off up the stairs. 'I suppose it's to be expected if you live in this kind of an area.'

I felt a spurt of anger. For the first time ever, it occurred to me that Anne despised our lifestyle and pitied us. Looked down on us because we didn't live in a grand house. I'd always considered us all equal before, in spite of Stonehill.

'We've lived here perfectly safely for years,' I pointed out. 'Everyone everywhere gets burgled at some point.' I refrained from mentioning the security precautions at Stonehill, the lights, the infra-red sensors and huge gates, even the hidden video camera that silently whirred over the front drive day and night. I considered telling her that she lived in a fortress, not a rural paradise.

Later, I began to realize that people always want to find a reason why someone has been picked out of the herd. You have to blame the victim, because if you didn't there'd be no reason why it mightn't happen to you.

On this occasion, though, as PC267 had pointed out, 'Nothing much taken, no one hurt; you've been lucky, if you don't mind my saying so. Not to make light of your experience, at all,' he'd added hastily. 'We'll pass your number on to Victim Support.'

'Cup of tea?' offered Max, looking concerned, as I closed the door behind the police. I nodded, feeling my legs tremble.

Stephen put his arm round my shoulders. 'It's over. Time to go back to bed.'

I shook my head. 'I couldn't possibly sleep. But you go ahead.'

He looked at me closely. 'Sure? You don't want me to stay up with you?'

'I'll be fine.' I didn't see the point in us both being knackered. Anyway, Max had offered to stay up.

Max prattled on about nothing in particular as he

searched the cupboards for a pot, mugs, tea and sugar, mixing it up like a chemist preparing a remedy. I sat there, as wide awake as if it was the middle of the day, watching my hands tremble every time I reached out for something.

'There.' He placed the pot on the table.

'Thanks.' I stirred the tea, to give myself something to do, trying to ignore the rattle of the teaspoon against the china. 'Are you sure I'm not keeping you awake?'

He cocked his head on one side, and grinned. 'I don't need much sleep.'

I remembered that. It was part of his restless energy – he was always last to leave a party, while my eyes had always ached for rest. It was one of the reasons why I'd finally given up the endless media parties he'd gone to. But I'd have thought that he might have changed over the years.

I tried to make a joke of it. 'I thought that now you're grown up at last, you might have turned into someone who goes to bed when they ought to.' But I suddenly felt a long-forgotten twist of pain at the memory of the times he'd come back, alone, so late, with the elusive scent of other women on him.

He instantly understood what I was talking about, although I hadn't intended to bring all that up.

'I'm sorry.' He placed his mug on the table, and looked directly at me. 'I'm very sorry. When we were together, I was too young. I wanted it all – everything – in those days. It's taken me until now to realize that very few things are really worth wanting.'

I was shocked at those words: 'when we were

together'. Since I had married Stephen we'd never said anything to recognize our former relationship. We'd never said 'Do you remember?' or 'What about that time when we . . .?' We simply never referred to those days. They seemed to have belonged to two different people.

My first instinct was to drink up my tea and hurry back upstairs to the safety of Stephen, but I was too paralysed by the shock of the burglary. It was as if my usual defences had been broken down by the assault, and I was no longer strong enough to rebuild them to hide behind.

'It wasn't just you,' I admitted. I'd been too in awe of Max, for a start. I hadn't stood up to him. I'd fitted in with everything he'd suggested. No wonder he'd felt free to do as he liked. I wondered if everything would have been different if I'd been more . . . or less . . . I didn't think so. But perhaps not.

'I was too young, too,' I said. Looking back now, I could see that once we had fitted together and then we didn't.

'Max?' I suddenly felt very fond of him. Those sparks, the last tiny embers of anger, finally burned out. Perhaps because Max had said, finally, that he was sorry. And I'd acknowledged, if only to myself, my own part in it all. 'I'm glad it's all worked out so well for you. Really.'

He took my hand. 'And you're happy too, aren't you?'

I slid my hand away. 'Of course, Max. I'm very happy.' I refrained from saying that I didn't think life was about happiness once you grew older. It was about being safe, not being alone, having something to fall back on . . .

Safe. Suddenly I didn't feel so safe after all.

But with the euphoria of survivors, we talked about nothing much for hours, except that, rattling around in my head, making Max's words sound intermittently distant and hollow as if I was hearing them through the echo of trapped water, was the question 'How did the intruder get in?' I shook my head repeatedly but I could not dislodge the inner voice.

We talked about those few things in life that were really worth wanting. For Max, of course, it was Stonehill and the family. I agreed with that. Home and family. For me, Polly and Jess, although they'd left home, were still at the centre of my being.

'At least,' I tried to ignore the deepening pains and aches that were beginning to throb through my body, 'Stephen would add having enough money to that, but you've always had lots, so perhaps it doesn't matter to you.'

Max loves a good argument. 'Oh, I don't know.' He marshalled his forces. 'Money is at the heart of most betrayals, which makes it pretty important. That or love.'

'Stephen and I have managed without betrayal so far. And I don't get the feeling that you've betrayed Anne.' This was really a question. Lack of sleep can make you reckless.

'Mm,' said Max. 'Of course, at our age, love divides into sex and love. Not like when we were younger.'

Does it indeed? I thought that said more about Max – and very possibly about his relationship with Anne – than about our age, but I let it go. 'And money?' I asked. 'Is money different, too, now we're older?'

'Oh, yes.' I could tell that Max was enjoying this. He loves talking about theories and concepts, and likes to make up the rules as he goes along. 'When you're older it divides up into money and power. And money is more dangerous than power,' he mused. 'You can be treacherous with power, but you have to be clever about it. But money, well, that's different. You can do any amount of damage with money.'

I laughed. 'I don't think we've got enough to get up to much with it. Although I suppose we could steal some if we knew where to start.'

He frowned slightly. 'But Stephen's very successful.'

I shrugged. 'Two children. A mortgage. Money just seems to vanish into thin air. I'm rather hoping things might pick up a bit financially with the Crown Project, but there's always some reason why almost everything he earns has to go back into the practice. I don't really understand it all.'

I could see Max thinking. 'You should,' he said. He looked as if he was going to say something and changed his mind. 'Stephen was always –' he paused '– careful.'

By now the pain in my shoulder had penetrated deep into the bone, and I was finding it hard to move my arm. There were other aches coming through too. I couldn't imagine why I hadn't felt them before. 'Do you want some toast?' I asked Max with difficulty. Perhaps some food would help. The breadbin seemed a long way away.

'Are you all right?' I saw concern in his eyes, and knew how terrible I must look. For a moment, I was back in the students' hostel at college with a high fever and Max was there to rescue me. 'You're hurt,' he said, realizing it before I had myself.

My eyes scraped against the inside of my head, and I could feel the edge of a hangover curling up my liver. 'All over,' I admitted, and my voice seemed to come from very far away.

He got up from where he was sitting to feel my arm and shoulder and move everything round gently. 'I think you'd have known by now if anything was broken. But shock does funny things. You ought to see a doctor.'

I shook my head. I couldn't face it. I couldn't face anything. I leant my head against Max's chest, and he stroked my hair for a while. It was what I needed. 'How about that toast?' he asked eventually.

I nodded. Food might help. I felt shaky.

'Don't get up.' He went to make some toast, taking a loaf of bread and a velvet pouch out of the breadbin. 'What's this?' It drooped against his hand, obviously empty.

With a crash against my chest, my heart leapt as I remembered the necklace. 'Oh, Jesus,' I whispered, going cold with horror. Nowhere in my memory could I dredge up any detail of where or when I had taken it off. It was as if the night's events had wiped a few hours out of my life.

We turned the house upside down, the four of us, as my arm and shoulder began to throb more urgently, scrabbling desperately amongst dusty bottles and cheap jewellery that cluttered up my dressing table, feeling deeply into pockets, lifting pillows and moving furniture. All we found was that a couple of other valuable things

– a pair of silver candlesticks from The Old Rectory and Stephen's grandfather's fob watch, both left to him in his mother's will – were also missing.

As the police said when they came back later: 'It looks like he knew what he was doing, after all.'

It's funny how money is a measure for so many things. The loss of the necklace – and its value, plus that of the watch and candlesticks – suddenly escalated the importance of the crime, promoting it from a break-in to a proper burglary. Now we not only merited another visit from the police, but also an interview with a detective. It was like being upgraded on an airline – you get more attention, but you get to the same place in the end.

And our destination was, indeed, unchanged. 'I'm afraid you can't expect to see your things back again,' we were told. 'With no leads and nothing to go on, it's very unlikely we'll find who's behind it. If they're pros they'll be in Europe already by now. The best you can do is claim on the insurance and try to forget about it.'

But the necklace, of course, was still not insured. We could have afforded it now, of course, but Stephen had decided that we'd just be paying double to insure it and store it, and that it was safer, by far, in the bank.

Discovering how catastrophic the night had been made the ache in my shoulder worse, so I had it x-rayed in Casualty after we'd ushered Max and Anne to their car with cries of 'Don't worry' and 'Have a good journey' and 'I hope you don't feel too grim after so little sleep'. I'd been stunned by the burglary, the pain and the loss of the necklace, and, like a chicken with its head cut off, kept on running round in the same old circles trying to pretend it was just a normal day.

'You've really got to go to a doctor,' said Max finally, standing on the pavement beside the car. 'Do you want me to drive you?'

'I'll take her.' Stephen sounded short.

'I'm fine. Honestly,' I told Max, sensing Anne's impatience from the passenger seat of the car. 'Goodbye.'

We waited for hours and hours in the casualty department. Nothing was broken, but the bruising was severe and might make it difficult to sleep for a few weeks. I was given painkillers and discharged, blinking, into the bright, cold winter sunlight. It was a supposedly ordinary Saturday morning, but the world no longer seemed safe. It was as if I had been thrust into a parallel universe, identical to my own world in every respect except that malice and violence, fear and anger, were the driving forces behind everything. Even with Stephen by my side, I flinched at the roar of a truck suddenly overtaking us, at a ball which flew in front of us when kicked by a group of young boys in the street. Everybody seemed to walk too close, and cars shot by at terrifying, death-dealing speed. When the wind seized the front door out of Stephen's hand and slammed it behind us, I screamed again, surprised to recognize that that first scream, at 3 a.m. when my arm had been grabbed, had been so forceful that it had left my throat hoarse and sore.

The noise made Stephen angry. 'Don't scream. And

why the fuck didn't you put the necklace somewhere safe?'

'I did. I think. You've always said that it's safest somewhere unexpected.'

'We can't have this happen again, Suzy, we really can't.'

'I don't know how to stop it,' I said, quietly. 'I wish I knew.'

'I knew we shouldn't have gone to that fucking party.'

'It wasn't the party. And don't keep saying fuck.'

'I'm just letting out my . . . my . . . anger. At these cunts.'

I put my hands over my ears. I wanted quiet and reassurance. Each remark was like another physical blow. I leant against the hall wall. 'Please, Stephen . . .'

He banged the wall with his fist. 'For Christ's sake, I've just lost a fortune.'

'*We've* lost it. It was my necklace. And you did decide that it was a waste of money to insure it.' I didn't really want to say that, but my nerves had begun to jangle uncomfortably.

'So it's my fault now, is it?'

I began to cry. 'No, honestly it isn't. I just can't take all this shouting.'

He looked at me sharply, and then took me in his arms. 'Sorry, Suzy.'

'If I'd had any sense at all, we would never have gone to the ball,' I sobbed. 'It's my fault, not yours.'

'Sh, sh.' He was back in control. 'Sh.'

'I'm so afraid of them getting in again.'

'They won't,' he said. 'They won't.'

I knew why Stephen was angry. I was angry too. I

could feel it burning beneath my breastbone. We should have spent today comparing our hangovers and passing on gossip from last night, not in this parallel universe of casualty departments and people with blood pouring from their heads and arms. The shadowy man had taken more than a necklace – he'd robbed us of our sense of security. And he'd left more than a cigarette end – he was causing arguments between Stephen and me.

I covered my face with my hands: 'I want to sell this house. Let's move. I can't bear to think that I don't know how he got in.'

He frowned more deeply. 'It costs a lot, just to move. Without the necklace . . .'

'But you asked me, last night, to move anyway, even without selling the necklace.'

He avoided my eyes, and went through to tidy up the kitchen.

'So you thought I'd come round about selling it. You were getting me to agree to look at houses in the hopes that I'd fall in love with one and sell the necklace to cover the costs of moving there?'

'Well, it's hardly relevant now, is it?' He sounded exhausted. 'Seeing as we don't have the necklace any more.'

I was silent, tiredness and guilt damping down my anger.

'Look, Suzy, I wouldn't have made you do anything you didn't really want to do. You know that. But I just wanted you to look at the options. Not dismiss them out of hand. That's fair enough, isn't it?'

It was. But I was left with the niggling feeling that he

hadn't been entirely straight with me. Unless it was just that everything suddenly seemed crooked. It seemed such an extraordinary coincidence to be burgled on one of only three nights in around sixteen years that I had a valuable necklace in my possession. It was as if someone had known about it, but the only people who had known were Stephen, Max and Anne. But could someone have followed me from the bank? Could I have been talking about it on the phone, overheard by someone delivering something to the door? Could someone have been listening through the letterbox? Or watching us as we came home drunkenly last night? The city had a thousand eyes in all the little windows that towered up to the sky above us, in the millions of footsteps passing the door, in the constant stream of cars that poured down the road.

No. I sat down at the kitchen table and sighed.

'Look,' said Stephen, 'I promised I'd look in at that exhibition of buildings for the twenty-first century and meet Sean there for a quick lunch, but I won't go if you need me here. Unless you'd like to come too.' Sean was one of his partners.

I shook my head. It suddenly seemed very important to prove to him that life could just go on normally, with him going to exhibitions and me cooking up something delicious for supper.

But once he'd gone I felt overwhelmed by the pile of cookery books almost toppling off the kitchen table. Even boiling an egg seemed too complicated, and with the corridor echoing to the sound of my feet, I couldn't quite face trooping up and down stairs with the washing in case something sprang out of one of the cupboards.

I had to tell myself, very firmly, that no one could have got in there during the night. There was nobody hiding there, with one of the knives, waiting until everyone went. The police had checked. But it seemed best just to hole up at the kitchen table with the telephone and call someone, anyone, to stop myself from feeling so frighteningly alone. The kitchen seemed brighter, stronger, more cluttered ... in every way more itself than it had ever been before, but it was as if the walls were paper-thin. There was, I sensed, something really terrible behind those walls, and I was powerless to stop it breaking through and overwhelming me. I dialled Vanessa's number with a shaking hand.

Vanessa was still in bed with the papers. 'Mm.' I could almost hear the crumbs of croissant on her lips as she swallowed. 'Great party. Hope you enjoyed it. Did you talk to . . .' And she was off, dropping names. Vanessa is such an operator. She talks to everyone who matters at a party. 'You just walk through all the people surrounding them,' she explained once. 'Then make your impression and leave. There's no point hanging around on their every word.'

But she was temporarily stunned into silence by our loss.

'Not your beautiful necklace!' she eventually cried. 'You loved it so much.'

'And he pushed me down the stairs,' I added, because by now the pain in my shoulder was higher on my list of priorities than anything else.

'How awful. Did you break anything?'

Once I had wearily told her that I was fine, she

returned to the more interesting aspect, the loss of the necklace.

'But why did he leave the case in the breadbin, do you think?'

I admitted, feeling horribly ashamed, that I couldn't remember exactly whether I had, in fact, put the necklace back in its case in the breadbin when we came home.

'But you must have done,' she squeaked, 'if he took the knife upstairs with the others. He was obviously grubbing round looking for the knife and got lucky.'

I added that I thought I might have just taken it off and left it on the dressing table, and that the police thought he might have come in through our room. Too many thoughts, none of them conclusive.

'Ugh!' She shuddered. 'Creepy. Suppose he'd seen your tits. Or do you sleep in a nightie?'

Just as I was confirming that I didn't sleep in a nightie, she passed the telephone to Barry, unexpectedly, murmuring something about 'terrible news'.

He chortled appreciatively, but added: 'What's up, love?'

I told him. When I got to the part about my shoulder, he interrupted. 'Are you all right? That sounds painful, I'd say.'

'Oh, Barry,' I finally let go. 'I feel so guilty. It's all my fault.'

While he was telling me that I had every right to wear my own necklace in my own house, I horrified myself by bursting into tears.

'The thing that really scares me – ' I tried to suppress the sobs ' – is that I just don't know how he got in.'

'Perhaps you left the door open,' Vanessa chipped in, grabbing the phone from Barry again, sounding brightly comforting. 'Lots of people do, you know. I've done it myself, left the latch up and pushed the door to without realizing it hadn't really closed.'

It had been latched by the time we opened it to the police. As we were talking, I heard a rustle at the door and my stomach contracted in terror. Something dropped through the flap. For a mad moment I wondered if it was a ransom note for the necklace. I screamed.

'Tell her to stay right there,' shouted Barry, who'd heard the scream even though the phone was clamped to Vanessa's ear. 'We're on our way round.'

I waited for them by the front door, sitting on the floor with my back against the wall and my knees protectively up to my chest, lost in the parallel universe where everything seemed like a threat. Crumpled up in my hands, as tears ran through my fingers, were two pizza-delivery leaflets.

8

I slept in bits and pieces over the next week. Dropping
with exhaustion I'd throw myself down on the pillow,
often quite early, around ten o'clock, only to be jerked
into frightened wakefulness by the sound of a car horn,
a dustbin shifting or the yowling of the neighbourhood
cats. In that other world I'd been thrust into, in the
darkness, there were no innocent explanations. Everything was a possible threat. I'd lie there, my heart
thumping in my head, trying to reclassify and understand
the sounds, slotting them back into their familiar roles
with painful slowness, listening to Stephen snore and
worrying about it getting later and later, then gradually
slipping back down into a darkness populated by faceless,
nameless, shadowy menaces.

The only time I really felt able to sleep was when I
quite clearly couldn't. At work. The school was dreary,
and smelt of floor polish, chalk and sweaty pre-
adolescent bodies, but it was safe. As soon as I entered
the staff room, I was overwhelmed by a desire to burrow
under a duvet, which turned every lesson into a battle in
staying awake. It was like some kind of torture. Yet as
soon as I got home, I'd fling myself down on the bed
and be instantly, totally, alert, with my heart thumping and
my mouth dry.

On the sixth night after the burglary, I woke up to the

soft, subtle sound of someone moving about gently on the boards outside the bedroom, and lay awake for a while trying to tell myself that Polly must have let herself in in the middle of the night. (Stephen for some reason was away.) My feet, of their own accord, wrenched me out of bed, and I opened the door. I must be brave. I mustn't let this burglary dominate my life.

'Poll?' Perhaps she had slipped back to spend the night.

I could hear someone breathing in the silence, and thought I saw a shadow from the top of the stairs.

'Polly?' I tried to speak again but this time the word didn't come out and my voice rasped like an old file. The phone, I thought, edging back into the bedroom, the phone. The key had been lost from the bedroom door, and it wouldn't shut. I tried to dial but my hands were so sweaty and shaky that they kept slipping off the buttons and I had to put it down twice to redial. It was no good. The line was dead. Time telescoped frantically.

As I finally dialled the last digit, there was a crash and someone seized my arm again, harder than before. This time I looked directly into his face, and saw that he was wearing a balaclava but that his eyes had been burned away. Maggots crawled out of his sockets and the freezing swirl of evil choked my throat and chest, squeezing the breath out of me.

I screamed again.

Stephen switched on the bedroom light.

'Suzy! Suzy! Wake up. It's a dream. Just a dream.'

'He had maggots in his eyes,' I gasped. Stephen pulled me to him, stroking my hair.

'It's all over. No one's here. No one's coming back.'

As I tried to stop shaking, I saw him turn the clock round. Half-past two. He was going to Amsterdam in the morning, leaving at six for a ten o'clock meeting.

'I'm sorry. You need sleep.'

He rubbed his hand over his face. 'I think I'd better sleep in the spare room while all this is going on. If you don't mind.'

I did mind, but I knew what strain he was under at work. It would be a long day in Amsterdam by anyone's standards. For someone who hadn't had a straight run of sleep for six days, it would be exhausting. Guilt knocked my conscience, and I lay awake for the rest of the night, as he slept again, determined not to fall asleep and have another nightmare. That night, as he sat at the kitchen table, ashen at eleven o'clock, having flown to Amsterdam and back in a day and hardly able to eat the reheated meal I'd saved for him, I agreed, shivering at the thought of sleeping alone, that temporary removal to the spare room was the only solution.

'Are you sure?' He squeezed my shoulder affection- ately, and I suppressed a wince of pain. It was only a bruise, after all, not dignified as a real injury. 'You'll probably sleep better on your own.' He must have seen that I wasn't entirely convinced because he added: 'Everyone gets burgled at some point. It'll be all right, you'll see.' I knew he meant it kindly, to reassure, but it underlined the way I'd found myself completely isolated in a tunnel of fear. There was no reason to react like this. As he had pointed out, everybody gets burgled at some point. The parallel universe should therefore be as densely populated as this one, but every time I slipped through to that other world, with its ultra-bright colours and deafeningly loud sounds, I always found myself alone or faced with strangers I couldn't trust.

He hesitated. 'Look.' He made one last attempt to get through to me. 'If you need me just call. I don't mind being woken.'

That would be pointless, I thought, dully, because he was moving from our room in order not to be woken. I felt a sick horror as he set off upstairs to the spare room, looking cheerful. He seemed utterly remote and irrelevant.

That night, when I woke up as usual, having faced the faceless man again and seen the terrible things in his eyes, I was too frightened to call out, and by the morning, decided not to mention it. There was no point in having both of us at the end of our tethers.

I tried to be practical. I got the estate agents in. Thomas Rupert, a thin, greying man with a bulbous red nose, who smelt of red wine, Mark Carruthers, a young, keen boy who had obviously practised his charm in front of a mirror, and two heavily made-up women, whose names I couldn't quite catch, separately walked round the house, nodding wisely and speaking optimistically of the quite dizzyingly large prices that houses like this were fetching. They loved the house, the garden, the aspect, the atmosphere, the off-street parking and even the decoration.

'Will you be looking for somewhere to buy in the area?' asked Mark Carruthers, just about to leave one evening as Stephen came in the door.

'Yes,' I said.

'No.' Stephen spoke simultaneously. 'That is, we'll be moving out of London.'

'Moving out is one of the options we're considering,' I amended.

'So shall I send you particulars locally?'

Once again Stephen and I spoke together. 'No,' he said.

'Yes,' I spoke as firmly as I could manage. 'There's no harm in looking.'

And I talked to my department head about doing more hours, suppressing the thought that I hated my job by thinking about how much money I'd thrown away by going to an expensive ball, and taking a valuable necklace out of the vault in which it had been safe.

He looked regretful. 'Our budgets for subjects like art are being cut as it is.'

Stephen, when I told him about this conversation, was irritated. 'There's no point in taking on full-time work when we're moving out of town. And could you discuss things with me in future, before just sailing ahead?'

'Well, you haven't discussed this move out of town properly with me. You've mentioned it but that's not the same thing.' I knew I was being sulky. I felt sulky.

And it wasn't Stephen I was angry with, I told myself. I was angry with the faceless man who had taken away my necklace.

At least we had Polly coming home for a weekend at the end of November. She dumped her suitcase full of washing down on me, seized the telephone almost as soon as she got in the door, and took it into a corner, murmuring incomprehensibly down it for most of the weekend. I suspected a love affair going right. She declined to answer any questions about her job, her friends or her social life beyond a small, quiet 'fine' and my heart ached for the affectionate, confiding little girl at the centre of whose world I had once been.

I cooked roast beef for lunch on the Sunday, something I could ordinarily have produced without thinking about it. This time my head ached, I burned the gravy, overcooked the meat, cut my finger on the carving knife, and the potatoes were like bullets. Stephen and Polly pushed the food around under their forks and looked baffled.

'Sorry,' I murmured. 'Just don't seem to be up to my normal cooking.'

'It's fine,' Polly assured me. Stephen had probably taken her on one side and explained that the burglary was affecting me oddly.

The phone rang. It was Ellen, who was married to Stephen's brother, Nigel.

My heart sank. If I put her off, asking if I could call her back, she'd be sniffy for months.

She took ages to come to the point, while Stephen and Polly began to shovel food in.

She'd seen the piece in the magazine.

'I'm very surprised you let the girls be photographed.' She made it sound as if we'd let them be raped by paparazzi. 'I've always thought children shouldn't be used as accessories.'

I struggled to keep my temper. 'They thoroughly enjoyed it.'

'Did you see that programme about photographers drugging girls and taking them to Milan?'

'So what are you doing for Christmas?' I decided to change the subject to prevent myself from being rude.

I'd fallen straight into her trap. 'I don't think we'll be having a Christmas this year. Nigel's been made redundant again. It's not his fault, some bloody man at work took against him. Our lawyer thinks we've got a case. But of course it means being very, very careful with the pennies.'

My heart sank. We ought to invite them here. Ellen was infuriating, but Nigel was Stephen's brother. And they didn't have much fun. I opened my mouth to suggest it, and caught sight of Stephen. In the light of our last argument, I'd better not do anything without discussing it first.

I made sympathetic noises and promised that Stephen would ring Nigel back.

'I'm not having them here.' Stephen was adamant. 'I need a rest at Christmas. The Crown Project . . .'

I pointed out that they didn't have any other family – Ellen's parents were dead, and their two adult children were both abroad, probably to get away from Ellen's constant proffering of advice. After the burglary she had gleefully sent me lots of brochures and cuttings about insurance, and had had great pleasure in telling me that no wonder we'd been burgled, living where we did. 'You should come to Croydon,' she'd declared. 'Nothing ever happens here.' Ellen had enjoyed telling me that it was extravagant to go to balls, but of course she expected I'd rather lost touch with reality now that Stephen had got so famous. 'Celebrity is very destructive,' she'd informed me several times. 'Look at Princess Diana. Or Paula Yates.'

'Anyway,' mused Polly, 'I might not be here this Christmas. Some of us might do something.'

This cut me to the bone. 'Oh, Polly,' I said.

She looked guilty. 'But I probably won't go,' she added hastily, looking at my face.

'I meant to tell you, darling,' Stephen stepped in suspiciously conveniently, having obviously been holding back until he thought the time was right, 'Max called the other day.'

My fork hovered on the way to my mouth. My new wary self wondered where this was leading. 'And?'

'He asked how you were.' My furious eyes forbade Stephen to have mentioned a single, humiliating fact about the way I woke up screaming after an ordinary little burglary.

Stephen glided over this. 'He said that as Jess wouldn't be coming back all the way from Japan, we might all feel like doing something else this Christmas. He asked if we'd like to join them at Stonehill.'

'Cool!' Polly instantly jettisoned plans for 'something'. 'They're stinkeroony rich. Will Jamie and Harriet be there?'

'Apparently.'

Polly glanced anxiously at me. 'Let's go. If Mum's okay about it.'

I took a deep breath. I knew it sounded petty, but

Anne's remark about expecting burglary if you lived round here had rankled. I remembered the time she'd passed on baby clothes, saying that she hoped it wouldn't make us feel like poor relations. Stephen had said she was just trying to be sensitive, but I'd pointed out that everyone else managed to bag up baby clothes and pass them on without having to mention relative wealth.

I told myself that I was being silly. 'I just don't think that it's very Christmassy having Anne endlessly scrubbing roasting pans with a pointy face, and never smiling if you talk to her. She . . .' I ran out of words, because criticizing Anne, wonderful Anne, was one of those things that no one ever did.

Stephen's face went stony with frustration. 'I'm absolutely astonished to hear you say that. Anne is the most hard-working, considerate hostess I've ever met. Everything is always done beautifully.'

'She doesn't like us. Or perhaps it's just me.' I enunciated the words clearly, because they had only just occurred to me.

Stephen stood up, tossing his napkin over the greasy plate on the table. 'Well, in that case, I'll just have to ring Nigel and Ellen and ask them to stay. I can hardly ignore my own brother unless we're going away ourselves.'

The thought of Stephen sulking in his study over Christmas in order to avoid Ellen and Nigel, with Ellen hovering over me and asking me if our marriage was suffering from his success – one of the implications she'd made in an earlier phone call – was more than I could bear. 'Don't blackmail me,' I snapped.

'Mum?' Polly put her hand out to my arm.

'All right.' I spoke with the bitterness of knowing I'd been outmanoeuvred. 'Call Max. They are our oldest friends, after all.'

Stephen started to say something, and sat down again. 'We can have pudding first.'

They pretended nothing had happened, but from the way Polly chattered, offering far more detail than she usually did, I knew she was worried about me.

After lunch Stephen sat down beside me, and took my hand. 'Look,' he said. 'What about seeing a doctor? They might have some idea of how long this –' he considered defining 'this' and obviously rejected it '– is going to go on.'

'So you think I'm going mad, do you?' Everything he said and did just seemed so terribly wrong.

He signed. 'No, Suzy. But I do think you need help. Beyond what I give you.'

At that stage, no one had told me that those who recovered most quickly from a traumatic event were the ones who could talk to friends and family about it.

'I'm not doing it on purpose, you know,' I tried to tell him, panic-stricken at the thought of having to 'get better'.

That day, on the way to buy the papers at the corner shop, a tall man dressed in black had suddenly appeared. 'It's time to die,' he'd said to me.

I'd gazed at him in terror.

'Excuse me, do you have the time?' he'd repeated, raising his voice slightly as if I didn't speak English. It was the distorting effect of the parallel universe, which heightened and changed speech, sound and colour, then evaporated. I'd snapped out of it, and I'd found myself looking at one of our neighbours, although admittedly not one I knew very well.

I'd scuttled off, my knees shaking, muttering: 'Quarter past eleven.'

I thought of telling Stephen about this, but decided not to worry him. He was looking bewildered enough as it was.

'Perhaps you need a new hobby.' He looked at his watch. 'Damn. Time to take Polly back to her flat.' He escaped, looking relieved, but, as he reached the door, he turned round to tell me that if I really didn't want to go to Stonehill, we wouldn't. 'But I did think you might find it easier to sleep in another environment.'

He might be right. I wearily agreed that, in the circumstances, Stonehill seemed the best option. Home didn't seem like home any more, so there was no reason to have Christmas here, especially without Jess.

9

'Going away for Christmas!' marvelled Vanessa on the phone a few days later. 'How lovely. You won't have to do all that arranging.'

But I liked the arranging, the feeling of being producer, director and star of a one-off performance titled The Perfect Family Christmas, the senses of anticipation and foreboding mingling deliciously in the definite knowledge, forty-eight hours beforehand, that you had done too much. There was a satisfying rhythm to the lists, the trudging up and down the high street and the supermarket aisle, the deliberations over a traditional turkey stuffing or the brief flirtation with one containing this year's fashionable ingredient. I suppose it was a reassurance that I had my place in the world and was needed. Without the arranging, I felt empty and useless.

I rang Anne to find out if I could bring anything from London, specialist cheeses, elaborately expensive crackers, organic hams or the fat, glossy chocolates that were hand-made in a little shop in Soho. She quietly made it clear that everything in Suffolk was so infinitely superior to anything you might find in London that there was hardly any point in bothering.

'Just bring yourselves.' She spoke in her calm, collected way.

I replaced the phone feeling raw. The burglary had

stripped off the top layer of my skin, leaving me vulnerable to the slightest hurt, even to something as trivial as a slur on the local cheese shop. It was silly, I told myself, brushing away an idiotic, irrelevant tear, just stupid tiredness or perhaps even hormones.

I decided to go for a walk, not because I had to go anywhere, but because the house seemed simultaneously dreadfully silent, yet vibrating with small, indescribable and menacing noises.

I found myself in front of a shop that I'd loved for years, because it had been such a good source of treasure: pretty old plates, an occasional extra dining chair that, amazingly, fitted in with the ones we'd got already, or the odd old Victorian glass. It was an Old Curiosity Shop in every way, except that it had the cumbersome name of 'The Past Is Another Country', shortened to The Past by locals and the girl who answered its phone.

She was on the phone as I went in.

'Really! It's a bit much.'

There was a twittering on the other end.

'Well, I don't care if you do have to go to Rwanda. The deal has been that you go to auctions and I mind the shop. That's the split. If you leave, I don't know what I'll do.'

There was more chirruping that went on for much longer this time, while I looked round. It had been some time since I'd found any good bargains here. It had been owned by this girl's mother, who'd had a magpie's eye for pretty things. And, of course, that was before the *Antiques Roadshow* led everyone to believe that even a little cracked teapot might be worth a fortune. Instead of genuine old plates and charming pieces of dusty bric-a-brac, the past that most of these things represented was not a very distant country at all. I picked up a blue-and-white plate and turned it over to read the back. Probably made in Taiwan some time over the last ten years. I replaced it and sighed. It was an afternoon for finding something to lift the spirits, something unexpected. There was nothing here, in this collection of heavy stained oak and cheap rickety pine, no surprises in the flat, dull green and blue plates and cheap lacy pieces of souvenir china that cluttered up the surfaces. But, as I knew, stock was hard to get. When the old woman had closed the shop on her last day, I'd been walking past. 'I've had the best of it,' she'd told me. 'There's nothing much left to buy except the really expensive stuff. Still, that's Alice's problem now.'

It was Alice, presumably, who slammed down the phone. 'Honestly! Some people.' She seemed to notice me for the first time. 'Sorry. Can I help you? It's just that my partner's backing out. She's going to Rwanda. Can you believe it?'

She repeated that her partner was responsible for stocking the shop. 'I suppose I'll have to do it now,' she grumbled. 'And close the shop while I'm away. Or find someone to look after it.'

'I'm looking for a part-time job.' The words were out of my mouth before I had time to think.

'Really?' She looked doubtful. 'It's not very ... exciting.'

I laughed for the first time for what seemed like ages. 'It'll suit me nicely then. I'm not looking for excitement.'

Almost unconsciously I checked the room. How safe did it feel? Surprisingly safe, because I couldn't imagine anyone wanting to steal – or buy – anything in it. Not even a crack-crazed fiend could possibly see any gain in this run-down shop. And the glass window on to the street made me feel oddly secure, in the same way that being inside my own home felt terribly exposed. I suppose that's because once someone is inside your home they can do anything and no one would see them. No one would know that you needed help. And I felt that anyone could get into my home now, they could seep up through the floorboards, or appear genie-like through the keyhole. But here, on view for the whole street to see, I felt much safer.

So we settled on an hourly sum that was rather less than Vanessa pays her gardener, and times that would be adjusted every week according to my teaching commitments and her auctions or house visits. I would start tomorrow so that she could show me the ropes.

I had found something unexpected to lift the spirits after all. There was something very undemanding and comforting about The Past's cluttered interior.

Stephen wasn't sure whether to be exasperated or relieved. 'A shop?' he repeated doubtfully. 'Are you sure it's what you want?'

Sure? I felt like snapping at him. Of course I wasn't sure it was what I wanted. I hadn't the faintest idea what I wanted, in fact, apart from a sudden burning need to earn some money to replace the necklace, and although this wasn't very much, it was something. I had resolved to save every penny of it. My teaching salary had always provided the housekeeping, but this, I resolved, was going to be for me.

'I'm going to save it.'

Stephen hesitated. 'You're always saying you need more money for the housekeeping.'

I ignored that. 'It's not very much,' I added. 'But it'll be useful for us to have a small sum in reserve.'

He nodded, looking uneasy. I think he thought I was so useless with money that I'd blow it all on some extravagant item. For a moment I even considered trying to shrink The Overdraft with it, but it seemed like trying to empty the ocean with a bucket, so I decided not to bother.

And so began one of the most peaceful, least eventful jobs imaginable. After facing a restless group of thirty children who saw art merely as an easier bet than maths, and a good opportunity to play up, I'd bicycle to the musty shop, and settle down behind the counter with a novel, occasionally looking up as someone wandered in. The most they ever did was turn over a few plates, or inquire about a chest of drawers, then go away again when they discovered the chest was rickety, or the plate not as nice as they'd hoped it would be from the window. There was very little to do, I thought, as I sat there two weeks later, beyond making calculations as to how many hours I could go on doing this before I made up the cost of the necklace again. Years, if you worked quite a lot of days each week. Pleasant as this way of earning money was, it still sounded like a prison sentence when you looked at it that way. It emphasized how incredibly irresponsible I'd been in wearing the necklace, in keeping it rather than selling it, in not insisting on insuring it, in not checking that the door was shut properly . . .

I could feel heat mounting in my cheeks at the thought of that night, and could sense the distorting mirrors of the parallel universe at the corners of my vision. I'd eventually been persuaded to see a therapist, who'd taught me deep breathing to calm me down when I felt panicky. It involved a complicated routine, which I never quite grasped, of making sure that the air filled one's stomach and not breathing in the top part of your chest. I never got it right, muddling up the in breath and the out breath until I felt suffocated, as if someone had moved a large stone on to my chest. But I had been assured that once I got the knack, I'd feel much calmer.

Just thinking about it all made my throat feel dry and my blood pump in my ears. The walls of the shop began to close in on me as a sense of panic began to rise. 'Think about trivial things, easy things, concentrate on something else, focus on something as simple as a tin of baked beans,' the therapist had said.

Still with a hand on my stomach, in order to breathe in the right place, I focused on the miserable collection of furniture in the shop, distracting myself by giving each item marks out of ten for hideousness. Suddenly, I realized that there was rather a sweet little chest hidden there behind a phenomenally ugly wardrobe. I could clean it up and put it in the window, and make an effort to dress it up with the plates, perhaps a couple of the lovely worn old orange Penguin classics from the 1950s that lurked in a box somewhere. As it was nearly

Christmas, the green plates, I thought, would be the best, and a little jug – the simple white one over there – would look charming if I brought in some holly and ivy from the garden. And, fired with a certain amount of enthusiasm, I thought the whole lot would look better if the windows were at least clean. The sense of weight on my chest began to ease, and I drew a breath of pure, clear air. When I look back on that moment, I think it was the first sign that I had been, in some way, ill, and that I was getting better.

I brought in some cleaning materials the next day – it was a Thursday. Alice claimed to be going to an auction in Bath and wanted to be away the whole day, although I was beginning to suspect that she just wanted time off from the shop. I couldn't imagine how she made a living from it, but it wasn't my problem, thank goodness.

I'd done the inside windows, perched perilously on wobbly stools and tables, and took a dusty stepladder outside on to the street. It was hard, invigorating work.

'Heavens.' I jumped as a familiar voice sounded amused behind me, just as I was finishing. 'Have you become a window cleaner now?'

I put down my polish and cloth, edging carefully down the stepladder. It was ironic to be worrying about what virtually imaginary burglars could do while genuinely risking one's life on a dodgy stepladder. 'Max, you bastard, that gave me a fright.'

He laughed and, amazingly naturally, kissed my cheek. He smelled of woodsmoke, lavender and newly ironed shirts. I realized that I'd missed him since those long, dark hours between the burglary and the dawn. It was as if he was the only one who would understand.

'Vanessa said you were doing something frightfully unsuitable, but I'd no idea it was window cleaning. You must find out some delicious secrets that way.'

'Did she now?' Bloody Vanessa was such a snob. 'Working in a shop?' she'd screeched. She'd have been thrilled if I'd been working in Prada and she could swan in and out. 'Well, as you can see, Max, I'm selling bric-a-brac. As I think it's called. Which would be absolutely fine with Vanessa if it was the sort of shop she could get discounts in.'

Max looked in the window – you could actually see in now that I'd cleaned it – and obviously tried to think of something to say. 'Mm.' He stood back. 'Very pretty shopfront, though.'

That's what was so nice about Max. He always found something positive to say.

'It is, isn't it?' It was a typical old Victorian shop window, which hadn't been touched since the shop was built in the nineteenth century. The big glass panels were framed by slender wooden pillars with flaking maroon paint, and a huge battered-tin shop sign, still with the old grocery-store name on it, stretched overhead ('The Past Is Another Country' had been painted across the window). A delicate, black metal awning stretched over the door, and there were cracked Victorian tiles on the step. When a customer pushed the old door open, it set off a brass bell, suspended overhead, which issued a comforting clang.

'So.' He turned back to me. 'You're going to be an antiques tycoon.'

I sighed. 'Why has everything got to be so important? Why do I have to be a tycoon? I'm just sitting in a shop, full of pretty horrible things, getting a bit of time to myself, and earning some money.'

His eyes crinkled up at the corners in a smile, and honesty forced me to add, 'Not very much money, I admit. But it's a job. That's all. Nothing dramatic. Nothing dynamic. No one's allowed just to be these days, are they?'

'Well, if you come out to lunch with me, I promise to allow you just to be.'

'Has Stephen sent you to talk to me?' I was getting paranoid, and, anyway, I couldn't think why Max was here.

Max looked genuinely surprised. 'No. What about?'

'He thinks I'm going mad. After the burglary.'

'And are you?'

I could feel the tears, now always too close to the surface, start up, and I turned away to pick up the polish and cloth. Max followed me inside, and I swallowed. The bell clanged twice, and the door creaked shut behind us. To give myself time, I didn't answer until I was in a little side room, where a cluttered lavatory and a butler's sink jostled for space with pans and brushes. 'No,' I shouted. 'I'm absolutely fine.'

I came out, feeling more collected. Max looked concerned, and I suspected he'd seen the edge of my tears.

There was an awkward silence between us. 'Good,'

he said. 'But your face is filthy.' He stroked my cheek with a smile. 'There's a big mark just here.' His thumb touched my nose. 'And more here.'

'If you keep an eye on the shop,' my voice sounded hoarse even to me, 'I'll wash my face.'

'I'll wait for you.' Max turned away and began to examine a very second-rate fruit bowl, a dull, thick piece of china printed with blunt, garish roses and rimmed with a band of peeling gilt.

I splashed my face with water and pulled a brush through my hair, deliberately avoiding any artifice. I would not put on my lipstick for Max, I didn't want to see his eyes light up, as they always did at any sign of femininity. Max loved women too much, and I didn't want to be a woman to him. At the last minute, though, I changed my mind and pulled a battered stump out of my bag. Just to give myself some colour. I looked too tired these days.

He put the bowl down as I came back. 'That was quick.'

I indicated the bowl. 'Pretty ghastly, isn't it?'

'Do people buy these things?'

'Hardly ever.' I flipped the sign to 'Closed' and turned the key in the lock.

Max raised an eyebrow. 'No burglar alarms? Just a little key? Aren't you worried about theft?'

He and I turned round at the shop behind us, and our eyes met in reflection over a cream melamine wardrobe in fake Louis Quinze style. The thought of anyone trying to steal it made us simultaneously dissolve into fits of giggles.

'No, well, perhaps not.' He took my elbow to guide me across the road. I relaxed. Lunch would be lovely.

We went to an Italian restaurant, all white walls, a black-and-white tiled floor, white tablecloths and slabs of modern art on the walls. Perhaps, in twenty-five years' time, we'd remember it with as much amusement as the Luigi's of our student days, with its ceilings draped in fishermen's nets and Chianti bottles dripping with wax.

Max listened to me talk about the house, as we ate rocket and Parmesan salad, followed by pumpkin-stuffed tortelloni, and I told him how Stephen and I had both agreed it was time to move on. I made jokes about the way we couldn't agree on what it was we wanted to move on to.

'So,' he leant back with a sigh of satisfaction, 'what do you really want to do?'

I gazed at him blankly. 'What do you mean?'

'What really gives you pleasure? Now that you have time. Or don't you?'

'God, I get far too much now that the girls have gone. That's probably half the problem.' I didn't really believe this, as my time seemed to be as eaten up as ever.

'And what do you do with it?' Max was so endlessly ambitious, I thought, that he couldn't even contemplate just sitting down and reading the paper.

'Well, you know. Teaching, washing, fetching the dry cleaning ... sticking bits of handles back on to old dressers, painting things a bit, seeing friends, Neighbourhood Watch, more teaching ... reading,' I added lamely. He would think me so dull and suburban. Just a housewife.

I flushed, as he looked at me intensely with those great dark eyes of his. He always gave the impression of being able to see right down into your soul, and I certainly didn't want that, because mine felt rather empty. I imagined it as full of broken washing machines and library books that had been returned too late.

'I said for yourself,' he replied gently. 'Things you like doing. Except for reading, most of those are chores.'

I wasn't ready to think about what I really wanted out of life, so I changed the subject and asked him about Stonehill, because even if I didn't know what I really loved, I did know what he loved. He told me about the latest improvements, and how much they were all looking forward to seeing us, that Jamie and Harriet were looking forward to having Polly for Christmas. I told him that we were looking forward to it as well, but wasn't it a lot of work for Anne?

'Oh, no.' He looked happy. 'Anne likes being at the centre of it all. It does her good.'

Perhaps it did. As a sense of peace and wellbeing crept over me for the first time for weeks, I was prepared to give her the benefit of the doubt.

10

But Max had the fugitive's habit of concealment. Or perhaps it was just the secretiveness of the very, very rich. He never told you any more than you needed to know. It was not because he wanted to mislead, I thought, but because he felt, deep down, somehow hunted. The less anyone knew about him, the less chance there was of someone taking something away from him. Twenty-five years ago, I had lived with him in the South Kensington flat for almost six months before I'd discovered that he owned the whole building, and the one next door, and that the source – or maybe it was only one source – of his wealth appeared to be the rents from the various tenants. His father had managed to get some money out of Poland when he left, and after the War, property had been very cheap, so Max's father had accumulated houses in Mayfair and Belgravia. I didn't know if Max still owned it all. A few were definitely sold when South Kensington became so hugely desirable in the 1980s, because that was exactly when Stonehill was soaking up cash like a huge, unquenchably thirsty sponge. But, of course, friends don't talk about money. Not if they've got a lot anyway.

And Max, during lunch, had not told me what would happen at Christmas or who would be there.

*

It crept up on us, surprisingly quickly, as people snuffled and sneezed their way into the Festive Season. There was the usual hysteria at school, as demands for angels' wings and ox masks threatened to swamp the art department, and children appeared more hollow-eyed with excitement and lack of sleep every morning. Vomit appeared more frequently on pavements at street corners, and the traffic got increasingly erratic, alternating virtually empty streets with grid-locked gloom. Occasionally yellow road signs proclaimed that a robbery, an assault or even, worryingly, arson, had taken place locally, and the parallel universe threatened to swamp me again, but I walked past them briskly, ashamed of my cowardice. I saw other people scuttle past, turning their heads to look at something else, and began to realize how many other people were afraid too. I still visited a therapist once a week, at nine o'clock on a Wednesday morning, but it seemed to me that we'd started to go round in circles. Bad things happen. Therapy can't undo them, it can only give you a few techniques for coping with them, and I thought I'd probably learned as much as I was going to at this point. The last Wednesday before Christmas, I didn't make another appointment, and, feeling slightly furtive, closed the door behind me without any intention of going back. But, I had to admit, it had helped me.

Eventually the day arrived to drive up to Stonehill – the night before Christmas Eve. Stephen took an extra day off to miss the traffic, and Alice, rather unexpectedly, agreed to cope with the 'Christmas rush' in the shop on Christmas Eve. A rush, at The Past, meant one person buying a plate in the morning, and another buying a small chest in the afternoon. This level of activity was rare, although the little chest had sold, along with the green plates and the little white jug, the day after my lunch with Max. I'd enjoyed the peacefulness of the shop at Christmas, rearranging bits and pieces for the window, or occasionally cleaning up and painting one of the more promising bits of furniture in the back yard behind the shop. Years of making papier mâché 'islands' and sculptures out of loo rolls with classes of school children had given me some useful experience when it came to smartening up cheap second-hand furniture.

But we left it all behind and drove Polly up to Suffolk, feeling liverish and slightly bad-tempered after a round of apparently identical Christmas parties. We were welcomed by the cool, soft air of Stonehill, a roaring log fire, Max's generous hugs, and one of Anne's most robust and warming stews. Jamie had turned into a pleasant, self-assured young man, who carried our bags upstairs and offered drinks with unusual grace, and Harriet was as tall as her mother, but with Max's striking high cheekbones. She was wearing baggy leather trousers, a torn top, and was, she informed me, having a great time at college organizing an exhibition of Vaginal Art.

I woke late on the morning of Christmas Eve, and stretched luxuriously under the linen sheets, the velvety langour of a blissful, brilliant sleep softening away all the tension in my muscles and bones. Stephen, I thought, joyously, had been absolutely right. Getting away from home, with its creaks and rustling noises, away from all those decisions about Life with a capital L, the arguments about where we should live, just away from the daily grind, had been what I needed to get me back to sanity.

Stephen wrapped his towelling dressing gown round him and strode across the room to see what sort of day it was.

'Good God!' He pressed his face to the tiny window-panes, wiping away the steam left by his breath. As he opened the window to see better, I could just see a frosty lacework of bare branches across an astonishingly pale turquoise sky. 'It's her. It's Max's mother.'

I sat up, amazed. I had never even met her. Max had hardly ever referred to her. I'd assumed, insofar as I gave it a thought, that she had died long ago. When we'd all met at college, it had seemed as if we were suspended in space, unfettered by parents or a past, or even, really, a home. Mothers tended not to come up in conversation.

'I haven't seen her since we were all about eleven. She used to come down in a huge great chauffeur-driven car and take us all out for a slap-up tea. She was quite young and very beautiful.'

'What's she like?'

Stephen started to get dressed. 'The sort of woman who wears full-length fur coats and parks her Mercedes in Disabled parking spaces, if I remember rightly.'

I laughed. Sometimes Stephen can be very funny. But then I suddenly realized what he'd said. 'You mean she never came down after then?'

He shook his head. 'No, Max used to come to us at The Old Rectory for days out and holidays. She got rid of Max's first stepfather, because he was dull and nice – even if he was very rich – and married a Count Kisfaludy, who was dangerously exciting, very good-looking and absolutely penniless. He swept her away to New York. I don't think there was any room for Max after that. He used to fly out once or twice a year, but I think it was more like visiting distant relatives than going home to a family. Sometimes he came back early because he'd had a row with the count. They absolutely loathed each other. And I think there was some resentment over money. Max and his mother had really valuable assets by then.'

'Poor Max.' It seemed sad that Count Kisfaludy, a grown man, could allow himself to 'loathe' a little boy. I visualized a pale, anxious Max in short trousers and a school cap, waiting on the school steps, eyes on the horizon, for the smart car that never came, then piling into Stephen's parents' battered Morris with their smelly, exuberant dogs and old newspapers piled up over the seats. Knowing Max, I could imagine him turning towards the warmth of a real mother like a sunflower to the sun. Stephen's mother, when she wasn't drunk, had been marvellously warm. His father had spent a great deal of the time travelling on business, and without his presence The Old Rectory had been a place where small boys could hunt for birds' nests, play cricket on the lawn and race about, stoked up by great slabs of bread and dripping or hearty sausage and mash. Stephen's childhood had not been perfect, but it had been a childhood before his mother's irregular bouts of drinking took over, and Max's, for all its privileges, had required him to be extraordinarily adult from an early age. It occurred to me that, as the relationship of Stephen and Max had matured over all these years, veins of envy must have shot through it sporadically like the mould in a fine Stilton.

Stephen pulled on his sweater. 'The worst of it was that she and Max used to be everything to each other. When Max's father died they were never apart, and Max said that the first stepfather never came between Max and Alexandra. She treated Max in those days as if he were the Baby Jesus rather than the averagely scruffy little boy he was. But once the count came along, that was that.'

'How terrible.' I thought of a small, vulnerable boy, adored by a beautiful, glamorous mother, then suddenly abandoned, left behind to fend for himself in a boarding school. 'Why is she here, do you think?'

Stephen went back to the window. 'She's probably been widowed and needs Max again.' He rubbed the windowpane once more. 'But no. There's someone with her. Maybe it's the count. Well, well. I suppose we'll find out at lunch.'

'Stephen!' Max's mother stretched out heavily ringed hands as we went down to the hall before lunch, and pronounced his name in a way that sounded more like 'Stefan'. With two well-placed air kisses, she added, 'Dahlink! It's been so long.' If Max occasionally gave the impression of being an English country landowner in a Noel Coward play, I thought his mother had obviously perfected the part of émigré Hungarian countess in a Hollywood musical.

She turned to me. 'Countess Kisfaludy.'

Stephen put his arm round me. 'My wife, Suzy.'

'Ah!' She shook my hand and I felt gold and diamonds

crunch beneath my fingers. 'My husband, Count Kisfaludy.' A tall, distinguished man with white hair and a military bearing shook Stephen's hand formally, his eyes sweeping over him dismissively and then assessing me at much greater length.

'My dear, I'm charmed to meet you.' He kissed my hand with an elaborate flourish, and Max's mother looked uneasy. By the way her eyes flickered over me, I suspected that this was a woman who rarely dared let her husband out of her sight. I thought again of the little boy at school, all those years ago, watching and waiting, night after night, as his mother became just a faded, scented memory of unconditional love. One thing I did know about Max was that the affectionate welcome that Stephen's mother had obviously provided could still never have been enough. Max needed love, not mere affection. But in those days there were lots of over-privileged, lonely little boys in the same situation, and they'd learned how to survive. Max had more than survived, he'd triumphed, surrounded here by his spectacular home and two wonderful children. And his competent, calm wife, of course.

Euphoric after that rare event, a full night's sleep, and feeling as if I could stride across the world, I asked Max what I could do to help.

'Entertain my bloody mother and –' Max jerked his head towards the count '– him in the drawing room until we're ready to go in to lunch.' A gleam of amusement came into his eyes. 'We're eating in the kitchen. Mother will be scandalized. I don't suppose she's eaten in a kitchen since—' The shuttered look came across his face just as I thought I might, for the first time, hear more than a few throw-away lines about his life as a child. 'Since heaven knows when,' he concluded quietly.

I managed to sheep-dog them into the drawing room, Max's mother fussing around until Stephen drew the count, who had urged us to call him Gedeon, into a corner to talk about property. Gedeon had interests in London, New York and Paris, he said, and was always interested in meeting architects who did not want to turn buildings into boxes. I saw Stephen showing him some particulars of one or two properties we'd visited and my heart sank. Surely we could forget about it all, just for Christmas. Stephen passed over the glossy folders, with their unconvincing colour photographs of dull, neatly arranged rooms, to Max's mother.

'We're thinking of buying this.' It was called Sackville House, a pretty Georgian house miles from the nearest village, too far from anywhere, in fact, and although it looked grand on the outside, it was mean in unexpected places. The rooms were smaller and darker than you might think. We'd have a garden and a paddock, but less space inside, and what had turned out to be a major road roaring only a few feet from the front door, and the cost seemed to be well in excess of what we could afford. But it fulfilled Stephen's idea of what a house should be like. I thought it was too much of a showpiece, and too inconvenient. We'd had quite a row about it, with him pointing out the wonderful views of the woods behind and me protesting that I didn't want trees in my life, I wanted people. I had thought that Sackville House had been consigned to the dustbin, so I glared at him over Max's mother's head as he ignored me.

'This is for your weekend cottage, yes?' She spoke in rich, guttural tones.

Stephen was taken aback. 'No, we're thinking of moving there. It's only an hour and a half from Waterloo.'

'Vell, never mind. It's a start.' She handed the particulars back to him without really looking at them and I hid a smile. She obviously thought that no one could contemplate living an hour and a half away from London unless desperate or heading for somewhere as splendid as Stonehill, and that anyway, she would have measured the distance from a shopping haven such as Knightsbridge rather than a dreary railway station like Waterloo.

Just as I was beginning to think I might enjoy her, she turned to me, patting the worn crimson velvet of a giant sofa to indicate that I should sit down beside her.

'And where do you live now?'

I told her. Surprisingly, she knew it. 'Ah yes. There are some sweet little houses. One or two of them are quite pretty if you like zat sort of zing.'

I asked her where she lived, and was treated to a litany of apartments, houses and villas in the US and the Caribbean. Perhaps they were all purchased with money from the houses in South Kensington. Max's father's money. That would be enough to create some family friction, I imagine. On the other hand, the count might have made some money himself. I could certainly overhear him talking big to Max. I turned back to the countess, and tried to think of something else to ask.

But she already knew what she wanted to talk about. 'So.' Max's mother pronounced it 'zo'. 'You are the girl who nearly married my little Miksa.'

For one astonished moment, I thought I'd misheard and that she was referring to some sort of small dog – a Yorkshire terrier, perhaps – on the mistaken assumption that I had a similar one suitable for breeding with. It seemed the only possible explanation for such an extraordinary outburst. I gazed at her blankly.

She waved a hand. 'Never mind, never mind, you can speak to me. I am completely discreet.'

It seemed most unlikely. Not if she was in the habit of opening remarks like that.

'It was a long time ago.' I was aware of sounding defensive.

'Yes, yes.' She sounded impatient. 'Time heals all wounds, they say.'

I wasn't letting her get away with that. Thinking that it had been Max who had decided not to marry me. It was I who had walked away from him, I thought, suppressing the memories of the late nights and the traces of femininity that had clung almost invisibly to him when he'd returned from parties during those last months together. 'I'm very happily married now. To Stephen.'

She took a sip of gin and tonic, and raised her eyebrows. 'So I see. Stephen is a very clever boy. Too clever, perhaps, I sometimes think.' (She pronounced it 'zink'.)

As she hadn't seen him since he was eleven, I didn't think she was in a position to comment on his cleverness or otherwise. There was a dismissive note in her voice that made me wonder if 'clever' was her way of saying 'poor', so I said, 'He's become very successful.' I'd have liked to mention the Crown Project, just to show her, but I didn't suppose it would have meant anything.

She looked amused. Very successful, in her world, meant having your own private jet, at the very least.

'And Max is very happy here with Anne, don't you think?' I was aware of goading her, of wanting to find out what this conversation was all about.

'Yes, yes.' The hand waved away Anne and Max's happiness. 'Anne is a vunderful vuman.'

I tried to imagine Anne and Alexandra locking horns in the traditional mother-in-law, daughter-in-law battles and failed. 'Max and Anne have done amazing work with the house,' I added. 'It was almost derelict when they inherited it.'

'Yes.' She looked thoughtfully up at the criss-cross plasterwork that divided the ceiling into elaborate squares and round at the dark-honey wood panelling and the large stone fireplace with its carved hood. 'It is a very fine house.'

'Do you usually come over at Christmas?' I still wondered whether the fact that Max never mentioned his mother was because there'd been some kind of feud, or whether it was just another instance of Max not telling people anything.

'This is the first time I haf been here.' At my barely concealed look of surprise, she added, 'Miksa comes often to New York and I am getting too old for travelling.' She sat up, suddenly alert as she saw Max walking towards her. 'Zo. As you say, everybody has a happy ending.' For a moment she looked at me intensely, a claw-like hand on my arm, before smiling and getting up. 'Miksa, dahlink, I have been so pleased to meet Suzy after all zis time.' Max looked uneasy for a moment, as if she might have said something she shouldn't, and ushered us towards the kitchen.

Stephen drew me on one side as we wound in a procession through the endless freezing corridors to the kitchen, Jamie, Polly and Harriet bullocking ahead and Max's mother wincing slightly at the noise they were making. 'What did you talk to the old girl about?'

I shrugged. 'Where we live. How long we've known Max. How marvellous Anne is. You know. Just that sort of stuff.' I was aware of lying to Stephen, just slightly. In spite of the count's 'loathing' and the distance to New York, Max had obviously discussed me with his mother. Enough for her to have remembered me.

But to be married for twenty-five years, and never have your mother to your house seemed incredible. And why was she here now? Beneath the calm, well-ordered surface of the house, the smell of beeswax, Christmas tree pine needles and good home cooking, I could sense undercurrents of distrust tugging and pulling against the atmosphere of bonhomie, and drawing Max down, away from the generous, confident persona he had so carefully created through the years.

'How charming!' Alexandra was looking satisfyingly scandalized as we entered the big stone-flagged room with one long wall entirely taken up with the house's original china-filled dresser. 'To eat in the kitchen! So delightfully . . . rustic.'

'We always eat in the kitchen, Mother. It's the fashion now.'

'Vell, I haf not had the time to catch up with your English fashions,' she retorted. 'In New York, ve do not eat at home, let alone in the kitchen. The kitchen is for the maid. Ve eat in restaurants.' She settled herself down as Anne slapped a plate of chicken in front of her, and looked across at the considerable expanse of worn, scrubbed pine table top. It was a huge table, with drawers all round, in which I'd once found old game books, dating back to 1812, listing the different kinds of slaughter – snipe, woodcock, rabbit and partridge – in an elegant black copperplate hand. The snipe, woodcock and partridge were rare now, but the rabbits were everywhere. Max and his children often shot them from the drawing-room windows, although he'd always imposed a cease fire while Jess and Polly were here, ever since Polly had knobbled him rather earnestly about *Watership Down*, the story of endangered rabbits, when she'd been around ten. Max had always been very kind and gentle to the girls.

'Yes, well, there aren't any restaurants round here, Mother,' Max boomed over my head. 'Not the kind you'd go to anyway. Help yourself to spuds.' He thrust a blue-and-white tureen, with a tea-coloured crack running across the lid, towards her.

Fortunately Anne seemed to have missed this exchange as she had spent most of it with her head in and out of the Aga, extracting a series of massive, steaming dishes from its capacious depths. Anne was, as Max's mother had so rightly said, a vunderful vuman.

But, just for a change, I was determined to make sure that she let me help with the washing up. She always did it all herself, which, while apparently so welcoming and cosseting, was curiously alienating, underlining the fact that we did not belong here by cutting us off from the real life of the household.

'So,' Max raised his glass in satisfaction when everyone was seated. 'All together. After all these years.' He turned to Stephen. 'Both our families.' He could get very sentimental. 'Shall we have a toast? To Christmas?'

'To Christmas,' we all echoed, while Harriet, Polly and Jamie scuffled with their feet under the table and giggled. Polly went pink.

I did help with the washing up, and Anne ran the girls and Jamie the way the army runs raw recruits — mercilessly dishing out chores and orders until everything was restored gleamingly to its place a mere fifteen minutes after lunch was finished, and the three of them loped off to their own concerns.

The evening of Christmas Eve was marked by a party at
Vanessa's house.

'Just a few drinks for the neighbours,' she'd said. 'Do
drop in any time from six onwards.'

By 'the neighbours' Vanessa meant anyone rich,
famous or in the possession of a seriously large or
historic house within a twenty-five-mile radius. Of the
actual neighbours – the half-dozen or so cottages that
bordered to the right and left of Merlins, their house –
only one was considered smart enough for an invitation.
Ironically, these were writers from London, whose snob-
bery was intellectual rather than financial. They'd indicated that they had come to the country to be alone, that
the concept of 'neighbours' was somehow intellectually
suspect, and irritated Vanessa by refusing the invitation
in Garbo-esque style. 'Really,' Vanessa had been miffed,
'I can't imagine who they think they are. Just because he
was once short-listed for the shortlist of the Booker.
They only live in a piddling little cottage, after all.'

She had also been unintentionally one-upped by Anne
on the subject of tree decoration on the afternoon of
the party. Vanessa's Christmas tree was a carefully chosen
Nordic blue pine, with evenly balanced bushy branches
that never dropped their needles, the decorations colour-
coordinated in violet and silver, with tasteful white lights,

naïve dangling wooden animals and purple velvet ribbons. Only presents that looked good under it were allowed round the base, and all others – and there were many, all prettily wrapped – were consigned to a table in the hall.

Anne, on the other hand, had simply hurled a mishmash of miscellaneous decorations at a tree dragged in unceremoniously from the Stonehill estate after lunch, with uneven branches that stretched almost up to the roof of the Great Hall. She and I were festooning it in the sort of decorations that Vanessa was so snooty about, and had always consigned either to the nursery or the dustbin – red, gold and green tinsel and flashing coloured lights. These were all mixed up with authentic Victorian Christmas tree decorations which had spent the last two centuries going up and down from the extensive Stonehill attics along with the children's loo-roll angels and paper chains from primary school. Vanessa had always allocated Anne 'good taste' because her house was so enormous and historic and her ancestors could be traced back to Edward the Confessor. She was not quite sure if this tree was a lapse of that good taste, or whether Anne knew something that she didn't about what was and was not acceptable in tree decoration.

'Goodness!' She sounded nervous when she popped over to cut some berried holly from Stonehill's bushes ('Honestly, it's such a bore having a tiny garden,' she tinkled of her acre-and-a-half plot), and found us tying on the last few balls. 'Are coloured lights in this year, then?'

She needn't have worried. Anne did not care a hoot

for fashion, Christmas or otherwise. For her, the aim of Christmas tree decoration was to cover the most amount of tree in the least possible time.

'I haven't a clue,' Anne said, not even prepared to give the matter a moment's thought. 'Here, hang these last balls up, will you? You're good at that sort of thing.' She handed Vanessa some tinny Christmas tree balls in garish colours with teddy bears imprinted on them, which had been given away free with petrol a few years ago. Vanessa looked at them in alarm, obviously feeling that even hanging them on someone else's tree was a crime against style. She looked particularly edgy when Max's mother came in, introduced herself and peered at the Christmas tree balls in Vanessa's hands. 'Are zese yours?'

'Absolutely not,' murmured Vanessa, and then, because she obviously didn't want to sound rude, 'that is . . .'

'Zey are quite horrible,' said Alexandra firmly, before tottering off in search of her husband.

'Well,' Vanessa gave a shrill laugh as she retreated. 'I can see I'm going to have to come and organize you next year.'

Anne stood back. 'Would you?' She sounded grateful as she prepared to shoot off to the stables. 'Bloody bore, Christmas trees.'

I'd sometimes assumed that Vanessa and Anne's friendship had endured because Vanessa was simply not prepared to let it go. Everyone has friends like these in their lives – people who always keep in touch, make future dates to meet up, are meticulous about birthdays and Christmases. In the end, the friendship is built on shared time and experiences rather than anything concrete in common. But looking at Anne and Vanessa in the Great Hall – one so tall and strong and the other so petite and blonde – I thought they needed each other a bit more fundamentally than that. Vanessa was Anne's feminine side, and without her, without the frippery and laughter, Anne, with her tractors and horses and the way she worked so constantly, lugging or carrying heavy things all over the estate, might have become a proto-man.

Vanessa had recovered from her Christmas tree crisis by the time she and Barry stood in their entrance hall, receiving guests in a line as if it was a wedding. Her dress was bright pink, encrusted with beadwork in the same shade. Her honey-blonde hair was cropped fashionably short, like a boy's, and the highest possible heels brought her almost up to Barry's rumpled shoulder. Until you were close up she looked about twenty-five, and even then there was just a suggestion of crumpled tissue paper rather than freshly ironed silk about her skin, perhaps the tiniest droop and sag around her eyes and lips, or the odd discolouration barely discernible through the expensive make-up. But with a bone structure like Vanessa's, the weekly facials, collagen injections to pump up her lips, and the personal trainer to keep her tiny buttocks firm, such minor imperfections seemed almost irrelevant.

A maid in a black-and-white uniform stood poised by the front door with a tray of full champagne glasses, and another whisked away our coats.

Max's mother, tiny and immaculate in red Chanel with real rubies at her ears, allowed herself to show as much approval as was possible on a face that had been surgically lifted so many times. 'This is charming, quite charming. My dear Vanessa, you are such a clever girl.' She raised a bony hand, the skin across it almost transparent like an x-ray, and adjusted her thinning, crimped curls.

The front door was flanked by two huge topiary urns, each festooned in delicate white fairy lights, there was a purple tartan wreath on the door and the tasteful Christmas tree stood at the base of a handsome circular staircase. In the double drawing room thick evergreen garlands, interwoven with pine cones, oranges and cinnamon sticks were draped lavishly from two fireplaces, and at least a thousand Christmas cards hung from ribbons topped with bows all round the room.

I saw the count trawling the room, his hand loosely trailing over any reasonably shaped bottom he passed, followed by a glassily cheerful Alexandra. Anne strode up to a group of her horsey friends and they got happily stuck in to shouting at each other about spavins and dressage and different kinds of bit, while Max worked the room like the seasoned party campaigner he was, Stephen in his wake.

People were often wary of Max until they got to know him well – the combination of the strong nose and powerful cheekbones with hair that still curled over the collar made strangers look twice at him. 'Who's that man who looks like Michael Douglas?' I heard one woman say to another, who looked surprised and interested. Then she frowned when she saw Max. 'Too dark and tall for Michael Douglas. Too wolf-like,' she added, and they both studied him appraisingly. 'Well, perhaps not,' said the first one, as they turned away. Stephen, on the other hand, only had to incline his even features and close-cropped hair towards someone, crinkling up the corner of his eyes in amusement, to have women hanging on his every word.

Polly, Jamie and Harriet disappeared almost immediately into the 'barn', an outhouse that had been done up with a snooker table and small 'home cinema'. I leaned against the mantelpiece, just watching it all, feeling uninvolved and relaxed, chatting about trivial things to people who I vaguely recognized. It was nice not to feel responsible for anything, but I couldn't resist envying Vanessa her life, just a little bit. With a husband who appeared to adore her, two adult children who were both 'doing incredibly well', the looks of a slightly ageing model, and more money than she could possibly spend, she had absolutely nothing to worry about in the world, except for the odd bout of agitation over Christmas tree decorations. But, even those were short-lived, because she had the time and the money to get experts in to ensure that everything turned out perfectly. She'd had her garden designer bring her eight different types of gravel, for example, she'd told me once, before deciding on exactly the right shade of greyish white stones for the Japanese garden in London.

I saw her intercept one of the dirty looks that the count's bottom-fondling had generated. She stepped in to head off any unpleasantness: 'Have you met Count Kisfaludy? And Alexandra, Countess Kisfaludy?'

The count clicked his heels, and kissed the hand that belonged to the bottom. Its owner cheered up at the thought that she had been groped by a title, even if it was a foreign one.

Barry appeared at my elbow. 'How are things?' I looked up to see his lined, brick-red face and sandy eyebrows, and felt a stab of affection. It was Barry who'd come in the taxi after I'd collapsed sobbing on the day of the burglary, Barry who'd opened a bottle of vintage champagne 'to bring you round' as Vanessa passed me tissues on the sofa.

'Things are much better.' I squeezed his arm. 'Thanks for asking. Really, it's just so wonderful to have one good night's sleep. I feel as if I could take on the world.'

He grimaced. 'Tell me about it. I'd give the entire balance of at least one of my Swiss bank accounts for a night without a party to go to.' He did look tired, under the high colour.

'Can't you slow down?'

He shrugged. 'With Vanessa around? Not likely. You know what she's like.'

We watched her marching the count across the room to meet the lord lieutenant of the county.

Outside there was a commotion and a great white light shone at the front door, obliterating everything around it. For a minute I thought it was something to do with Christmas, perhaps, for a brief, mad moment, the coming of Jesus or even aliens landing. Everyone stopped talking and turned towards the door. Vanessa fluttered away from the count with cries of joy to greet an immaculately coiffed woman in a bright-orange trouser suit, who was followed by a man holding what looked like a giant sausage over her head, and the rest of a TV team, including lights.

'Television,' sighed Barry. 'They're doing some comparative programme about people's different Christmases. For some mad reason Vanessa's let them go ahead. We shall look like right berks.'

Out of the corner of my eye, I saw Anne and the horsey types melt into the back study. Publicity, of any kind, was Simply Not On, in their world.

I didn't particularly want to appear on television either, so as the party split into those who did, clustering around the cameras and trying to look casual, and those who didn't, I edged into Vanessa's conservatory, and decided to sit down for a moment.

'Oh, there you are.' Max appeared at the door. 'I wondered if you were all right.'

Stephen had obviously been talking to him about me. I wished he wouldn't.

'I'm absolutely fine.'

'You're looking better.'

'Better than what?' I asked, defensively.

He came to sit down beside me. 'It's okay not to be perfect. All right? People do get very shaken when they're robbed. When they first find out the world isn't a safe place.'

'I'm not stupid, you know,' I told him, sharply. 'I've always been perfectly aware that the world is a dangerous place.'

'Intellectually, of course. But you don't feel it in your heart until you've been threatened.' That's when he told me about society having to make victims feel guilty for getting caught, getting hurt or getting robbed. That it's much easier for everybody if crime is seen as a kind of joint project between victim and criminal because then everyone can sleep a little sounder in their beds, knowing it won't happen to them, because they would never be so foolish, careless or unwise.

'Really,' I told him after I'd listened carefully, 'it was just a very ordinary burglary. I wasn't hurt badly at all.' I remembered the dispassionate, hard violence of the man's arm as he pushed me out of the way. He hadn't cared whether I broke my neck, perhaps had wanted me to, even pushed me that bit harder than he needed to, to make me fall. It must be what enemy soldiers feel like, to be aware that someone you have never met feels a cold, merciless hate for you. The police had found my handbag, thrown into a bush down the road, with every little piece of paper and photograph torn up angrily into tiny bits. Even pictures of Polly and Jess as babies. Like the arm against mine, that angry gesture had felt personal. Not just your average burglar doing his thing. But perhaps there aren't any average burglars. Perhaps they all hate the people they're robbing because they couldn't do it otherwise.

The room suddenly seemed rather hot and bright. The parallel universe was always more extreme than the real world – colder than cold, hotter than hot, brighter than bright, and full of strange threatening noises that roared and spat and rustled, but never revealed themselves for what they truly were.

I didn't want to slip into it now, not when today had

been so blissfully relaxing. 'Really,' I repeated. 'I'm fine. It just spooked me that I didn't know how he got in. That's all. It just turned everything upside down for a while. I'm not sure why.'

'That's because once you know bad things can happen, you don't know how to stop them happening again. You know you don't know how to keep it all out. You've gone through a door that can never be closed behind you.'

I tried to imagine what Max's fears were. He read my thoughts. 'When I was small, there was always a feeling of menace. As if we were about to be moved on, or chased away. I grew up with that. The feeling of not belonging. Of people you don't even know hating you. Of not having a safe house.'

'But you're safe now?' I queried. 'At Stonehill.'

He smiled. I love Max's smile. Not the twisted, ironic one, but the one that creases up his face completely, as if he was amused by the world, and everything in it, and most particularly by me. He settled further into Vanessa's comfortable sofa, inclining towards me. I could feel the warmth of his body. It was a comforting feeling, and I felt the parallel universe slip away. 'Yes. I am, now,' he said. 'And you will be, too.'

I decided to confide in him. 'But when, Max? I just want to go back to the person I was before, the one who fell asleep without feeling frightened, or walked to the bus stop without looking over her shoulder. People say you feel much better after a year, but that seems such a long time to be so wired up.'

He paused, then obviously made a decision to go

ahead. 'You can't go back, Suzy, I'm afraid. You have to find your own way forwards. That happy, lovely Suzy who danced with me before the burglary has gone for ever. But you won't go on feeling the way you feel now for the rest of your life.'

I wondered why he seemed to know so much about it all. It was a long time since I'd had a conversation with someone who seemed to know exactly what I felt. To whom I didn't have to explain things. But then, I'd never had to explain anything to Max.

Perhaps he'd been burgled too, and we hadn't heard about it. I had discovered that being burgled or attacked was a bit like joining a club. Other people who'd had similar experiences gravitated towards me at parties, to tell me their stories. It often gave me nightmares but I was always too fascinated to tell them to stop. There was always the chance that their stories might make some sense of it all.

'Did you want to go back ever?' I asked him. 'Like to where your father's family came from in Poland?'

He shook his head. 'I wasn't talking about going back in the physical sense. I was born here, but I don't feel completely British.'

'How amazing that you've married someone in exactly the opposite situation – someone whose family has lived here since the Normans.'

He grinned. 'Not at all. The Normans were considered the most frightful *nouveau riche* Eurotrash when they first arrived. I've just come about a millennium later to carry on the family tradition.'

We both giggled because we knew he'd never have

said anything like that if Anne had been anywhere near. 'Honestly,' he added, 'I've got interested in local history, just because I started by trying to make sense of where I belonged, and where my children belonged, and all that. Not that they give it a second thought.'

We sipped our champagne, and I could feel tiredness overwhelm me as I relaxed. I intended to bank sleep in my time at Stonehill.

'No, you can't go back,' he repeated. 'We can't go back.'

Then it suddenly occurred to me that he might also have been talking about him and me. Us. Although it wasn't quite clear. Was this a final, final goodbye? An expression of regret? An admission that I'd been more than just one of his girls?

Or a warning? I stood up, hastily, smoothing down my skirt as it rode up. Suppose Max thought I was still in love with him? He couldn't, surely. It had been me leaving him, not the other way around. Not, of course, that that had fooled anyone much, but still. Girls, in my experience, did not leave Max.

Stephen appeared, pushing through the crowd that had now packed into the conservatory.

'Max!' He clapped him on the shoulder. 'Here's someone who wants to meet you.'

'All right, darling?' He gave me a solicitous look. There was a woman behind him, baring lipsticked teeth at me.

'Your husband's so successful these days,' she crooned. 'You must be so proud of him.'

'I've always been proud of him,' I assured her, having met her several times before, when she had always ignored us both. This recognition was part of the rewards of the Crown Project, I supposed. I took Stephen's arm to reassure myself that everything really was fine. I could feel myself shaking slightly from the conversation with Max. He was the first person to tell me that life would never be the same again. That the burglary had changed me for ever. But he hadn't been telling me, as so many people did, that I'd soon forget about it, and that everything would simply return to normal. That was a surprising relief.

Stephen ushered me towards someone else.

'Have you met Marcie?' One of the party's lost lambs had strayed hopefully up to Stephen, and I knew from past experience that he would shine his charm on her, deftly introduce her to me, and then almost seamlessly disappear.

She smiled eagerly. 'Now, don't say a word. You're a sun sign Sagittarius. I can always tell.'

I hoped she hadn't tried that opening line on any of the horsey crowd. They'd have snorted like stallions on the rampage.

'Well, actually . . .' I heard myself say, wondering how I could politely explain that I wasn't.

12

Christmas wasn't quite Christmas in such splendid sur-
roundings. It was lovely, of course, almost like a scene
from a film, but without the frenzy and work, it had lost
its bite. All I had to worry about were the presents. Polly
had long since passed the age of tantalizing parcels in
brightly coloured wrapping paper and had begged for a
cheque. Anne and Max were impossible to buy presents
for, because they had so many possessions stored away
in the attic that they never needed anything new. I'd been
driven to buying expensive soap.

'You shouldn't have,' said Anne, with a smile, laying
it aside.

I hadn't brought up any emergency presents and was
mortified that the countess had been shopping in New
York. She'd bought soft cashmere shawls for all the
women, gloriously cosseting wisps of luxury in beautiful,
jewel-like colours.

'But this is amazing,' murmured Anne. I saw her
exchange a glance with Max. 'So generous of you.'

Max's mother shrugged. 'I love to buy presents. And
you've made us very . . .' I thought she was going to say
'welcome', but she finished with 'comfortable'.

The presents between the couples were honed by
years of experience. Anne and Max had apparently
'bought' each other something for Stonehill – Anne's

'Christmas present' was to have the stables refitted. Max's 'present' was to have the fence in the South Field repaired. Stephen and I exchanged items of clothing, the choices fine-tuned by our knowledge of what each other needed and wanted over the years. The count received a magnificent smoking-jacket from Alexandra, and she, in turn, was given a tiny exquisite brooch.

'It's Alexandrite, you see, for my name,' she told me. 'Far more rare and precious than diamonds.'

I felt a giant stab of regret for the necklace. If only I had been more careful. It wasn't just the threat of violence that made me walk so carefully down the street. I no longer had my necklace to fall back on. I felt exposed, to anything life might throw at me.

Max looked sharply at it. 'Beautiful, Mother, beautiful.' He seemed angry about something, and she caught the look. For a moment I held my breath, waiting for an explosion.

Anne put her hand gently on his arm, and he looked up at her. He nodded, and the moment passed. Like so many couples they operated wordlessly after twenty-five years.

I joined Anne in the kitchen to help with the final frantic phase of boiling sprouts, stirring gravy and coord-inating everything so that it emerged hot together.

A couple of glasses of pre-lunch sparkle made me feel light-headed.

'Thank you so much for having us here,' I said to Anne, although she usually brushes off gratitude. 'I can't tell you how blissful it is not to be responsible for anything. It's so kind of you.'

Anne passed me a whisk. 'Could you just keep the bread sauce going? Frankly, it's a relief to have people who can come between Max and his mother.'

'They don't get on?' I ventured, thinking that at least I'd now found out why Anne had invited us.

'Oh, they adore each other.' Anne drained some sprouts. 'Which is irritating for me, as you can imagine. But they don't approve of each other's choices. Max hates the count, and Alexandra disapproves of me.'

While Anne was hardly easy to warm to, I was astounded that Max's mother could actually go as far as disapproving of her. 'But that's so unfair. How could she possibly object to you?'

Anne shrugged. 'I couldn't give a damn, frankly. She didn't come to our wedding, and she hasn't been here since.'

I knew from experience that, unless I asked, Anne would leave it there. 'Why did she come now?'

'Oh,' said Anne, stirring the gravy with fierceness. 'After twenty-five years she's realized that I'm here to stay, and that unless she makes an effort to get on with me, she's not going to see much of Max.'

'So this Christmas is olive branches all round?'

Anne smiled. 'That's the sort of thing. I hope. Well, that's pretty much all sorted. Can you tell everyone to come in for lunch?'

As we walked in Max asked me if I'd slept well.

'Brilliantly.' Once again it had been wonderful. Something heavy and dark seemed to be falling off my shoulders.

'Good. Call me if you ever need a chat. I know what it's like.'

Did he? How? I wished I knew.

Still, the idea of calling Max for a chat warmed me. Sometimes because Stephen was so busy, he could be impatient, and the people I saw every day – friends in the staff room or who lived in the street – were likely to say things like 'You ought to be over that by now', or 'Lightning doesn't strike twice in the same place', both of which made me feel more, not less, frightened and isolated.

I watched him playing the part of Master of Ceremonies in the Great Hall at lunch time, urging us all to pull crackers and wear our paper hats as he helped Anne dole out luke-warm portions of goose (nothing so common as turkey at Stonehill) from the heated hostess trolley. When they finished he kissed her, and squeezed her arm.

'Well done.'

She flashed a look at him that might have been gratitude.

Max settled down between me and Harriet with a flourish of his napkin, which was when Harriet got the chance to tell us more about her New Age beliefs. I wondered what Anne made of that. She launched into a spiel about the importance of the Age of Aquarius. It reminded me of some of Max's passions: the I Ching, for example, or a brief, intense interest in Tarot cards.

'No one knows exactly when it started, but we're in it now. It's a time of great creativity, especially for women.'

'Women,' murmured the count, sitting on the other

side of Harriet, and trying to peer down Polly's cleavage on the other side of him. 'How delightful.' Polly shot him an embarrassed look and buttoned up her cardigan.

Harriet took no notice. 'Women today are giving birth,' she told him. 'To themselves. As people, that is.'

He looked taken aback. 'Indeed, indeed.' He detached himself from Polly, and his hand dropped down on to Harriet's thigh.

With a deft move, she jabbed it with her fork, turning on a surprising 100-watt smile. 'I'm so sorry. I'd no idea your hand would be there.'

I met Max's eyes, and we smiled. Harriet had clearly inherited her mother's determination and her father's sense of humour.

As people peeled themselves away from the table to find vast, cavernous armchairs suitable for over-stuffed snoozing, I decided that a walk would be better than sleep to displace the hefty load of fatty goose, and went upstairs to find a warmer jumper. As I returned down the back stairs I could hear angry voices behind the closed door of Max's study.

I stopped, not wanting to intrude on a private argument.

'Vell, ve none of us haf any money, Miksa, you know.' Max's mother had opened the door, obviously intending it to be a last remark.

Flattening myself against the wall, I saw Max's hand take the door out of her hand and close it again to stop her from leaving. 'If you hadn't . . .' The door closed on what she hadn't done.

I crept past, edging towards the back door, where a long row of brass hooks were piled with coats, and around two dozen pairs of wellington boots were lined up underneath. It took me some time to disentangle my coat, and select a pair of wellies that were around my size.

The countess click-clacked out of Max's study and up the stairs, looking angry, and Max came flying out. He stopped when he saw me, his eyes very dark in a white, white face. I knew that look, although I hadn't seen it for twenty-five years. I deliberately made my voice sound casual. 'I'm going for a walk. Fancy coming?'

He looked incredulous for a moment, and then seemed to recover himself. 'What a good idea. Have you found a pair of boots to fit?' He was back to playing Max Galliard, host of Stonehill, and, tugging on his boots, he strode out towards the woods. 'Better hurry. The light's going to go soon.'

The sky was already olive green, but Max knew every inch of the Stonehill gardens, and could have made his way through them in the darkest of nights. I followed him across the moat and out through the wild garden, which had paths snaking through it to the bluebell wood. A solitary statue, a graceful abstract piece like a curved arrow, marked the boundary between the gardens and the wood, and my fists curled into tight, frightened balls as I passed it. Nothing bad could happen here, I reminded myself. Nothing bad.

I racked my brains for an opening remark. Max might be the life and soul of the party when there were people around, but I remembered the long, silent hours when he used to lie on the waterbed and stare at the ceiling, smoking interminably. He no longer smoked, except occasionally at parties, and I had no idea if he lay under the huge four-poster in Primrose, the room he shared with Anne, looking up at the faded, light-stained fabric. The easy camaraderie of last night seemed like a dream. That was what I had always found so difficult about him. One minute you could be as close as people could be, and then he'd flip back to remoteness.

I scrambled after him. We were now striding through the wood, carpeted with fallen leaves and already in a twilit gloom.

Almost every opening remark I could think of seemed loaded in some way or utterly fatuous. 'It must be nice to have your mother over' was just one of the idiotic comments I considered and discarded. 'Do you see her often?' was another. 'Is anything wrong?' seemed nosy. 'The count seems pleasant' could get me shot, at the very least. Apart from anything else, it wasn't even true. The count, as anyone could see, was a creep.

From time to time a dried twig crunched under our feet in the gloom. I could still, just, see our breath curling up in the air.

Eventually I settled on 'It's a beautiful wood. So peaceful.' Such conversation would hardly set the world on fire, but, with any luck, perhaps Max's brain, like mine, was numbed with food and drink.

He stopped and sat down on a pile of logs, neatly arranged as if to form a natural sofa, but waiting, presumably, to be chopped up for the fire. I sat down beside him.

After a few minutes of silence he rummaged around in the pocket of his waxed jacket and brought out some

Rizla papers, a packet of cigarettes and a small lump of silver paper.

I sat there, relishing the clarity of the cold air, while he rolled a joint, as intensely occupied in the action as he had been twenty-five years ago.

As he lit it, with a sigh of satisfaction, I spoke. 'I thought you'd given up smoking.' I kept the remark deliberately ambivalent, so as not to seem uncool.

'When you get past thirty, everything's about abstaining and giving up. I get tired of it.' He didn't enlarge further, and passed the joint on to me.

I worried that it would make me feel sick. All that wine at lunch, and I hadn't smoked anything, not even tobacco, for at least fifteen years. I eyed it nervously, debating feeling nauseous versus possibly feeling young again. Max treated joints like expensive Havana cigars, lighting one up occasionally after a good meal. I worried about it more than that.

'Well? Do you want some, or are you going to give it back? I don't see why the birds should enjoy it.'

'Oh, sorry.' I inhaled a quick stabbing puff, relishing the sharp sweetness of the dope inside my mouth, and wishing I hadn't also enjoyed the tobacco hit. 'Here.'

He drew the smoke into his mouth, savouring it, and exhaling in three, coiled rings. We sat in silence for a few minutes, while I tried another, longer, more enjoyable inhalation.

When he eventually spoke, it was as if he was dropping pebbles of sound into an echoing pool of silence. 'I love it here. It's the only place I've ever really belonged.' The words lingered on the smell of ferns, of cold, rotting leaves, and the soft, whispering silence of the trees around us.

'The wood itself, or Stonehill?' My voice came out a long time after he spoke, and floated away into the darkness, apparently unconnected to my thoughts. As the words died away, I'd have liked to call them back. You could never quite tell how far Max wanted to take conversations.

He put his hand out, shadowy in the dark, and gently stroked a curl of hair away from my face, then straightened my collar, leaving his hand on the nape of my neck. I could feel the warmth of his breath drifting past my ear.

It was as if he was breathing on dead flesh, bringing it to life. I had fled from intimacy with Max for twenty-five years.

'All of it, Suzy. The whole thing.' His voice seemed both very close and terribly far away, as if he was a ghost from the distant past. 'How amazing. You still wear the same perfume.'

'Sometimes.' I pushed my hair back from my face to give myself an excuse to turn away slightly, but the movement was made with limbs of concrete.

'It's what I used to buy for you.' He contemplated the thin coil of smoke spiralling up through the dusk.

As if in a black-and-white film, I remembered Max all those years ago, standing holding my hand, on the side of a high street somewhere, and being splashed by a bus with an advertising hoarding of a girl striding out, proclaiming her independence. She'd been advertising a new perfume that women bought themselves. Today's girls, it had implied, no longer stayed at home, waiting for men to bring them gifts. 'I might get some of that,' I'd said, drawn by the image of freedom.

'It's cheap,' Max had said. 'Never wear cheap scent.' Instead he had bought me a magic potion, subtle and lingering.

'You didn't want me to wear cheap perfume,' I repeated back to him, so many years later.

'No.' He passed me the joint again. 'You're different. Complex. Sweet.' Each syllable seemed to last for ever. 'Bitter-sweet, not sugar-sweet. That's why I chose what I did.'

I didn't understand what he meant and vaguely assumed it was something about being a nice-ish person who felt cheated or angry. 'Oh,' I said, and he heard the reproof in my voice.

'Bitter-sweet,' said Max, 'is balanced. The best of sharp and sweet together.'

I smiled, feeling happy again, until I remembered seeing Anne's perfume on their bathroom shelf.

She, too, never wore cheap scent. She always dabbed a hurried splash of Chanel No. 5 behind her ears and on her wrists. I wondered if Max had ever given her something mysterious and rare to wear instead, and whether she'd put it aside with a quiet smile. Or perhaps, like so many of Max's passions, the interest in scent had passed, to be replaced with an equally intense obsession related to shoring up Stonehill. The dovecotes, perhaps, or the crumbling wall that wound for miles along a road around the edge of the estate.

I began to feel the lappings of nausea at the edge of my consciousness. 'We ought to go back.'

'You've got so sensible,' mused Max, taking the joint gently out of my fingers. 'You used to be adventurous.'

'Was I?' It sounded unlikely. I tried to remember what I'd been like before I'd drowned in nappies and teaching and school runs, then GCSEs and A levels. I could dimly recall, as if in a film seen long ago, laughing all night and sleeping all day, having chocolate cake for breakfast and huge fry-ups for supper. In contrast to my organized, regimented life, it had been a world where practicalities seemed not to have existed.

'Do you know?' I turned to Max, because what I was about to say suddenly seemed terribly important, deep and meaningful. 'I can't remember myself at all. Somewhere along the line, something got lost.' I paused.

His dark eyes, deep pools of memory, understood it all. 'I know what you mean. That's what I found here. Myself. At Stonehill.'

'Did you?' My thoughts drifted over the concept for a few moments, until I suddenly wanted to know more. 'Whereabouts in Stonehill, exactly?'

We both immediately dissolved into giggles at the thought of hunting for one's true self as if it was a lost sock.

'In the house or the garden?' I gasped.

'Oh,' he waved an arm around. 'Under one of the four-poster beds, perhaps. Possibly in that frightful old wardrobe of Anne's mother's. Certainly not the stables.'

I wiped the tears of laughter from my eyes. 'You've

always been very fond of the morning room. Could it have been there?'

'Probably the piggery.' He stopped laughing suddenly. 'I hope it wasn't in anything like the linen cupboard or the second pantry. It would be terrible to be the sort of person whose spiritual essence was in the second pantry.'

We giggled incoherently over this, which seemed quite the funniest thing anyone had said for decades.

Max stopped laughing and leaned back, throwing his arm casually round my shoulders, drawing in deeply again. 'Here. Finish this off.' He put the joint between my lips.

I was aware that his hand, so close to my face, seemed bigger and stronger than in those days. The new, more wiry Max had worked hard. He was no longer a slender, poetic boy, but a well-built man who could drag logs through a forest, walk for miles and camp overnight in the open.

There was a rustle as a bird fluttered heavily out of a tree, and he stood up, shrugging his hands into his pockets. I buttoned my coat up tightly, suddenly embarrassed at the return from what seemed like intimacy. Was there anything wrong about sitting on a log, with a man's arm around you, if that man was not your husband? It was scarcely adultery, but where exactly did adultery start? Max didn't seem at all concerned. Perhaps he was more drunk than he appeared. He was not the sort of person who reeled and slurred his words. He just got more intense when he drank.

I was glad it was too dark for him to see my expression properly, and we stood there, curiously elated, as the silence between us began to echo uncomfortably. 'If we make it to the end of the track before the light goes, we can pick up a few more logs for the fire. It was getting low when we left.' He sounded normal and unconcerned. Perhaps I was turning into a hormonally challenged middle-aged hysteric. All he'd done was adjust my collar, and put his arm round me. You'd have thought he'd propositioned me at the very least by the sense of embarrassment I was suffering. Embarrassment, and something else I couldn't quite identify.

I concentrated on the logs. Neither Max nor Anne did anything or went anywhere without tagging on some kind of practical purpose. Nothing could be wasted, not even a stroll in the woods after Christmas lunch. When they wandered round the gardens in summer, they snatched at any weed they saw, even if they were holding a drink in the other hand. When they went for walks they always checked on something – a stile, a piece of fencing that had been reported broken, some tiles allegedly missing from the roof of a shed. I felt a stab of shame that I'd even contemplated thinking that he might want me again after all these years when it was so clear that everything he felt passionately about was tied up in Stonehill.

We trudged back, inhaling air that was as cool and stimulating as champagne, and as we pulled logs out from a clearing in the woods at the end of the path he told me about coppicing with the men only a few months back. That meant thinning out the young trees from their bases – rather than cutting them down – so that the light could reach the forest floor. 'Or the bluebells get so deprived of sunlight that they stop flowering. The lily-of-the-valley are more resilient. They flower here whatever.'

As we passed individual trees, he showed me how to tell the difference between a virgin tree – it has one trunk rising up from the base, clear and clean – and a coppiced one, with its muddle of several whip-slender beginnings going in different directions.

'Like us, I suppose,' he mused. 'We start out so straightforward, then life knocks us down, and we spring up again in different directions.' Then he piled my arms with as many logs as I could carry. Our shoulders jostled together as we turned back, and I tried not to flinch away. The silence seemed awkward again, or perhaps Max was lost in his own thoughts. The lights of Stonehill twinkled ahead of us through the bushes and trees. With the outlines of the tall chimneys in the night sky, I thought of a fairy-tale castle in a magic spell, surrounded by thick vegetation.

But sitting with Max on the logs had felt bitingly personal and I felt deeply disloyal to Stephen for coming out on this walk, especially as I'd told Max that there was something missing from my life. It was as if I'd admitted that my sex life with Stephen wasn't up to much or that our relationship wasn't working, although, of course, I'd said nothing even remotely to indicate either.

I decided that it had been a completely ordinary conversation and it was the feverish workings of too much wine and dope that were making me paranoid and over-imaginative. There was nothing wrong with

Stephen and me, with either our relationship or our sex life.

And Max's? Pretty good, I thought, in spite of his remark about 'knocks'.

I tried not to remember his love-making, his mixture of eagerness and sensuality, his curiosity and tenderness, the way he could draw a response out of me even when I'd sworn, absolutely sworn, that I was tired, or ill or wanted to get on with studying. We used to look at each other, and know that that was what we both wanted.

Now, with the icy crunch of ferns and dead leaves under my boots, I could remember the way we'd hardly been able to wait long enough to take our clothes off.

No, I couldn't imagine Max having middle-aged sexual problems, although, conversely, I couldn't imagine Anne having sex at all, except for the purpose of reproduction. Perhaps she majestically allowed Max to mount her once a week on Saturday nights.

When we got back, after depositing the logs, we found Stephen snoring in an armchair, Harriet curled up on a sofa, dozing over a book on aromatherapy, and even Anne was stretched out on a 'daybed'. She looked composed, with her hands on her chest, reminding me of Lady Eleanor Dewarson, 1536–1582, lying in commemorative stone on the sarcophagus in the little Stonehill church. Anne and Max would be buried there one day, while Stephen and I would be ashes, blown away by the wind over Tooting or Aldershot, or Golders Green, even. Depending on where we finished up.

'Sleeping Beauties all round.' Max grinned.

I flushed with the sudden blaze of heat from the fire

after the cold outside, and made an excuse to go upstairs, where I lay restlessly staring at the ancient Jacobean cornicework and the zigzag cracks across the ceiling.

There was nothing normally wrong with our sex life, of course, but Stephen and I had not made love since the burglary. It's not that either of us was keeping track or anything, but six weeks is a long time. When I thought about sex, it seemed as bland and unenticing as a re-heated rice pudding, or, in an oddly contradictory way, menacing. I felt too vulnerable and he felt . . . well, whatever he felt he wasn't telling me. I thought he was just too busy. Too tired. Travelling too much and arriving home jet-lagged, and sleeping at odd hours. It was my fault, I knew, because the burglary had switched off my sensuality like a light, and I spent most nights trying to go to bed at a different time from Stephen in order to avoid it. But I should have felt more relaxed at Stonehill.

The worst of it was that I hadn't, until now, missed it. Not one little bit. Perhaps that's why suddenly talking to Max so intimately, and feeling the warmth of his body against mine had seemed so imbued with sexual meaning. I had to remind myself that Max always touched people – lightly on the arm or back to indicate friendship, or even putting his arm around your shoulder to emphasize a joke. It was a world away from the count's gropings, perhaps because Max hugged old ladies and friends from school, as well as pretty young women, whereas the count tended to specialize. It was just repressed people like me who read anything into it.

But that half-embrace had woken something deep

inside me. It was about an hour before I fully recognized it as sexual frustration.

I lay on the bed, as the wine swirled around my head, and found myself thinking about sex. Wanton, random sex. Stephen walking in and suddenly ripping my jeans down to my ankles, and the deep, deep satisfaction of feeling him coming into me. We wouldn't bother to undress or slide between the icy linen sheets, or get goose pimples down the hairs of our arms. It would be just us and a tangle of partly discarded clothes. I waited for him, knowing that he must come to find me at some point.

When I eventually went downstairs to look for him, he was playing chess with Max. I massaged the back of his shoulders, and he eased into my touch with a sigh of pleasure, but didn't take his eyes off the board. I could hear him telling Max about one of the 'people of influence' parties he'd been to in Downing Street, and what the Prime Minister had said to him. I left them to it, and wandered into the kitchen to pick a sliver of cold goose off the huge carving dish in the kitchen.

Polly was in there, tucking into a sandwich with a rampantly youthful appetite.

I sat down and stroked a piece of hair behind her ears, aching with love for her, and feeling that this Christmas had somehow taken her away from me.

'Nice Christmas?'

'Brill,' she mumbled through a piece of thick, crusty bread. Then, after she'd finished chewing, she added: 'But I miss home, though. It isn't the same, is it?'

'No, it isn't.' I admitted. It would never be the same

again. The thought stabbed me once, sharply, before I could muffle it with the words: 'But there are lots of good times ahead.' I kissed the top of her head, wishing I could still smell those childhood scents of well-washed clothes and baby lotion, and left her to it.

13

The house in London, when we returned after New Year, was sulking. What with being burgled, put on the market, and then left alone for Christmas, it had developed an air of pained neglect, cloaked in shabby greyness. As we stepped in the door, we could smell a sour, rotting undercurrent beneath the usual closed-house scents of dust, old polish and stale air. The sitting room merely looked untidy instead of pretty and bohemian. Truffle, who'd been staying with a neighbour, jumped disdainfully out of her cat basket and stalked off with her tail making a question mark in the air. For the next few hours she pretended not to know us.

Stephen sniffed accusingly. 'Did you leave something in the fridge?'

'Probably.'

We discovered several things in various states of decay but nothing that quite accounted for the penetratingly sharp odour. As we rummaged, the butter compartment slipped off the door and smashed on the floor.

'If we lived somewhere sensible these things wouldn't happen,' grumbled Stephen.

I pointed out that butter compartments did not smash according to postcode.

We found out what was up as soon as we started to

run baths and put on the washing machine. Blocked drains. The smell became a stench.

'For God's sake.' Stephen opened windows and shut doors, while I worried about whether we would suffocate to death on toxic fumes if I was to shut them again, or whether, if I left them open, there'd be a greater chance of being burgled again, and also found dead in our beds, this time with our throats cut. So the parallel universe had not gone away. It was still waiting for me, a trapdoor opening into a world of dangerous mirrors, just hidden round the bend of the road ahead.

I plumped for the fume-filled death, and shut the windows again.

'What on earth are you doing?' demanded Stephen.

'Shutting the landing window. In case of burglars.'

He looked exasperated. 'There's a sheer drop of three storeys from that window. How were you expecting them to get in? Drop on a line from a helicopter? Abseil down from the roof?'

'Well. We don't know how the burglar got in last time.'

Stephen sighed. 'Honestly. I thought you'd got over all that. That's why we went to Stonehill for Christmas. Anyway, you don't die from drain fumes.'

'In that case it won't matter if the windows are shut. We can live with the smell.' In my fury at the implication that our Christmas had been designed to sort out my 'problems', and a mild sensation of panic that I was obviously now expected to be completely 'better', I wrenched the window lock closed and it snapped off in my hand. Now how was I going to keep it locked? The fear washed back over me, in a freezing fog which penetrated deep into my bones.

It was a comedown after the seamless days at Stonehill, free of either responsibilities or arguments. I looked back at the past ten days, when we'd all had such fun. Stephen and I had been happy, I thought as I carefully poured One Shot down the plughole of the kitchen sink with a slightly shaky hand.

Stephen found me sitting on the kitchen floor in a state of despair, and bent down, stroking my cheek. 'What's up? I'm sorry if I snapped.'

I buried my head in his arms and tried to smell the security of his warm body. There was only the diminishing pong of drains.

'I'm sorry, too. I just feel frightened. Of losing things. Of everything we've got slipping away.'

'Silly girl.' But he said it quite gently. 'We're not losing. We're winning, at last. We'll sell this house and go somewhere where we can both be happy. Where you'll feel safe.'

We stayed there, quite still for a few minutes while I worried about where this might be. Where we both belonged. And how we would find such a place. We couldn't go back to where we came from – we didn't want Birchington-on-Sea and couldn't afford The Old Rectory – and there didn't seem any particular reason to choose anywhere else. We suddenly lacked so many of the usual anchors. The location of the children's schools was no longer important. No one could pretend that my work was of the least consequence as I could get similar jobs anywhere, and Stephen's work was now so peripatetic that it was beginning to matter less and less where he was based. We didn't have any aged parents we needed to be near, or hobbies that needed the sea, the countryside or even any particular attachment to the city's museums, theatres and galleries. We could go where we had friends, of course, perhaps to Suffolk near Max and Anne, but I knew, deep down, that that would have been a bad idea. We would just turn into Stonehill satellites, without any real life of our own. Even Vanessa seemed smaller and less glamorous against the imposing Dutch gables of Stonehill and Anne's statuesque gravity.

It all made me wonder who we really were, what we stood for. Where we were going.

'Look at me.' Stephen spoke softly, and I obediently drew back. 'The hard times are over. We've survived. Things are going to get better and better. We've got enough money to buy a really beautiful home, somewhere we can be proud of. This is what we've been aiming for all our lives.'

He was right. We'd nearly gone bankrupt, struggled throughout the children's schooling, fretted over what we should be doing in life, and whether Stephen would ever get the recognition he deserved. Now our problems were basically over.

I hugged him as the parallel universe receded, and the real world came into focus. 'I know.' I kissed his cheek. 'I know.'

The drains were followed by the total breakdown of the boiler, and then the gas leak. The house appeared to be determined to fight our efforts to sell it. I constantly had to cancel arrangements to be in for plumbers, gas men and central heating engineers, and Stephen not only insisted on my finding a plumber who would turn up, and do the job without wrecking the place or leaving all his tools there for weeks while he left the job half done, but he also got infuriated if I didn't get three quotes. I was supposed to show them to him, and we'd decide which was the best value before eventually booking someone. By this time, the chosen plumber/electrician/craftsman was 'on a big job' and unable to make it for another three weeks.

'For heaven's sake,' Stephen would say. 'Count yourself lucky that you're not a site manager. They manage to get plumbers and electricians by the dozen.'

Eventually I snapped. 'If you ever did any of this yourself,' I checked my watch, because yet another workman was half an hour late again, and although I could put off the shop, my teaching commitments had to be honoured on the dot, 'you'd soon discover that there's a world of difference between getting an individual plumber for an ordinary house, and commissioning an entire plumbing company for a huge development. They're just not on the same scale of things.'

He took this as an accusation that he wasn't pulling his weight. 'Well, I can hardly do it. Have you any idea what my time is worth nowadays?'

My interest sharpened. 'No, I don't have the faintest.' I read our bank accounts, of course, but hadn't noticed that Stephen's income had gone up all that much. Not as much as you might think, but then these prestigious projects don't necessarily bring in much cash, do they? 'I'd love to know.'

'Oh, for heaven's sake. You wouldn't understand. You have to take overheads and running costs and staff salaries and everything out of it. It would seem a lot if I told you, but it doesn't add up to much. In real terms, that is.'

I raised my eyebrows. He was painting himself into a corner.

Alice, whose New Year's Resolution had probably been 'spend less time in the shop' judging from the scarcity of her appearances there, was not happy about it all, either. 'Staying in for the plumber?' she demanded, when I phoned her. 'Can't your husband do that?' I told her, truthfully, that he would be in Belgium.

'Oh.' She sounded as if he'd gone to Belgium deliberately to inconvenience her. 'But I've got a consignment of stuff coming in from the house clearance in Esher that I wanted you to do.' It had been agreed that part of my job would be to clean up anything that was particularly dirty, and polish the odd bit of furniture. Alice had told me where to find the Supaglue, and suggested I stick back any bits that were obviously falling off. 'I've got ten thumbs, couldn't possibly manage it,' she'd brayed. 'You're obviously so practical.'

I didn't mind. It made a pleasant break from reading. So I offered to take a couple of pieces home and sort them out there.

She didn't bother to thank me. As Alice herself would say, 'Really! Some people!'

*

The domestic disasters did not impress prospective buyers, and it was quite impossible to control the estate agents' visits in any way. However much I begged them not to bring anyone round while the man with the sewage tank was actually pumping out the drains, or when the gas man was sealing up the hob with a large notice in Arabic, Swahili and English saying 'Do Not Use This Appliance', there'd still be a shrill ring at the door and Mark Carruthers, accompanied by anxious, smart-looking women or keen young men would appear. Interested, eager expressions would quickly collapse into an appalled exchange of glances, and within minutes I could see that all that the visitors wanted was Out. Now. They'd scurry out on to the windy, wet February pavements, literally chased down the streets by the scraps of litter scudding along in the breeze.

And the ones with stamina were invariably the rude ones.

'Oh, we wouldn't want a sitting room like this,' asserted a stern woman in tweeds, who reminded me of a younger Margaret Thatcher. She didn't specify what was so terrible about it.

'The place is absolutely falling apart,' declared one man indignantly, as if we were trying to deceive him in some way. 'I'd make an offer but it's ludicrously over-priced.'

'That's what houses cost round here,' I told him through gritted teeth. 'I suggest you try further out if you want cheap accommodation.' He marched out without a word, and I enjoyed slamming the door behind him.

'We'd have to gut this, of course,' said a very pregnant blonde to a man with a shaven head and a nose-stud.

'Nah,' he looked around, clucking slightly under his breath. 'Not worth it.'

Others were distracted by detail – most of the men were extremely anxious to know if there was a garden tap, for example, while the women obsessed over whether the windows would take certain kinds of window treatment.

The house, wilting under the strain of these insults, looked sadder and more battered than ever, and its real assets, its generous red-brick solidity, the space in its high airy ceilings, and the soft greeny-grey of the original tiles inset into a handsome Art Deco fireplace, faded into nothingness.

The headlines in the newspapers proclaimed that family houses were going for a premium, particularly in London and the South East, just around the time that Mark Carruthers suggested dropping the price. I asked him how this could possibly be.

He cleared his throat, his Adam's apple bobbing up and down. 'Ah. Well. It does need Work.'

I asked him, again, whether it would be worth smartening everything up a bit.

'Oh, I wouldn't say that,' he said, hastily. 'Good money after bad if you ask me.'

I phoned up the agency with the two overly made-up women again.

The one I managed to catch, after leaving several messages, was cautious. 'Oh, we don't like to advise. Generally purchasers don't want anything too extreme.'

Stephen put his finger on it when I mentioned it over supper. 'But what would we do exactly?'

'Oh, I don't know. Paint everything white. Just clean it up a bit.'

'It is white.' Stephen looked at the sitting-room walls. 'I don't think making it any whiter would make any difference. Anyway, it costs too much.'

14

Early in March Stephen and I were invited on a corporate weekend in Paris for him to receive an award. Some wives grumbled about corporate travel, but I got so little of it that I revelled in every minute of the expense-account pampering, and besides, an award was an award, although Stephen said it was quite an obscure one. This was a famously chic hotel in Paris, paid for by the organizers (the award was attached to a conference), with a dinner beforehand, a wives' programme all day, then another dinner in the evening, and the chance to tag on the rest of the weekend just for fun.

And hotels felt safe. People didn't burgle hotels. Admittedly, the door chains looked horribly flimsy, so anyone who did want to get in wouldn't have much trouble, but I felt comfortably and securely anonymous. Any men in balaclavas would have an awful lot of doors to try before they found mine. Or perhaps I was just getting better. The endless troop of workmen in and out of the house had been remarkably good therapy in some ways, because sudden, unexpected noises made by strange men now usually had a perfectly good explanation. It usually meant they'd put their foot through the ceiling trying to fix the water tank in the attic.

The hotel was rambling and pretty, and the room had rich red wallpaper. The bed took up almost all the floorspace and was hung with velvet swags. A tiny marble bathroom had a pull-out bidet, and there was a carefully concealed mini-bar and a television in an ornate armoire. Long French windows opened on to a balcony over a courtyard, amazingly like a tall lift shaft. I was just trying to decide whether to indulge in a quarter bottle of champagne or a gin and tonic, when Stephen, channel surfing in his boxer shorts, caught a snatch of the British weather report.

'There's been a freeze in Britain.' It was one of those freak weather events that appears to take the entire British infrastructure by surprise – trains had derailed, roads had iced up, schools had been closed and hospitals were bursting. The news announcer made it sound as if the London we knew had gone for good. We felt comfortably remote in our cosseting luxury, as if it was something that had nothing to do with us.

I was puzzled. 'It's only a drop in temperature. However sudden. Thank God I didn't prune the roses.' Controlling the flow of workmen and potential buyers in and out of the house had left me little time for my usual chores.

'I turned the central heating off,' muttered Stephen, looking worried. 'I mean, it is March, for heaven's sake.'

'Oh, it'll be fine,' I assured him. 'We're only away for two nights.'

Two nights. Nights. They were suddenly very important to me. I wanted to quench the feverish feelings that had been ignited so casually by Max in the bluebell wood on Christmas Day.

Whenever Stephen wasn't around, I would be suddenly seized with a desire for sex. But somehow it never came off when he got home. Either he was too tired, or I was too tense, or we'd get entangled in some domestic argument about plumbers and dishwashers.

I'd even wondered whether I should take the initiative to spice up our sex life. I mean, it was all very well him being obsessed with his work, but he might look up from his desk and see some beautiful young thing who was just as interested as he was in the specifications of lift shafts. I hadn't noticed it until Max and I had started talking, but now that I had, I needed to quench that indeterminate restlessness, that warm, damp, irresponsible feeling that would suddenly wash over me while reading in The Past, or while shoving an unwieldy pile of clothes into the washing machine. When I was asleep I'd have dreams where I wanted – desperately, gluttonously, painfully wanted – him, but where everything melted away as soon as he came into me; yet I'd wake up in the morning with my head full of lists about grouting or pipes.

I acquired, furtively, a book showing an unlikely looking airbrushed couple with identically flawless peach skins engaged in a number of obviously posed positions. It told me to surprise my partner with candle-lit meals, sexy clothes, murmured endearments, or taking the initiative. I contemplated recommendations such as licking Stephen's ear, or suggesting that he licked mine. But it sounded slobbery and irritating, and the taste of ear potentially sharp and fuggy. What about a little light bondage, they suggested, with clean, clinical photographs to illustrate, which looked remarkably like washing-powder advertisements. Blindfolds, as neat as the eye patches given away on aeroplanes, were suggested. But what, exactly, did one tie one's partner to? Especially if you sleep on a divan bed with a comfortable padded headboard. Perhaps that's why people request the four-poster bed when they go away for romantic weekends.

And in real life, when it really gets down to it, there just isn't the time or the energy to go around murmuring that you're not wearing knickers or whipping out a blindfold. After a long, tiring day, there's something more appealing about a drink or the thought of supper, rather than dressing up and rampant passion. Candle-lit dinners for two, with music, were out, because the phone went constantly, even in the evenings, because projects on the other side of the world hit a hitch, or he needed to give final approval to a bid that had to go out in the morning. Zara, the PR, phoned in the evenings, too, with requests for him to participate in a television programme on architecture here, appear on the radio for a debate on the environment there, for a press quote on a new, controversial development or the opportunity to review some other architect's book. The fruits of success were many and varied and Stephen clearly loved tasting them all. He deserved it, after all these years of watching his dreams appear to wither.

So Paris was the perfect opportunity, because that niggle of desire, although it had never quite blossomed, had never gone away either. Stephen and I, I promised myself, deserved some serious sex. The headboard was solid carved mahogany, pretty – although admittedly without anything you could tie anyone to – and Stephen was now lying back, contemplating the glass of champagne with satisfaction, and wasn't even reading a boring document.

I snuggled up to him, and he stroked my head as if I was a favourite dog. This was where the sex manuals would suggest a little 'manual stimulation', so I edged one hand down the V of dark hair on his slightly softening stomach. He smelt of man – clean man – with just the faintest tang of sweat above the scent of washing powder. My hands traced around a torso that was still lean, with a smattering of dark, slightly greying hairs. They felt rough under my fingers. Suddenly it all seemed too much bother. The niggle of desire vanished, just as he smiled and pulled me to him, checking his watch. 'We've a couple of hours to spare.'

As he kissed me, tasting of red wine and garlic and other good things, I struggled to retrieve some sensuality out of the afternoon. The trouble with real life is that it's just too real. My dreams of love-making had been suspended in time and place, without having to think about the bad back that twinges or normal human smells. They'd been about disembodied cocks, and magically understanding hands.

It wasn't too bad, actually, because he did know what I like, it was just that I didn't seem to like it as much as I did. Perhaps it was a bit like the pipes at home – everything had got a bit furred up with time. But gradually I could feel pleasure tugging away inside me, mounting with each slow, loving thrust rising towards a peak of ecstasy. Then, without any warning, it suddenly fell away. Gone. All the delicious sensations had melted into nothing more than the feeling of something going in and out, in a deadening rhythm.

But Stephen didn't notice, and later on that evening he looked so gorgeous, taking his award in the spotlight and murmuring a few self-deprecating words of thanks, that I suppressed a sense of mild disappointment over the weekend, and wondered if it might have to be four-poster beds and blindfolds after all.

'You must be so proud of him,' everyone told me, and I was. Very. Perhaps a different future, but a better one, had begun to dawn like a late sunrise.

As quickly as it had come, the Big Freeze vanished, and before we got back from Paris the pipes in our house had burst. The water had flooded from the tank through the spare-room ceiling, our bedroom ceiling, and then the sitting-room ceiling below, possibly for as long as a day, bringing down plaster, wrecking carpets, drenching sofas, leaving great tidal marks on the wood, rotting odds and ends like silk flowers or tapestry cushions and generally destroying three of the house's major rooms.

Minutes after we arrived back, Mark Carruthers appeared with two more prospective purchasers. After one look, they scuttled off, aghast, but Stephen managed to collar him for long enough to tell him we were taking the house off the market. 'Just till we get it straight.'

Mark Carruthers adjusted his collar and made a noise like a bath emptying. 'Very, ah, wise. Do call us when you're, er, ready to, er—' He looked at the house doubtfully, as if he thought it might self-destruct, and fled after his clients.

'More workmen?' asked Alice disbelievingly. 'Surely you've had everything done by now?' I explained about the Big Freeze, and she did agree that she knew several people who'd been caught short by it. Her boyfriend, Augustus, had been skiing, where it had actually been hot, she said, while his pipes burst in Clapham.

A trail of loss adjusters, furniture restorers, reupholsterers, plasterers and carpenters followed the plumbers and electricians, not very speedily, because the Big Freeze had caused so much damage that they all had too much work to do.

'Bring back the recession,' muttered Stephen on one of his brief walk-throughs between home and work. 'I want to get on with moving.' He handed me a pile of brochures of houses that seemed well out of our price range.

'There's no point in looking at houses we can't afford.' I pushed them to one side.

'We can afford them.' It was odd. Stephen was usually so careful about money, and never stopped telling me that things cost too much. I did hope that success wasn't making him rash. I couldn't face another twenty years of worrying about bankruptcy.

I resolved to have fun decorating on the insurance, regardless of what might happen to the house after that.

That was when I discovered that if you don't know exactly who you are and where you're going, if you've lost track of how and where you want to live, then you can't create a home. Even small, unimportant, irrelevant decisions, such as what colour to paint a wall, seemed inscrutably beyond me, and, as for the bigger things, such as where we would live and when we should move – well, I could hardly bear to think of them.

15

I decided to call Vanessa. Her encyclopedic knowledge of interior decorating should inspire me with some kind of vision.

She picked up the phone immediately, as if she'd been sitting next to it, sounding thick and coldy.

'Vanessa?' Even her voice sounded different. 'Vanessa, are you all right?'

There was a pause, followed by a series of snuffling and gasping sounds. It took me a while to work out that Vanessa was crying. What on earth could have happened? Surely *Vogue* hadn't decreed that Japanese gardens were 'out'? Or had she been bumped to the bottom of the five-year waiting list for the latest Hermes handbag? There were few other possibilities for disaster in Vanessa's life. Her next words struck me with guilt.

'Barry's left me,' she eventually choked. 'He's gone.'

'Surely not.' My brain couldn't take it in. Perhaps she was joking. Dear, kind, adoring Barry. 'Perhaps you've just had a row and he'll be back.'

She sniffed. 'No. It's the whole thing. The mid-life crisis. The thirty-something secretary. It sickens me, it really does. It's all so predictable. So common!' she shrieked. 'He's just found some silly little thing who's got no sense of shame, and run off with her. I suppose he can't see any further than the end of his willy. I feel so humiliated.'

I'm not being selfish when I say that a break-up, anyone's break-up, feels like having the Bad Fairy come into your life, waving her wand apparently at random, striking one couple and banishing them from The Land of Happy Endings. I visualized thousands of little sparks flying from her wand, flicking past all of us, Vanessa and Barry's friends, acquaintances, even Vanessa's facialist and hairdressers. These sparks would briefly land on us all and then fizzle out, like sparklers at Guy Fawkes night. But sparks could be very dangerous. I shivered. Some of them might catch, and start another fire. I murmured something ineffectual, while, like everybody who hears about the end of a marriage, I feverishly examined my own for cracks. 'It could have been me,' echoed faintly in the hallway. It might be me.

'What happened?'

'It's just so fucking typical of men,' she fumed. 'It's the old story.'

A torrent of unconnected facts spewed forth. It had been going on for a year. A year! 'Or two!' she shrieked again. And none of us had noticed. Except for his tiredness – and now we knew it was the strain of living a double life, rather than Vanessa's incessant party-going – he'd been the same apparently happy, successful, proud Barry he'd always been. She came from Essex, such a cliché, wailed Vanessa. 'She's probably just interested in his money.' They'd met at a family wedding of his, one which Vanessa hadn't gone to because they'd been double-booked. 'And I could hardly miss Lord and Lady

Hartington's do, could I?' she wailed. 'I mean, it was the wedding of the year. You ought to be able to let your husband go to his niece's wedding without him falling in love with his niece's best friend.'

'Is she?' I was beginning to lose the drift of where this woman had appeared from.

'Something like that. It's disgusting, it's practically incest. And you'll never guess what he said.'

I waited.

'You'll laugh, you'll really laugh.' She took a deep breath. 'He said he'd never belonged in my world and he wanted to go back to his own kind. Isn't that rich? As a way of justifying the fact that he's gone off with a younger woman? Someone who's firm and smooth, with a flat tummy and no cellulite on her thighs. His own kind, indeed. You have to laugh.' And she made the bitter, braying noise of the deeply damaged.

I rather agreed with her. Weren't we supposed to live in a classless society? And Barry had made it into Vanessa's world with his own money. He had apparently belonged there for over twenty-five years ('Thirty years,' gasped Vanessa, crying again now. 'I was only nineteen when we got married. I'd never really known anyone else.') without showing any signs of being out of place. I thought of him at parties, casually joking with everyone from the supermarket lords to captains of industry, the odd backswoods earl or even the occasional Royal. No, he had no reason to feel out of place – everybody always loved Barry, so I suspected that Vanessa was right. He was making excuses for having found firm young flesh.

I checked my watch. 'What are you doing?'

'What I've been doing since he left. Sitting here, crying.'

I asked when he'd gone.

'Tuesday morning. I thought he was going to tell me he'd make his own way to the Hartingtons' – you know, Lady Hartington was having one of her regular salons,' she couldn't help name-dropping even now, 'but he sat on the edge of the sofa arm and said he was sorry, but he'd met someone else and was going to leave me. As if it was all part of a normal day's work, except that he had a suitcase. And I had an appointment at Eve Lom's for a facial and there's a four-month waiting list, so I couldn't cancel it.'

That did sound unnecessarily cruel. Barry could be quite calculating and I wouldn't put it past him to have known about the Eve Lom facial and to have made his announcement directly beforehand in order to escape as quickly as possible. I thought of the man who'd always been the most considerate, caring human being over the burglary, and tried to equate it with a man who could shave, shower, pack a suitcase and calmly inform his wife of thirty years that he was leaving for ever. Leaving her absolutely alone. Didn't he worry about her, even if he didn't love her any more? I felt a spurt of anger. Vanessa might be brittle and over-fond of parties, but she was partly what Barry had made her, and she didn't deserve to be treated cruelly, and it was now Thursday, so, apart from the facial, she had obviously been crying for two days.

I'd set aside the morning for dealing with insurance, taking damaged furniture to the restorer, doing the weekly shop, picking up Stephen's suit from the dry cleaners, getting a birthday card for Ellen-the-sister-in-law and having the car serviced, but it could all wait. I offered to go round.

Vanessa had literally shrunk with crying. She looked older, and when I hugged her she felt like a bag of bones. The tissue-paper fineness of her skin was crumpled and dull, and her eyes were red-rimmed and bruised with tears. The bubbly champagne-blonde hair had gone brown and lanky, smelling unwashed and neglected, and it was the first time I'd seen her in baggy, unflattering clothes. She sat down again, curled up in a defensive ball, a tiny scrap of human misery in her great empty ballroom of a drawing room, on one of two white sofas placed at right angles. A small portable phone sat on the arm of one sofa, and she fingered it like a talisman. 'In case he calls,' she admitted, brushing a tear away from her cheek. 'You see, I don't even know where he is.' I could see that Vanessa, usually so smart and confident, had gone into a parallel universe of her own, filled with pain and bewilderment. Once again, I couldn't understand how Barry could leave her suspended like this, with no idea of where he was. He'd obviously skipped off to find his own happiness and couldn't give a damn that she was sitting alone, sobbing her heart out. What if she needed to contact him for something urgent? But no, I supposed this was all about getting the message across to Vanessa that she was truly on her own now. Having moved smoothly from her father's London flat and generous allowance at the age of nineteen to the protective wealth of Barry's empire, she was totally ill-equipped to start looking after herself at the age of fifty. I felt furious with Barry again. Maybe he didn't love her any more, and maybe she was shallow, vain and frivolous, but simply abandoning her after so long without any kind of planning was like tipping a faithful dog out of the car on a motorway because you were going on holiday and wanted to save on the kennel fees.

'Had you noticed things going wrong?'

She shrugged. 'He was bad-tempered. But he's always bad-tempered. She'll find that out for herself.' I had never seen Barry bad-tempered. Other people's marriages are extraordinary.

'And sex was fine. Well, you know.'

I hoped I didn't. Fine sounded suspiciously like what we had. Slightly better than what we had, in fact. 'Have you eaten anything?'

She shook her head.

'We'll start with a bath,' I decided, and went upstairs to a vast room, done out entirely in wall-to-wall granite, with a huge cedarwood bath that reminded me of a coffin. I turned on the taps and poured in Jo Malone's Lime and Basil Bath Oil, briefly observing that the potions and lotions that she had arrayed around the room hadn't saved her. Poor Vanessa. But at least she'd be all right financially, I reminded myself. The courts would award her a big chunk of Barry's wealth.

She was afraid not.

'Barry's very clever,' she said dully. 'And I'm not. He knows how to hide his money away. I wouldn't begin to know where to start with what to tell the lawyers. He's quite capable of declaring himself to be virtually bankrupt so that he doesn't have to pay me. He's quite ruthless about money.'

I thought of how kind Barry had been to me. 'I'm sure he'll be fair. He won't leave you with nothing. And you know some of his assets, surely? I mean, this house, for example, and Merlins. And your joint account.'

She snorted. 'Joint account? He sees to all that. We could have sixty joint accounts for all I know. Except they'll be sixty of Barry's accounts and I'm sure he'll have them stashed away offshore or something. I think even the houses are in the name of some kind of trust, but don't ask me how or what. There's nothing as simple as a house in my name. Or even his.' She must have seen how appalled I was at her complete ignorance of any of the realities of life because she burst out: 'Barry never let me near any paperwork. He said I hadn't got the head for it.'

I thought of how Stephen and I had gone through the bank statements together at the end of every month. We'd often had rows about it, but at least I knew about every penny we possessed. I was especially intimate with The Overdraft, which seemed a positively benevolent figure in comparison to these secret offshore accounts and anonymous trusts. In spite of all her shopping sprees, Vanessa had never had any financial freedom. She'd been shackled with gilded chains. I suppose, in the end, nobody really has it easy. It just looks that way.

'The credit-card companies say that he's put a limit on my spending, so when my cheque book runs out I won't have any money, and he won't send me another.' She looked around at the vast room in panic. 'I daren't leave the house in case he takes possession of it, but I don't think I've even got the money to heat it or pay the rates.'

Jesus. Vanessa really was vulnerable. 'You need a lawyer,' I told her. 'Now.'

She wiped her eyes. 'That's what Annabel said. She gave me this name.' She went to the desk and took out a card. 'These people. They did her divorce, and she said they were terribly nice.' She met my eyes guilelessly. 'But have you heard of anyone better?' I swallowed. Annabel was one of Vanessa's more rapacious lunching friends. These were London's heaviest-hitting divorce lawyers. Even I'd heard of them. Poor Barry. Being chased by that lot. Perhaps Vanessa wasn't quite so vulnerable after all.

'They'll be awfully expensive,' I warned her.

Vanessa shrugged. 'Oh, Barry'll have to pay that. He's the one who's responsible for all this, after all.'

'Do the children know?' Even at twenty-seven and twenty-five respectively, Rob and Emily were still children to us.

'They're devastated,' Vanessa twisted her tissue in her hand. 'Emily's cancelled her wedding. She says it's destroyed her belief in marriage.'

I was appalled. 'Oh, no!'

'She's still living with him, of course,' added Vanessa. 'I expect they'll probably get married some day. I told her not to bother.' She started to cry again. 'And if Barry marries this tart, then she'll get all his money when he dies. The children will get nothing.'

Rob was a merchant banker, and his firm had been in the news at Christmas because the gargantuan size of the Christmas bonus awarded to its employees had astonished even a jaded press. He lived in a penthouse which Barry had carved out for him at the top of one of his 'loft' developments, and which had been given to him outright. Emily worked for an interior designer, and had an allowance, a house in Fulham bought for her by Barry, and a diamond the size of a knuckleduster to proclaim her future union with another successful banker.

'They've grown up,' I pointed out. 'They've got their own lives. They can look after themselves now. It's you that matters.'

'They've promised not to see him.' Vanessa seemed dry-eyed suddenly. 'Emily will never forgive her father and neither will I. And, as for Rob, he knows which of his parents is really thinking about his welfare and which one has gone off to indulge himself in an irresponsible fling. I'll tell you how I intend to protect the children,' she leant forward. 'I'm going to take Barry absolutely to the cleaners. I'm going to wring every penny out of him, and I don't care what it costs in lawyer's fees. Because he's the one who's going to pay them. It's the only way I can keep their money, the children's money, out of the hands of that scheming little tart.'

On the way home I got stuck in a traffic jam, and had

time to read the advertisements on the billboards. 'Fun-loving criminals', ran the strapline for a television pro-gramme. The world tilted sharply on its axis, dislodging my concern for Vanessa and replacing it with that cold, empty feeling I'd come to dread. In my mind's eye, I could see the curtain to the parallel universe flapping in the brisk April winds, and I looked away to concentrate on my driving, trying to keep the dark images out of my brain. Crime as fun-loving. What sort of crime? Knocking fragile old people to the ground for their pensions as if they were coconuts in a funfair? Knives in the kidneys of young boys who ought to know better anyway? Perhaps they were now considered disposable, these young men on council estates, and could be allowed to have fun killing each other, like gladiators in Roman times. I clutched the steering wheel very hard, so my knuckles went white, and thought about what I would cook Stephen tonight. Steak would be easy, because I had to go to the shop this afternoon, and wouldn't have any time for shopping. We had some steak in the freezer. Steak, I thought, like a baby carefully placing one brick upon another, steak, and low-fat oven chips. And broccoli.

'But what I couldn't understand,' I told Stephen later on, after he'd expressed considerable sympathy for Barry and none at all for Vanessa, as he grappled with the steak, which had turned up at the edges like a curling piece of shoe leather, 'is how Vanessa comes to know absolutely nothing about their joint finances. I mean, didn't she ever wonder where the money was coming from, or how much she had to spend? Surely Barry should have told her something? I mean, what if he got run over by a bus?'

Stephen put his knife and fork together with a clatter, murmuring something about Vanessa being too busy shopping to think about where the money was actually coming from, in tones of such dismissal that I wondered if he'd secretly despised her all along. It was something I later noticed in other people over the next few months. When Vanessa had been rich and beautiful and part of a couple, she had been fêted and indulged. Broke (relatively, in her terms), ageing (also in relative terms) and single, her problems were deemed to be all her own fault. I said as much to Stephen.

'For Christ's sake, don't waste your pity on Vanessa,' he replied, rather too sharply. 'If you're really feeling like playing bleeding hearts think about people who really don't have any money. Single mothers in council flats. The homeless. Refugees.'

It was like being told by Nanny to eat up all your tea because there were starving children in India. I could see that single mothers in council flats had more problems than Vanessa, but Vanessa was our friend – my friend, anyway. 'Just because she's rich it doesn't mean she's not suffering. She's in terrible pain. You've no right to criticize her,' I snapped back before realizing that I was allowing the fallout from Vanessa and Barry to affect us. It seemed that I was on Vanessa's side and he was on Barry's. Predictably, perhaps.

'Well, at least they can afford to get divorced.' He spoke with a grin, reaching out for another glass of wine.

This was a standing joke between us. When friends had started divorcing, dividing up their assets and swapping four-bedroom houses for two two-bedroom flats, we'd hugged each other and giggled that we couldn't afford to get divorced because what with our debts and living in an unfashionable part of town, our assets divided wouldn't even make two one-bedroom flats, or even two lots of rent. The Overdraft was clearly a great believer in family values, because it certainly did not permit divorce, and wouldn't even allow either of us to have an affair. Affairs cost money – all those lunches, and the occasional night in a hotel, I assumed, never having given it much thought. The careful scrutiny of credit-card statements and cheque stubs that was required in our lives would not even have allowed for the odd bunch of flowers. So we'd laughed, barely bothering to conceal the slightest sense of superiority. 'You're stuck with me,' we'd told each other joyously. 'There's no way out.'

It occurred to me with a sudden sense of mild alarm that if we paid everything off some time this year, and slowly grew richer on Stephen's new success, then that no longer applied. We, too, could afford to get divorced. A tie between us had been loosened and released. Still, after the years of penny pinching, perhaps it would be a nice change to have problems like that. We were strong enough, I thought.

'Well, anyway,' I retreated, relieved that most of the failings in Vanessa and Barry's marriage didn't seem to have echoes in our own, 'at least we don't keep secrets from each other. I know everything about our finances, except for the stuff that belongs to the business.'

'Did you get my dry cleaning?' Stephen changed the subject so quickly that I felt a sudden thrust of fear. Perhaps he, too, had a girlfriend, hidden away, waiting her time until she could take him from me.

'No, I told you. I didn't have time.'

'Really,' he sighed, picking up his blue-and-white plate and taking it to the dishwasher, 'I don't know what you do all day.'

'Stephen,' I knew that this was the question that could blow apart our life, but I'd been hit with a sudden, terrifying thought. 'Look at me.'

He stopped, irritated.

'Please be honest. Are you having an affair too? Is that why you're so sympathetic to Barry?'

He threw back his head and roared with laughter. 'Look,' he came back to sit beside me, and took my hand. 'Please believe me. I don't have time for an affair, I don't want an affair, even if I did want one, there's no one I could possibly have an affair with, and finally, no, I am not having an affair. Now is that good enough, or would you like me to swear on a bible or something?'

And I laughed too, at my own paranoid suspicions – because even when he worked late, I could call him any time of the day or night and he was always exactly where he'd said he'd be – and suppressed the feeling that there was still something about the conversation that wasn't quite right.

'I'll tell you who really can't afford to get divorced, though,' he said, half an hour later, as we switched off the TV and started to go upstairs to bed.

I felt affection for the way we slotted together, the way the unspoken language of couples meant you could start and stop a conversation at any point over a six-week period and the other would pick it up without having to go back over old ground. 'No. Who?'

'Max and Anne.'

I stopped. 'But surely they wouldn't want to?'

He shrugged. 'Probably not. But the fact is that they can't. Not without losing Stonehill. The word is that Max has ploughed all his money into it over the years, and they've got a cash crisis. They couldn't buy each other out, so they'd have to sell up, and neither of them would ever do that, would they?'

'God, no.' I thought of the static, enigmatic quality of their relationship. Perhaps that was why it seemed so carefully and perfectly balanced. They were married to Stonehill as much as to each other.

'You do tell me everything, don't you?' I turned to Stephen one more time before switching off the light.

'Of course. I promise.' He flicked his side of the room into darkness, kissed me and we turned on to our sides away from each other and slept soundly, like an old pair of bookends.

16

Against the backdrop of intermittently appearing (or non-appearing) gas fitters, electricians, brickies, plasterers and carpenters, life rolled on. The wisteria showed tantalizing promises of small, slender green buds, promising elegant lilac plumes later on. Brightly coloured bulbs jostled each other for space against the even more garish colours of the crisp packets and lager cans that blew into the garden from the street. Stephen picked them all up on his way out in the morning, dropping them into the dustbin with an expression of distaste. 'We must move,' he muttered. Later I noticed a used condom by the lamppost which he'd failed to spot. Directly under a lamppost is a curious place for sex. Perhaps it was some middle-aged couple desperate to pep up their flagging sex lives with a little exhibitionism.

April turned into the cruellest month as far as everything in the house was concerned. My 'to do' list threatened to swamp me. Video repair shop on Monday (the smaller pieces of equipment had caught the breakdown bug and were taking it in turns to fold in an electronic dance of death that had me endlessly trudging to dusty shops in impossibly located parts of town, only to be told that they weren't 'worth' repairing).

The video shop was followed by the dentist, the perpetually deferred car service plus the dry cleaning on

Tuesday, then the supermarket and the cheese shop – if I could get there in time – after which I needed to drag my bicycle through the side alley of the house to get to The Past in time for Alice to leave for a house clearance in Surbiton. With the school on Easter holiday, I had time to take all these things to be mended, or to buy other things to replace them. More importantly, Polly was coming home this weekend, and I could feel the spring sun on my back. I missed the girls terribly, and occasionally I'd remember that if we'd had another, had the last one, there'd still be a child at home needing me. That child would have been fourteen by now.

Still, all the machines and gadgetry in the house seemed to need me. I consigned the car to the joking care of two enormous men in overalls and dreadlocks, who would clearly enjoy making a doom-laden phone call later on in the morning about its big end collapsing, or the need for the clutch to be replaced, and headed for the Underground with a sense of satisfaction that at least one thing I'd meant to do for ages could finally be ticked off.

Even wandering along in a dream, I couldn't have missed the lovers by the mouth of the Underground. It was Barry, on the side of the Clapham Road, holding a girl's face in his hands, stroking her hair as if he was afraid to let her go. They fitted together, as if they were in a world where no one else existed. I stopped, uncertain what to do.

'I couldn't bear it if you saw Barry,' Vanessa had implored. 'I think he really ought to realize how irrespon-sible he's been, and if he knows that all his old friends disapprove I'm sure he'll think again.' I'd opened my mouth to protest, when she'd added: 'Not that I would ever take him back. Not now. She'll find out what he's really like and chuck him out as soon as she's got her hands on some money.'

I'd tried to say that of course I wouldn't take sides, but that . . .

'I trust you,' she'd said. 'I know you wouldn't be disloyal.'

Barry and the girl stopped. She wasn't the gilded harpy of my imagination. She seemed very young, pale and slim – almost transparent, with an oval face and straight brown hair. She was quietly dressed and wore little make-up.

'Suzy!' Barry put his hand out to my arm, hanging back from his customary kiss.

'Hello, Barry.' What can you say? I pecked him on the cheek, feeling Vanessa's invisible, disapproving eye.

'This is Kelly.' The girl smiled hesitantly, and stretched out a hand to shake.

'Pleased to meet you.' She turned to Barry, and stretched up to kiss him again. 'I'd better run. I'm late. See you at seven.' When she smiled it was as if she was lit from behind. I hadn't seen two people look so adoringly at each other since the girls were toddlers and loved their Mummy 'more than all the stars in the sky'.

He obviously forgot about me for a second while he kissed her briefly back. 'Bye, love. Take care. Ring me on the mobile if you want me to pick you up.'

She laughed. 'I'll be fine.' And she hitched her bag over her shoulder, swinging round to address me: 'I'm sorry it's all had to turn out like this. I never wanted anyone to be hurt. But I'm glad to meet one of Barry's friends.' And she was gone, almost flying through the barriers at the tube station, with a final wave and a dazzling smile to Barry.

We stood there, Barry and I, until she'd disappeared from sight. 'I'm sorry,' he touched my arm. 'So sorry about all this. How is she?'

'She doesn't know where you are.' I was determined to make sure he knew how much he'd hurt Vanessa by walking out so suddenly.

He looked surprised. 'I'm at work. During the day. Where I always am. She can always reach me there. But I didn't think it was wise to tell her where Kelly lives. She can be a bit impetuous. Here, look . . .' And he steered me into a trendy coffee bar where we ordered and sat down.

Barry told me that he'd stopped being in love with Vanessa years ago.

'I don't know when I started to get tired of it all. The endless parties. We were never alone. We went on holiday with friends. Apart from our honeymoon, we've never been anywhere that was just us in the whole thirty years of marriage. Even when she had Rob and Emily, she had to have the top consultant, the society midwife and the most fashionable maternity nurse, and the whole thing was more like a coming-out ball rather than a birth.'

I started to say that he could surely have discussed that with Vanessa, asked her to make time perhaps, but he swept over me. He couldn't stop talking. It was as if years of discretion had been unstoppered.

'That wasn't the only thing, of course. Vanessa's in a different world. I always felt apart, as if I was always one step behind her. I suppose I was entranced by it at first – completely dazzled by her – but in the end, it just wasn't me. I'm not shy, or ashamed of myself or anything. I simply want to be me. Not Sir Barry, the property developer. She was always on at me to do things to get a knighthood, but frankly I don't care about any of that. I never have. When I first met Vanessa she seemed so full of life, so sparkling, but then I discovered that was all there was. Party sparkle. We don't have anything in common.'

You'd think a property developer and someone whose obsession was decorating houses would have something in common. I was reminded of the old question: 'Is she happily married or is she an interior decorator?'

'What about the children?'

He smiled, slightly. 'The children –' he paused and swallowed '– are grown up. Anyway they're her children, they always were. I never had time to get to know them when they were little, and now they don't want to know. There's nothing of me in either of them. All they care about is the money.'

I started to deny it, but he looked directly at me, and I could see the pain in his eyes. 'They've told me that. As good as. They said they were worried that if I married Kelly then she'd get everything if I died. They want me to put it in trust for them. They think she's some kind of gold-digger.'

I was silent.

'And she isn't. You saw her. I've offered to buy her a

car, but she just laughs. She says it's easier to go by tube.'

'It is, mostly.' Barry did have it bad. He obviously considered this view of Kelly's to be an insight on a par with the development of penicillin.

'I've got her a credit card. I have to make her use it.'

I wondered how long the unworldly Kelly would maintain her principles before she, too, started comparing swatches of material and ordering three-hundred-pound tassels for her bedroom windows. 'I think what hurt Vanessa,' I spoke carefully, 'was that it all seemed so sudden. She had no idea.'

Barry stirred his coffee thoughtfully. 'I did try to talk to her. I asked her to come to counselling, twice. Once before I met Kelly, then again as a last-ditch attempt when I knew I was falling in love with her.' Nessa refused point-blank. She said counselling was common, and, anyway, she didn't have time.

'Still,' he added. 'To be fair to her, she may have sensed that I just wanted out, and was going to use counselling as a way of saying so, so perhaps I shouldn't blame her.

'The thing is . . .' He looked at me again. 'I'm fifty-six. I don't know how many years I've got left. Twenty, perhaps. Hopefully more. Perhaps less. And I couldn't face the idea that what I had with Vanessa was all there would ever be. I couldn't accept not having passion. Love. Joy. I could see it all stretching on the way it was, for ever. Parties. More parties. Then funerals. I kept asking myself "Is that all?" It's not enough, Suzy, it's just not enough.

'What I mean is that I want to live. More than live.

Enjoy life. While I've still got it. And Kelly is my life. She's everything I ever wanted.'

'She's very young,' I blurted out, still wondering whether 'enjoying life' was a euphemism for 'enjoying sex'.

'She's thirty-three. Old enough to know her own mind.'

I was surprised. She had the untouched, innocent look of someone ten years younger. 'And what about children?' I murmured, unkindly, perhaps. It just slipped out. It still didn't seem quite fair that Barry could walk away from an unhappy marriage to someone new and young, while Vanessa, for all her faults, faced years of loneliness and pain ahead of her.

He leant back. 'You mean are we going to have babies? And how will I manage that at fifty-something? Well, we don't know about the future. We're just living from day-to-day at the moment. But if Kelly wants babies, she can have them. I just want to make a better job of fatherhood than I did the first time round.'

'She's very hurt,' I said of Vanessa. 'It's knocked her confidence. And she feels so vulnerable.'

'No one with those lawyers is vulnerable,' Barry grinned. 'But you're right. I'm glad she's got you. I wish there was something I could do to help her.'

I thought of Vanessa telling me that he'd cut her credit-card limits and refused to send another cheque book.

'I think she's a bit worried about money,' I murmured. 'She's frightened that you'll leave her without anything. It's just that she's never had a proper job, and fifty is no time to be launching a career from scratch.'

'Oh, I've let her have plenty of money. I know what she's like, don't forget.' He looked at me sharply. 'Don't tell me she's run through it all already? For God's sake, what's the woman doing? Bathing in liquid gold?' He shook his head in irritation.

'But she's been a huge part of my life, and I still love her, even if I'm not in love with her any more,' he added. 'And I know I've hurt her. But if I ring her to see how she is, if I tell her I care, she may think I'm weakening, coming back to her even. The sooner she realizes it really is over between us, the faster she'll move on.'

'I don't think "moving on" is exactly something you can do quickly after thirty years,' I reminded him.

'No, you're right. Even I've found that. But, Suzy,' he touched me on the arm again, 'you will look out for her, won't you?'

With a sense of inadequacy, I promised that I would.

'And how are you?' When Barry asked this, he really meant it.

'Not bad,' I acknowledged. 'The house is falling apart, which takes my mind off . . . you know.' He did know. The dark side. The nightmares, like a ripple in a pond, were gradually ebbing away, but occasionally something would happen that I couldn't instantly identify as safe, and it would be as if someone had thrown another, albeit much smaller, stone in the lake of fear.

'How's Stephen?'

'Busy. Happy. Frantic with giving soundbites on every aspect of modern and not-so-modern design. Now that the newspapers have to have lifestyle sections, he seems to be in great demand. He got an award the other day, you know.'

'Good. I'm glad it's working out for you both at last.' Barry got out his wallet to pay the bill.

'I just wish we could sort out where to live. What to do now. I can't see a way ahead somehow.'

Barry put the wallet back, looking concerned. 'What do you mean?'

'It's not as simple as him wanting the country and me wanting the city, because I don't, necessarily. He's obsessed with a certain type of house, and I suppose that's all right, but he seems to want to spend a quite horrendous amount of money on it, and I'm not prepared to mortgage everything we've got just for that.' It occurred to me that, like Barry, I was beginning to count the years I had left, and I did not want to spend them worrying about money. It was like a splinter working under my skin. Every time I thought about where we were to go next, I just couldn't visualize it.

Barry hesitated. 'You'll probably find a house one day and fall in love with it. And that'll be that. And nobody else will be able to see what's so different about it from all the other houses you've seen, but there'll be something about the way the light streams in a top window, or some old tree in the garden, and you'll know you've come home.'

I was surprised that Barry, who saw houses in terms of profit per square inch, could be so lyrical. 'It sounds as if you've fallen in love with a house as well as with a woman.' Without warning, Max came into my mind. Max and Anne.

'It's not much,' he grinned. 'Nothing compared to Stonehill, or even Merlins or our London house. But it's right for us. We're exchanging contracts soon. It's got a one-hundred-year-old mulberry tree in a walled garden.'

'Congratulations.'

'But I'll tell you one thing,' he added. 'You're right not to settle for the one that looks right, but doesn't really grab you. All the houses Vanessa ever bought were her houses – she chose them, and decorated them, and I paid for them, though I never felt anything for them, except perhaps for Merlins. I could see they were good buys, that was all. And then we always moved on, to a better address usually. But none of them ever felt like home. That's why I always loved coming to your house. It was warm and crazy, and falling apart, and completely untidy, but it was real.'

Feeling slightly crushed at the 'falling apart and completely untidy', I told him he must come again, and then thought of Vanessa, and amended it to: 'You must both come round when we've finally finished decorating.'

'Yes,' he took my hand as he kissed my cheek. 'I understand if that takes some time. But whenever that is, we'd love to.'

It's strange seeing someone you know in love. There was a light behind his eyes that I'd never seen before. It made me feel switched off and shut out in comparison. I just hoped that Kelly was as loving and well-meaning as Barry clearly believed she was.

Perhaps Vanessa would find someone too. But it

wouldn't be easy for her. As she'd said, crunching a tear-sodden tissue into a tiny ball, 'Starting again at fifty isn't the same as doing it at thirty.'

17

May's gentle, warming sunshine struggled through the gardens along my road, encouraging the frothy bridal plumage of pyracantha to bloom in the neat town hedges, the scented jasmine to wind through a few early rose buds, and an air of pale pink expectation in the blossom of scrawny cherry trees. The wisteria fulfilled its promise with abundant lilac tassels. Ugly buildings disappeared behind green blankets of ivy, Russian vine and Virginia creeper, and self-seeded green shoots of lavender began to sprout alongside the broken glass between the paving stones. People smiled and spoke to each other, usually to compare notes on slashed tyres or new graffiti, nodding their heads gravely. The parallel universe remained muffled, however, by the birdsong and blossom, and I managed to sleep longer, and better. The plasterer assured me that the main rooms would be dry enough to paint within ten days.

Which meant choosing a colour. All my feelings of inadequacy came flooding back, as I remembered the dark days earlier in the year when I'd been unable to make a decision on what to wear or what to cook in the evening. It had been as if my decision-making abilities had been disabled by the faceless man and the bruises down my shoulders and ribs. This sudden block about making a choice on paint at home was all the more startling because at The Past I was enjoying myself doing outrageous things with some of the most worthless pieces of furniture. Seized by a feeling of total hedonism, I'd painted a fake chipboard-and-vinyl Louis Quinze dressing table in a glorious Schiaparelli pink, because I thought that, as a background, it might draw attention to some relatively nice scent bottles that had turned up from a house in Reigate. Alice had hooted with laughter, and suggested adjusting the dosage of 'whatever you're on'. When it sold in two hours, she told me she didn't care if I painted everything sky blue pink if it made me happy, and went off to stay with some friends in the country for a few days. I then painted two hideous wardrobes tangerine and lime green, added tassels to the keys and changed the handles to glittering coloured glass. They, too, had sold within the week.

But I couldn't decide whether to paint my own living room white or cream.

'Why don't you ask Vanessa?' Stephen suggested. 'Just don't let her talk you into buying something that's three times the price because it's got a stylish name.'

Stephen's new-found success didn't seem to have stopped him worrying about money, but perhaps that would come. The mention of Vanessa reminded me how lucky I was to have a husband who told me everything and who didn't seem to have the slightest interest in firmer, younger flesh. I'd talked to him about Barry, saying that he and Vanessa no longer had anything in common.

'We still have plenty in common, don't we?' I'd asked, suddenly struck with worry.

Stephen had laughed. 'You are funny. We've got a whole life in common.'

I liked the sound of that. A whole life. Everything was fine.

I called Vanessa once a week to see how she was coping. We'd invited her to dinner once or twice, scraping up the odd 'spare man' from Stephen's office, and she'd bubbled and laughed with them as if she hadn't a care in the world. But during the day she wore sunglasses, even when it was grey and rainy, and when she lifted them up her eyes looked sad and fragile.

Fortunately, Vanessa's life was charted by parties, and May was a great party month. She read articles on 'The Ten People You Must Have to Your Party', or 'London's 100 Most Invited Party Girls' as obsessively as a stockbroker follows the market prices, and was delighted to be able to tell me she had acquired a team of the top 'walkers'. These were personable men who were free in the evening, who could squire married women to parties while their husbands grappled with breathtakingly profitable mergers, takeovers, deadlines and foreign travel. Walkers were harder to find if you were genuinely single, Vanessa explained, 'because they're frightened you'll pounce on them', but when Vanessa was bent on acquisition she usually succeeded. 'I mean the last thing they'd want is sex,' she added, because sex was going through one of its unfashionable cycles according to *Harper's*. 'So it's not too bad, being single,' she said cautiously. 'Although I was terribly hurt not to be invited to the Cavendishes. People always side with the man, don't they? Although I don't suppose That Floozy would be exactly their cup of tea.' Fortunately we hadn't been invited to the Cavendishes either, so I wasn't able to say whether Barry had been there or not.

This party-going was punctuated by a guerilla war with Barry. Barry had the money, and Vanessa had Rob and Emily, both of whom had refused to see him, or meet Kelly. ('I'm not surprised,' Polly had said, with unusual venom. 'If you or Daddy ran off with someone else, I certainly wouldn't go and meet your lover. Imagine!')

I thought, hearing Vanessa seething, that taking Barry to the cleaners was, perhaps, deep down, a ploy to get him back. 'He'll probably have to sell, or at least re-finance his company, to pay me off,' she'd say, repeatedly, as if trying to dredge up some satisfaction from it. 'Bet that makes him think twice about whether it's really worth it to stay with *her*. But he'll really have to convince me if he wants to come crawling back,' she'd add, wistfully. She refused to admit that she loved him or missed him, but she brought his name constantly into the conversation, in a painful parody of the newly in-love who can't stop mentioning the person they've fallen for.

Having promised to come shopping for white paint with me ('there are so many different whites these days, and some of them, frankly, are quite ghastly') she returned to her second favourite subject after Barry, asking what parties I'd been invited to, in case she was being crossed off guest lists for being unsuitably single.

'Have you been invited to the Hendersons'? In early June?' She asked me this every year, and every year I'd been forced to admit that we didn't really know them well enough. We didn't, in fact, so it had been with some surprise that I'd picked out the understated little 'At Home' card from the usual pile of bills and brochures a few weeks earlier. The Hendersons. Stephen really had arrived. Since getting the Crown Project our usual social round of casual suppers with friends and occasional drinks parties had been considerably supplemented by grand parties like these. I was childishly excited about it.

Lavinia Henderson and her husband, Hector, were generally considered to be 'terribly nice' in spite of being so rich. This was often discussed by Vanessa's friends in tones of wonderment, as if niceness and wealth were simply two qualities that you wouldn't expect to find together, particularly in such abundance. Hector and Lavinia really were rich, by anyone's reckoning.

'But they're the sort of people,' Vanessa had told me in hushed tones, 'whose sons all got scholarships at schools like Westminster and Eton, but they refused to take them so that they could be offered to children who really needed them.'

But as if to prove that niceness didn't have to mean hair shirts and simple pleasures, their annual party, in their huge house in Holland Park, was famous. There'd been the Egyptian party, when the garage had been covered by a pyramid and camels had been tethered by the entrance (they'd eaten the entire beautifully land-scaped planting in the front garden, which had all had to be replaced afterwards). There'd been the Rose party, where the marquee, along with each individual chair, had been wound with roses, and balloons with rose petals had bobbed up from every table. We had heard about these parties from Vanessa, but this was the first time we'd been invited to one. Stephen's new fame was opening doors for us both.

The Hendersons did not do anything as vulgar as hold a fancy-dress party. The theme was referred to by Lavinia as 'a few decorations', so it was a question of waiting until you stood on their sweeping front steps, bounded on either side by grumpy stone lions, and were announced – in this case by an Indian butler wearing a turban. This, it seemed, was to be the Indian party. Everyone was too cool to gasp when they saw the wide hall flanked by thousands of jewel-coloured lanterns and the staircases hung with brilliant silks. The queue shuffled forward in a caterpillar of immaculately clad size 8 women in dazzling gowns and bald men in suits. Rich women seem to be a completely different size and shape from everyone else, quite apart from the designer clothes. The slender hips and fragile-looking upper arms on display made me feel three stone heavier and horribly concerned about the possibility of threads dangling from the hem of a dress I'd bought, at Stephen's bidding, that would 'do' for smart events such as gallery openings. 'With the Crown Project, you'll need to look well turned out. We'll be going to a lot more evening events from now on.' I'd prised myself away from a romantic gypsy dress with a floaty hem and a low-cut neckline that promised fun and flirtation, and into a green damask number that made me feel like a reasonably glamorous headmistress on Speech Day. Very grown-up, very sensible. Possibly it made me look a bit like a giantess, but never mind. I was hardly going to seduce anyone.

We edged through to a huge drawing room which had been tented to simulate a maharaja's marquee. All the furniture had clearly been put in storage, with lavish cushions, tiger skins and low carved tables replaced in their stead. All the waiters and waitresses were Indian, in traditional dress ('Wonder how they got that past the Equal Opportunities laws,' muttered Stephen). There were a couple of elephants, complete with elaborate howdahs, in the garden, to give guests rides.

I spotted Vanessa almost immediately. 'You look terrific. Much smarter than usual. Is Barry here?' she asked, trying to crane her golden head over the crowd.

I admitted I didn't know. 'Who do you have as a walker?' I wanted to get off the subject of Barry.

'Max.' She beamed at me.

He stepped forward and kissed my cheek. 'You look fabulous.'

We stood there, grinning like idiots at each other, while I tried to think of something to say. I was vaguely aware of Vanessa standing between us like a referee.

'How's life?' He sounded as if he really cared.

Life, I told him, was pretty marvellous. It was the truth at that moment.

'Good.' He went on looking at me. 'Don't forget, I said call if you need a chat.'

My stomach lurched uneasily and then swooped back to its correct position again. 'I will.' A part of me registered that this was strange behaviour. This was good old Max, I reminded myself, my husband's oldest friend. He started to ask me if I'd read anything good recently, but Vanessa let out a shriek of recognition. 'Nigel! Have you met Max?' Max was dragooned into his escort role, and the sheer weight of party-goers pushed us apart. I was finally dislodged from his side by a woman with a backless black dress, who was trying to claim him to hear 'all about Stonehill'. He looked over her shoulder, and mouthed, 'See you in a minute.'

I then got entangled with a woman called Portia who, after looking faintly puzzled on hearing where we lived, quickly established that we were both trying to sell our houses. 'It's so frightfully difficult to sell these days. Honestly, I think we might as well just keep our place in London so we have somewhere to stay when we go to the theatre.'

Stephen appeared at my side at this point. Once she'd drifted off, he hissed at me that their house had been priced at one and a quarter million pounds. 'Million! A place to stay after the theatre! Oh, look, there's Max.'

By this time, the party had filled out with quite a lot of stout, middle-aged people, in sturdily respectable party attire, who looked incongruous amid the exotic Indian finery. It was as if two different films were being shown overlaid on the same screen – possibly a Hollywood spectacular about India and something like a training video for the Post Office. The headmistress outfit began to feel more glamorous in comparison.

'You must meet Louise,' Lavinia Henderson swept down on me. She was famous for her introductions. It was said that government ministers could rise or fall, and great corporations merge after she'd introduced exactly the right person to someone else. And, being so terribly nice, she introduced everybody, not just people who could appoint editors of national newspapers or arrange star parts in films. She dragged me towards a frighteningly sophisticated blonde in an understated black trouser suit. 'You've got so much in common.'

'Louise Robertson. Suzy Everett. You've both been . . .' She trailed off, looking faintly embarrassed. 'Kingsley! Darling! You must meet Stephen Everett. You know, the Crown Project . . .' She made her escape by lunging towards someone else, Stephen in tow, leaving Louise contemplating me with deep brown eyes. She offered me a cigarette.

I shook my head, wondering what on earth we had in common. I was quite sure we didn't both work in bric-a-brac shops or schools. 'We've both been . . .?' I inquired.

She raised her eyebrows and exhaled smoke. 'Attacked? Raped?'

I froze. 'I haven't been raped.' I was puzzled. 'Have you?'

'Oh, God, I'm Lavinia's pet rape victim. The Ferret?'

I realized why she looked familiar. She'd been in the news when she'd been attacked by a serial rapist and had given up her anonymity to call for women to come forward. As a result he'd been arrested and convicted. The judge had called her 'an outstandingly brave young woman'. I felt ashamed of my cowardice after a mere bruised shoulder.

'It was very courageous of you.'

'That's what everyone says.' She spoke dismissively. 'Brave. I'm shit-scared half the time.' She seemed very cool about it. 'But it gets better. So what happened to you?'

Feeling rather a fraud, I told her.

'Jesus, I'd hate to find someone actually in my own home. Ugh. That must have been terrible.' She looked at me intently and seemed to mean it.

'Well, it's nothing compared to what you went through. Compared to what you read about it in the papers.'

'What you went through wasn't nothing.' She spoke quite sharply. 'Don't let anyone make you think it was nothing. Especially if you don't know how they got in.' She gave a shiver. 'That gives me the creeps. How are you now?'

'Not bad,' I admitted. 'I just hate that sick, lurching feeling I get when something gives me a sudden fright. It stops me sleeping, so I get very tired.'

'Mm. I remember that. But it wears off.' She told me that The Ferret had been sent down three years ago, but that it was only recently that she'd felt a sense of normality creeping tentatively back. 'But don't you find that it made you rethink everything?' She stubbed out the cigarette, pulled another one out of the pack immediately, and lit it. I noticed her hand shaking.

'Everything?'

'Life. I was a solicitor. Now I own an art gallery.'

This woman was terrifyingly together. 'Er, wasn't that, um, a bit difficult?' was all I managed, although what I was dying to ask was: 'How did you manage to afford it?' I mentally kicked myself. I'd obviously caught Stephen's appallingly dull habit of measuring the cost of everything.

'Oh, God, it was absolute hell at first,' she said. 'I could only do it by selling my house, finding somewhere I could live over the gallery and then persuading someone to invest in me.' She raised her eyebrows. 'Which was not easy, I can tell you. And it's still a bit touch-and-go.

'But I'd thought I was going to die. The . . . The Ferret kept telling me he was going to kill me, especially when I wouldn't—' Her eyes clouded over, as she failed to finish her sentence. 'So when he didn't, I just stopped being afraid of what might happen if I gave up my sensible job, and decided to make every day count. It sounds trite but it's true. Oh, and I left my husband, so now I have lots of lovers instead.'

I never quite believe women who talk so casually about ending their marriages. I suspected a great deal of pain lay behind the decision, and wondered if the lovers were a cover for the way The Ferret had taken away her trust in men. It had been a hideous experience, as far as I could recall from the press clippings.

'An art gallery!' I suddenly laughed. 'I think that's what Lavinia thought we had in common. I'm an art teacher.'

She grinned back. 'And now we've told each other all our secrets. Although I have to say, I'm completely open about it all.'

'People must be fascinated.'

'Yeah. It's like being some kind of exhibit on show.' She struck a stagey pose. 'Ta-ra! The amazing raped woman. People always want to reassure themselves that it could never happen to them, so they want to know all the details.'

We chatted for a bit, until an impossibly handsome man came over to claim her. Louise Robertson had really got her life together. She'd been afraid – still was afraid if what she said was true – but she wasn't a victim. Something clicked inside me.

'I'd love to see your gallery.'

She fished a card out of a tiny, fashionably beaded bag. 'Come any time. It was great to meet you.' She smiled as if she meant it, and scribbled my address down on a pad. 'It goes on getting better from here. And don't forget about the life change.'

'I like my life.' I thought of how much happier Stephen was, how much less worried I felt now about everything. And how well the girls were doing.

'Good.' She smiled. 'I think you recover faster if you do. But if there's anything really wrong, something like being attacked certainly makes you notice it. Here, come to my next private view. Bring friends. Or not. Whichever.' And with a cheery wave she was gone into the crowd, folding into the arm of her lover as if she really belonged there.

'It's time for the fireworks.' A turbanned waiter slid up quietly on slippered feet. 'Can I refill your glass?' It was real champagne, I noticed, not supermarket fizz. I accepted a sliver of something delicious with caviar on it, and followed the cooing crowds out to the terrace. The end of the garden had been covered in panels to make it look like the Taj Mahal, and two long ponds had been inset, just for the evening, with fountains. A series of bright white stars shot into the air in sequence, followed by an explosion of vivid lilac, a cascade of tiny pops like champagne bottles being opened, and intermittent slow, arcing rockets in the shot-silk colours of an Eastern bazaar. Illuminated in the cascade of falling stars, I could see Stephen, head-to-head with two serious types, entering something into his Palm Pilot, completely oblivious of it all.

I remembered the last time we'd seen fireworks properly together, around ten years ago, on Clapham Common on 5 November. Polly and Jess had slipped their gloved hands into mine in the dark. We'd had sausages and cheap wine at home afterwards, with an assorted rag-bag of friends, and laughed so much our sides hurt.

I suddenly wanted terribly to be with him. Unlike Louise Robertson, I didn't want to exchange my husband for lots of lovers. I worked my way round to him, nodding and smiling at people as I went.

'Having a good time?' He squeezed my hand.

'I was just thinking of the fireworks parties we used to go to on Clapham Common.'

'Mm?' He looked puzzled, as he sifted through his memory. 'Oh, yes,' he eventually said in a vague way. 'Well, we've come a long way since then. Thank God, we don't have to go back to those days again.' He put his arm round me. 'Have you seen Max?'

'Briefly.'

'The brewery's failed. Well, at least don't tell anyone yet, but if they don't find a buyer, it'll almost definitely go into receivership in a few months.'

I gasped. 'But how awful. Poor Max and Anne.' I thought for a moment. 'He didn't say anything to me about it.'

'Well, it's all very hush-hush.' Stephen didn't look quite as sad as he might have done. 'Anyway, Max hates anyone knowing these things. By the way, he's asked us down for a weekend in June.'

I felt like saying that I wasn't 'anyone', but, of course, the days when I was special to Max were over. There was no reason why he should not have told Stephen, rather than me. I decided to try to find him to . . . well, cheer him up, I suppose.

Max had left early, according to Vanessa. 'He wasn't his usual self, darling, I do hope he's not worried about something.'

18

A few days later, I was sitting at Stephen's big bureau, where he keeps all his paperwork, when Max called.

'Max! You left early the other night.'

'I had to get back to Anne. I don't like her being on her own for too long.'

Every so often Max says things that make me realize that he does love Anne. Anne, the most independent, least vulnerable person I'd ever met, was more than capable of being on her own, but Max seems drawn back to her, protectively.

'Stephen said things were bad at the brewery. I'm sorry.'

'Well, it's a bit of a bummer. But we'll survive. Just have to start making Stonehill pay its way a bit.'

I wondered how Anne would enjoy that. I could see her organizing enormous tea urns for open-garden events.

'Still,' he added. 'You're coming up to see us for the mid-summer weekend. It's the best time of year.'

We'd been before in June. Sitting on Stonehill's lawns listening to the birds, sipping home-made elderflower cordial while the children raced about had always been balm to my soul. With its heavy clay soil, Stonehill's gardens were paradise for roses – creamy white Albertines created a magical tunnel of fragrance along the Rose Walk, clumps of fragrant pink Old English roses were underplanted with glorious drifts of yellow santolina or lavender in the beds, and cascades of cream or blush-pink ramblers tumbled exuberantly down every faded old brick wall. June at Stonehill was England at its most perfect.

'We haven't seen you properly since Christmas,' he reminded me. I thought of the undercurrents then, the occasional slam of a door, the way Max's eyes would turn dark with anger, and how Anne's brow had furrowed when she thought people weren't looking.

I twirled the phone cord round my fingers and listened to his plans for a barbecue in the bluebell wood, and for inviting Vanessa over for supper if she was 'up'. We talked, idly, about arrangements and bedrooms, and times of arrival. I liked the sound of Max's voice. There was a warmth about it – a certain timbre that seemed to make him sound very direct. 'Are you sure you want us up if things are difficult?' I'd asked him eventually, as we said our goodbyes.

'That's exactly why I want to see you. Gives me something to look forward to.' He spoke lightly, as if joking. 'Come and cheer us up.'

Max would survive, I reflected as I put the phone down. Fish a last few million out of some untapped source. I turned his last sentence over and over in my mind, like a pebble found on a beach, knowing that there was no value or use in it, but feeling its smooth, tactile surfaces, treasuring it anyway. I knew his words had been directed at Stephen and me together, as a couple, as his 'oldest friends', but somewhere, deep down and from very far away, an old wound, one that I'd almost forgotten about, was soothed, eased, and finally healed.

I began to go through the desk, to sort out the last paperwork connected with the burglary. The necklace hadn't been insured but some of the other stuff had been covered. There'd been six months of wrangling over exactly how much and what, and Stephen had reminded me that there was just one more thing to sign and send off in order to get the cheque. I couldn't find it, though, not on my desk, so I'd decided to check his.

One of the envelopes looked about right for the insurers, although as I pulled out the contents I noticed that it had an unfamiliar logo franked on the front. So probably only junk mail, I thought.

It seemed to be some kind of a statement. I read it without understanding it. There were rows of figures, bewilderingly large, and something that looked very much like an 'End Balance'. Stephen's name was on the top.

He'd obviously brought one of the company accounts home. I tried to understand it a bit better, because I'd always been curious about the company and the way it worked, but it didn't seem to be anything to do with a company. Deeply uneasy, but sure there was some kind of explanation, I slipped it into my bag and waited for Stephen to return home.

I pushed it to the back of my mind while I stirred a coconut chicken dish. My cooking faculties had returned, although, oddly enough, not on teaching days. While The Past was so laid back as to scarcely constitute a job, teaching was leaving me more and more frazzled. I wanted to leave, and had wanted to leave for years. Not long now, I told myself, maybe next year; but when you count the time you've got left, like Barry had, it seemed a terrible waste to be spending two days a week doing something you absolutely hate.

Stephen got back late, and pleased with himself. The Crown Project, so far, was ahead of schedule and there was a sniff of another prestigious piece of work to follow. He had been asked to appear on a late-night programme about architecture, and if it was successful it would be the start of a six-part series, for which he could be paid a considerable sum.

I waited until we'd finished our food, because I was still sure that there was some very ordinary explanation, and produced, hesitantly, the bank statement.

He looked at it. 'We don't normally open each other's mail, Suzy.' There was accusation in the tone. 'I thought we agreed that there had to be some basic privacy in our lives.'

'It was an accident. But I want to know what it is.'

'Ah.' He seemed unworried and I relaxed, watching him pick up our plates and stow them in the dishwasher. 'I was going to tell you about that. As a nice surprise.'

I raised my eyebrows without meaning to.

'It's a bank account.'

'I can see that.' I felt myself going hollow and cold.

'It's a savings account. I've managed to claw back a few expenses.' He sat down beside me, and took my hand. 'So you see, we really can move somewhere an awful lot better. There's no need to worry about the price of those houses we've been looking at.'

'We plan all our finances together. Shouldn't we have discussed this?'

'Well, I don't tell you everything.'

The hollow grew. 'Don't you? How long has this been going on?'

He laughed. 'Suzy, you're making this sound like some kind of affair with my secretary! This is our money, it's for both of us. And, of course, I do tell you everything. Everything important, that is.'

I looked at him. He was sleek, convincing, successful. But he'd let me worry about money for so long when we had all this. And I didn't think he'd ever intended to tell me. He'd have come up with the money without telling me where it came from, murmuring something about a bonus from a long-ago completed job. He'd done that before, I realized, looking back on another couple of occasions when there'd been some crisis and he'd suddenly 'discovered' exactly the right amount to sort out the problem. 'How long, Stephen?' My hand shook as I held out the account to him. 'How long have you been doing this?'

'Oh, a few years now. Does it matter?'

'Yes, it does matter. Very much.' I stood up. 'This would easily pay off an overdraft forty times the size of the one we've got. We didn't need to have an overdraft. I didn't need to wake up worried about it all in the night. I don't need to be trudging along in a job I hate. I could have resigned and retrained several years ago. Be established in something else now. But most of all,' my voice rose so high it was almost breaking, 'it's a lie, Stephen, you've been lying to me.'

'Hang on a minute.' He rose too, his face darkening. 'Not so fast. You've missed the essential point – we wouldn't *have* this money if we'd done everything we wanted to do. If we'd paid off the overdraft, and you'd left your job, that would have cost money. Suppose you couldn't find anything else and found yourself sitting around the house all day?'

I gazed at him in horror. 'Is that what you think of me? Unable to stick at a job unless forced to? Don't you have any belief in me at all?'

He began to bluster. 'That's not what I meant. Of course, I believe in you. It's just that people's best work is usually produced under conditions of adversity. I did this for our benefit.'

'Crap. I've never heard such utter crap. You don't trust me.'

'On the contrary,' his voice had grown hard, tight and dry. 'It seems to be you who doesn't trust me.'

'So how long, Stephen, how long?' I could hear my words shaking with shock and rage. He shrugged.

I waved the paper at him. 'You could check. And if you don't, I'll know you have something to hide.'

'Ten years, perhaps, maybe longer.'

I looked at the bank statement again. 'You saved *all* this in ten years?' Disbelief corroded my question.

'Well, as I said, probably a bit longer.'

'A bit, Stephen? A bit? How much, exactly, is a bit?'

We both knew what was at stake. The baby.

'Around fifteen years.' He swallowed and didn't meet

my eye. 'But –' and he waggled a finger at me '– don't forget, if we'd done everything we wanted to do in that time, *we wouldn't have this money.*'

'I wasn't thinking of doing *everything* in those days.' We had started to shout, the way you do when you know you're not being heard. 'I just wanted one thing. You led me to believe that we couldn't afford a third child. And we could have. And we took the decision together to end it. But you never told me the truth.'

'As I said,' he began to wash up viciously, clattering dishes together and rattling things down, 'if we'd had another child we wouldn't have had this money. We'd still be worrying about every penny we spent.'

'Tell me.' I could hardly bear to look at him as I dried up the salad bowl. 'Just one thing. Did you start that account – siphoning money straight off from the partnership separately so that I'd never know it even existed – when the question of the baby came up? To take away my choices?'

'Don't be so melodramatic. I simply can't remember exactly when I started it.' He assumed a lofty tone. 'It really isn't important. *I* have put aside a sum of money for us – money I've earned, I would add – to help us have a decent old age, and *you* seem to think this is some kind of crime. Most women would be delighted to know that there was more money in the bank.'

'Then I'm not most women.' I walked out, grabbing my keys and slamming the door behind me. I didn't usually walk round London late at night but if a mugger wanted to take me on, well and good. I was so angry that I would positively relish the idea of a fight.

As I paced furiously, I tried to understand that Stephen had lied to me. Stephen never lied. Never. That's what I'd thought until now. What else wasn't he telling me about? It was as if someone had just told me that my home was made of paper and had blown away.

And I tried to be rational, and to think about it from his point of view. As Stephen said, it was not as if he'd been having an affair. What I couldn't get over was that he had obviously started siphoning money off into the secret account when I found I was pregnant again, in order to force the decision. The timing would be about right, and he hadn't denied it. I thought of the long, watchful nights, the overwhelming sense of emptiness and regret, and of watching the girls grow up, always aware of a little shadow that should have been following them. All for money. Or rather, for a house, a house like The Old Rectory.

In my mind's eye, I saw the study of The Old Rectory, with Henry Everett, Stephen's father, sitting in front of a blazing fire while the rest of the house froze. Stephen's father roaring by in his Jaguar while his mother cycled furiously into town to get the groceries, or chugged along in a shabby old Morris, kept permanently short of petrol, to get the boys from school. Stephen had been angry enough about his father to tell me all about it.

Now, perhaps, he was turning into him. If I'd still had the necklace – that little chunk of financial freedom that was mine alone – I think I might have left him there and then. But I couldn't afford to, so I returned to the house. Stephen looked up from a pile of papers but didn't speak.

'Firstly,' I tried to prevent my voice shaking, 'the overdraft goes.' I noticed, with a small part of my mind that was standing back observing the scene, that the overdraft had lost its capital letters. It was no longer a personality in its own right. Just a sad little debt. It had lost its power to frighten me.

'Secondly, I'm giving in my notice at the school tomorrow. I'll leave at the end of this term.'

Stephen nodded, with exaggerated humility, I thought. 'You see,' he spoke gently. 'This money is a help. You couldn't have done either of those without it.'

There was no point in prolonging the argument and going over the same old ground again. If it hadn't been a secret, we could have done it a lot earlier, and we could have planned it together. If we weren't together, I didn't know where I was. Floating, unanchored. All the money in the world makes no difference to something like that.

As I slipped into sleep, my back determinedly turned against Stephen, I thought how ironic it was that, in twenty-four hours, Max's situation and mine had been reversed.

He hadn't got enough money, and I now had too much.

19

I was still fuming the following day.

I stormed into the school to give in my notice. Tom Johnson, the head of my department, looked faintly fazed by my resignation.

'What is it with you forty-somethings?' he muttered. 'You'd think it'd be the younger teachers swanning off to Australia or leaving to have babies or whatever, but you lot never stop retraining to be aromatherapists or deciding to become organic farmers in the Hebrides. Don't tell me . . .' (I wasn't going to.) 'You want to change your life. Set up a bed and breakfast in Norfolk. Get out of the rat race on the North Devon coast. Start an animal bookshop. Breed hamsters.' He gave me a reasonably kindly but exasperated smile.

'They're all quite good suggestions,' I said. 'But I haven't quite decided yet.'

'Oh, well, I suppose you've had a lucky escape,' he grumbled. 'But I'll have to advertise. Again.' It seemed there'd been some government rethink in the last few weeks, and a study had come out proving that pupils who did art were less likely to end up in prison or on benefit. So Art would be upped in schools, along with lots more paperwork to ensure that the right pupils were getting the right sort of art. Thank God it wasn't my problem. I'd escaped just in time.

I informed the staff room of my departure in tones of some defiance, and several people looked at me enviously. 'Wish I could afford to resign,' said Marie, the French teacher.

'It's not so much a question of affording,' I began to say, but I realized I didn't want to tell any of them about the money. So I compromised with: 'I should have done it years ago, whatever the finances.' Which was sort of true. But I still slightly despised myself. I could see that the money was quickly becoming a legitimate part of my life.

The following day I told Alice I was resigning from the school. She was never very interested in anything that didn't concern her directly. 'Oh, yah,' she said, vaguely, without asking why. 'Well, there's plenty to do here.'

I looked round at the deserted shop – we seemed to sell anything that had been painted, distressed or in some way altered, quite quickly, but it was still incredibly quiet – and felt a giggle rise in my throat for the first time in forty-eight hours. 'Plenty to do' was Alice's way of saying that she really didn't want to spend a moment longer here than she had to. Stephen had asked me if I was also going to give up The Past, and I'd said 'No' in a tight voice. 'Not until I find something else.' But I still wasn't sure whether that was because I enjoyed it, or because I was determined to prove to him that I wasn't just going to sit around. Or, perhaps, in spite of the fact that we could now officially call ourselves 'wealthy', I feared that it still might all be snatched away from me. Tiny as the sums were from The Past, they were mine.

*

Perhaps that was what Stephen had felt about the secret account. As I furiously took out my feelings on a harmless, if hideous, cabinet, sanding it down in order to cover it with a retro floral wallpaper I'd found in a box at the back, it occurred to me that maybe this was Stephen's only way of mapping out a little of his own space in the communal hurly-burly of family life. Then I remembered the baby, and my heart hardened again. Personal space was one thing. Using it to control other people – people you purport to love – was quite another.

This was no good. I would have to get a grip. In less than a week's time there would be a shared three-hour car journey up to Stonehill. I would have to stop simmering with rage by then or we'd finish up murdering each other.

In the end I drove up alone, through the choking, fume-filled tangle of the Friday rush-hour traffic. Stephen was in Brussels again, and would take a train from the airport on Saturday morning. I suspected he was avoiding me.

At the moment, the sight of him made my stomach curdle. I couldn't trust myself not to snap at him and make everything worse. For the last couple of nights, I'd taken to going to bed early, genuinely aching with tiredness, and pretending to be asleep when he came in. When I did sleep the nightmares churned round my head in an endless loop, facing the man without a face, struggling against the sense of being dragged down into somewhere dark and terrible, panicking at the feeling of nowhere to run to.

In the morning we were bright and breezy with each other, but every request to pass the milk or comment that the toast had popped up was pregnant with unspoken accusations and resentment. We'd never stayed angry with each other for this long before – even though we'd been snappish with each other in the months after the abortion, we'd been angry at life, not at each other. At least, I'd been angry at life. Now I knew that he'd merely been relieved. The anger cramped inside me again, sharp and furious.

When I reached Stonehill, I nearly fell out of the car, stiff with being confined in a tight box for what had turned out to be over four hours of stopping and starting. I gulped down the crystal-clear air, as if I'd been rescued from drowning, feeling sticky and sweaty when Max hugged me. I drew away, not wanting to smell of confined car journey and dank human.

I told him that Stephen would be here tomorrow.

'So.' Max took my little case. 'It's just us.'

'Where's Anne?' I could hear my voice coming out too high, sounding false. Stop it, I told myself. This is Max. Good old Max. Stephen's oldest friend.

'Over near Towcester delivering a horse, then bringing another one back tomorrow morning. She's staying with a schoolfriend.'

I had a bath, feeling unusually apprehensive. What would Max and I talk about? My sense of self, and of my relationship with Stephen, had been so rocked by finding the money that conversations came out of my mouth sounding silly, fake and detached. I kept forgetting myself in the middle of sentences, while my mind, apparently uncontrollable, trooped round in the same old circles.

In the end it was easy. Max prepared an omelette and salad, deliciously light and fragrant, accompanied by an ice-cold bottle of delicate, flowery white wine. We sat out on the terrace, looking at the walled garden, and watching the colours of the flowers deepen and darken as the twilight gradually gave way to a moonlit night. The lawn was a severe oblong of grass and the banks of flowers on either side clumped in soft drifts of blue, pink and white. The scent of roses and jasmine blew softly over us in the night air, and I could sense nature settling itself and folding its wings for sleep. The anger slowly seeped out of me, leaving me drained and peaceful.

Max got out a bottle of brandy, and switched on some music. The haunting notes of his favourite operatic aria spiralled out on the balmy air.

'Max?' As the warmth and relaxation crept up from my toes, I felt brave enough to mention the brewery. 'How are things working out?'

There was a silence. 'Fine.' Max sounded weary.

I didn't know how to respond to the change in tone, and said nothing.

'Actually, Suze. This is strictly one to be kept away from the grapevine. We've really got to focus on keeping Stonehill afloat too. It costs a packet to keep up.'

'How awful.' It seemed a rather trivial response.

'The farming is hopeless, all farming is hopeless now . . .' I'd never heard him sound so tired. 'Might as well sell that too. Then invest the money in something that'll keep Stonehill going so we can pass it on to the next generation.'

'It'll be all right, though, won't it? I mean you're not really worried about having to sell Stonehill itself, are you?'

'It's not out of the question, but I don't think so. It's depressing, though.'

Depressing? Max depressed? Max's depressions had always been fire-storms of gloom, force fields of despair emanating from the depths of his soul. Not this grey miasma of resignation. Everyone was falling apart. Barry and Vanessa. Max and Stonehill. Only Stephen seemed to be going from strength to strength.

'I suppose I'm just tired.' Max smiled and took my hand, so naturally that I hardly registered. 'There are things we can do. Upmarket bed and breakfast. Renting the house out as a location. Renting out the West Wing. Doing weddings and conferences. Selling everything we don't need. Opening the gardens. Turning the barns into holiday cottages. Taking livery in the stables. All that. They'll change the fundamental way we live here, and it may not be enough, but we've got to try them out. There are a couple of friends from the City who are coming up this weekend, in fact, with their wives, on a purely informal basis, just to see what the scope is for making the most possible money with the least possible change, if such a thing can be done.' He talked for ages, as I listened, soothed by the sound of his voice, about his plans to save Stonehill. At least his money, now apparently almost gone, had meant that it had been restored beautifully. It should last several generations, as Max had intended that it should. Several generations of Galliards.

'I simply couldn't bear to lose this place. To be the one who lost it for the next generation.'

'Will you be able to manage it all? You both work so hard anyway.'

'I think so. We'll sell off whatever we can from the brewery. I don't expect much money out of it, but at least it means I'll be able to be here full-time. Provided that nothing happens to either of us, it should just about come together. But I dread the day Anne injures herself in a fall out riding, or I do my back in. It could happen so easily, and we certainly can't afford to hire anyone.'

I was impressed. I realized that Max had been the spoilt child of a rich woman when I'd first known him. Now he worked hard, day and night, and wasn't afraid of working even harder.

He squeezed my hand. 'Thanks for listening, Suzy. Now it's your turn to tell me why you're so miserable.'

I was startled out of my contemplation of the roses, shining a luminescent white in the moonlight as they tumbled down the old walls. 'What do you mean?'

'I have known you for thirty years.'

'Oh, I'm sorry, I . . .' I must get better at acting.

'Don't be sorry.' My hand stayed in his warm, strong one. It seemed quite natural, not wrong at all. 'You don't have to tell me what it is, but if you do, I promise not to judge or tell anyone.'

Well, I had to talk to someone, so I told Max.

'Ah,' he said, once I'd finished.

'Don't tell me you knew.' I could feel the anger start up again.

'No-o-o.' He spoke slowly. 'But I had wondered why you always seemed so broke. Stephen's actually been quite successful for some time. I thought there must be something I hadn't heard about to account for it.'

He took my other hand. 'I don't know if this will help, but I'll try. When Stephen was at school, there was a gang of boys who were very rich. Very dominating personalities. They took the mickey out of him. Relentlessly. Because his mother turned up in a battered old Morris. Because he had an outdated tennis racket that was thirty years old. Because he never got new uniform until his wrists and ankles were poking out yards from the bottom of his cuffs and hems. I told him not to worry about it, told him they were just the jumped-up parvenu sons of garage owners and porn kings.' He grinned. 'In their hearing, of course, which didn't make *me* very popular. They used to call me a dirty little foreigner, but I didn't care. Stephen cared about it, he really did. He was humiliated. And it was relentless.'

I could imagine that. And I suspected Max had cared too, for all his bravado.

'What about The Old Rectory?' I'd always thought that living there had been a golden period in his life.

'The Old Rectory was the one thing he could be proud of. You know it – it was a truly beautiful, huge, rambling Georgian house, the kind of thing that goes for millions now. He always visualized renovating it – he used to talk about saving up enough money so that he could buy Nigel out when they inherited, and how he'd bring up his own children there. Then his father married that woman Jean, and he got nothing. You remember how hurt he was. He just wanted to restore it, make it glorious again. But of course he never got the chance.'

I did remember Stephen's almost animal pain, at his father's death, at the way the old man had never, for one moment, acknowledged his son's love or ability, and his howl of anger when he heard that Jean would get The Old Rectory. It had, I thought, been cripplingly unfair, and perhaps I had forgotten how deep the scars ran.

'Poor Stephen.' I became aware that Max and I were still holding hands across the table. 'But that didn't mean he had to lie to me. I've always been on his side, after all.'

'His mother was always on his side,' Max pointed out. 'But he could never quite trust her. If she was drinking, she'd be late, or arrive in a terrible state. He once drove us home from school, when he was only fourteen and had hardly driven a car before, except for playing around on the drive at home, because it was obvious that she was completely incapable. I think that's also part of his not trusting people about money.'

I still couldn't quite forgive Stephen's lies, but I could, perhaps, stretch myself to understand them. 'It's the secrecy I mind, when he knew how I've worried about money almost constantly, waking up in the night thinking the house was going to be repossessed. Terrified every time I read a piece in the papers about pensions and having to provide for one's old age. And we had rows about it when he knew we had money all along.'

'Suzy.' Max spoke softly. 'Everyone is capable of betrayal. It doesn't mean there isn't love. It doesn't mean the end of everything.'

'So you think that if you love someone, you have to forgive them everything?' I thought of Max, that night he didn't come back, the morning I'd left him and walked out into the rain.

Max shook his head. 'No. I don't mean that at all. I just mean that you *may* forgive them. It's one of your options.'

Dear Max. He may not be faithful, but he is loyal to his friends. I picked up the hand in mine and kissed its palm. Gently, in case he didn't want me any more.

I'd never have done it without the brandy. Without the grey-and-white light of a summer moonlit night that made me believe I could be in *Brief Encounter* or *Casablanca*. And I wouldn't have done it if I hadn't felt so betrayed about the money.

But Max, as he had said, did want me. 'Suzy.' He took my face in his hands, kissed my neck and the top of my breasts, gently freeing the top button of my shirt. It felt so right. Almost-forgotten feelings flared up, as tendrils of pure desire snaked up through my body. I realized I'd wanted Max, desperately, since that evening in the wood. He took my hand. 'Let's go upstairs.'

I would never have gone to Max and Anne's room, or even to Bluebell, where we always stayed. But Max led me up a last winding flight of stairs behind a door to a room I'd never seen before, with views over the walled garden. The floorboards were so old that they sloped away under my feet, and there was just a bed – a French *lit bateau*, with polished walnut carved at the head and foot, gleaming in the darkness – and a delicate cherry-wood chest of drawers. There were white linen sheets on the bed, crisp and inviting. The ceiling was low, and it, too, sloped crazily, as if the room had been there for so long that it had settled into the folds of the earth below it. There were no curtains at the windows, so in the silver moonlight I could see that one whole wall was filled with books, and that over a stone fireplace was an oil painting of a woman. There was an iron candelabra on the mantelpiece. Max let go of my hand to light each of the five candles one by one, and I saw that the painting was of his mother, as a slender, dark beauty of twenty.

'This is my room,' he turned to face me. 'No one else comes here.'

I was too dizzy to ask why not, or whether this meant that he and Anne slept apart. I knew I was doing something very dangerous.

'Take this off.' He touched my white shirt and my hands trembled as I unbuttoned it.

'And this.' But I wasn't going to let Max be in charge of everything. I unbuttoned his shirt as well.

'Don't fight me, Theo,' he whispered, and my body remembered the old name he had for me. 'I love you.'

We were a tangle of limbs and hair, of powerful movements and gentle words. My skin felt new where he touched me, and where he touched me, it took my breath away. I couldn't tell where he stopped and I started, and I realized that until now I had only been half alive. I remembered what I had forgotten, which was that love had nothing to do with positions or gadgets or elaborate games, and everything to do with the slow, gentle exploration of intimacy and trust.

He drew me closer. 'There hasn't been a single hour,

of a single day, since you left me, that I haven't loved you.'

I laughed, out of sheer joy. 'There must have been a few.'

'Well,' he kissed my nose. 'Perhaps one or two.'

Like the birth of Jamie and Harriet, or the birth of Polly and Jess. There were so many times, important times, that we hadn't been part of each other's lives.

He knew what I was thinking. 'But we're together now. And we'll be together in the end. Somehow. I promise.'

And I agreed. It seemed obvious. Max and I were made for each other. A love that had lasted three decades could survive anything.

Without curtains, the sunlight hurt my eyes long before six the following morning. I jumped up. 'Christ! What if somebody comes?'

Max pulled me back, and kissed my hair, drawing me into the crook of his shoulder. 'Nobody will. I told you no one comes here.'

Morning is harsh reality time. He saw the question in my eyes, as I looked up.

'I go to Anne. I sleep there as well.'

I go. The present tense. Nothing was over between him and Anne. Or me and Stephen.

'I know,' he said, understanding the look in my eyes. 'I know. It'll take time to change things, but have faith in me. Have faith in us.'

I could see the painting above the fireplace now. 'Does your mother know how much you care about her?' I asked him. She'd seemed quite frail, I'd thought, and there'd been such tension between them.

He kissed my neck, my shoulders and my breasts. 'Do you know why my mother and I had that terrible row?'

I shook my head.

'When I told her I was marrying Anne, she accused me of doing it for Stonehill. Which wasn't quite true. She didn't see how I could love Anne as well as loving you, and she knew how much I loved you. I told her that passionate love wasn't necessarily the best basis for a marriage, and she said that, after my father died, she married a nice, kind, safe man with lots of money who could look after us both, but she knew she didn't love him and she was absolutely miserable. When Gedeon – you know, the count – came along, she discovered real love again, and she's never looked back.

'I was so angry. If her relationship with Gedeon Kisfaludy was the epitome of true love, I told her, then she could keep it. My marriage would be based on sounder principles. So she asked me what I meant, and I finally told her that he was using her money – my father's money – to spend on his mistresses. The argument went downhill from there.'

'Oh, Max.' I knew what he meant, but he'd obviously been rather blunt about it. 'Couldn't you have been more tactful about it?'

He laughed. 'Still determined to make an omelette without breaking eggs, Suze? Anyway you needn't worry, my mother carried on with her life as if I'd never said anything – she just refused to come to the wedding or to come here until recently. When I see her in New York, we're fine together.'

I began to pull on my clothes, feeling the perfection

of the morning slip away from us. 'Why did you make it up now?' I only asked out of idle curiosity.

He laughed. 'I hoped I could sting her for a loan, or something. It turns out that she was hoping for the same from me. We've both run through everything.'

I left him at the window, looking over the gardens. 'I just have to get Stonehill sorted,' he murmured. 'And Anne.'

'Well, at least Anne's pretty resilient.'

'I'm afraid she's not,' said Max. 'Unfortunately.'

'Max?' I suddenly felt frightened.

He turned to me. 'My love.'

'We will finish up together, won't we?'

He came over and held me close. 'Of course. We'll find a way.'

I shut the door, and beyond the click I thought I heard him call out my name again. I paused, but there was nothing there.

I went back to my life, and he to his.

20

I moved through the morning in a dream, with happiness singing in my heart. I scrubbed the adultery off me, wishing I could keep the smell of Max on my skin all day.

I met Stephen at the station with a genuine smile on my face. 'Good trip?'

He looked alarmed at my change in mood. 'Not bad.' He eased himself cautiously into the car. 'Shall I drive?'

'No need. You've been travelling. I came up last night, and had a relaxing evening.'

And I smiled to myself again. The memory was still warm, still special.

'Oh?'

I looked at him, innocently. 'Oh, what?'

'Oh, what did you do?'

'Ate omelette in the moonlight. Max told me about his plans for Stonehill.'

Stephen shifted uncomfortably, but if he suspected anything he didn't dare say so.

'So,' he ventured after about five miles, as we drove down twisty lanes banked high with greenery and studded with the scarlets, blues and yellows of wild flowers. Poppies, pointed yellow lupins and blue geraniums seemed to have escaped from the pretty cottage gardens and self-seeded themselves along the hedgerows. 'Are we friends again?'

I turned to look at him, at his chisel-cut features and ash-grey hair, and saw, in his face, the complete and utter lack of any understanding that what he had done had hurt me. In his eyes was the belief that he'd been right.

And I realized that this was where the lying began. I hadn't thought about that. About actually telling lies. It's not something I'm very good at. And neither Max nor I had mentioned Stephen back there in the little room. Stephen, who couldn't bear to have anything taken away from him. When I look back now, I can't help wondering what on earth I was thinking when I thought it was all going to be so easy.

I suppressed my moment of doubt. Nothing was going to happen immediately. I must have faith. I suddenly remembered something Vanessa'd said to me once, when I asked her if she still hoped Barry would come back. 'You can't put the toothpaste back in the tube, darling,' she'd said sadly, studying her reflection in a mirror. 'You just can't.'

So all I said, with a shrug, was: 'Friends. If you like.'

He drummed his fingers on the dashboard.

Let him worry about it. I just didn't want to think about any of it for the time being. I wanted to be back at Stonehill with Max.

'I've got some fantastic news.' He sounded surprisingly restrained for 'fantastic'.

I tensed up. Now what?

'We've had an offer on the house.'

My heart dropped suddenly into a hard, cold pit. An

offer. Crunch time. We couldn't put off the decisions about the future any longer. I kept my voice calm. 'A good one?'

'Asking price. Cash purchaser. Couldn't be better.'

'Have you accepted it?' I clenched my hands on the steering wheel. I had visions of him taking all the decisions without asking me. I just didn't trust him any more. And, to be fair, that may also have been because he couldn't trust me.

He sounded the epitome of a caring, sharing husband. 'I was waiting to hear what you thought about it.'

My hands relaxed. 'Oh, take it, definitely.' A step closer to freedom.

Out of the corner of my eye, I saw him smile. Stephen really did have a very nice smile, all crinkly at the corners of his eyes. 'Thank you, darling.' He squeezed my knee affectionately and I let him. I was aware of a slight sensation of life moving forward, accelerating out of the pit we'd found ourselves in.

'It's rather a relief, really,' I said. 'To have an offer at last. I was beginning to think no one would ever want it.'

We both smiled, in partnership again at last. Up to a point.

The electricity between us switched off. My heart lifted as I turned into Stonehill drive.

Of course, I had completely forgotten Max mentioning that there would be others this weekend – two people who had something to do with money, with their wives, on an informal visit to see whether Stonehill had any potential for big investment. When we got back, they were parked outside the moat. A heat haze was beginning to shimmer beside a church tower on the horizon, just where two gently curved fields folded and merged into each other. I jumped out of the car and took one last, slow breath before the socializing started. I couldn't see another house anywhere. It was a perfect June day.

They were confusingly alike, the two couples. The men both wore new, immaculately pressed, 'casual' wear, and the two women were smart, slim – one slightly slimmer than the other – faded blondes with huge diamonds on their fingers. I was reminded of my necklace. If I still had it, I would be free to leave Stephen without worrying about how I was going to survive the first few months until Max could join me. If I had the necklace I wouldn't have to be so careful. I could hear the soft coo of the doves over the stable block, and the occasional rustle of a gentle breeze through the trees. It all seemed so peaceful that I couldn't believe that I was planning to tear my life apart. I turned to chat to them. From now on, almost everything I said would be some kind of a lie. I might as well start as soon as possible.

All four visitors covetously eyed Stonehill's red-brick Dutch gables, generous stone-framed windows and tall chimneys, looking it up and down as if they'd come to buy it.

'It reminds me a bit of Hampton Court Palace,' murmured the plumper of the two women, who I later discovered was called Belinda. 'In style, that is.' She flashed a sweet, worried smile.

The other, Tina, had a sharp, spoilt line between her

eyebrows, and perfectly painted red toenails, which she jiggled up and down furiously whenever she wasn't getting enough attention. 'The Westinghams have got a place like this, only bigger,' Tina looked at the gardens disdainfully. 'Now that's what I really call a house.'

'Must cost a packet to maintain,' murmured Anthony.

'Well,' Mark raised his eyebrows meaningfully. 'I expect we'll find out.'

Stephen, as the owner's oldest friend, set out towards them with a welcoming smile. They looked at him, trying to assess whether he was a fellow guest or someone who could safely be ignored. Belinda gave back a wan smile, just in case. 'The moat looks awfully murky,' she called anxiously to her husband. 'Do you suppose there are any ancient diseases in it?'

'Moats always look murky,' I said. 'Nobody's died in it or of it. It's been there for about five hundred years, as far as I know.'

Belinda looked faintly disgusted. 'Urgh. How unhygienic. But the house is pretty,' she added, obviously not wanting to upset anyone.

Tina merely swivelled round so that her designer sunglasses faced the patchwork of brilliant green and deep-lavender-blue fields that stretched across the horizon. 'I wonder if there's any decent shopping round here,' we heard her say. 'Some of these rural places have terrific factory shops. But it doesn't look hopeful.'

The heat began to trickle down the back of my neck, and my bones started to luxuriate in the warmth. I love summer. And I love Max, and Max loves me. That was enough to be going on with.

Still on a cloud, I floated inside, followed by the others.

Lunch was tedious. Tina and Belinda talked about shoes most of the time. Tina told Belinda that there really wasn't any point in buying shoes from shops any more, not if you wanted something really special.

'I'm having a pair of evening shoes made, with diamonds stitched into them,' she explained. 'I can't tell you who you get to meet in the fitting rooms. All the stars are getting them.'

'Gosh, they sound a bit expensive,' worried Belinda.

Tina flashed a complacent smile. 'Under twenty thousand pounds a pair. Just about.'

I thought Belinda was going to faint. Then they started yapping on about the differences between Designers Guild and Colefax & Fowler. Their idea of conversation was to include Max by occasionally asking him whether one should forget about fabric altogether and go modern, or asking him what his favourite shops in East Anglia were.

Anthony and Mark kept shouting names back and forth, accompanying each with a potted career history and the inevitable conclusion: 'And now he's sold out for a fucking fortune.' All four indulged in a regulation, although slightly half-hearted, discussion of property prices in Suffolk, but Max damped this conversation down by claiming to know very little. 'Anne's ancestors got the land for this place a thousand years ago, and it's certainly gone up in value since then,' he reminded them, with a flash of malice, I thought. However, it seemed to be exactly the right thing to say, as the thought of all those pound signs over so many years drew a brief respectful silence. The conversation started up again when Anthony remembered another friend who'd bought a derelict estate nearby, and was selling it, divided into flats, with 'executive' houses packed into the gardens, for 'an absolute bomb'. Stephen's face grew more sombre with every sum mentioned, and his fingers tapped impatiently on the table top.

Anne and Max, as usual, were perfect hosts, whipping away plates and topping up glasses with such speed and efficiency that it seemed as if there were butlers and maids, rather than just the two of them. I now slotted into their team as an extra member, but when Belinda tried to hop up and down, Anne gently pressed her back into her seat, and she subsided, looking more anxious than ever. Tina merely bared her teeth in thanks every time anyone passed her anything.

Max, of course, behaved impeccably that weekend, and so did I. We acted the parts of two old friends, but we were careful not to be left alone with each other, if possible. Once I looked up, while I was talking to Anthony, and saw that Max was watching me with a softness in his eyes. I quickly looked away, but my heart glowed.

But I started to watch him more carefully when he was with Anne. He was gentle with her, and I could see that he had one eye constantly alert for her. I wasn't quite sure if he'd always been like that, or whether this was something new, but I still wondered what he meant when he'd said that Anne wasn't as resilient as I'd thought.

At one point I was reading a magazine, completely concealed in a huge armchair, when Anne clattered through with a tray piled high with glasses from the dining room.

'Darling?' Max came out of his study. I don't think either of them noticed I was there. He went over to her and touched her shoulder. 'You're doing too much.'

'I'm fine.' It was the same blank, polite, but essentially empty response that I so often got.

'Let me take these.' He took the tray off her.

'If you like.' I heard her footsteps mount the main stairs, and ten minutes later, on my way to my room, found her sorting a linen cupboard.

'Can I help?'

'It's easier if I do it all myself. I know where everything is.'

If it hadn't been so typically Anne, I'd have thought she suspected something, but she couldn't. We'd left no clues.

After lunch Max and Anne talked to the two venture capitalists about money, and I took 'the girls' over to Vanessa's. They settled down happily to talk about shops, and were much more relaxed by the time we returned in the evening.

The two husbands ignored me entirely. I sat between them at dinner, and politely asked each in turn where they lived, what they did, whether they had any hobbies, where they were going on their holidays and what their opinion of various snippets of current news was. They didn't ask me anything.

Eventually, because we'd run out of conversation, I told Anthony that I was an art teacher and had two grown-up children.

'An art teacher!' He hastily detached his gaze from the tapestries, which he'd fixed on at the beginning of our conversation, and looked at me as if I'd suddenly revealed a very exciting takeover tip. 'How fascinating. Where?' He was a bit disappointed to discover that I mainly taught children, but told me that when he retired (in only two years' time, 'because you don't last longer than fifty in my profession'), he was going to be an artist. 'Not sure if I'll be any good, har, har, and, of course, Belinda's not keen. Not keen at all. Worried about the money, you know. But,' and he dropped his voice in a way that made it carry far more effectively than normal speaking would have done, 'to be honest, I'll leave with the kind of money that means my children, and possibly even my grandchildren, will never have to work.' As he raised his eyes across the table, he caught Stephen's eye and held it for a second too long. These men, like the boys at his school, knew what they were doing to him with their talk of huge sums so casually disposed here and there. With a sudden flash of pity, I saw the insecure prep school boy again, being teased for his lack of possessions. Stephen was doing well, but the goalposts of wealth had moved away from him again, and he couldn't hope to catch up.

Anthony helped himself to some more broccoli from the tureen that was being passed round. 'My folks stopped me from going to Art College, said the law was the thing, and then I went into the City. Never had time for art classes. Never forgotten it though. Nearest I've got to painting is getting the firm to sponsor things. Least I could do, har, har.'

He asked me where I'd trained, and I told him that Max had been there too. He looked at us both as if we'd been canonized. 'You must be bloody good. Bloody good.'

'Not really.'

He took my denials for modesty, and, for the rest of the weekend, gave me imploring doggy looks as if I'd got his favourite bone concealed about my person. There was, however, a limit to the morale-boosting conversations I could convincingly summon up about it never being too late to start, and if you don't give it a try, you'll never know if you can do it.

The other banker, Mark, was also planning his retirement, he informed me, and he was going to spend six months of the year on a golf course on the Algarve. Tina, his wife, looked up from where she was spearing her food with a fork, elbows on the table. 'You know you'll be at the bar by midday, darling. You have absolutely no self-control.' She turned to me. 'He'll be an alcoholic before he's sixty.' Her eyes were like a child's glass beads.

I agreed that the Algarve would all be very nice, and wondered if Stephen was the only person at the table who actually enjoyed what he did. You had to admire him for that. He hadn't gone off the boil the way everyone else seemed to have done.

And between us that weekend there was a civilized politeness that I could almost mistake for warmth. He was very considerate, dropping little kisses on my shoulder, deferring to me and laughing at my jokes. I tried to be as nice as I could back, which wasn't difficult because I felt so happy.

'I'd like to drive around to look for houses,' he'd said, on Saturday afternoon.

I didn't see the point of going to look at houses I would never live in. So I'd just smiled and merely told him I felt a bit tired. 'If you find anything you like you can always take me back to see it.'

He returned whistling, looking satisfied. I avoided asking him if he'd found anything because I felt too dreamy to go and look at anything we had no intention of buying. I just wanted to laze away the weekend, with the chirrupings of Tina and Belinda drifting over my head like the sound of the birdsong.

Sunday morning dawned in a haze the colour of moon-stones: a shimmering opalescent blue that promised real summer heat later in the day.

Tina and Belinda appeared at around eleven o'clock and began to go through the Sunday papers with enthusiasm.

'Isn't that darling?' Tina passed over a page showing the latest cashmere coats. They both mused over them reverently.

'Terribly *expensive*,' worried Belinda. 'I couldn't possibly afford them.'

Tina gave a short laugh. 'Just use your credit card. Make *him* pay for them.'

They thumbed through a few articles about kitchens, and Tina came to the conclusion that their London one was looking a bit 'tired' and ought to be ripped out. 'Nothing makes you look more dated than an unfashionable kitchen,' she muttered, looking around at the huge plates on the big oak dresser. 'Mind you, I don't suppose this one has been touched since 1985. They really must be on their uppers.'

'I don't think it's been done since 1885 actually,' I told her.

Tina looked irritated. 'Well, they must know that the whole country-kitchen business is hopelessly passé. I'm amazed they can live with it, frankly.'

Belinda was on to the food pages by now. 'Did you say you were going to France next weekend?'

'Yah.' Tina flicked through a Sunday supplement. 'Shopping.'

'If you're getting some nice French cheese would you bring some back for me? It's so much cheaper over there.'

'Not that sort of shopping,' Tina slapped the supplement shut. 'We're buying a boat and a house.'

'Oh.' Belinda seemed crushed. 'Quite a lot for one weekend.'

'Yah, well, he's had an affair.'

Belinda was appalled. 'Oh, no! Poor Tina!' She stretched out a hand, as if to comfort her friend, and then withdrew it again, blushing.

Tina shrugged, apparently not caring. 'Well, he's had to buy me a villa in Provence to make up for it. And the boat. I think I'll have a motor cruiser. Something with enough room to sunbathe on deck. I can tell you –' she opened one last colour supplement '– he's not going to be grumbling about *my* credit-card bills for some time. Not if he knows what's good for him.'

I imagined Tina stalking the streets of Knightsbridge, venting her anger on shop assistants and imaginary faults, whipping her credit card out and slapping it down on the table like a lethal weapon. Belinda obviously shopped to feel safe and Tina out of anger. And Anne didn't shop at all. She had everything she needed.

'Well, I'm going to get some sun.' Tina got up. 'Where are the sun loungers?' She directed this at me.

'Er. I don't think there are any.'

Tina gave me such an incredulous look that I added: 'Max and Anne never seem to do any lounging.'

'Well, neither do I,' she replied in a sharp tone. 'But when I do manage to get away, I expect some sun. It's hardly unreasonable.'

After a hurried consultation with Max, we did find a dusty plastic sun lounger in one of the outhouses, and I gave it a brisk wipe with a cloth.

No sooner had Tina settled down in a bikini in the courtyard with a pile of glossy magazines than the sun was almost blotted out, and we were plunged into a fierce, pale grey gloom.

'For heaven's sake,' cried Tina, returning to the kitchen, her glossy magazines covered in giant gobs of rain. 'This place is unbelievable.'

Belinda, whose sweet nature I appreciated more every minute, looked alarmed, and tried to change the subject. 'Whose is the black dog? I love Labradors.'

'Who was it who called them nature's equivalent of the cardigan?' asked Tina, shaking the water off the magazines with a sharp tutting noise.

Belinda blushed. 'Well, I like cardigans too. You know, those cashmere ones that are such good value from — where was it . . .?'

'I don't think Anne and Max have a dog at the moment.' I was beginning to feel like one of Stonehill's ancient retainers doing an extended guided tour of the house with a particularly difficult coach party. 'Their last one, Tansy, was buried in the pets' cemetery in the bluebell wood last November.'

Belinda looked puzzled. 'Well, there's definitely been

a black dog nosing around. Quite a big one. We're so far from the road, I wouldn't have thought it'd be a stray.'

'Perhaps it's the Black Shuck.' Max's voice behind us made us all jump.

Tina took off her sunglasses, and gave him a long, assessing look that might have been meant to be sexy. 'Do tell.'

'The Black Shuck is seen all over Suffolk, according to a couple of the local history books in the library. It's a black dog stabbed by forked lightning, and it heralds all sorts of disasters. Storms, floods, anything like that. It's been known to drag children out to sea, or go into churches and tear out the throats of the worshippers.'

Belinda gave a little scream. 'I can't bear it. Too spooky.'

Tina merely flashed a sardonic smile. 'Well, I hope you're going to defend us. I simply adore protective men.'

'I'm sure there *was* some lightning just now . . .' Belinda fretted, looking agitated.

'It was probably a fuse,' drawled Tina. 'I don't suppose this place has been wired this century. Talk about Gormenghast.'

'Max redid it all ten years ago,' I said.

Tina just about managed to restrain herself from calling me a very dreary little person indeed.

Max squeezed Belinda's shoulder. 'I'm sorry. I didn't mean to frighten you. It's probably just a smugglers' legend. They needed ways of keeping people inside on dark nights.' Belinda blushed with pleasure at the touch, and glowed gratefully at him.

Tina drummed her painted fingernails on the table. 'Well, I can't imagine what we're going to do here if it's *raining*. I mean we can't sit around reading the papers *all* day.'

22

When we got back to London, I crashed down into reality again. I'd floated through the weekend on a bubble of happiness. Stonehill has a magical quality, as if it was sealed off from day-to-day life, the moat a barrier to the realities of the outside world. But the euphoria had slowly subsided to a dull ache as we drove down the A12. It had hurt to say goodbye to Max, and to drive away from Stonehill. It had hurt so much I didn't even want to think about it.

At home, my now clean, magnolia-white, mended home, where everything, or almost everything, worked, I had to face up to ... well ... the future, I suppose. Max's love was a distant dream. The gritty reality was my relationship with Stephen, with all its imperfections and irritations. I picked up Truffle and buried my face in the cat's soft, dark fur. 'We're back.' She purred, forgiving us a few days away. I held her tight, as a barrier between me and Stephen. We'd chatted casually in the car, from time to time, but had both been wrapped up in our separate silences for most of the way. It was only now, walking through the door, that real life would start again.

The first night home the nightmares came back, but I now knew that they would go away again. The memory of the burglary was growing fainter, and the yellow street signs asking for witnesses to assaults, arson or even the occasional stabbing were losing their power to frighten me. I no longer scoured newspapers to find out everything I could about people who'd been burgled or attacked in order to reassure myself that it couldn't happen to me again.

The immediate destination was The Past, on Monday morning.

'I've been rushed off my feet,' exclaimed Alice crossly. 'It's just not on. Couldn't you give up the school early and come full-time?'

I said no, firmly. 'It would be letting the children down.' That's the one advantage of doing a job like teaching. You can always step up to the moral high ground whenever it's convenient to do so. 'Anyway,' I wasn't prepared to let Alice get away with grumbling all the time, 'surely that's a good thing? If the shop's doing well.'

She sighed. 'Yes, but who had to be stuck behind the counter on Saturday? Muggins here.'

I reminded her that I was doing next Saturday, as agreed, and she looked only slightly mollified. 'The real problem is that we've sold out.'

'Sold out?' The shop seemed almost as piled-high with junk as ever.

'Of the stuff you do. The, you know –' she waved her hands around '– the arty stuff.'

I couldn't help feeling pleased. 'Well, I'll do some more. If you pay me the hours, I'll take a few pieces home and do it in the evening, as long as we're not going out. Just until the end of term.'

Clearly irritated that she was going to have to pay me more, rather than get me to do it in the shop time, Alice reluctantly agreed.

I had the sneaky feeling that I was taking on the conversion of ghastly wardrobes, wonky chests of drawers and tasteless chairs with screw-on legs simply in order to be too busy to think, but what the hell? When I wasn't dreaming about Max, my mind still worried at the issue of Stephen and the secret account. I knew that some people wouldn't consider it such a very major crime – I knew several friends who kept financial secrets from their other halves, although I'd always thought it was dangerous. It wasn't the money, it was the trust. He'd lied to me and he'd tried to control me with those lies. I just couldn't forgive it, no matter which way I looked at it.

As July came without ever quite turning into summer, I left the school, without regret after nine years. It just slipped out of my life, accompanied by a signed card from all my colleagues, a bunch of flowers and a huge sense of relief. My ears strained continuously for a call from Max, and every few days, developing a pattern as we gradually honed our awareness of when it would be 'safe', he called. These calls were our reality. Nothing else existed. Stephen, the shop, the bank account and even the house sale seemed like remote irrelevancies.

Outside it rained. It was cold, but not chilly enough for a sweater. The roses threatened to bloom, but instead merely curled up into tight, sodden balls. Plants grew big and fleshy, almost aggressively green, but failed to flower. Roots began to rot. Then slowly, over the month, the heat came, baking the pavements in short blasts before the clouds blanketed us again. The street came alive with the sound of distant half-heard conversations and television programmes as people began to open their windows against the airlessness of it all. And the traffic dropped away as everyone who could afford to left town, leaving behind, as in an evacuation, only the poorest and the worker drones. I buffed and sanded my way through the heavy days, picking out the soft summery pastels of gulls' eggs and ice cream to paint my furniture, experimenting with driftwood effects to conjure up the beaches near Stonehill. They stretched out in my memory in long, generous, deserted curves, fringed by dune grass, their creamy sands patterned with shingle.

'I hope you're getting some decent money for this,' said Stephen one evening, getting in, as he usually did, at ten o'clock. He stood at the door of the sitting room, his white shirt still crisp and fresh in spite of a twelve-hour day, looking relaxed and easy as he pulled off his tie, rather than rumpled. He didn't crumple, my husband, you had to give him that.

I pushed my hair back, leaving a bit of paint on my face. 'She's paying me by the hour.'

'Hmm. You're worth more than that.' He walked around a low coffee table which I was studding with shells. 'You should value yourself more.'

I was warmed by his concern, and sat back on my heels. The awful, terrible thing about having discovered sex again was that I wanted more of it. And because Max was miles and miles away, I put my hand out to

Stephen. It shouldn't be like this, I told myself. Taking a lover shouldn't make you want your husband again, but I did. I thought of Max while I lay under Stephen, and although it was never what I craved, it satisfied an itch. It was a double betrayal, but nobody need ever know.

But I'd wake up in the morning, worrying that I was leading Stephen to believe that I'd forgiven him, and that we had a life together. I'd comfort myself with the thought that at least it was making him happy for now. And then the phone would ring, and it would be Max, and with the selfishness of lovers, I'd forget all about it.

The following day I set up my stuff – my sandpaper, scrapers and strippers – in the little lean-to at the back of The Past. It had originally been the alleyway between the shop's back extension and the garden wall and been glassed over at some point. Alice had used it as a storage dump, but, as it had a door straight into the shop, I'd cleared it as a tiny workshop. It was freezing in winter, and baking in summer, but in this indifferent weather, it was tolerable. What I really needed, I thought as I sandpapered a bookcase before painting it the soft grey of a dove's wing, was someone to talk to who would understand.

But who? Sadly, my closest friend and neighbour, Helen, was currently posted with her husband to some-where in the Middle East. There were friends from Art College, mostly now happily ensconced around Britain with their growing families, but although we all regularly exchanged visits, I could hardly ring them up out of the blue and say that I'd fallen in love with my husband's oldest friend. Some of the other teachers at school had become good friends at the exchange-of-supper-parties level, and we'd even, over the years, been on family holidays with some of them, but it would be letting Stephen down to discuss it all with anyone who might pass it on. I didn't want to humiliate him.

We went out several times a week, to smart parties and intimate evenings, we went to the theatre or the cinema, or even to restaurants, with other couples, and exchanged hundreds of Christmas cards with people but, in the end, it all came down to the fact that Stephen was, or had been, my main confidant until I discovered the secret account. My fury, damped down by the cloudy warmth and general laziness of July, boiled up again. You just don't expect your best friend to lie to you, consistently, over a number of years, about really important things. The bookcase wobbled against the last ferocious thrusts of sandpaper.

Then I realized. I did have someone to talk to. I knew exactly who would understand what I felt: Barry. Barry had fallen in love. Barry knew how I would feel.

I must speak to Barry. I got it into my head that he would have the answer, or at least some answer for me. I had been drilled never to disturb people in offices unless necessary, but I dropped the sandpaper, and returned to the shop to find the telephone directory. It was underneath a pile of reference books that had come with the bookcase, and I was seething with impatience by the time I dialled the number. I just knew, in my heart of hearts, that what Barry would say could really help me.

The switchboard operator hesitated, but I assumed that she was just handling a large volume of calls. 'I'll put you through now,' she said in a low voice.

'Who's speaking?' demanded another subdued, wary voice, almost immediately.

I told her.

'Are you a personal friend?' I was surprised. It was Barry's company, and I thought it was strange that his employees were allowed to interrogate callers in this way. But perhaps it was just a way of keeping unnecessary calls away from busy men.

'Yes,' I replied defiantly, wondering if I should have pretended to be the secretary of some captain of industry, just in order to get through.

There was another silence. Eventually the girl on the other end spoke in a rush.

'I'm terribly sorry to inform you, but Mr Tanner died last night.'

'What?' I nearly screamed down the phone. 'It's Barry I want to speak to, not his father.' Daft response really, because Barry hasn't got a father.

'I'm afraid,' the voice sounded wooden, 'that Mr Barry Tanner, our managing director, died very suddenly of a heart attack late yesterday afternoon.'

'It isn't possible,' I begged. 'It can't be. He was fine when I saw him last. He was such a lovely person.'

The voice sketched out the bare, brutal facts. They'd had a phone call only this morning. He'd collapsed over his lunch. A massive heart attack. He'd never regained consciousness after being rushed to hospital. I thought of Kelly, and the way her eyes had shone when she looked at him.

'Could I possibly have Kelly's address? I must write to her.'

The silence echoed.

'I did meet her. Please.' I could feel tears beginning to start behind my eyes. Not Barry. Not Barry, please. He had been counting the years ahead, and was planning to fill them so happily.

'I'll have to talk to someone.' There was a great deal of conferring, and a more senior, but even more emotional voice came to the phone. I realized that the silences were because Barry's staff couldn't trust themselves to speak, beyond giving the facts. In the end, a complete stranger and I were talking in halting gulps, assuring each other that it would be fine for me to call Kelly.

'Anyway, I'd like to know when the funeral is. Has it been set yet?'

There was more hesitation, but, of course, it wouldn't be, not so soon.

'I thought Kelly was very nice,' were my last words.

'Yes. She made Barry very happy.' The voice at the end of the phone ended on a choking noise.

I put my head in my hands, out there in the open shop, and cried and cried and cried. I wanted Max to cry with; or even Stephen to offer a comforting shoulder. But no one came in, and eventually I washed my face and finished the cabinet, thinking of Barry, praying for him, constantly suppressing the desire to write him a letter or call him up, just to tell him how sorry I was that he had died, and how much he'd come to mean to us all. I wanted him to know that I didn't totally condemn him for going off with Kelly, that I could even understand it, however cruel it had been to Vanessa. I wished, desperately, that there had been a chance to say goodbye, but, above all, I just wanted him back.

23

When I got home, my first action, surreptitiously, was to ring my lover. My second was to ring my husband.

'I don't believe it!' said Max. 'Not Barry. I don't believe it.' Then: 'Poor Vanessa. Poor, poor Vanessa. Now there's no hope of them ever getting back together.'

'Do you think she wanted to? I thought she'd given up.'

'Oh, yes,' Max sounded so sad. 'Underneath all that hard talk, she loved him very much.'

I couldn't speak without crying.

'My darling,' said Max. 'We must meet. I can't bear to think of you being alone during all this.'

When I got through to Stephen, he breathed out a great puff of disbelief. 'Good God. Barry. Well, it's just as well we've finished the Meadowfields Project with his company. Dead? Are you sure?'

I assured him that it was difficult to get the wrong end of the stick about 'dead'.

'Stroke of luck for Vanessa, though. Chances are that he hadn't changed his will, and now she'll get the lot.'

I put the phone down, having established that Stephen's next overnight trip to Brussels was in a few days' time, and rang Max back. We were going to risk a meeting at home. I couldn't bear not knowing when I'd see him again. In the face of death, love seemed the most important thing in the world.

That's what Vanessa said, too, about her relationship with Barry when I went round to see her a few days later.

We perched on high stools in her vast, anonymous glass-and-concrete kitchen, which had featured in several design magazines. A designer coffee maker spat and rumbled behind us, and eventually disgorged two steaming cups of coffee.

'*Thank you* for coming round.' She sank down on the stool. 'Thank you *so* much. Because Barry and I weren't living together, people don't seem to realize that I've got feelings too. I suppose everyone's expressing sympathy with that woman. It's as if I don't exist as far as everyone else is concerned. I feel that our thirty years have been completely wiped from everyone's minds.'

I was shocked. 'I'm sure nobody means to ignore you. Perhaps they don't know what to say.'

'You're too nice. They just assume I don't care, that's all.' Her voice broke. 'We had the most terrible argument the day he died, and all I want is to see him again and say that we didn't mean it and we love him. Anything he's done – absolutely anything, even living with Her – would be all right if only he was at least still alive. This . . . stupid infidelity is nothing, I'd have let him have his games, let him do anything he wanted, just to know he was still there.'

Vanessa was able to tell me what had happened. He had collapsed at Kelly's flat. 'She was obviously putting him under enormous pressure,' she told me, blue eyes wide with indignation. 'The hospital called me. As the next of kin. She didn't even have the guts to tell me herself.' Vanessa twisted her ring round her finger. 'I was next of kin,' she repeated, as if the words were a talisman that could bring Barry back again. 'That's a great comfort to me. It shows he still really thought of me as his wife. He'd have wanted me at the end. He was –' her voice faltered at the memory '– all connected to tubes and gadgets. He looked old. I've never thought of Barry being old.' She took another sip of coffee, and stared out at the Japanese garden, temporarily in another world. 'I told him how sorry I was about everything. How much we all loved him. But he was unconscious. Even so, they say hearing is the last thing to go, don't they?'

I murmured something. There are no words that are really appropriate. Poor Vanessa. 'The funeral's going to be up in Suffolk. Barry loved Merlins, and that's where he'd want to be buried. I've bought a double plot in the local churchyard – they're terribly difficult to get these days – and that's where I'll be buried when I go.'

As visions of Vanessa buying grave plots in the same way she purchased exclusive designer handbags drifted through my mind I remembered Barry telling me that he'd never felt anything about any of the houses he'd lived in with Vanessa, and my throat constricted. But what could I say?

'It'll be a small funeral. Just family. And close friends, like you and Stephen, of course. We're keeping it fairly secret. We don't want . . . anything inappropriate.'

'What sort of inappropriate?' I was perplexed.

'Well, you know.' Vanessa avoided my eye. 'Her. I mean, she could hardly . . . not with the children there. It wouldn't be right.'

'But Barry and Kelly loved each other!' I burst out, without thinking.

Vanessa sounded shocked. 'What do you know about it?' She spoke sharply. 'Barry was my husband, you know. He may not have been faithful in the last few months of his life, but lots of middle-aged men go through a sort of . . . a Thing. But he was back with me at the end, and that's what matters. That's how he'd want to be remembered. As a loving husband and father. A successful businessman. And a good friend. That's what I put in the death announcement. Barry Tanner, loving and beloved husband of Vanessa, and dear father of Rob and Emily.'

It sounded plausible – up to a point – but then the separate accounts of Vanessa and Barry's marriage, or divorce, had always sounded convincing. I had occasionally wondered whether they were actually talking about the same relationship when I'd heard each side of the story.

I made one more attempt. 'Don't you think that, well, she ought to say goodbye to him? In her own way, of course.'

Vanessa's face darkened. 'I don't know whose side you think you're on. Barry would be alive today if she hadn't worn him out. I mean, can you imagine, a man of fifty-six with a girl of thirty-three? Of course, it was always going to end in disaster, and she knew it. She just wanted the money. And the awful thing is, she's probably got it. She never stopped going on at him to change his will, and when he left us that afternoon, he told us that he was going straight to the solicitor's to make sure that she got every penny.' Vanessa wiped her eyes again, carefully, so as not to smudge the make-up. 'Do you think he had a premonition? I'm sure it was probably her nagging, and all that sex that killed him. And now I'm going to be penniless, and the children won't inherit anything from their father.'

Calling Rob and Emily children was beginning to irritate me, but if what Vanessa said was true, then she might be right. Perhaps Kelly wasn't as unmaterialistic as she seemed.

'I'm sure you wouldn't be left penniless. You were still legally his wife when he died,' I pointed out.

Vanessa snorted. 'Yes. Exactly. I was his wife, and I'm the one making the funeral arrangements. Now I know you mean it kindly, because you can never see anything but good in everyone, but I would really be very grateful if you—' She must have caught sight of my stricken face, because she stopped and grasped my arm. 'Oh, God, I'm so sorry, Suzy. Death does this. It makes people argue. And I know you miss him too. Sorry, Suzy, sorry.' She took a handkerchief out of her bag and blew her nose. 'Forgive?

'I can't tell you how awful it's been, dealing with Her. She tried to kidnap his body, that's the horror of it. She'd already started making funeral arrangements, until I called her up and told her she could jolly well stop arranging. I've got the death certificate, I told her, and you won't get far without that. I don't care if you lived with him for four months, four years or four decades. Legally, he's mine. What's more, I said, I'm arranging the funeral Barry would have wanted, so please leave us in peace to grieve as a family. She was trying to sneak off with him, just as she did in life. She had no right, you know. No right at all. I checked it all with our solicitor.'

Of course, I had to forgive Vanessa. She was trying so hard to do the right thing. I did wish we could ask Barry what he really wanted, but, of course, Barry wasn't there. I tried to communicate mentally with the vastness of death, but if Barry was floating above us, hearing everything, understanding our feelings, trying to convey approval or disapproval, there was no sign of it.

The following day, Kelly phoned me. 'Thank you ever so much for your card. Nobody else on Barry's side has got in touch.'

'Well, I don't suppose they knew where you were.' My heart sank. Why had she phoned me? A part of me wondered about the will – I had seen that Barry adored her so much that he probably would have given her anything if she'd asked. And why else would he suddenly go and change it, rather than leaving it until all the divorce finances were finalized?

She must have heard some reserve in my voice. 'Please.' She sounded urgent. 'Please, I wouldn't ask this if I didn't have to—' She broke off. 'Perhaps I could come round?'

Now what? It was all getting too complicated for me, and Vanessa was primarily my friend. But then I saw Barry's kind, open face again, his concern for me, and for Vanessa, as well as for Kelly, the last time I saw him. I knew he'd have wanted me to look out for Kelly, however unscrupulous she might turn out to be.

I looked at my watch. 'I'm working at the shop this afternoon. Come for a drink this evening.'

Kelly seemed even paler and thinner when she appeared on my doorstep, wiping her feet very thoroughly on the mat, although, for once, it was sunny outside. She sidled in, looking embarrassed.

'This is very good of you.'

'Not at all.' Once again, Vanessa's image of a gold-digging floozy was so at odds with this gentle, quiet girl that I wondered if perhaps Vanessa had got the wrong end of the stick about her attempts to arrange the funeral. Perhaps they should meet.

Kelly sat on the sofa, looking like someone who had recently been in an explosion or washed up after a natural disaster. When I offered her some wine she made a small movement with her head which could have been 'yes' or 'no'. I poured her the wine anyway, and she drank it like a thirsty child.

I waited.

'I'm sorry.' When Kelly looked directly at me the pain in her eyes made me turn my head away. 'I'm so sorry.' She began to sob, and, feeling helpless, I went out to find some tissues. When I got back she was rootling around in the bag and had one out.

'Sorry about this,' she said, again, sniffing. 'I need to know where the funeral is.'

'What?'

She gulped. 'The last thing Barry said to me was that he'd had this terrible row with Vanessa and the children. They'd been on at him to turn his assets into a trust so that Rob and Emily's inheritance would be protected if he died after we were married. He thought they only cared about the money, not about him at all.' The words brought on a fresh bout of sobbing.

She recovered again. 'Anyway, I tried to calm him down, because it wasn't good for him to get so upset. I always thought his colour was a bit high, that he overdid it. And I didn't like those indigestion pains he kept having. I'd been nagging him to get a coronary check-up practically ever since we'd met, but he wouldn't listen. He was a stubborn old bastard all right.' She gave a watery smile at the memory.

'That was the last thing he said. I went into the kitchen to get him a drink, and came back to find him lying on the floor. I dialled 999, and I held him in my arms. I told him it would be all right and I'd be with him all the way. The ambulance took him away, and they don't let you go in it too, so I had to find a taxi. It took ages. By the time I'd got to the hospital, they'd found Vanessa's name as next of kin on some document in his wallet, and contacted her. She was already there. He was in intensive care, and they wouldn't let me in to see him. Family only, they said. Vanessa'd obviously left strict instructions.

'In those last few months I *was* his family. More than that money-grabbing lot anyway. I tried to get the hospital staff to tell Vanessa that – well, not about the money obviously, but that he'd need me. They told me that he needed to be kept quiet. No excitement, they said.

Doctor's orders. I've been seeing him for two years, living with him for four months, we were buying a house together, we had plans for children, a wedding date . . .' She wiped her nose with the back of her hand. 'And suddenly I've been erased from his life. I'm not even allowed to see his body. Or go to his funeral. Or give him the burial he asked for.'

'She was just very upset herself, she . . .'

'I'm not surprised.' Her voice hardened. 'She killed Barry, you know, she and that Rob and Emily. He was so upset about that argument. He just didn't believe they cared about anything else except the money. I've never known him so angry.'

I explained that Vanessa bitterly regretted the argument now.

'I doubt it. Now that he's dead, and she gets the lot. Which I assume she does.'

I decided to keep quiet.

She went on with her story. 'Vanessa got security to escort me away. She wouldn't even speak to me – I asked them if they could get a message to her, for her to come out of the ward and talk to me, but she simply refused to come anywhere near me. I thought that if I met her I could explain. In the end, I managed to call the ward sister and explain the situation, but by then he'd died. She'd gone by then, of course, so I went in to see him.'

She looked at the ground again, tearing part of the tissue into bits. 'I told him, you bastard, we've only just found each other, and now you're leaving me. But he wasn't there. He just wasn't there, if you know what I mean. I kept thinking about him lying in hospital for hours, unconscious, wondering why I hadn't come to him, thinking I'd deserted him. I'd wanted to tell him how much I'd loved him. He might have heard that, even in a coma. I'll always hate her for not letting me do that.'

I was trying not to cry myself, so I didn't point out that people in comas probably didn't wonder where other people were. We sat in silence for a bit, just remembering Barry.

'And I know how he wanted to be buried. We were on his yacht a couple of weeks ago, you know the one?'

I did, vaguely, but Vanessa hated sailing so Barry'd usually gone out alone, never with the rest of us. It was moored up the East Anglian coastline.

'He said, when I go, love, you'll have me cremated, won't you? And take the yacht out with a few friends, and throw my ashes into the waves. You'll do that for me, won't you?

'I told him that I hoped I'd be too old to sail by the time that happened. I told him that when he was in his eighties, I'd be in my late sixties and getting pretty doddery myself. He'd be thinking of trading me in for a younger woman. He laughed. We so much wanted to be in our eighties and sixties together.'

I thought of Max. We wanted to be in our eighties together. Our nineties, even. And I imagined Barry talking, one arm casually round Kelly and the other at the helm. I could see the rough skin on his face, his yellow oilskins rustling as he talked, and the sound of halyards tinkling against the masts. It still didn't seem possible that he'd gone.

'And now she won't let me near the funeral arrangements. I explained that Barry had told me how he wanted to go, and she said I was talking rubbish. She says he was probably just joking. She won't even tell me what is being organized, but I should be doing all that. He should be in his home, the one we're completing on next week. I can't bear to think he'll never be there. He wanted that house so much.'

'I know he did, he told me,' I said, unwisely.

She grasped me. 'So you understand. Tell Vanessa, please.'

I explained that I had tried, feeling like a coward. But at least Kelly deserved to say a final goodbye. 'Look, I'll tell you where and when the funeral is. Provided you don't . . . you know, don't do anything.'

She shot me a bitter look. 'What do you think I am?'

'I think you're someone who loved Barry, I promise. And I know Barry loved you very much.' I spoke gently. 'That's all I think. But you're very upset. And I will have another go at Vanessa, but at the moment she's like an automaton. I don't think anything is getting through to her.'

'She's a cold woman,' said Kelly. 'I've been to that house in London, and it's hard and cold. I'm not surprised Barry wanted to leave.'

Vanessa, when I called her, was busy erasing all memory of Kelly from her life. The only way she could get through this was to pretend that Barry's departure had never happened, or, at least, it hadn't been more than a quick fling with a younger woman. Vanessa would be a widow now, not a divorcee. And that's the way she intended to stay, particularly if she was planning – and she was definitely planning – to contest the will.

On the other hand, knowing Barry, he'd have sewn it up in a watertight way. Poor Vanessa. And poor Kelly.

I sat alone that evening, in our garden, finishing off the white wine and waiting for Stephen to come back. It had made me realize that Max and I couldn't just drift on, with no real idea when we would be together. We were running out of time.

24

August was dreary, weighting down my shoulders like a thick grey blanket. It was stifling, itchy, and the dull heat drained my energy. Every so often the heavens opened and a torrent of rain drowned everything. The litter floated in huge puddles in the streets, and the roses balled up into tight mildewed fists, while the more steely greenery – the ivies and creepers – wound round relentlessly, choking the buildings, prising apart bricks and pushing up pavement stones or roof tiles unless they were constantly stripped back. One day this city would be covered by ivy.

Everything came to its usual summer halt. The phone no longer hummed constantly for Stephen, and the demand for media soundbites withered away. Although he'd grumbled about it, I think Stephen missed the steady stream of requests for an instant viewpoint on inner-city versus green-field planning or requests for four designers each to make up a different style of Christmas tree (or floral centrepiece or window box, or whatever) for a magazine article. Friends fell away, to their holidays and second homes. We closed The Past for the last three weeks of August because no one wanted to think about buying anything, although Alice agreed to pay me to catch up with 'sorting out the stock' as she called it.

Max and I managed one evening together, respectively stealing a few hours from Stonehill and Stephen.

He stood at my front door, looking evasively over his shoulder to avoid being seen by the neighbours. I closed the door behind him before kissing him.

Our back garden is overlooked by several other houses, so we couldn't sit outside, although it was one of the few sunny evenings of summer, and stiflingly hot. We couldn't risk someone saying something to Stephen about me entertaining strange men on my own, even as a joke.

So we sat inside, with the curtains drawn, which, as it's light at that time of the evening in August, seemed fusty.

'This is impossible,' said Max, fumbling to unbutton my blouse while I looked nervously over my shoulder. Our bodies pressed together, hot and sticky.

I nodded, desire killed by concern over where exactly in the house we could make love. I mean, I know you're supposed to be carried away, but it seems a bit much to do it in the bed you share with your husband, and, as for using the children's rooms for illicit sex, well, I couldn't bear the thought. And the sofa was uncomfortable – we were too tall and too wide, and no longer as supple as we were. I couldn't quite shed the idea that Polly, or our cleaner, might just come in unexpectedly for some reason and catch us at it. Or that the window cleaners, who occasionally worked late, might suddenly materialize with mops and rags. While I luxuriated in the thought that Max was here at last, his body against mine,

I just couldn't quite manage to recreate the glorious sensations of Stonehill.

I kissed him, and was just beginning to enjoy it when the doorbell rang. It was the organic box delivery, considerately carried out in the evenings so that working people would be at home to receive it. I paid the delivery man fifteen pounds with a shaking hand, and realized that my buttons were done up crookedly.

I wouldn't be able to relax until we'd successfully had sex and were safely dressed again. That's how sad and bourgeois I'd got.

Eventually, rearranging the sofa cushions on the floor we achieved something that could vaguely be called comfortable. We wrapped ourselves round each other with the feeling of coming home, and, as I could feel a delicious sense of wickedness mounting inside, the phone rang. The answering machine took it, but the voice of the caller blared out my other life, my married life, as we stopped, freeze-framed with guilt. We paused and listened to a change-of-venue message from the organizer of the Neighbourhood Watch. Max laughed as it flipped off with: 'Er, I hope you won't be too tied up to come.'

'I too hope you won't be too tied up to come,' he muttered, with a glint in his eye.

But only one minute later, it rang again. The Grants at No. 37 were inviting us for drinks next week, then three minutes later a friend of Polly's wanted to know if she'd be back this weekend.

'If you don't mind,' he murmured, 'I think we'd better make this a quick one.'

I couldn't get into the mood after that.

Five minutes later, we buttoned up our clothes, giggling.

'Is it completely impossible to expect five minutes' peace to have an affair round here?' Max kissed me to soften the slight irritation in his voice. 'Never mind, one day we won't have to worry about all this.'

But I could see what would happen in the years ahead. Max and I would steal hours, kisses, even whole days, lying to the people we love, like Polly and Jess or Jamie and Harriet, going to cheap, tawdry places that we didn't really want to be in, just in order not to be recognized. Always afraid that we'd become the latest gossip, a juicy gobbet of scandal to be laughed over, or that we'd really hurt someone because the girls, or Stephen, or Anne, would get to hear. I didn't want to be the ageing, painted mistress and I didn't want to have a secret that I could never tell anyone. I didn't want to have to hide my receipts from Stephen, or to have to count the cost of finding neutral territory where we could be together.

I loved Max too much for that. And I didn't want his love to wear out, as we both got older. At least we had something good to remember now. I didn't want him to be making excuses about needing his space in five years' time.

'Is it madness?' I asked him. 'Mad to think we'll ever really be able to be together?'

'Not madness at all,' he replied firmly. 'That's what I'm here to talk about. I need to sort out the finances for Stonehill, so that I can get some money out, and as soon as I've done that, I promise you we'll be free.'

'Money?' I had forgotten that money would have to come into it.

'We need money, dearest.' He stroked my face. 'We have to live somewhere, on something. Neither you nor I have a real income at the moment, you may have noticed.'

'I don't mind not being rich. I never have been. It doesn't worry me.'

'Well, we won't be rich.' He poured himself a glass of wine. 'All my money has gone on repairing roofs and fences and all the rest of it. The estate is in Anne's name. It always has been.'

I remembered how incredibly wealthy he'd seemed. 'Surely it hasn't all gone?'

'A place like that eats money: two hundred thousand pounds for a new roof; repairs to the stonework and repointing, one hundred thousand; renovate the book bindings in the library, one hundred thousand; re-landscape the gardens, a hundred and fifty thousand – darling, I'm sorry to sound like a builder's estimate, but I cannot tell you how much running an estate like Stonehill costs. I inherited my wealth early – too early – and I'm proud of what I've done with it, but there is really very little left.'

I started to say that I could earn. And then I remembered. I've never earned enough to keep myself, let alone two of us. If only I still had the necklace, it would be different.

I would have the proceeds of a split with Stephen, though. It seemed terrible – to leave him and to take the money that he treasured so much. But I'd worked for it too.

The impossibility of it all overwhelmed us both into silence.

'Whoever gets out first can set up a home.' Max rubbed my hand. 'Just have faith.'

I nodded. It seemed unlikely. On the other hand, the fact that Max and I were meant for each other seemed so blindingly obvious that something would come up. Surely.

Barry's funeral was in the middle of August, in Suffolk near Merlins, as Vanessa had promised.

Stephen told me, only the night before, that he couldn't go. I gazed at him in amazement, my hand tightening round the bottle of wine we were sharing in the garden.

'There's a meeting in Paris. I'll leave to catch the Eurostar at about six o'clock.'

Getting rid of Stephen would make it easier to see Max, but even so, I was shocked. 'Is it a very important meeting? Too important to miss Barry's funeral?'

'Darling.' He sat down next to me on our stone bench, and put a hand on my shoulders. 'Believe me. I wouldn't go unless I had to. There's a great deal riding on this.'

'But Barry's one of our greatest friends. Was.' I tried to suppress my irritation at Stephen's self-important meetings. No one else seemed to be trying to do any work this month, and certainly not in Paris, which was supposed to be empty in August for heaven's sake.

'Yes.' Stephen sounded sombre. 'I'm just trying to

handle it the only way I know how, okay? I care very deeply about Barry ... and about you. It's just that I have other responsibilities too, you know.'

Invoking his job always put me in the wrong. I reminded myself how hard he worked and that these arguments were trivial in the face of terrible things like Barry's death. He was the first of us to go. Normally, that is. There had been a car crash at Art College, and one of the women in my post-natal baby group had committed suicide. Another couple of friends had contracted cancer, tragically early, but Barry's death, of a heart attack, seemed like the start of friends beginning to die naturally.

'Barry wasn't old.' I spoke aloud.

'No,' Stephen massaged my knee. 'It makes you think, doesn't it, that we have to make every second count?'

'By going to meetings?' I retorted, unable to keep the sharp criticism out of my voice.

'Sh, Suzy. That's not like you.' We sat in silence for a little while until Stephen spoke again.

'Jess'll back soon, and we'll be a family again.'

No, we wouldn't. We'd floated away from each other. In the last year, I had lost my necklace and found my love. I was on a different planet from the rest of the world. Everyone else seemed to have stayed the same. I'd changed. If I could, I would have called back my old, happy, unquestioning self, the faithful wife, the involved mother, the pillar of the community. Suddenly I wished Stephen was coming to the funeral. I wished we could be a family again. 'I need you,' I told him.

'Darling, you'll manage. You're strong. That's what I love about you.'

I felt like saying, yes, but that's not the point.

So I made the long stop-start journey by myself, through the East End of London, along the grubby suburban roads further out, and eventually bursting into the winding green highway that denoted Suffolk. My hands trembled from driving, and my legs ached, but I arrived, only ten minutes before the service began, outside a square grey church, surrounded by a hedge with a lych-gate and a flower-filled graveyard. The sun broke out, hot and brilliant, a proper August at last. It seemed a terrible thing to be buried below the earth in bright sunlight, and the hearse, parked with its coffin just beyond the church, seemed so impossibly not Barry that I couldn't believe he was lying there.

It was like a wedding, as smartly dressed mourners hesitated in groups at the church door, waiting to be shown where to sit, except that instead of the more familiar question, 'Bride or Groom?', the ushers dropped their voices respectfully to ask 'Friend or Family?'

Ahead of me was a pair of thin shoulders and a glossy brown bob.

'Partner.' Her voice was quiet but defiant.

The usher smoothly indicated a row of seats to the left. 'You'll find your other colleagues along there.'

Kelly looked taken aback, but went meekly to an empty row behind the 'colleagues', with a quick bob to the altar before sitting down. In front of her a dark girl handed out wedges of tissues to the rest of Barry's staff with a practised hand, obviously relishing the opportunity of a good cry. Kelly simply sat there, staring straight ahead. She looked older, now, nearer forty than thirty. No one looked at her.

I was shown to a pew in front of a row of old codgers, who obviously hadn't seen each other for years. They carried on a whispered interrogation until the coffin was carried in.

'How's Madge?'

'Madge died twelve years ago. A heart attack.'

'I'm very sorry to hear that. How's Cyril?'

'Prostate,' hissed the voice behind me. 'They think they caught it in time, but he's had a lot of . . . you know . . . treatment.'

'Probably best that Madge went first then,' mused another voice. 'Has anyone heard about Betty? Betty was a one.'

'Breast cancer,' a fourth voice chipped in. 'Lost one breast, oh, five years ago, then they took the other one last year. Doing very well, they say. What about you, though?'

'Oh,' the first voice sighed. 'Mustn't grumble. Had a bypass two years ago. Wonderful thing. Feel like a youngster again. They . . .' I lost the rest of the detail as a smartly dressed couple I vaguely knew from Vanessa's parties came into the pew and I shuffled up in front of the third and fourth voices, who were muttering about different treatments for arthritis.

The husband and wife glanced at me with two identical glittering smiles, not too broad in order to show respect, and then turned back to hiss amongst themselves. I caught the words 'Wonder who's got the money?' and 'Is she here?' I tuned into the other conversations around me, and heard the words 'mistress', 'money' and 'will' swooping around the church like swallows.

A dowdy woman in a squashed black hat got up from the pew at the front and went painfully down the aisle with a stick, to lean over to whisper to Kelly, who shook her head. I watched as the woman seized her elbow and steered her forward, into the 'family' rows. I didn't recognize any of them, but I heard one of the old men murmur something about Pamela. 'Barry's sister, don't know who the other one is. A cousin, perhaps.'

'Pamela? Someone told me she was in hospital having her hip replaced. So she made it out?'

The arthritis conversation got louder and louder, as it became obvious that the sufferers were both also quite deaf, and continued after all the other whispered conversations stopped. The smart couple beside me turned round and glared at them just at the point when Voice Three was saying he'd even had to give up eating his own tomatoes.

With a roll of the organ the pall-bearers began to inch down the aisle, followed by Vanessa, in black Armani and a wisp of a veil, with Rob and Emily at either side. The veil suited Vanessa – she looked beautiful and tragic, and about thirty-five. I caught sight of Kelly's eyes, hollow in a gaunt face, as Vanessa passed. Once again, I was reminded of a wedding, with Vanessa in the role of victorious bride.

'Is that the girlfriend next to Vanessa?' hissed one of the old codgers.

'No, it's the daughter, you fool,' was the whispered reply. 'Looks just like Barry.' This last really wasn't true, although Emily did have Barry's rounded, slightly pudgy nose.

An old schoolfriend of Barry's got up to speak. Barry, he said, had been a great builder, a great friend and a great man. He'd built up his business from nothing, and turned it into an inheritance. 'Ah, but who gets it?' muttered one of the old codgers, slightly too audibly, and the smart woman beside me whipped round with a glare. Her husband nudged her and whispered something.

The old schoolfriend rumbled on about Barry's achievements. 'Barry loved beautiful things. His wife, Vanessa . . .' The congregation stiffened with anticipation at this point, expectant of some mention of Barry's last four months of life. They were disappointed. The old schoolfriend cranked out a few clichés, such as 'devoted' and 'family man', and when he concluded with the words: 'Having lived abroad for the last twenty years, I didn't see as much of Barry as I'd have liked, but I know that . . .' I realized that Vanessa had deliberately chosen someone who knew nothing about Kelly.

'Wasn't it lovely?' Vanessa asked me tearfully as everyone milled around outside, their formal black suits unequal to the sudden blast of true August heat. Sweat trickled down the sides of their faces. Men mopped up with handkerchiefs and women stoically ignored their smudging mascara. 'It was just how Barry would have wanted to be remembered.' She indicated the freshly dug hole. 'Such a good location for the grave. The best view in the whole churchyard, *and* it's next to the family tomb of the Avonshires.' This was a huge stone coffin with an eagle on top, and various inscriptions on metal plates. I read that Lady Hermione Avonshire had lived from 1840 to 1936, then my eye was caught by a tiny little grave under the yew tree. 'James Edward. Aged 9.' I read: 'Dearest little son of . . .' I turned away, as tears filmed over. Dearest little son. A round-headed little boy whose parents had adored him. I thought of Polly, and Jess at nine, so full of life and love.

Dearest little son. I had to get away. I slipped past Vanessa as she was being reassured that Barry had had a 'good innings', and that at least it had been quick. 'Wonderful way to go, really,' the smoothie-chops from my row was telling her. I didn't think I could face Merlins for a drink, and I didn't want to have to talk to Max when I was feeling this vulnerable. He and Anne were just coming out of the church, his hand protectively on Anne's elbow. One day it might be Max in the coffin, and I would be expected to sit there and talk about illnesses and praise the address, staying in the background and not saying anything about what he had been to me.

It took about ten minutes to work my way through the crowd, murmuring that, of course, it was so sad, yes, sad, very sad. Vanessa's idea of a very small 'secret' funeral was about two hundred people, and she fluttered amongst them, her cries of recognition muted only slightly by grief. 'We'll all miss him so much, I don't know how we'll manage without him,' I heard her trill to someone. I could hear Vanessa's friends reverting to conversations about house renovation and cosmetic surgery as soon as the regulation 'terribly sad' exchange was over. I ducked between two magnificent black hats to hear the words: 'They cut my nipples off and put them in saline solution.' The broader brimmed of the two, whom I'd met several times before, caught my startled expression, and gave me a steely smile: 'It's so important to get the right man, don't you think? I've got a very good address if you need one.' Nobody seemed to be talking about Barry, about who he really was and what he'd meant to us, and my throat tightened again. It was just another of Vanessa's parties, except for the old men. Heaven knows where they fitted in. Perhaps they were funeral groupies, turning up to everything to relish their own survival. I'd just about got to the lychgate when a hand dropped on my arm.

I whirled round. 'Anne! How are you?'

'This is a farce.' Her face was flushed. I remembered how honest Anne always was, and, for once, didn't resent it. 'Barry left Vanessa over four months ago, making it absolutely clear that he had no intention of coming back. What is this . . . charade?'

'I think it makes her feel better. Just because he left her, it doesn't mean she's not devastated by his death.'

'Oh, I know that,' said Anne. 'But I wish she wouldn't try to pretend that it all hadn't happened.'

'We're not all as good as you at coping.'

She looked at me steadily. 'Is that how you see me? Coping?'

I wished I hadn't said anything. 'Well, you're always so marvellous. Everyone says so.'

'If only.' She fumbled in her bag, and for a moment I

thought Anne, impassive, indestructible Anne, was going to cry. 'Could you talk to Vanessa?'

I was startled. 'She's your oldest friend.'

'You're better at talking to people. I always say the wrong thing. You just bounce in and say any old thing, and people love it.'

I tried to work out whether this was a compliment or a criticism. 'Well, I suppose I do tend to gabble a bit. To fill holes in the conversation.'

'Yes,' said Anne, not contradicting me. 'It must be very useful. I wish I could do that.'

I felt like telling her that I'd often wished I could be like her, but suddenly realized that I didn't want to be like Anne, I just wanted what she'd got. I felt ashamed.

'Have you talked to Max recently?'

My heart executed an uncomfortable somersault in my chest. Had she discovered something?

'A bit,' I replied cautiously.

'He's got very worried about the brewery closing, and everything at Stonehill,' she said, watching me carefully. 'He's always been so fond of you, I thought you might be able to cheer him up.'

Fond. She had certainly cut our relationship down to size. 'I . . . don't quite know, I mean . . . I'd do anything I could, of course . . .' I dug my hands into the pockets of my cream linen jacket, wrapping it tightly round myself, as if defending myself against the possibility of 'cheering him up'.

'You're probably frightfully busy. But if you do get the chance, give us a call. And come and stay again soon. Properly. Even if Stephen's busy.'

Max appeared at Anne's side. 'Suzy.' He bent forwards to kiss my cheek, and I felt his slight roughness against my skin. 'Aren't you coming back to Merlins?'

I wanted to fight back tears. I couldn't bear the thought of Merlins without Barry. And Anne riding shotgun at Max's side. 'Do you think Vanessa would mind if I didn't?' My voice came out hoarse with trying not to cry.

'Not at all,' boomed Anne. 'Quite understand. We'll look after her, won't we, Max?'

As she took Max's arm to steer him back into the crowd, he looked at me, and I looked back. And Anne saw it all. I met her eyes in a brief stab of recognition and shame.

But she waved me off cheerfully, her arm still on Max's.

I was trembling as I slid the key into the ignition of the car. I thought that, very possibly, Anne was letting me know that Max was allowed to be with me, but that she had ultimate control. Otherwise what was all that about?

25

I decided to take the long way home, in memory of Barry. I wanted to wish him – well, what can you wish a friend? Rest in peace? Barry wanted to soar out over the sunlit water from his yacht, Kelly's hand as his last human contact. He didn't want to be rotting away in a picturesque graveyard, next to Lady whatevershewas-called. I wished I'd tried harder to get through to Vanessa. I wished I could stop crying. It was as if I was finally facing up to the whole of the past year: the burglary and the lost necklace, finding Max and losing Stephen.

I drove to Southwold and bought some fresh fish wrapped in ice from John's the fishmonger. Max had brought us here, one year when we'd all been invited to Stonehill for a summer holiday.

I hadn't been into the town for over a decade but it hadn't changed in a hundred years. There was still the old coaching inn, the cobbled triangular town square with its pump, the Georgian and Victorian houses lining the seafront, and the bright white flash of a distant sail catching the sunlight on the horizon. A few people were drinking pints of beer outside: it was Adnams, though, not Anne's family's. I could see why the brewery had gone under. I'd never seen anyone stock it.

Pleasant-looking women, in sensible navy or cheery pink, strode up and down the high street trailed by tots clutching buckets and spades. We'd been those women once, Vanessa and Anne and me. We'd eaten fish and chips down by the harbour, and paddled with the children in the greenish-grey sea. We'd bought ice creams from the shed tucked away on the beach, and brewed up strong, workman-like mugs of tea from a miniature cooker in a tiny, brightly painted beach hut.

I walked past the ancient cannons on the common, and on towards the marshes, which stretched out ahead till they fell off the edge of the world. We used to walk along here, while the children learned to ride their bicycles. I remembered one golden day in August, very like today – sunny but surprisingly sharp in the shade – when we'd crossed the river at the old railway bridge, and gone on to the medieval church at Blythburgh. I would walk that way again to remember Barry.

The narrow path was still there, forking right through the bracken after the bridge. There was honeysuckle twined amongst the ripening blackberries, and, as the gravel path opened out, clumps of startling purple, pink and orange heather shot through the scrub like bolts of Indian silk.

'It's not heather,' Barry had told us twelve years ago. 'It's sea lavender.'

Vanessa had contradicted him. It was definitely heather, of course, he knew nothing about plants.

But it had been the only cross word in the afternoon, and we'd drifted on, chatting idly with the sun on our backs, as the children's short legs pumped away ahead of us on their little bicycles.

It was all still there, the honeysuckle and sea lavender,

along with the feathery purple plumes of an elegant weed, and the harsher, sculptural shapes of fern and gorse. On either side, flecks of gold and brown speckled the fading green, a sign that summer was drawing to a close. Candelabras of cow parsley were already turning dry and brown. I tried to remember more about that afternoon, so long ago, to see if I could spot where the shadows of today had come from.

Firstly, Barry. He had walked a few steps ahead of us all. He always did that. In all our walks I remember seeing him striding ahead. Even then, perhaps, he wasn't wholly with us.

Then Vanessa. She'd been elated, because she'd bumped into some countess she was on a charity committee with, and exchanged brief, if slightly puzzled, hellos with a minor actress: 'Everybody comes to Southwold,' she'd exclaimed happily.

Max. Max had loved being a father, I remembered now, and had always included all other children around him in that love. He was always the first to hoist a tired child on to his shoulders. I recreated pictures of that week, when we were mainly together, in my mind. It was the only time that Max and Anne, and Stephen and I had spent time together as a foursome, rather than as part of a bigger party, and we must have seen beyond the usual ideal host and hostess act that Max and Anne had perfected together.

Max had been the ringleader, always laughing – sometimes a little too loudly, I thought. He was the planner: a picnic in the woods, a trip to the beach, a treasure hunt in the gardens . . . his enthusiasm seemed endless. Anne followed quietly behind, making it all happen. 'Fine,' she'd say, to his latest idea. 'All right,' was another response. She was serene. In her own world. She only really emerged from it to chat about compost and pruning with Vanessa, who had decided that gardening was getting fashionable and that she ought to know about such things in order to talk about them at dinner. Then Max would suggest treating all the children to ice creams, or going back across the open fields. 'If you like,' Anne would reply.

But Max did seem to like. He had seemed happy. It was like trying to put together a jigsaw puzzle with half the sky missing. I still didn't know if Max loved me more than anything in the world, or if he loved us both.

I was jealous of the past that Max had had with Anne, but perhaps she was also jealous of the past he'd had with me. Once I walked into a room at Stonehill, as dusk was falling, and found Anne in there, sitting alone in the dark, not doing anything. I remembered Max's hearty welcomes to us all, as Anne hovered in the background, dishing out food and drink without comment. Did Anne dislike us because we were Max's old friends, and I'd been Max's girlfriend, or was she like that with everyone?

On the way back, as I leant on the tiny railway bridge across the mouth of the river and looked out across the marshes. I thought of Stephen. What had he done or said that holiday? All I could remember was a tetchy debate about whether we should take sandwiches or have fish and chips at the Harbour Inn. Stephen had lobbied vigorously for sandwiches because fish and chips were 'expensive', and the washing machine needed replacing. But I knew that sandwiches meant more work for Anne, and could see, by the way she suggested fish and chips, that she really didn't want to do it. I reluctantly threw in my vote for the fish and chips, and Stephen had looked blackly at me.

Suddenly I remembered that that was when I had realized that the necklace could represent a little bit of freedom, that I could leave him, if I wanted to. I could sell it and take Polly and Jess to a new home, getting divorce lawyers, another job and new schools.

How could I have forgotten it all? When the girls were young, his temper had got worse and worse, as he worked longer and longer hours, for less and less reward (according to him, although I now knew that that hadn't quite been true). The girls and I had been utterly dependent on his moods, as he turned into a domestic tyrant. 'What's this mess?' he'd shout, if their painting or homework wasn't cleared up by the time he got home. I'd scurry forward, apologizing. I remember him walking into the house once when Jess was a toddler. She'd raised her arms for a hug. 'Daddy!'

'That child's face is filthy,' he'd said, walking straight past her.

And I'd suddenly thought of the necklace. I'd realized that I could now get away. If I sold it we could survive at least six months until everything was settled. The necklace could buy me time.

And why hadn't I? Well, we'd talked about it. The balance between Stephen and me had shifted slightly as we talked. He hadn't realized, he'd said. He was so worried about money, and so tired. Under stress. But he understood that it didn't justify that kind of behaviour. He'd try harder.

And to give him his due – and you must give him his due – he did try very hard indeed. And he'd talked to me, having thought it through very carefully, about the effect – 'both emotional and financial' – that divorce would have on the girls. Then Max had invited us to Stonehill for the week, and we'd had one of the happiest holidays of our lives. Stephen had made a great effort with the girls, and they had responded so lovingly and gratefully that I couldn't have torn it all apart. Everyone has faults, after all. It's not as if anyone is perfect.

I stopped to nibble a blackberry, but it still wasn't quite sweet enough. It needed a little more sunshine.

I drove through the back roads on the way home, twisting and winding through the quiet little villages. That's how I found the old shop, a pretty Georgian flat-fronted cottage crying out for love and attention. It faced a triangular village green, with a cannon and a flagpole, opposite a grey stone church, a thatched pub, and several rows of smaller, but beautifully cared-for, cottages with tiny front gardens bursting with giant hollyhocks.

It was a long pretty building, mainly a Georgian cottage, with a delicate, dilapidated metal porch and awning framing a battered classical doorway, and, at one side, a Victorian shop. The shop side occupied around one third of the building and had tall windows, while the living quarters had smaller square-paned Georgian ones, mainly covered with peeling brown paper. There was a tree poking through the roof, and the back, by the looks of it, was collapsing. Peering through a broken window I could see timber beams criss-crossing the walls. In a decent-sized garden behind, a wilderness stretched, overlooking fields. It had a For Sale sign outside.

'Last time I were in there was 1924 when I bought three-farthings' worth of sherbet,' said a quavery voice behind me.

I jumped, and turned around to see an old man leaning on his stick to talk to me. I hated strangers talking to me now, even ones as unthreatening as this one, but he was determined to tell me that the shop had been closed some twenty years ago. 'Nobody lives there now. It's falling down. You can't even get into the rooms to see what they're like. It's too dangerous.'

As he rambled away, I gazed past him through the murky and paper-covered windows. I thought how I'd love to buy a house with rooms that hadn't been entered for twenty years. To bring it back to life. As I peered through the windows, I could almost taste the house at the back of my throat, earthy like freshly dug potatoes, but as sour and rotting as old vinegar. It would need a great deal of work to turn it into a home.

Home. The very word overwhelmed me with nostalgia for the colourful, crowded, laughing place where I used to live. Now it was an empty, elegant, magnolia-tinted house waiting for us to get on with the next stage in our lives. After the Big Freeze, I'd cleared the rooms, sorting everything as I'd meant to do for so many years. I'd thrown away stuff that was essentially rubbish, and bagged up other things which I hadn't the heart to unbag now we were moving. We hadn't replaced anything, because there didn't seem any point, and the rooms seemed neat, tidy and soulless. They were just waiting rooms now. I felt as displaced as Max must have felt at college, with his one-room flat and no place to go back to. I'd already outgrown Birchington but it had still been there, with a welcome, a warm meal and a washing machine whenever I needed it. No wonder he'd wanted me to live with him, although he clearly hadn't been ready to settle down. He hadn't had a home. I tested the pain of his betrayal all those years ago, like a child assessing a wobbly tooth. There were no twinges. It was all too long ago. Then I thought of Max, now, and my heart twisted painfully.

Perhaps we could buy The Old Bakery, and live in it together.

But it was without much hope that I took down the name and number of the estate agent. Neither of us had any money.

When I got home Stephen was fizzing with excitement. He kissed me, and opened a bottle of champagne.

I felt warmed. Perhaps he did care about Barry, and was trying to comfort me.

'How was your day?'

I was surprised. 'You mean, Barry's funeral?'

An expression of sadness flitted over his face in a way that made me suspect he'd forgotten about it completely. 'Of course. Terrible. Terrible. What else did you do?' He assumed a look that denoted riveted interest.

It occurred to me that he was softening me up for

something. He wasn't usually interested in my day. I considered saying 'Spit it out', but that would only delay things while he protested that there was nothing to spit. So, instead, I asked him how his day had been.

Without noticing that I hadn't answered his question he took some estate agents' particulars out of his brief-case with a flourish. 'Look at this! And provided we move really fast, it's ours!'

I gazed, horrified, at a photograph of the most perfect Georgian manor house you could possibly imagine.

26

A silence shimmered between us.

'What do you mean "ours"? I measured out each word. I would not lose my temper.

'You remember that weekend . . .' Stephen sounded as glib as a salesman determined to install double glazing in a listed building. His voice flowed on, and I watched him through a haze of anger that billowed up and clouded my vision red. He'd seen the house that weekend in June, when we'd been at Stonehill, but it had been under offer. He'd asked the agents to let him know if anything changed, and just today they'd contacted him. The sale had fallen through, and if he could exchange by the end of the week, he could have it. The sellers just wanted to get rid of it. Otherwise it would go back on the market for fifty thousand pounds more. As it was we'd be mortgaged and in debt up to the hilt if we did buy it. There was no fifty thousand pounds more. It was our only chance.

'So you see,' he concluded. 'We have to move quickly but that shouldn't be a problem because all the paperwork's in place from the sale that fell through.' He was gabbling, I thought, at the sight of my expression.

Sounded convincing, didn't it? Once I would even have believed it. Now I didn't. If he'd found the perfect house under offer last June we'd never have heard the last of it.

'You could have called me today on the mobile. I could have gone round after the funeral to see it.'

He looked evasive. 'Well, I couldn't interrupt the funeral service. And I thought you might not be up to it. I know how fond you were of Barry.'

'So you were thinking of me? All along?'

'Of course, darling.' His eyes were guileless. 'You've been through a lot today. It was the least I could do.' He always had an answer. I thought he'd just manoeuvred the house this close to the exchange of contracts so that I didn't have the chance to say no.

Now that I could see my marriage more clearly, I realized how often things had been concealed from me or rushed through our lives under a blanket of protectiveness. I was sickened. By myself. For letting it all happen.

'No,' I said, trying the word out. 'Not until I know what I'm in for. The money. The plans. Everything.'

'You're being deliberately obstructive. This house is beautiful. Nobody could find anything to dislike about it. Nobody.'

'I didn't say I disliked it. I said I didn't know it. I have a right to choose my own home, you know.' Once we were installed, Stephen would never let me go. He'd never let his dream of a perfect house be torn in two by divorce. Panic filled me.

'Sometimes I don't understand you.' His face had clouded over. 'I work my guts out to give you everything a woman could want – money, a beautiful home, a social life that any woman would envy – and you talk about rights.'

'You're not working to give me things. You're working for yourself. I'm incidental to all of this. It's easier and cheaper to have a wife, that's what I sometimes think you feel.'

'I don't know how you can say that. I've done everything for you. Earned every penny for us.'

'I earn some of it. You earn more. It's supposed to be a partnership.'

'Hardly.' He sounded cold. 'Our lifestyle is reliant on the money I earn. Which I work bloody long hours for. I spend nothing on myself.'

'No, you hoard it instead. You lie about it. My money, what there is of it, is "ours", and yours is "yours". That seems to be the way it is.' I tried not to point a shaking finger at him. The anger about the secret account hadn't gone away, just underground.

'Don't be so fucking dramatic, Suzy, it doesn't suit you. I've provided everything for you in the last twenty-five years.'

'I've done what I could. And you never wanted me to earn much money. You wanted to stay in control.'

'Been going to a shrink, have we? Trying to blame your little panic attacks on a dominating husband? You're just jealous, because I've overtaken you. You were talented once. You wasted it. You were so busy wanting children and a family that you just . . . squandered your talent. You always found an excuse. The latest one is this idea that I'm keeping everything a secret from you. You can blame me.'

'I'm not blaming anyone. I just want to know what I'm going into. And I don't want to be so tied up by the financial commitments of a house like this over the next few years that we can't do anything.'

'Like what? Shopping? Lunching? Decorating? Holidays?' he sneered. 'Really important things like those?'

'That isn't fair. I shop for us. You couldn't have got where you've got to if you'd had to shop for yourself. Had to iron your own shirts. Take your suits to the cleaner's. Have the car serviced.'

'Anyone, my dear little Suzy, anyone, can stick a shirt in a washing machine and drop a suit off at the cleaner's. It's not rocket science. I can't believe I'm hearing this. All those years when I compromised on what I really wanted to do so that you could have children.'

'So that *we* could have children. It's a joint activity, you know.'

'I don't think so. You were the one who mucked up the contraception. The one who forgot to take her pill.'

'Are you saying that you would never have married me if I hadn't been pregnant?'

'Well, welcome to the world, Suzy. Welcome to the world. It's time to wake up. Twenty-two-year-old men still in full-time education *don't* want to get married.'

'Max did,' I whispered. 'Max did.'

'Yeah. Max. It's always been Max, hasn't it? Sometimes I think *you* married *me* to stay close to Max. You could have forgotten your pill with some other guy, couldn't you? But you didn't. You forgot it with me. Max's best mate. The one who gets what Max doesn't want any longer.'

'That's not true. You know that Max asked me to marry him. After you and I moved in together.'

There was a silence, while we glared at each other, breathless.

'Is that all he asked you? Are you sure you haven't been having a bit on the side with him all along?' He slapped his forehead with his hands. 'How very convenient. Max gets Stonehill *and* you.'

I couldn't tell him he was wrong. So I told him he was sick, instead. But he saw the truth in my eyes.

'You two-faced bitch,' he shouted, as I slammed the door, sobbing. 'You evil, two-faced bitch.'

I had to go back, of course, because all I had in my pocket was a one-pound coin, and I couldn't get far on that.

I stormed the streets for half an hour, and had the humiliation of ringing the doorbell because you don't exactly remember to take your keys and cheque book when you storm out of a house, blinded with tears.

Stephen looked exhausted when he opened the door. I went straight upstairs, pulled down a small suitcase and began to pack.

He propped himself against the door. 'I didn't mean it, Suze.'

I checked the bag. Knickers. Change of clothing. Toothbrush. God knows where I was going. I wiped my nose with my hand. I didn't want Stephen to see a great gob of snot land on the suitcase.

'Let's talk about it in the morning. Work it out. Go to counselling. Even pass up on the house if that's what you want. Okay?' He was back to being the charming, understanding, attentive husband, the one all my girl-friends envied. The man with family values, who worked so hard for us all, who never had affairs and was kind to old ladies. Only I got to see the bitter, envious, greedy man underneath.

Envy. The most corrosive of all the emotions. He had envied Max too much. He'd even had to have his girl. Perhaps Stephen had never really loved me. He'd just wanted to show Max that he could succeed where Max had failed.

I looked up. 'Stephen. Once you've let the genie out of the bottle, you can never get it back in again.'

But he still didn't believe me, offering drinks, coffee, sleeping pills, even; then barring my way. 'I don't want you to go, Suzy. That's the truth.'

I picked his arm away from the door. 'The truth is expensive, Stephen. And you've never wanted to pay full price.'

'You think you're so fucking clever,' he shouted after me, as I lugged the suitcase down the road to the tube station. 'So fucking clever. But you won't last two minutes on your own. You never have.'

A few window sashes were raised, but lowered again when it was obvious the fun was over, and then I was alone. The parallel universe, kept at bay now for so many months, shimmered out there on the dark streets, populated by drunks and thieves, rapists even. Gangs of boys who threw women into canals for the fun of it. People with knives and guns. Paedophiles and pederasts. Gremlins who only came out at night. I walked past a yellow sign asking for witnesses to a robbery, and three youths stopped shouting loudly at each other and looked at me curiously, assessing my worth. I trudged on towards the underground station. I'd find a cheap hotel near one of the big railway stations. I could see their neon signs and tatty stuccoed fronts in my mind's eye. It didn't really matter, any longer, what happened to me.

As the tube clattered through the tunnels with the hollow sound of an empty train, I thought about how much truth there was in everything we'd said. Too much, I thought. Perhaps I had gone to Stephen as a way of staying in touch with Max. I'd never thought of it that way. And forgetting my pills? Had I unconsciously done that on purpose? Had my drive to have a family over-ridden everything – even down to whether Stephen and I really loved each other?

I hadn't fulfilled my dreams because bringing up the girls, the darling girls, took up virtually all my time and energy, so I'd plodded on in a job that didn't set me alight. But if I thought about it, Stephen had also discouraged me at every turn. Most of the excuses why I couldn't do this course or enter that competition, or turn a tiny attic bedroom into a studio or a darkroom had come from him. He usually cited the girls' wellbeing, or my own health. He'd sounded caring, strong enough to take the weight of having to achieve off my shoulders. But it was because he wanted to stay in control.

At the heart of it, though, was the fact I'd been Max's. That must have been attractive. Anything you can do I can do better than you. Comfort your girlfriend. Go to bed with your girlfriend. It had just all gone too far when I got pregnant.

But I had to accept that by going straight from Max to Stephen I had started the whole thing off. I wasn't just the victim of the long friendship between Stephen and Max. I had played a part in it too.

Now I had to survive on my own. I left the tube at Victoria and found a cheap hotel only a few steps away, as I'd expected, a grubby little guest house in a run-down terrace, with swirly brown carpets, cream paint and internal windows made of wired glass, without the faintest idea of what I might do next.

The following morning I rang Vanessa because I had no idea how you got divorced. She gave a scream of amazement, and couldn't really understand the vague reasons I gave.

'Darling, they all lie terribly about money and things. It's not quite divorcing grounds. And it is very difficult being a single girl again at our age. People still don't like uneven numbers at the table.'

I murmured something about it being more complicated than that. How would I find a lawyer, not a top-whack one like Vanessa's, but reliable?

'Oh, darling, you must get the best lawyers. After all, Stephen's heavenly, but he's as tight as a duck's arse, you know what I mean? Well, you must do, being married to him for all these years. He's frightfully good company, so one doesn't mind, but stingy is the word. You'll have to fight tooth and nail to get what you're entitled to.'

I was rooted to the spot with surprise. Mean. Stingy. Not broke. It always amazed me what someone inside a marriage doesn't see, when it's obviously perfectly apparent to everyone outside it. I just never thought it would apply to me. I'd made excuses, all the time, for Stephen's attitude to money. Suddenly it reminded me of a friend who refused to believe her husband was alcoholic, asserting that his two bottles of wine a day were due to work stress.

Stephen and I had had so little, all those years – or at least I'd thought we had. I'd thought it was perfectly reasonable – if sad – to fret over the difference between fish and chips and sandwiches. I'd looked forward to the day when he – when we both – could just enjoy life.

Now Vanessa was saying that he never would. Henry Everett had, after all, bequeathed something to his son. His attitude to money.

'We all think you've been marvellous about it,' she added. 'Come and stay, darling, to give yourself a breather. I'll stop you doing anything you might regret.'

I bleated something about her not wanting guests so soon after the funeral, but she cut me off: 'Nonsense, it'll do me good to have someone else around. The house is awfully echoey when I'm on my own. There's a bed for you here any time you want it. Although heaven knows how long I'll be here. I'm expecting to be turned out by that woman at any moment, as soon as we hear what's in the will, but my lawyer says I have an excellent case for hanging on to the house as long as I stay put.'

Next I would call Max, and tell him I'd done it.

27

I couldn't get through to Max. There was only an answering machine, and, of course, I could hardly leave a message, and his mobile was either switched off or out of range.

So I dragged my suitcase to Vanessa's London house, which was, as she predicted, echoey. It had been redone by a fashionable architect in the latest tones of stone and steel, with Perspex stairs and huge skylights above the stairwell. It was like being in a dazzling spaceship, with Millie the Filipino maid pushing her mop around like someone who'd been accidentally transported from the nineteenth century to the infinite future.

Millie let me in. 'Miss Vanessa out. She leave you key.'

I was shown to a bedroom that reminded me of a cross between a luxury hotel room and a cell in a Buddhist monastery. It was plain white, with a huge, stark double bed, sunken lights in the ceiling, and no other furniture. It was all rather unsettling, but exciting, as if by throwing off a normal bedroom you could throw off your life and be someone completely different.

The door slammed downstairs. 'It's wonderful to have you here.' Vanessa came bustling up the stairs to kiss me on both cheeks. 'Now I have the most utterly fabulous news, so we're going to open a huge bottle of champagne this minute,' she said. 'Although we'll have to drink it outside. Do you know what they told me the minute they'd laid the limestone floor? That it permanently stains if you spill champagne on it! I'd *never* have chosen it if I'd known. Can you imagine?

'But at least it's summer,' she burbled on, as I followed her out to the garden. 'In the winter the only place we can drink champagne is in the en-suite bathroom. I think champagne's all right with marble, don't you?

'Salud!' Before I could offer my views on champagne and marble, she'd opened a bottle unbelievably quickly, sloshing it into two tall glasses, and indicated what looked like a couple of very large concrete turds in the garden. 'Make yourself comfortable.'

It was a command almost impossible to obey, considering that the choice was between the turds or a severe Japanese-style black teak bench without a back or arms. I perched, feeling my bottom-bones pinch (how nice to discover that there were still bones there), and waited to hear Vanessa's news.

'Anyway,' she raised her glass to me, 'I expect you're dying to know what I've got to say.'

I couldn't believe it was hardly more than twenty-four hours since she'd been bravely tottering up the aisle behind her husband's coffin. I felt a pang for Barry, for his affectionate smile and gentle way of sending Vanessa up.

'He didn't change his will!' She leant forward and hissed with delight. 'That Woman gets nothing! In fact – and this is even better – she's in a real pickle because they've just exchanged on a whopping great house in her name – presumably Barry was trying to keep assets away from the divorce settlement – and she hasn't a penny to complete the purchase with. So it serves her right. It's about time these young girls realized that taking someone else's husband isn't all sugar-coated. Even if she gets out of the purchase, she's got all the legal fees and the deposit to pay.'

My heart sank for Kelly. 'Surely if he incurred the fees, his estate should pay them?'

'Rubbish,' declared Vanessa. 'If you think I'm paying his mistress's legal fees, you've got another think coming. It would be ridiculous. No, she got herself into this, and she'll just have to get herself out. Which won't be easy on the salary of a dental nurse, or whatever she is.' She sounded satisfied.

'All we've got to do now, dearest,' she sat forward with an expression of determination, 'is to sort you out. Because you've got yourself into a ridiculous hole, and it's up to me to drag you out of it.'

With the guilty feeling that I ought to stand up for Kelly, but being too preoccupied with my own problems to address the matter properly, I sat there while Vanessa made me add up everything I possessed or had immediate access to. Five thousand pounds, a part-time job, and the joint account cheque book ('and I wouldn't count on him not cancelling that,' she added darkly).

'I'm afraid that it simply won't last two seconds,' she declared. 'I mean, have you seen where you'd have to live on that sort of money?'

As I'd trawled a few estate agents on the way over to Vanessa's I had a very good idea. The only thing I really minded about it was that I couldn't afford more than two bedrooms. The girls wouldn't be able to come home whenever they felt like it, throw their laundry at me, and go into their own rooms. There would have to be endless negotiations about who would be on the sofa bed, and whether there was a spare mattress. It meant, effectively, that either they wouldn't have a home, or their home wouldn't be with me, it would be with Stephen. That, above all, terrified me.

I reminded myself that I just had to hang on until Max could join me. Even if he hardly had anything, we could probably get somewhere together with three bedrooms. My heart quailed at the thought of Max moving from Stonehill's sixteen bedrooms to a squalid little basement somewhere. Or a boxy little cottage near the coast. Uncomfortable pinpricks of honesty began to puncture my belief that he would leave his beloved Stonehill without a backward glance. Have faith, I reminded myself. Have faith.

'If you're really serious about this,' Vanessa's voice jolted me out of my reverie, 'and I have to warn you that it's not easy – you've got to get some money out of that skinflint. But, financially, you would be miles better off going back to him. To be honest, you'll both be much worse off apart.'

'No. We said some terrible things.'

'We all say terrible things. I mean Barry and I used to say the most ghastly things to each other all the time, and we stayed together for years. It's really not a reason for splitting up.'

I stared at the ground, determined not to say anything like 'and look where that got you'.

'Now I do hope you don't have any romantic notions about marriage? Not at your age. Being madly in love with your partner and longing for him to come home in the evening, all that thing? I mean, most couples have very little in common after the children grow up, but they don't let that spoil their happiness. You just get on with it. Stephen's out a lot, isn't he? Away, even?'

I admitted that he was.

'Well, there you are then. You've got no real reason to leave him. Don't do it,' she said, obviously reluctant to reveal that her life was no longer one long round of glittering parties. 'I have a pretty good life because I make myself have one, but I'm incredibly lonely sometimes. Last Saturday – it seems ages ago, doesn't it – there wasn't anything on the box, I'd finished supper, and no one was around to phone. I went to bed at nine o'clock and I just couldn't get to sleep.'

'I know, but . . .'

'It's always the man who comes out best. Take Arabella, for example.' She mentioned a friend I'd met occasionally at her parties. 'Her husband, Ian, has a brand-new sports car, *and* a new woman he goes to country house hotels with, and she's trying to bring up two children on £150 a week. And they, theoretically, got a fair divorce settlement, not like poor Cecily who's even worse off. And then you get friends' husbands feeling under your skirt when they think no one's looking.'

I was shocked.

'They all do that,' Vanessa told me. 'They come to "give me a hand" with something, and then press me against the wall with claret-smelling breath, or they just suggest, quite bluntly, that they have an hour to spare and there are a number of inventive things that could be done with it.'

I protested. 'Vanessa, it's just that you look so gorgeous.'

'Nobody of fifty looks gorgeous,' she said. 'And anyway this isn't about how I look. It's about the fact that they know I've had sex for the last thirty years, and now I'm not getting it. And they presume I'll miss it. Which makes me an easy target.'

I bleated something about surely not.

'The trouble is,' Vanessa added, 'I do. Miss it, that is.'

'And are you ever tempted to take up the offers?' I was dying to know.

Vanessa looked sad. 'Oh, Suzy,' she sighed. 'I don't think there's any point in discussing it, do you?'

Which I assumed meant yes, on occasion. I tried to think about the husbands Vanessa knew and tried to sift the pouncers and propositioners from the balding, paunchy family men and distracted tycoons. It was impossible to imagine any of them – particularly with their clothes off – so I resolved to keep clear of situations where I might find out.

'I'm only thinking of your own happiness, darling, you know that. I mean, I'd love it if you were single and we could spend giggly Saturday nights together comparing the ghastliness of the occasional man we manage to sleep with. Do you know, I went out the other day with this divorced man who wore his pyjamas under his suit. He smelt all stale.'

I put my hands over my ears. 'Stop, Vanessa! For goodness' sake.'

'There you are, then. Much better just to stick with it, and live more or less separate lives. I'll even lend you some of my walkers if you like. You can still have a social life.' She took a swig of champagne, and gazed nostalgically over the white gravel. 'I remember the day I married Barry. It was the happiest day of my life. I knew I'd never be poor again.'

I was shocked. 'Didn't you love him?'

She looked dreamy. 'Oh, madly. I mean who wouldn't? He was handsome – really good-looking in those days – and absolutely stinkeroony rich. What more could a girl ask for?'

An awful lot, was my instinctive response, but I kept it to myself.

But she saw my face. 'Look, my parents really had to make sacrifices to send me to a good school. My mother never had any fun. My father died of sheer weariness at the age of fifty-five. I didn't want a future like that, not for me or for my children.'

With a spurt of interest in the never-revealed fact that Vanessa's life hadn't been as privileged as she liked to make out, I thought of the way they'd spat at each other over almost every issue, of his happiness with Kelly, and of the flower-covered coffin waiting yesterday beside the church. It seemed unutterably sad. 'But I don't think Stephen and I will ever again have the things that really matter to me . . . trust, equality . . .' I drifted off. It all sounded so naïve, surrounded by Vanessa's sophisticated modern architecture.

'Good heavens.' She sounded brisk. 'I'd have thought you'd have grown up enough by now to know that you never get those sort of things in life. Much better to have achievable goals like a car with a brand-new registration every three years.

'I mean, look at me.' She refilled our glasses. 'One of the reasons why I'm so thrilled about the will is that it gives me another chance at marriage. Let's be frank, as a broke divorcee, I wouldn't have been as attractive as I am as a rich widow.'

I could see the strain in her face under the elation and the carefully applied make-up. She obviously did want someone new, but I thought her aims were pitifully low. A man who'd be after Barry's money.

'Vanessa. Of course, you can meet someone else. Whether you're rich or broke. If he's worth it, he'll love you either way.'

She gave a little shake of her head. 'Darling, I don't do illusions. That's why Barry and I suited each other very well, you know. Neither of us had any illusions. I don't think I could bear to have any now. They're luxuries for the young. At our age, it's much better to face facts. That's why it's so daft to leave Stephen just because he had a secret account, and tried to buy a house without consulting you.' She giggled. 'Just think of all Barry's secret accounts and houses!'

Put like that, it did sound silly. I tried to articulate what I really meant. 'It's not exactly the secret account. It's just brought everything to a head. Our marriage has been dying for years.' I surprised myself with the words, but I knew they were true the minute they left my mouth.

And, as I'd said to Stephen, once you've let the genie out of the bottle, you can't get it back in.

Vanessa goggled at me. 'You always seemed so happy.'

'Or perhaps I mean that I've been dying in the marriage.' I thought of the way Stephen and I had been unable to communicate over the burglary and the nightmares, how remote and irrelevant he'd seemed. How I'd dragged myself to teach at the school, how little enthusiasm I'd had for sorting out the house, how I hadn't wanted to buy another one. Now I knew why I hadn't been able to visualize us living somewhere else. Because I didn't want us to live somewhere else.

All I'd done, for twenty-five years, was go to work and bring up children. Looking back on it, I couldn't recognize myself. Leaving, even for one day, felt like opening a door and breathing in pure, fresh air. 'I'm not going back, Vanessa.' I almost shouted the words, as a great, fizzing bubble of joy rose up inside me and burst free. 'I'm going to live.'

She gazed at me, puzzled. 'I think there's something you're not telling me. I know!' She gave a scream of delight. 'You've met someone else!'

I went pink. 'No, honestly. I promise. No one else. If there was, would I be here? I'd be tucked up in my little love-nest drinking *his* champagne.'

'Hm. I suppose so.'

I suppressed the thought that I ought to be honest with her about Max, but it would be all over town if I did. And talking to her about it all had made me realize that Max wasn't the only cause of my leaving. He'd merely triggered off something that had been inevitable.

'Even if there was someone else,' I added, explaining it to Vanessa, 'he would be a symptom of all this, not a cause.'

Vanessa looked cynical. 'In that case, dearest, decent lawyers. If you're to have any life at all, you need money.'

I stood up. 'If I could possibly afford to walk out of this marriage without taking any, I would. As it is, I'm going to find out what's fair, and that'll be that.' I thought of the necklace with a pang. I really needed it now.

I tried to call Max again, for about the sixteenth time. I got the answering machine again, and his mobile was still switched off.

28

My resolve stayed intact until supper time. Millie stir-fried something low in calories – a contradiction in terms – and discreetly left us to it at the table, a slab cut from surfboard material. When the phone rang, Vanessa had to hunt for it, as, along with everything else, it was cunningly concealed so as not to clutter up the clean lines of the design.

'Hello? Hello?' She shot a look at me. 'Yes, she is here, actually.' She passed it to me, looking thrilled at being part of a drama.

'Yes?' I braced myself for a tirade of accusations about selfishness and ungratefulness.

'Suze?' Stephen's voice sounded hoarse, almost a whisper. 'I'm sorry. I'm so sorry about all those things I said. I didn't mean them. I didn't mean any of it.'

'Are you all right?' This broken whispering undercut my brave intentions more effectively than any shouting could have done.

'I feel as if my life has been shattered. Being here without you is—' There was a long pause, in which I thought he might be crying. 'It's just terrible.'

My first instinct was to tell him to talk normally and not to over-dramatize, but there was real, terrible pain in his voice. I'd never heard him like that. The horror of what I was doing to him began to sink in.

'Stephen? This is awful, I mean you can't . . .'

'Please come back, Suze. I mean it. I don't care about the house or the money, or any of it. I just want you back. I love you, Suze, I didn't realize how much I loved you.' And then he started to sob, helplessly, great jerking grunts of agony that didn't belong to him, shouldn't belong to anybody.

'Stephen! You don't mean that. It'll be all right, I promise.' I stopped myself from saying anything more. What was I promising?

'Just come home, Suze. Just come home.' The line went dead.

I gazed with horror at Vanessa. 'I'm worried he might do something to himself.'

'It's so romantic,' she cooed.

My hands felt icy. When I'd made those resolutions about living my own life, I hadn't thought about what it might mean. I'd simply erased Stephen from my mind as if he stopped existing when I left the house. But he did exist.

'It's not bloody romantic,' I fumed. 'I mean the whole marriage has been as dead as a dodo since God knows when. We've been functioning as – oh, I don't know – a sort of limited company to bring up children or something. I thought he'd feel the same way.'

I wasn't even angry at him any more, that was the sad thing. I just felt terribly, terribly sorry, and awed at the prospect of dismantling our twenty-five years together.

'You mean, you're not going back? You mean you've got a handsome, successful, solvent man who loves you and you're not going back to him?'

'No.' I felt like a criminal. But it had to be done. I faltered briefly, and nearly phoned him back. How would I feel if Stephen committed suicide in the night? He wouldn't, I told myself. He wouldn't. 'If I go back now, he'll think I don't mean it. I'll never get away again.'

So I went upstairs to my white, empty bedroom, clenching my fists so that my nails dug into the palms of my hands. The temptation to go home and sort it all out was so strong that I had to feel pain to stop myself doing it.

Suddenly I fell into the deepest, soundest sleep I'd enjoyed since the burglary.

I woke up with light flooding into my room. Instead of a twinkle of subdued creamy sunshine trickling under ordinary curtains, the walls were washed in an explosion of brilliant whiteness as the August sky shone through a vast skylight overhead. I felt almost new as my bare toes turned up against the unexpected sensations: a paper rug beside the bed and a criss-cross wooden bathmat in an otherwise apparently empty shower room. I wondered if the architect had set himself the goal of using nothing in its original way: glass for the stairs, wood for the bath, surfboard for the table, paper for the cushions. Nothing was as expected – it was, as Kelly had said, hard and cold, but its courage suited my mood.

It took me ages to find the shower controls, pressing successive identical studs on the wall which serially turned on the lights, several different radio stations and the extractor fan before a sudden whoosh of water from an unexpected corner made me leap. But once I'd got the hang of it, it was fantastic, just as you'd expect from Vanessa's house, with a baking stream of water pounding down my back like a fierce, invigorating massage. Each part of my body twitched, bubbled and sparkled, as if coming back to life after a long sleep. My skin was alive – acutely sensitive to the slightest change in temperature or the touch of the different hard, shiny surfaces of the shower room. I felt that I could have clambered on to the concrete window ledge and flown over the city for the sheer joy of it.

I went downstairs to find Vanessa drinking a mango smoothie and frowning over a glossy magazine that had come with the post.

'Oh, dear,' she looked carefully round the room with a worried expression. 'Do you think this is all looking a bit dated? A bit Year 2000, if you know what I mean?'

I laughed. 'No, Vanessa, I don't. Your house is wonderful. It's exciting, and it's different, and I don't think you should even think about fashion when you've got all that.'

She didn't seem convinced. 'Mm. Well, I suppose you should know. You're so artistic.'

'Look,' I added. 'Just being here has made me feel differently about myself.'

'Cripes.' Vanessa took a swig of smoothie. 'I think you'd better go and stay at Merlins in that case, to bring you back to your senses.' We both giggled.

My senses. They all suddenly registered the reality, which wasn't hot showers in blazingly sunny bathrooms. The reality was a mess. 'I'm still not going back.' I spoke more to myself than to Vanessa.

'Well, I think you should think about it.' Vanessa was determined not to give up. 'And I should think about having some curtains. It says here that the new softness . . .'

As I set off for The Past, I couldn't help thinking that Vanessa had adapted to Barry's death with amazing speed.

29

There was an enormous bunch of green and white flowers – lilies, guelder roses and something fluffy and sweet-smelling – waiting for me at The Past.

'Oh, no!'

Alice, who was sorting the post, looked up at my exasperated tone. 'Yah, flowers are always *frightfully* bad news,' she agreed. 'Has he been unfaithful or did he just buy something terribly extravagant like a sports car?'

'Neither.' I sighed, as I took off my coat. 'I've left him.'

This penetrated even Alice's armour of self-absorption. 'You've *left* your husband?' She was astounded, as if one simply didn't leave useful things like husbands lying around. I mean, one never knew who might pick them up. Then she brightened. 'Does that mean he'll be a spare man for dinner parties?'

'You can have him. For God's sake, introduce him to someone gorgeous so that I don't have to worry about him.' As I spoke, I was aware of a spark of jealousy igniting. Aha! Feelings, at last. A positive feeling towards Stephen. That was a good sign. Perhaps there was hope. After all, part of me didn't want to tear everything that Max and I each had apart. I was like anyone else, I wanted to be part of a couple, to go on doing all those things couples do, like accepting invitations to barbecues in the summer and Sunday lunches in the winter. Getting videos out for quiet nights in. Planning summer holidays. I just didn't want to do them with Stephen. I clung on to the jealousy spark in the hopes that it might light a fire within me. It expired almost immediately. No, the fact of the matter was that I wanted to do all that with Max.

With resignation, I read the inscription on the card attached to the flowers. 'Please forgive me. Loving you always, S.'

'Grr!' I clipped off the stems and rearranged them in a vile jug in the window, which did make everything seem a bit better.

'He must have done something,' queried Alice, obviously hopeful of a little more detail.

I ignored the implied question. 'Do you want me to do any more hours, by the way, on a regular basis?'

She brightened at the opportunity. Once again, I couldn't imagine how she made a living. 'Well, I did think ... as you're so good at tarting all this stuff up,' she waved a hand at the still impossibly revolting shop-full of furniture, 'you might find it fun to buy it in the first place. Of course, you'd have to do it in the evenings or at weekends, as I can't possibly spend any more time in the shop, but I suppose you won't have much to do now.' She was obviously struck by another thought. 'Unless you've left him for someone else, of course.'

Irritated at the assumption that if you didn't have a man, then you didn't have anything to do, and that finding someone else was the only justifiable reason for ending a marriage, I was nevertheless pleased to be asked to start buying. There wasn't a chance, these days, of finding antiques, but there was definitely furniture out there with more potential than we were getting.

And I wanted to do a bit of scouting on my own account. The beginnings of a plan were forming in my mind. But, first, I had to get hold of Max.

I'd phoned so often since I walked out of home, only to get the answering machine, that I was completely taken by surprise when a human being picked up the phone. Anne.

'Oh, er . . .' Damn. She'd heard my voice. Now I couldn't just put the phone down. I tried to pull myself together. 'Anne?' I could hear myself sounding surprised, which was a giveaway.

'Suzy.' She sounded resigned, as if she had been expecting me to call.

'This is so silly,' I said, groping for something to say to her. My mind was a complete blank. 'I didn't mean to call you at all. I meant to call the name just below yours in my telephone directory. The . . . er . . . Gordons. Who live just down the road. So I suppose I shouldn't really have used the phone at all. It's probably easier just to walk along the street and knock on the door. Ha, ha.'

'I see,' said Anne, who probably did, as even someone misreading a telephone number isn't likely to confuse a London dialling code with a number in Suffolk.

I pulled myself together. 'Er, are you all right after Barry's funeral? I know you were both so fond of him.'

'We're fine, thank you,' replied Anne, with the faintest suggestion of emphasis on the word 'we'. 'Have you spoken to Vanessa at all?'

'Sort of.' I certainly didn't want to reveal that I was staying at Vanessa's, as that could trigger off a potentially lethal avalanche of questions and explanations. 'She seems fine. Considering.'

'Good.' Anne waited, as Anne does, for me to continue or stop the conversation. She creates these huge craters of silence, and I have the overwhelming temptation to fill their emptiness with gabble. I restrained myself from pouring the whole story about me, Stephen and Max into Anne's listening ear. 'Well, er.'

'Did you want to speak to Max?'

'No, no. No. I mean . . . no. I didn't want to speak to either of you . . . if you see what I mean, it was an accident, I mean, it was jolly nice to talk to you, but . . .'

'Goodbye, Suzy.' Anne put the phone down. If it was anyone else, I would have said she knew about me and Max, but that was just the way Anne was. Honestly. I sat there looking at the telephone as if it was about to explode, which even Alice noticed as odd.

'Are you all right?'

I shook myself. 'Absolutely. Fine. Okay.'

My freedom lasted less than forty-eight hours. Like an escaped prisoner, I was cornered after lunch.

Stephen, who was supposed to be in a meeting in Milton Keynes, according to my diary, walked into The Past, looking gaunt, unshaven, and, if you like that sort of thing, even more attractive than usual.

It just irritated me. How had he managed to do such a good imitation of a shattered man in such a short time? With pale, papery skin under a pepper-and-salt stubble, his cheekbones were knife-edge sharp and high. Very suffering film-star, I thought.

'Darling.' He obviously didn't dare kiss me, but put a hand out to touch my arm.

I twitched away.

'We do need to talk.' He settled himself down. 'Now I quite understand if you can't stand the sight of me, but I want to ask you just two things.'

I waited, tense.

'Firstly, would you just come and see this house? I absolutely promise not to put you under any pressure to buy it.'

'There's no point, Stephen. I want a divorce, and that means splitting our assets. It's pointless even looking at a house that costs every penny we've got.' The very word 'divorce' made my stomach curdle. Was I doing the right thing? I didn't see how I could do anything else.

I thought he'd press the point, but he didn't.

'Secondly, Jess is coming home on Friday week. Back from her travels at last.'

Jess! How could I have forgotten? My heart somersaulted with joy. Darling Jess. She was so beautiful and sensible. For a moment, I almost believed that once Jess was back everything would work out.

'I think it would be only fair on her if we met her together, and took her home as a couple, and waited a while before telling her what we intend to do. I don't think she should walk straight back into this situation after being away in Japan for a year.'

Of course she couldn't. The reality of looking Jess or Polly in the eyes, and telling them I was going to tear the family apart was horrifying. Totally horrifying. I couldn't imagine how I could ever have thought I would be so cruel. I must have been mad. Obviously I'd have to do it some time, but not now. When the time was right. The world flipped back to its usual shape in seconds. There would be no concrete baths, steel skylights and clear Perspex stairs for me. Meekly, more like a stray sheep than an escaped prisoner, I allowed myself to be led back to the world of occasional tables and standard lamps.

I did try, though. 'I want to stay at Vanessa's until then.'

He nodded, a wise doctor placating a mildly deranged patient. 'Of course, darling. A break will do you good. Give you space to think.'

'And I'm not looking at the house you want to buy. There's no point.' His face darkened at that, but he pulled himself together. 'Very well. But I would remind you that we're supposed to exchange on selling our house in the middle of September, so we'll be homeless from about mid-October.'

A crack of light appeared through a half-open door. Every prisoner knows that a journey offers more potential for escape than being shut in one place. I offered him a compromise. 'If we bought two places – one in the country, and one in London – then we could have a sort of temporary separation, to see if we can slowly get back together, and the children never need know about it. Spend some time together rediscovering each other, and some time apart for a bit of space.' I thought this all sounded pretty good, even if it was the most outrageous lie. The awfulness of my behaviour began to overwhelm me. Unfaithful. A liar. Betraying my husband with his best friend. And then not facing up to the consequences. I had this sudden sneaking suspicion that I didn't even deserve to live. And I certainly deserved some terrible punishment, like losing one of the girls. My heart stopped in terror. Surely God wouldn't be so terrible.

I told myself that my affair with Max in no way endangered the girls' safety. My inner voice of conscience pointed out that it definitely threatened their happiness.

I waited, holding my breath, to see if Stephen would take the way out offered. Perhaps, in reality, we could all come to some civilized agreement, where we all . . . what was I thinking? There was no easy way out of where I stood now.

Stephen did not want two homes. 'We wouldn't have such a good place if we split our money in two. And anyway, we'd be buying two compromise houses, rather than anywhere that either of us wanted to live. We'd only have to sell them both again once we'd decided what we wanted to do.'

A vision of The Old Bakery in Eggleton suddenly came into my mind. An enchanting place like that would never be a compromise for me, but I knew Stephen would never see it that way. It was Georgian, which Stephen would have liked, but it was a shop, which he wouldn't. In Georgian times, he wouldn't have been 'trade'. He'd have been at the Hall, the Manor House or the Rectory.

'Anyway.' Suddenly I felt weary. Anything to get him out of here. 'We can rent if we can't agree on what to do by the middle of October. Separately.'

I thought he would say that rental money was just thrown away, but instead he nodded. 'Together would be cheaper.' He looked at me, and I looked away. 'Unless, of course,' he added, 'you think we should pull out of selling.'

'Oh, no.' I could see, from his face, that this was one thing we did agree on. We just thought it would achieve different things. I thought I might be able to escape again, in the muddle, and he thought he would finally get me to The Old Rectory or something like it.

And, with an apologetic kiss on my forehead that made me want to kick his shins, he gave me a tragic, misunderstood smile, picked up his newspaper and left.

'Golly,' said Alice, emerging from the back room where she'd been hiding. 'What an attractive man. You can't possibly be thinking of leaving him.'

The door of The Past closed behind Stephen, rattling its Victorian bell. I sighed. 'It's a bit complicated.'

The rest of my time at Vanessa's turned into a holiday rather than a life change. I refused to go home one minute earlier than I had to. I still didn't dare tell Vanessa about Max, because she was so famously indiscreet, and I didn't want to risk phoning Stonehill again, so it would be a holiday without Max's calls, but apart from that I felt freer and lighter than I had done for ages. The parallel universe vanished almost completely. There was something about the sparse modernity of Vanessa's house that made me feel safe. Possibly because any burglar could see that there was very little to take away.

Vanessa spent her time with the solicitors and accountants trying to unravel the complexities of her inheritance, filling in any gaps left by pestering her architect to do something about the limestone floor. 'It's just too ridiculous that I can't drink champagne. I mean, what else would one serve at parties?' she berated him. From the bleating sounds on the other end, I gathered that he thought she should have said something when the house was done two years ago. I felt sorry for him, because I knew that the real problem was that she'd read a feature in a glossy magazine that said that dark hardwood floors were coming back, and she was terrified of looking outdated.

'Still, it'll take at least a year before the finances are properly sorted out,' she decided. 'So I can have the whole house done again from top to bottom then. I won't use him again though, he's been absolutely foul about this champagne business.' I thumbed through her magazines, hoping to visualize my own future from the articles about makeovers and life changes, but the pages danced in front of my eyes in a series of meaningless photographs.

After three days, Max finally called me at The Past on his mobile.

'Where've you been? I've been calling you at home,' he said. 'Every day. I couldn't leave a message. You weren't there.'

I explained. 'But it was a very brief burst of freedom,' I concluded. 'Didn't Anne say that I'd called?'

She hadn't. I wondered if that was proof that she suspected something, or that it simply hadn't been an important enough call to mention. You could look at it either way.

'Do you really have to go back to him?'

'I can't let Jess come back to this kind of a mess.'

He agreed. 'It's a pity, though. Look, once you sort yourself out, I'll be there. I promise.'

I mentioned the house in Eggleton. 'It's very cheap. It needs a lot of work, but I thought we should look at it.' I remembered Max's experience of old houses, of the cottages he had done up and sold off on the estate. I was thinking of his local knowledge, that he would be able to deduce something from the outside of the rooms that had been closed up for twenty or thirty years. I couldn't immediately see how either of us could afford to buy it, but I wanted us to try.

He managed to escape for a few hours the following day, and I took the day off from The Past to drive up to Suffolk.

We had to wear hard hats. The estate agent obviously thought we were married.

Neither of us corrected him.

Max and I went to a local pub afterwards. While he got our drinks I looked round. I could spend time in here. It was simple, with low dark beams, worn stone floors and a roaring log fire. A handwritten menu promised home-cooked stews and filled baguettes, and, judging by the smells wafting towards me, as someone walked past with a plate, the standards were high.

'Are you serious about it, Suze?' He put his pint and my half of lager down on the dark polished table.

My heart failed at the tone of his voice. 'Don't you like it?' My hunger vanished.

'It's pretty,' he was cautious. 'And it's quite big – those rooms we couldn't get into because they're unsafe are all probably quite a decent size, so there'd be four or five bedrooms, even six, and quite a lot of living space with the shop end opened up. But, Suzy, I don't think it's realistic. It's basically a rebuild job, and you could spend two or three times the price doing it up. And you'll be quite restricted on what you can do because of the historic side.'

The handwritten menu lay untouched between us. The future seemed very far away.

We discussed how we could get in touch with each other. Max could ring me safely at The Past, and probably at home, because if he got Stephen he could pretend he'd been ringing him.

'Do you feel guilty about him?' I asked.

'Desperately.' Max looked sombre. 'But I tell myself that you were mine first. And also, if he hadn't stepped in so quickly when you left me, then I might have got you back.'

That was true, although I didn't think that was Stephen's fault. Mine, if anyone's.

I asked Max how the new plans for Stonehill were going. He sighed. 'We're still exploring all the options: renting it out for films and weddings seems about the most profitable now.'

He finished off a cheese sandwich. 'I wish I could get more enthusiastic. I don't seriously want to have the place stuffed with location photographers and wedding ceremonies, let alone bouncy castles. If only Jamie was a bit older perhaps he could take it all over but, frankly, it's not a job for a twenty-four-year-old. Still, I've got to get it financially viable enough for me to get some money out.'

What I really wanted to know, but didn't dare ask, was whether he still loved Anne. Whether he slept with her. Whether their marriage, like mine, had been hollow for years. And how he could bear to leave Stonehill, the only place he'd ever been able to call home.

I didn't dare, partly because Max still had a core of privacy, that part of him deep down that still remained an enigma to me, and partly because I was afraid of the answer.

He looked at his watch. 'I'd better go.' He briefly kissed my cheek, and we both looked hastily round the pub in case someone was looking. 'I'll be so glad,' he sighed, 'when I can actually claim you for my own. Kiss you without looking over my shoulder.'

'Not long now,' I said, hoping it was true.

'No.' But he looked worried, and I didn't like to press it.

It was rather a depressing day, really, one way or another, except that as we left the pub Max caught my shoulder just before I unlocked the car door. 'Just a minute,' he sounded hoarse.

'I have to do this. Even if somebody does see.' And he kissed me, beside the village green under the late-summer sun, so thoroughly that he took my breath away, wrapping me up in a Max hug – deep and warm and all-enveloping. 'I promise you,' he whispered, 'I promise that we will be together. Soon.'

I sang tunelessly, but joyously, to the radio all the way home, stopping off at a bric-a-brac barn to find some plain but promising bits and pieces from junk shops. I had an idea of what I might do to them for the shop.

As I got back in and switched the ignition on, I heard the fragment of a song. 'You're a link in my daisy chain,' rasped the singer.

I thought about Max linked to me, and me to Stephen, and Stephen to Max. A daisy chain.

I drifted along in a glorious dream for the next five days at Vanessa's, sleeping late, working at The Past, and occasionally joining Vanessa when she went out in the evenings. One night she had a 'Girls' Night In'.

'Lots of champagne and gossip, darling,' she promised me. 'You'll love Clarissa, she's frightfully nice. And there's a friend of the Hendersons with a dear little art gallery. Louise.' Vanessa dropped her voice. 'She's so brave. The Ferret, you know.'

From eight o'clock, the doorbell rang continually. Clarissa arrived first in a swirl of voluminous fabric concealing a stocky figure. She peered at me with interest, and I knew, with a sinking heart, that Vanessa had told all of them everything about why I was there. Several other women, whose names I barely noticed, flooded into Vanessa's drawing room after her, followed by Louise, wearing the same black trouser suit I'd seen her wear at the Hendersons' and looking tired, but elegant. She looked round at Vanessa's walls. 'This is a wonderful space for paintings.'

'I thought so, too,' replied Vanessa. 'But my architect

thinks you should leave everything bare.' She looked doubtfully at the vast white expanses.

I was delighted to see Louise again. I'd meant to follow up her invitation to visit the gallery, but hadn't had time. She and I settled into a corner to talk about her business, and I was just going to confide my idea to her when Clarissa boomed across to Vanessa: 'I've got some gossip that's just too delicious. Hot from Suffolk.'

Suffolk. I caught my breath. Everyone stopped talking.

'Well.' Her eyes were alight at being the centre of attention. 'You'll never guess. Max Galliard is having an affair!'

'No!'

'Does Anne know?'

'I don't believe it.'

Clarissa poured herself another glass and allowed the babble to die down. I felt a tight, wrenching sensation grip my insides.

'Sh, girls, one at time. Podge' – apparently Clarissa's husband (she was just the sort of woman who'd marry a Podge) – 'saw them kissing in front of the pub in Eggleton. Passionate stuff, he said it was. Not a social peck.'

Everyone looked suitably stunned and I stared at my drink, hoping that Vanessa wasn't looking at me.

'Well,' continued Clarissa. 'What do you think?'

'Who was it?' One of the others leant forwards, and Clarissa shrugged. 'Podge's never seen her before. He says that they were so wrapped up in each other he couldn't see her properly anyway.'

Phew.

'Darkish hair, quite untidy,' Podge said. 'Tall. Long legs in nice boots. I think Podge rather fancied those legs. I told him he'd better keep his hands off Max's women. You know what Max is like.'

'Max's women?' I tried to make my voice sound normal.

'Suzy went out with Max at Art College,' explained Vanessa. Everyone looked at me, and I went scarlet.

'It was ages ago,' I mumbled.

'What was he like?'

'Oh,' I tried to sound casual. 'Clever. Talented. Funny.' My voice was drying up and fading away. 'Unfaithful.'

There was a collective moan. 'Not much change, then,' someone trilled.

'Anne had a terrible time with him when they were first married. No one gave that marriage a cat's chance in hell. But she's been very clever.' It was another of the women whose name I hadn't bothered to listen to.

'Or stupid,' said Vanessa. 'She either doesn't know about them all, or she chooses not to know. She just pretends it isn't happening, and sooner or later, Max comes back. But she absolutely never says a word, not even to me, and she's my oldest friend.'

'Well, she knows he'd never leave Stonehill,' shrugged Clarissa, 'so perhaps it doesn't matter.'

'It was all a business deal for her anyway, wasn't it?' chipped in a sharp little voice from the corner. 'She married him for his money, to restore Stonehill. That's what Daddy thought, anyway. Frankly, if you're going to do that sort of thing, you have to put up with a few affairs.'

Someone else sniggered. 'But not quite so many, perhaps. Or maybe there ought to be a quota per million pounds you bring to the marriage? Little millionaires could be allowed three or four affairs a decade and really, really rich men might be permitted up to thirty or forty?'

This was howled down by everybody.

'Does he have a lot of affairs?' I made my voice sound as even as I could, but still didn't dare look at Vanessa, who was the only one who knew me well enough to detect a wobble.

'They seemed to have died down recently,' said Clarissa. 'Until this last one. I think he just loves women. I mean, you have to admit, it's great fun sitting next to him at dinner. But sometimes I suppose it all goes just a bit too far. I expect it's because he's a foreigner. They have different ways of doing things.'

'Max is English,' I said, but no one heard me.

I left the room to deal with the heaving, sloshing and wrenching that gripped my stomach in waves. I felt as if I was going to be turned inside out, and stood by the lavatory bowl willing myself to be sick. Anything to stop this churning. But eventually the nausea subsided, and when I came back, everyone was talking about something else.

Louise touched my arm. 'Okay?' she murmured.

I nodded. 'I'd like to talk to someone about setting up a business. Would you mind if I picked your brains?'

'Not a bit. Come any time.'

Her neighbour on the other side then claimed her to talk about whether modern art was all a con. 'My son Oliver could do better than some of these things I see. And he's only five,' she asserted.

Funnily enough, hearing that Anne had married Max for his money should have made me feel less guilty about her, but, in fact, I was furious. Max deserved love. A great deal of love. The little lost prep school boy and the thin dark intense youth I'd first met at Art College had both been starved of it. Getting married and having a family should have fed that need in him. Nobody had the right to deprive him further by marrying him for his money. At that point I hated Anne, really hated her. How dare she?

But then I remembered that this was just idle gossip, and that Stephen's father had said similar things about me getting pregnant in order to get a leg up in society. Stephen had nearly hit him for it, but I knew that that was what Henry Everett had told his friends. Merely because it was gossip didn't mean it was true, although I knew that the talk of affairs almost certainly was. I'd known that about Max, although I'd hoped – and believed – that people really do grow up and change.

Half of me believed that Max had had affairs because he'd never really loved Anne. The other half told me that Max was an incurable romantic, who fell in love, over and over again, always believing it would last for ever, but whose attention would always be distracted by the next glittery toy that dangled before him. And that Anne, because of Stonehill and their shared life together, was his anchor.

Either way it was not something that could be discussed over the telephone.

It brought me down to earth with a crash. The next day, Stephen picked me up from Vanessa's on the way to the airport, where we would meet Jess off her plane. I packed my suitcase, leaving a few clothes in Vanessa's spare wardrobe in case I needed to bolt again. 'You don't mind, do you?' I asked her, as I packed up.

'Of course not, dearest. Just come flying back here any time, even in the middle of the night. I never mind being woken. But –' the drop in her voice warned me of dull, sensible advice to come '– I do really think you should give it all another go.'

Stephen, from the moment I opened the front door to him, treated me as a particularly fragile convalescent. 'Would you like to drive, or shall I, darling?'

He'd better drive. I couldn't trust myself. I slid into the passenger seat, wondering what on earth we were going to talk about all the way to Heathrow. There didn't seem any topic that could be entirely relied upon to be one hundred per cent argument-proof.

Eventually I settled on: 'It's a lovely day, isn't it?' It was. The sunshine of early September sparkled with a hint of cold, unlike the heavy, drizzly grey days of August. A few leaves had begun to turn brown, and were drifting across the road.

'You must be feeling better,' Stephen replied. 'About things. I'm so glad.'

I didn't want to say that I'd only meant the weather so I let it go.

A few minutes later, I tried: 'Have you seen anyone we know?' It was equally unsuccessful.

'I didn't have the heart to go out without you. I had a very quiet time. Thinking, you know, of all the good times we had together.'

The thought of trawling our memories suffocated me so much that I could barely breathe. Was it my imagination, or had Stephen always sounded like a complete creep? The conversation faltered again.

'I've been thinking . . .'

Oh no, I pleaded inwardly. Don't think.

'. . . that I'm away too much. You've been left on your own, and that must have been very isolating.'

It had been. It would now be more isolating *not* to be left alone. I said nothing, wedging myself even further down into the passenger seat and scouring the passing horizon for some neutral topic.

'So if we make it back together again . . . and I know it's a big "if",' he added, sliding me a glance, 'I'm really going to cut down on my commitments.'

'Oh no!' I was so horrified that my resolve not to be drawn on anything, no matter what, flew out the window. I tried to retrieve it. 'I mean, look, you're absolutely the only person I know who loves what they do. Who's still excited by it all. You can't throw that away. Look at everyone. Vanessa. Hasn't a clue what to do with her life. Those bankers, counting the minutes till their retirement. Barry. Only found the woman he really loved a few months before he died. Max. Tired and depressed.' I stopped. I shouldn't have mentioned the Max word.

Stephen pretended not to notice. At least, I think he did. Change the subject, quickly, I thought.

Third time lucky. I would talk about road works. He couldn't possibly bring that round to 'us'.

Wrong again.

'There seem to be an awful lot of cones for this time of year,' I ventured.

'Mm. It reminds me of all those journeys we used to make up the A12 to visit Max and Anne. Do you remember? When we travelled at night so the children would be asleep, and the A12 used to do its "Million Cones for Jesus" act?'

I dimly remembered a journey with an apparently endless line of cones diverting us into Colchester and out the other side, muddling us so that we went twice round roundabouts and making our journey so complicated that we arrived elated to have actually got there. I wouldn't say it was one of the highlights of our marriage, though.

'Those were great times,' added Stephen.

I refrained from adding, 'and now they're over'.

'We ought to arrange another visit to Max and Anne soon.'

I froze. Last time he'd mentioned Max he'd accused me, with some justification, of sleeping with him. Was this all going to be brushed under the carpet? Just part of their great shared friendship? Now was not the time to ask. I grunted, trying to make a noise that didn't commit me either way.

'You seem a bit tired. Have you been burning the

candle at both ends?' I couldn't tell whether this was another attempt at polite conversation or an interrogatory technique to discover if Vanessa and I had been holding orgies. It took me a few minutes to formulate a safe, non-revealing reply.

'Not really.' It's extraordinary how long it can take to think up two little words. And we were only at Hounslow. Aargh. At least twenty minutes to go until we were safely chaperoned by Jess.

Dearest Jess. Dear, darling girl. Suddenly I longed passionately to see her, to find out if she'd changed or grown up. She must have done. In a year. The thought cut me sharply. Jess had survived a whole year without us. When she'd first told us she was going to do Oriental studies at university, it hadn't occurred to me that she'd have to spend a whole year away learning to speak Japanese. It seemed extraordinary to have a daughter who could speak such a completely alien language, presumably quite well by now.

Just as I thought I might have to jump out of the car and hitchhike to the airport, Stephen spoke: 'I know this is hard for you, but I really do appreciate it, you know. Let's just try to get through the next few weeks, until the girls go off again, then we can talk properly.'

A dull, dragging ache started up at the thought of talking. Feeling like the biggest bitch in the world, I mumbled something.

'But,' Stephen seemed to be taking the responsibility for this conversation entirely on his own shoulders, and I was only too relieved to let him, 'I want you to know that all I want is for you to be happy. I hope, very much, my darling, that that means being happy with me, but if it doesn't, well . . .' He swallowed. 'I'll just have to deal with it.'

I felt the pressure ease. He wasn't going to force me to stay, after all. The next few weeks would be fine, because Jess would be back and Polly was going to leave the flat in Clapham for a few days to spend some time with us to be with her sister. We'd be a family again, and I'd be so busy piling supermarket trolleys high with food again that I wouldn't have to think about the big things in life.

And Stephen was being so sweet about it all. I looked at him with new respect. Perhaps it was going to be all right after all. I managed a smile, and he smiled back as we arrived at Heathrow.

Jess, taller and browner than I'd ever imagined, with her long, dark hair flying around in the air, and a tiny stud in her nose, enveloped us both in the biggest hug I'd had since she went. She talked non-stop, laughing, shrieking, breathlessly trying to compact a whole year into a few paragraphs. I couldn't take my eyes off her.

She flew into the house and whirled round it, like a cat inspecting its marked territory. Within moments she was back in the kitchen, puzzled.

'Everything's changed. It's different.' It was an accusation. 'It's sort of –' she looked around again for a few moments while searching for the right word '– boring.'

'Well, darling, you know we told you about the burglary, and the flood . . . and with the house on the market, we've put quite a lot of stuff into store, and it didn't seem worth . . .'

'Mm.' She wandered round the kitchen, picking things up and examining them, smiling at a postcard she'd sent in March. 'It's funny. It's as if there was something here, something special, but I can't quite remember what it was. But I can't find it again.'

She didn't seem too bothered, though, and when Polly got back from work, they disappeared upstairs, to Polly's unchanged, cluttered bedroom with the rose-print wall-paper and I heard the rise and fall of their voices fill the air like the chatter of happy starlings.

And what was it like for me, going home? It was just that. The door closed behind me as if I'd left only a couple of hours ago. Very little had changed. Stephen had been considerate, and had tidied up, filling a vase with flowers and the fridge with food. Really, I had no grounds for finding fault with him at all. Everybody makes the odd mistake. I felt humble. If only I could be as nice as him about it. I resolved, again, not to be drawn into any arguments.

I switched on the kettle.

Stephen swept in. 'Fancy a coffee? Don't worry. I'll make it. You put your feet up.'

I blinked at him. My resolution not to argue meant that I couldn't reply, 'But I don't want to put my feet up.'

He took the mug out of my hand. 'Just relax, darling. Where will you be? I'll bring it in. Would you like the paper?'

And we had a whole weekend of this ahead before he went back to work.

He continued to be helpful. I did, once, remonstrate, along the lines of: 'You can just behave normally, you know, you don't need to treat me as if I was an invalid or something.'

This deteriorated quickly into an exchange along the lines of: 'I am behaving normally.' 'You don't *normally* make me cups of tea/scrub the potatoes/put the sheets through the laundry.' 'Are you saying that I haven't been pulling my weight in this marriage? Is this what it's all about?'

'No,' I said, wearily. 'That's not what this is all about. Forget I said anything.'

'I can't just forget it. You've said it now. We should discuss it.'

I soon learned it was easier to let him make the coffee or mow the lawn for the final time before putting the mower away, or whatever. Stephen whirled through the weekend like a domestic dervish, pushing me down on to a sofa with a magazine whenever he could. I learned to keep a watch on my tongue, and not say anything that might cause an argument until I'd thought it through very carefully. It was so difficult that in the end I didn't say very much at all, and spent my time thinking about Max. My belief in 'us' wavered from day to day. Sometimes it seemed obvious that we would be together in the end, and at others, I couldn't help wondering if he just wanted to get me away from Stephen one last time.

*

We decided to spend the last fortnight before Jess went back to university on holiday at home, instead of in the Algarve or Tuscany, because she'd been travelling all summer anyway, and 'it's the last time we'll be in this house'. Polly, too, arranged to take a week off from cooking in the restaurant, and spend it with her sister, packing up for the move. This was a huge relief because I couldn't have faced Stephen over a sun lounger every day and stayed sane. As it was I could take refuge at the supermarket for hours at a time. Add in the fish shop, the Italian deli and conjuring up some chore – all too easy, like having the toaster repaired or going to the dry cleaner's – and I could stay out of the house all morning. Stephen and I had agreed that we wouldn't bring work home, but I itched to get my hands on the stuff I'd bought on the way down from Eggleton.

It was extremely difficult for Max and me to talk. I didn't dare ring him, in case I got Anne again. When he rang me, he got Stephen. They had a long, pally conversation and Stephen came in looking satisfied. 'Max is on good form. We're going up to stay in early November.'

I avoided his eye and mumbled something. Suddenly the day seemed flooded with brilliant sunshine.

On the last day of the holiday, my mood lifted. The girls had decided to clear their rooms, consigning old theatre programmes, homework books, headless Barbie dolls, rosettes and *Jackie* annuals to big black dustbin bags, and boxing up a sadly tiny amount of stuff that they wanted to take from their childhood into the new house. Stephen helped them – I could hear them all joking and reminiscing, as his baritone voice provided the depth to their high-pitched giggles and squeals of horror at this outdated frock or that old school report.

'Where *are* we going to live?' Polly asked anxiously at lunch. I was warmed to hear the 'we'. I'd feared that 'home' to Polly was the untidy flat she shared with three other girls in Clapham.

Stephen and I looked across the table at each other.

'Your mother and I are still trying to decide.'

'But it's likely to be somewhere in the country,' I added, to be rewarded by a look of such sweetness from Stephen that my heart turned over. I wished, with every fibre of my being, that I wasn't such a spoilt bitch, and that I could be grateful for all that I was being offered.

'But not necessarily,' he said. We were saying each other's lines.

'God, not the country,' said Jess. 'It's so uncool.'

'I think it would be nice,' Polly mused. 'It would be lovely in the summer to get on a train and be in the middle of fields and things.'

'Can we have a tennis court?' asked Jess. 'If we had a pool and a tennis court, I could bring my friends back to stay, couldn't I?'

'Your father's doing brilliantly,' I said, 'but I don't think we're quite in that league yet.'

Stephen looked pleased at the 'brilliantly', and I was glad I had, at last, said something that he was prepared to hear without analysing it.

'Oh well,' she added. 'In ten years' time, you'll probably have loads of grandchildren, and it'll be perfect for them.'

We all looked at her sharply. It was a most un-Jess-like remark to make.

'Don't look at me,' she grinned. 'I'm going to be sterilized as soon as they'll let me. But I bet Polly'll start breeding the minute Paul proposes.'

Polly turned deep pink and glared at her. I wanted to meet this Paul.

'Well, it's all up to your mother,' said Stephen.

Three expectant faces turned trustingly to me.

I knew I shouldn't have done it. I shouldn't have let them think that everything would be all right. But I was drawn in by the warmth of the meal, and by the love on their faces. I just couldn't bring myself to tell them that there would never be another home for us all.

So I lied. Just temporarily. Until I could sort myself out. Until we could sort ourselves out.

I smiled, warmly at the girls, hesitantly at Stephen. 'Perhaps, in that case, we should start looking in the country. If Daddy goes on being so successful –' I managed to up the wattage of my smile at Stephen '– and I work more, which I'm going to, we might even get a little flat in London too, one day.' Everyone beamed. Family life was restored, happy and complete, just the way it ought to be, but so seldom is.

Like Jess, I knew that there was something very special that ought to be there, but wasn't. But wanting it didn't make it happen.

We spent the rest of the day looking at estate agents' particulars, and between the four of us, established a shortlist of possible houses. Now that the summer was over, there seemed to be lots more choice.

Was it very bad of me to allow Stephen and the girls to think we were all going to move, when I was just waiting for the right time to tell him it was all over?

Or did I think, deep down, that our marriage still deserved another chance?

Either way, I was lying to someone, even if only to myself.

30

I was surprised at how easy the next few months were. We moved, which was hard work, but took my mind off anything else, put all our furniture in storage, and took a short lease on a small, convenient, well-equipped mansion flat not far from Stephen's work. It was safe (three floors up, twenty-four-hour porter, rather smart area), close to a very good delicatessen, and all I ever had to do, apart from make the beds and do the washing up, was change the odd lightbulb. Any more fundamental problem would be fixed by the landlord. The temporariness of it suited my mood. I didn't feel committed or that anything was expected of me. It was like being on a permanent holiday.

The girls adored it because it was so near the centre of London and Jess came home as much as she could, cramming herself, her friends and a mound of sleeping bags into three very small bedrooms. Polly took to dropping in more often, too. My heart blossomed. This was what family life was about.

Stephen treated me as someone who'd nearly died, and I myself felt weak and wobbly, as if convalescent from a long illness. Sometimes I felt feverish, as if burning up with love for Max – usually after one of our long phone calls – then suddenly drained again by the impossibility of it all.

Stephen and I didn't exactly 'talk', but we did, briefly, talk about talking. We discussed going to counselling. I didn't want to. We seemed to have established some temporary status quo, and I didn't see the point in examining it closely. The last thing I wanted was to unbalance things.

Even so, I still had to watch what I said, very carefully indeed, partly because of my secret life with Max – confined to the telephone, and a very occasional lunch when he could get into town – and partly because Stephen seemed to be able to read an insight into the state of our marriage in the most harmless remark. I hardly dared offer to make a cup of tea, until I'd examined the consequences of doing so from all angles. Even something like taking the rubbish out generated a competitive round of supportiveness.

'I'm just going downstairs with the rubbish.'

'Don't worry, darling, I'll do it.'

'That's fine, I'm halfway down the corridor already.'

(Door of study opens, Stephen appears and wrests the rubbish out of my hands.)

'Sweetheart, it's far too heavy for you, it won't take me a moment to pop down with it.'

'Really, I can manage.'

Weighed down with guilt, it was usually me who gave up first. 'Thank you, darling.' And I trailed back to finish emptying the dishwasher, only to find that, too, whisked out of my hands. 'You're looking tired. Let me do it.'

Once or twice I tried to give something back, to show him I appreciated the effort he was making. I bought wild smoked salmon and champagne, and spent all afternoon cooking an exquisitely worked dish with steak and wild mushrooms and a little pastry hat. It looked like an illustration in a cookery book.

Stephen took off his coat, and saw the candles.

'What's this?'

'I just thought it was time we had a treat. You've been working so hard recently.'

'Champagne? Suzy!' I could see irritation beneath the words, but he quickly wiped it away. 'Suzy,' he repeated, making an obvious effort to be nice. 'That's really sweet of you . . .' He swallowed, and I realized that such treats would not build any bridges between us.

'Just this once,' I added.

'Good,' he said, more forcefully than he'd intended. 'Of course, I'm thrilled . . .'

And he closed the bedroom door behind him while he went to change.

When he came back, looking irritated and apologizing, he'd clearly made up his mind to be pleasant, but the evening was forced and tense. I was slowly beginning to realize that the shadows of his childhood – the financial ones – were long ones.

Yet when I talked to him, reluctantly, about my business plan, we finally found something we could talk naturally to each other about. He was surprisingly helpful. He listened carefully while I explained.

'You know I've been buying valueless junk? Then painting it up and selling it in The Past?'

He nodded, scribbling things down on a pad of paper.

I'd kept track of the costs, and worked out that because the furniture itself was so cheap, I could do it up quickly, and still sell it on quite reasonably, even allowing for a shop's mark-up and a more commercial rate for my time. I'd been inching the prices up at The Past, and people seemed happy to pay them.

I wasn't going to try to do something tasteful or chic – there was plenty of that around already at prices I couldn't compete with. What I wanted to do was create outrageous or fantastical fashion pieces, zebra-striped chests of drawers, tables covered in a riot of roses, dressing tables in fuschia, magenta or violet, or trunks covered with fur fabric, comics or Astroturf. I thought people would buy them for children's and teenagers' rooms, and fashion-conscious people like Vanessa might buy the odd, almost disposable, piece to keep for a season or two and throw away. It would be fun, quick stuff. I'd use scraps of fabric and wallpaper to save painting – I'd even covered one wardrobe entirely with copies of the *Financial Times*, varnished it and sold it to a young man who worked in the City.

Stephen couldn't back me with any money, but he went patiently through everything I needed to create a business plan, what cash flow I'd require, what future expansion I should look at, and even whether the prices would allow me to subcontract work if necessary. Together we fretted over where we were going to sell the furniture. It would have to be in town, because it needed to be somewhere fast and fashionable. Best simply to supply other shops rather than have your own, he suggested, and I thought he was probably right.

'I met a girl called Louise, who's just started an art gallery – Lavinia Henderson introduced us,' I told him.

'She said she'd tell me what it was like starting up. She might even sell some stuff for me.'

'Good idea,' Stephen agreed, looking wistfully at the contents of his own briefcase which he had hardly touched all weekend. 'Would you like me to come with you?'

Feeling that taking Stephen to Louise's art gallery would somehow be letting the side down, as if it would underline the fact that I hadn't been brave enough to change my life completely, I was anxious to persuade him not to come.

He seemed equally anxious to support me in every possible way, but said he was actually quite busy . . .

With a sigh of relief, and after the usual time-consuming dance around each other ('Of course, if it would help at all I'd be delighted to.'/'No, no, honestly I'll be absolutely fine on my own.'/'Are you sure, darling, would you like me to at least drop you off?'/'No, really, it's not far, I might even cycle and get a breath of fresh air.') we agreed that I would visit Louise on my own.

Apart from that, we looked at houses. He'd come down a fraction in his aspirations, so we now looked at houses we could just afford without making ourselves too miserable. It was as if he'd realized that some prices were too high to pay. You'd think I'd have been victorious, but all I felt was a mild regret that another dream had had to be consigned to the dustbin of life.

We started looking at nice, well-built Victorian houses – retaining many original features, of course – with well-appointed gardens in convenient suburbs or villages.

All these houses seemed perfect for our needs, and Stephen and I had to work hard to find reasons for not buying any of them. We managed, however, colluding in some invisible, unspoken way that made me think we must be a pretty good partnership after all.

Every time we went to a new town or village, or received a comprehensive list of particulars from an estate agent, or the 'Property Advertisements' were laid out in front of me, I played a game with myself. I'd cut the amount we had to spend in half, and see what we could each have got for it.

The results were depressing, but occasionally I found myself going into elaborate fantasies of what I'd do to make them nicer.

One day, rather to our surprise, we found a house that Stephen adored, and I liked. In fact, it was lovely. The light streamed into a big, wide hallway, and a pile of tiny wellingtons were lined up at the back door. There was a cat asleep on the boiler, and a garden that, even at the end of the season, was so exuberant that you knew that this was a home full of love and laughter. I looked at the piles of coats on the coat-hooks, and heard a child sing happily in the bath.

'I could live here,' I said, thoughtfully, forgetting, for once, to watch my tongue.

'Of course, it needs loads doing to it,' said Stephen.

'Do you think so?' I was surprised. 'I rather like it as it is.'

'Shall we put in a bid for it?'

It was the weekend before we were due to visit Max and Anne. I had to discuss this with Max. The possibility of us finishing up together was beginning to look more and more like a childish dream, while Stephen and I were slowly behaving more normally with each other at last. The choice was between going on as we were, living comfortably, getting my business started, staying close to the girls and eventually looking forward to grandchildren, or turning everything upside down and going God knows where with Max. Perhaps Max would hang on to Stonehill and I should settle for Stephen. Perhaps that's what people do after a mid-life crisis.

It was time to decide.

'Let's think about it over the weekend.'

But I could see, from the look in his eyes, that Stephen believed this was a 'yes'.

I had had butterflies in my tummy for days at the thought of the coming weekend, and had been choosing, cleaning and pressing clothes endlessly, in order to boost my confidence. I did think it was strange that the question of whether I had slept with Max had been raised, not wholly denied, and then completely ignored, but perhaps it was part of the careful way Stephen was treating me. Or, perhaps, I thought, with a surprising pang of pain, that his friendship with Max was too precious to tarnish. Either way, I certainly wasn't going to bring it up. Sex had become remote to my life again: one of those odd things, like pot-holing or Morris dancing, that other people do.

Stephen would join us after shooting a new programme in Norwich. He was successfully setting himself up as a style guru, taking every opportunity, however trivial – and some were very trivial indeed – to appear in the media. In the last few months, he had been on several radio programmes about inner-city regeneration, which had led to his inclusion in a government think-tank. He was often in those magazine columns where 'experts' are asked to choose the best door handles, coffee tables or kitchen worktops. Houses he'd designed now featured in the newspapers, and he was beginning to appear in articles with titles like 'The People Who Shape The Way We Live'.

'Dad may only be in the foothills of fame,' commented Jess one day, 'but it's amazing how often he seems to pop up in the papers these days.' Our flat became strewn with obscure kitchen or bathroom magazines, their pages falling open at postage-stamp-size pictures of his head, and his comments on taps, or correct grouting, or the use of windows. Two different sets of publishers were talking to him about a book and he'd been asked to give a couple of prestigious lectures. Every day I could see the tangibility of this success boosting his confidence.

Anyway, it all meant that I had a blissful drive up to Stonehill alone. I was determined to stay on the main road, not to turn off into Eggleton to see if the old Georgian shop was still for sale.

Anne greeted me as I parked the car.

I suddenly wished for the support of Stephen, for the protection of being half a couple. 'Anne! How are you?'

We kissed, unconvincingly. As I followed her inside, I tried, desperately, to think of a way to start a conversation, but I'd talked so much to Max over the past few months that almost anything I asked might reveal a greater knowledge of the situation at Stonehill than I really ought to have.

Anne, apart from offering a cup of tea, didn't bother with small talk, but I found the silence so unsettling that eventually I asked who else was expected.

'Just you two.' She whisked a kettle off the stove. It was a big old-fashioned one, with a curved spout like a swan's neck, always warm on the Aga. 'And Vanessa's coming over this evening. Along with Podge and Clarissa Fairfax, who live locally. Have you met them?'

Oh no! I felt rather sick. Podge was the one who'd seen me in the pub with Max, although all he'd seen were my legs. Thank goodness I'd brought a long skirt. And I'd try to make my hair specially tidy, although it was always a challenge.

I cautiously admitted to having met Clarissa at Vanessa's, and tried to change the subject by asking if there were any developments at Stonehill since I was last here, which seemed a safe question. I was briskly told that a local company was taking over the West Wing of the house as an office. 'They'll be using other parts of the house on an occasional basis for conferences, taking bedrooms to put up visiting VIPs and so on. So it'll be quite a change for us,' concluded Anne in a bright voice. 'If they expand, we'll probably convert one of the barns to offices and rent that out too. We're delighted – it means we have the weekends to ourselves; and business people are so much more organized, it's better than having to get involved with individuals.' She made the word 'individuals' sound like 'hooligans'.

I already knew all this, of course, but tried to look

surprised and asked her if that meant that everything had all been sorted out for Stonehill's future. I received a hard look that conveyed that even if I was vulgar enough to talk about money, she, Anne, was not going to stoop to my level. 'But you must be thrilled to have sold *your* house at last,' was all she said. 'Do you think you'll manage to buy something in a better area?'

I gritted my teeth at the implication that there was a great deal of difference between her home, which must be preserved in the family at all costs, and mine, which was a 'relief' to sell. 'Well, of course, we've been very happy there,' I said pointedly.

'But I expect you've got tired of all the crime and the litter,' said Anne. 'We've got some friends who moved away from your area a few years ago because their car got vandalized six times in one year.'

'Really? How extraordinary. Our car has never been touched,' I countered.

'Still,' mused Anne. 'It must all be very wearing.'

'I don't know,' I was determined to fight back. 'It's just as tiring to live in the country and have to drive for twenty minutes before you can even buy a roll of loo paper.'

'Oh, that's no problem.' Anne's superior position remained unassailed. 'You just get more organized about shopping. You must come to live in the country – it would be such a relief not to have to worry about burglary all the time, and virtually anywhere in London is obviously a nightmare these days.'

Max swept into the kitchen. 'Suzy!' He sounded gratifyingly pleased to see me, and gave me a kiss on both cheeks. The touch of his skin was soft and cool against mine, just for one second. 'Have you just arrived?' He turned to Anne. 'That was Geoffrey on the phone. They've been done again. Just mindless vandalism, apparently. The barn was set on fire. The sheep were terrified, and there's paint everywhere. He reckons the damage could add up to ten thousand pounds, and both tractors were stolen.'

'Geoffrey always makes such a fuss,' replied Anne, fixing him with a look that should have turned him into stone. 'It's probably a bit of graffiti and a few sheep that got out.' I tried to look as if I hadn't heard, but she added, with difficulty: 'These ... yobs ... come from the city, of course.'

Inwardly I felt like going 'Yess! Goal!' until I remembered the poor, terrified sheep, and hastily murmured something like, 'How awful.'

'Darling!' Anne calling Max 'darling' was like anyone else shouting 'Heel!' to a large dog.

'Mm?' He rummaged through the newspaper, standing up.

'Are you listening to me?' she demanded.

'Absolutely.' He folded the paper and tried to look attentive, but his eyes kept darting down to a story on the front page.

'Have you sorted out that paperwork from the council? I know it all seems rather trivial to you, but unless we get enough lavatories for these beastly little people, the deal will be off.' She removed the paper, folding it under her arm.

I'd never known Anne sound this poisonous. She must have found out about us, somehow. On the other hand, she might just be furious at having to share Stonehill with 'beastly little people'. I wondered if I could get straight back into the car and drive away again. In her current mood, I wouldn't put it past her to add ground glass to my porridge.

Max, gently but firmly, took the newspaper back from her, and she turned away, and began to put things away in cupboards, making, I thought, rather more of a clattering noise than was strictly necessary.

I wondered if they'd just had a row, or whether it was like this all the time at the moment.

She disappeared down a corridor to put something away in the long-term freezer, and Max folded his arms, leant back against the dresser and looked at me – and I mean, really looked, in a way that made me feel warm deep down inside – with a soft expression in his eyes. 'So how are you, Suzy?'

'We've got to talk.' I kept my voice low.

'Did you see that the place in Eggleton's under offer?'

'Oh, no.' I knew it had just been a dream, but it was still sad.

'Suzy was just saying that she's frightfully glad to get away from that dreadful area,' intercepted Anne, bustling in from the long-term freezer with an armful of food for the short-term freezer. 'Now I'm sure you're keeping her hanging about when she's dying for a bath.' With that she practically pushed me upstairs, instructing Max over her shoulders to do something about something else. I got the impression he didn't take much notice, because later he emerged from his study, and she snapped at him.

'I promised Suzy a walk to stretch her legs,' I heard him say. 'Do you want to come?'

'No,' she shouted in return.

So we pulled on our boots, and headed out to the bluebell wood. Rust and copper leaves slithered and rustled under our feet. Overhead, bare branches were beginning to sketch shapes against the sky, interrupted by clouds of yellowing leaves as the trees prepared themselves for winter. My hands felt cold, and I pushed them deep into my pockets. I had to know about 'Max's women', and how things stood with Anne. So I asked him.

He sat down on one of the logs, and thought for a moment. 'If I tell you, I'll have to break a promise.'

I thought about it. 'Whatever happens, I won't tell anyone anything. Whatever happens between us.'

He would have to trust me. Otherwise there was no future for us.

'But before you say anything,' I added, 'I think I ought to tell you what I heard in London.' I mapped out the conversation at Vanessa's house – except, of course, the bit about Anne marrying him for his money, which was too cruel – and watched his face darken.

'I'd have thought you were too intelligent to listen to gossip.'

'No one's too intelligent for gossip. And I do care. I don't want to be just part of a game you're playing.'

'You're not,' he said, angrily. 'Is that really what you think?'

'No,' I admitted. 'But I would like some answers.'

He thought for a few moments. 'It's difficult to know where to start.'

'Start anywhere?'

'Very well. Anne. Well, I'd never met anyone like her. You know. Self-contained to the point of being mysterious. Calm, competent, pleasant, but always that feeling of something stormy underneath. I wanted to –' he struggled to find the words '– to get beyond that tranquil exterior. Get under her skin. Possess her, I suppose. I found it all very seductive – the ruined estate, that sense of belonging that she emanates, the feeling that if you lived here you'd really be part of something solid and permanent . . . I'm not saying any of this very well, am I?'

I swallowed. 'Go on.'

He squeezed my hand. 'It think it's better if I'm truthful. If I just pretend there was never anything much in my marriage, you'd know I was lying.'

I nodded, as the cold outside crept in icy fingers up to my heart.

'Anne was like a princess trapped in a tumble-down castle,' he continued. 'I suppose I thought I could be the prince that awakened her.'

So it had been a marriage of love, after all. On his side, anyway.

'And I was fascinated by Stonehill. It really is somewhere that money can't buy. I wanted to stop travelling. I wanted a home.

'So we got married. It took me a long time to discover

the real Anne, and I still don't think I know her yet. She has depression.'

I was mentally knocked off balance. Whatever I'd been expecting him to say, it hadn't been that. I'd known, of course, that I didn't know Anne very well, but I had never thought of her as vulnerable.

'It's corrosive, unreachable, clinical depression,' added Max in explanation. 'Not just feeling a bit miserable about things. There is a glass wall between her and the rest of the world, and she's trapped behind it. It started with Jamie's birth, and when we consulted specialists about it, they said that it would eventually go. Eventually it seemed to, but then we had Harriet, and the post-natal depression started again. I'd always wanted three, or even four, children, but we didn't dare trigger off this terrible condition again.'

'But that was years ago,' I said, sympathy already tinged with doubt. Could she really have been ill, for so long, and have managed to conceal it from everyone except Max?

'Things have been up and down since then. Recently, very down, possibly because of the money worries. Sometimes she doesn't speak for days on end. There's no colour or taste in her life. She gets up at five to work, and sometimes doesn't go to bed till eleven or twelve. Or maybe later, I don't know.'

Uncharitably, my heart flipped at that. Didn't know when Anne went to bed.

'In the old days, I was afraid that she'd actually harm herself or, when they were younger, the children. It's like living with a robot when she has bad days. If I talk to her, she answers in a bare minimum. Yes. No. Over there. That sort of thing.'

'Oh, I thought that was only to me,' I interrupted. 'I thought I'd done something.' And then blushed, because, of course, I had.

'She's better at Stonehill,' he continued. 'That's why we hardly ever go away. I've tried to take her on holidays, but, away from home, it's as if the darkness in her mind completely stifles her.'

I thought of the veiled, confident young girl stepping up the aisle to marry Max. And I'd always thought that Anne had always had everything. Poor Anne.

'Is this anything to do with the affairs?' A small part of me wondered if I was being softened up for a typical male excuse. That he'd say that he had affairs because of the strain of living with Anne.

'Maybe. I did want some uncomplicated comfort sometimes. But I suspect I just married too young. I'm probably the sort of man who shouldn't have made a commitment until my thirties at least. And I don't want to give the impression that my marriage has been totally bad, because that would be untrue. There's a lot I admire about Anne. We've rebuilt Stonehill together, and we've enjoyed doing it. She's a fantastic home-maker . . .'

I felt guilty about the times I'd inwardly criticized Anne for seeming cold and distant. I felt even more guilty about wanting to take away the one person who knew her secret, and who would look after her. But it was painful, too, to hear Max's concern for his wife. It hurt, because I knew how hard he would have tried to make her better, and how reluctant he would be to leave her suffering anything more. Max has always been very protective, and it was beginning to sound as if he was still deeply involved with her.

He caught the expression on my face. 'But she's not you. You are, and always have been, the one I love. And the affairs have ended, I promise.'

'And now?'

'Now, I've re-established Stonehill so that there's an income coming in, and a few more things we can sell. Anne is ... well, she's in a bad mood today, for some reason, but that's not depression. Depression is despair, not anger.' He sighed. 'Or hers is, anyway. I expect everyone's different. So I think I'm ready. If you are.'

We gazed at each other, incandescent with joy.

He looked at his watch and kissed me. 'Shit. It's getting late and I promised to light the fires.'

'One last thing . . .' I caught his sleeve. 'Does Anne know about us? Or suspect anything?'

'No.' He looked thoughtful. 'I'm absolutely sure she doesn't.'

I bathed that evening with a delicious sense of anticipation, combined with a terror of everything coming to a head.

Stephen had been so sweet, and, apart from the odd outburst, had tried so hard, that it seemed sheer selfishness to leave. Everybody else thought he was wonderful. In spite of my happiness, I still didn't know, truly, if I was doing the right thing.

*

Even I was impressed when Stephen swept up to the door an hour later in a chauffeur-driven car. I suddenly realized how much his success had polished him. He had that burnished look that went beyond his gleaming shoes and beautifully manicured nails, and was more than merely wearing well-cut clothes in perfect condition. Perhaps it's about being able to radiate calm because you're being driven, rather than racing to catch a train. Most of all, though, it's a light within. Confidence. Stephen had arrived.

'Darling.' He kissed me full on the lips in front of Max, and guided me confidently upstairs to the bedroom, hand firmly on the small of my back. Over his shoulder, he excused himself to Max with the words: 'I must just quickly change and say hello properly to my wife. We've been apart for a whole two days, you know.'

I tried to suppress a sudden feeling that Stephen had contrived this weekend, including its tie-up with the television programme, to prove to Max that he had won. He'd got the fame, money, and his wife back. Max's business had gone bust, he'd never fulfilled his early promise as an artist, and there was a threat hanging over his home. After all those years of Max being the leader and Stephen the follower, Stephen was ahead.

I hunched up on the double bed, as he pulled off his tie and unbuttoned his shirt, sitting down next to me and tracing his finger down my cheek.

It was irritating, like having a gnat buzzing round your face. I didn't want to say anything, though. I didn't want to jeopardize his good mood.

'The series is going ahead. That'll be a nice little extra lump sum.'

I moved my face fractionally away from the stroking. 'Well done.'

He used the opportunity to kiss my neck, murmuring: 'We'll be able to get a new kitchen in the house after all.'

'Look, we must talk . . .' Now was the wrong time to say anything but I couldn't let him go on thinking that we'd buy this house and be a happy family again.

'Not now.' He looked into my eyes, with what I always thought of as his 'caring' expression. 'We'll have a good long chat when we get home.'

I could feel the word 'unfaithful' writing itself in fire across my forehead under his gaze, so I gave him a quick, but firm, hug back, using the positioning to wriggle out from under him and head for the door. 'I promised Anne I'd help lay the table. She seems a bit tense, so I'd better go.' Just to make it seem less like running away, I blew him a kiss. Perhaps it would help to get really drunk.

31

Dinner was formal. We all dressed up, and I laid seven places at the long, thin table in the Great Hall.

Max and Vanessa were in the drawing room in front of the roaring fire, laughing at something. I kissed them both. Anything to feel Max's cheek against mine again.

'I've decided to do something with my life,' explained Vanessa happily. 'Before it's too late.'

I looked at her, questioningly. She was fizzing with excitement. 'I'm going to do a degree,' she burst out.

I nearly spluttered into my drink. The idea of Vanessa, dripping with jewellery, slumming it as a mature student, was a surreal one. 'What in?' I wondered if you could do a BA in choosing handbags.

But she surprised me. 'English literature. I've always loved reading, but I've never really tackled the greats, so I think it's time I started. I've got the time, and the money. And no ties.'

I was impressed. 'Brilliant.'

'You never know,' she tinkled, 'one day, I might be one of the oldest people ever to get a PhD.'

I laughed. 'You're not old. For goodness' sake.'

Vanessa smiled back. 'Well everybody has to get old some time. I'm just going to defer it as long as possible. Anyway, I can't start until next September, so I've got nearly a year to go round the world. I've suddenly realized that there's so much out there that I haven't done. I'm going to start with Hong Kong early in the New Year – because the Hendersons have been posted out there – but then there's the Great Wall of China . . .'

She began to map out a journey that combined staying at the houses of her smartest friends with some really quite daring adventures. 'I'll get to a friend's place every three weeks,' she explained. 'So that I can be sure of at least one decent bath a month.' For someone who usually expected at least one decent bath a day, this was quite a development. Max and I exchanged pleased glances over her head. I could see that he was as delighted as I was. It all sounded so much more fun than redecorating her house every two years and waiting to meet a man who might marry her for her money, which had been the sum of her ambitions since Barry left her.

'The only thing I feel sad about is that Barry won't be with me,' she continued.

I stiffened, but she caught my unease. 'I do know,' she added, with a tremble, and the suggestion of wateriness about her eyes, 'that he'd left me months before he died. But I'd still have liked another chance.' She stared down at her glass. 'I do miss him.'

'So do I,' Max put his arm round her and gave her a hug, and I could see her melt into him like someone who hadn't had a hug, particularly not a male one, for a long time. She gave him a quick peck on the cheek.

'You're a darling to say so. I just don't want people to forget him, that's all.'

I felt tears sting my own eyes. 'Nobody will forget him, Vanessa, I promise. He was far too nice for that.' I could see that she was still on the rollercoaster of grief – elated one minute, desolate the next. In spite of her apparent ability to cope, she was very fragile.

I touched her arm. 'He'd be so proud of you, doing a degree and going round the world. He really would.'

We all had another swig of our drinks and gazed into the fire, and by the time Stephen appeared in the doorway, emanating expensive aftershave, we were talking about more mundane things again.

It was like looking at a stranger. At first I thought perhaps he'd put on weight without my noticing it, but I realized that it wasn't that. His personality filled the room in a way that it hadn't before. His teeth seemed whiter, his shoes more polished, his voice louder, and his opinions more pronounced, as, without asking her how she was, he immediately started to tell Vanessa about how long it had taken the chauffeur to find Stonehill. 'Nobody's properly trained these days.'

Vanessa gulped down her drink, and nodded, hardly getting a word in edgeways.

Shortly afterwards, he was followed by Podge and Clarissa, who were ushered in by Anne. Together they looked like Tweedledum and Tweedledee, with almost identical pug-dog faces, except that Clarissa's was framed in a stiff, coiffeured bun, and Podge merely had a few stray wisps on top. They beamed at us.

'Haven't we met before?' asked Podge, obviously rummaging through his memory with difficulty.

I tried to sound carefree. 'Probably. Stephen and I have been coming up here for years.'

'Of course, of course.' He accepted a huge whisky from Max with a shout of appreciation, but continued to give me thoughtful looks from time to time. Anne asked everyone to bring their glasses into the Great Hall.

I was seated between Vanessa and Podge, facing Stephen and Clarissa. Max and Anne sat at either end.

'Darling,' Stephen's voice was definitely louder than it had been this time last year. 'Tell everyone about our new house.' We were picking our way through a delicious roasted pumpkin, parsnip and sweet potato salad, all grown in Stonehill's own vegetable garden.

He made the word 'darling' sound like a poisoned arrow.

I could feel myself go pale. 'We haven't put in an offer. Yet.' I couldn't bear it if he got too excited about this house. 'And even if we did,' I warned him, 'we've no idea whether it would be accepted.'

Stephen waved my comments away and, emptying his glass in one big gulp, left me with the suspicion that, once again, he'd gone ahead and bid for it without telling me.

'So what's this house like?' asked Anne.

'It's nice,' I said, in a small voice, thinking what a bitch I was, sitting in Anne's house, eating her exquisite food and planning to run away with her husband.

'Nice! It's . . .' And Stephen was away, monopolizing the conversation with a discourse on architectural detail.

Max sat back and watched, refilling everyone's glasses as soon as they were even half-emptied, as if he was detached from the evening. I couldn't help catching his eye from time to time, and I didn't think I could ever get tired of mapping the distinctive contours of his face. Clarissa and Anne seemed to be paying rapt attention to Stephen, who hardly drew breath.

'Didn't I see you in the King's Arms at Eggleton the other day?' Podge asked Max, with a twinkle in his eye.

'Did you?' Max was bland. 'I don't remember it.'

'What's that, Podge?' Anne obviously wasn't quite as gripped by Stephen's explanation of why the proportions in classicism were so important as she'd seemed to be.

Podge went a deep, brick red. He'd obviously intended to tease Max privately. I suspected that he was basically too kind to want to stir things up, but possibly a little too dim to realize what even a gentle tease could unleash.

'Er, I was just asking Max if he fancied a drink in the King's Arms at Eggleton one day.'

Anne gave him a stony look. It was extraordinarily stupid of him to change his story like that. Anne would now be much more suspicious if she'd heard him properly the first time.

Max created a distraction by jumping up. 'I think we need another wine bottle opened, darling. Have you got some out, or shall I check the cellar?'

Stephen drained his glass again, with satisfaction. 'Bloody good wine, Max. Any more where that came from?' He was obviously enjoying himself. I knocked back another slug, too, to get me through the evening.

Podge tried to start a conversation about politics, but in that way that conversations do, it quickly swung round again to the one topic that Podge, Max and I were now all trying to avoid. Adultery. A cabinet minister was considering resignation after the press had discovered that he had not just one, but two mistresses.

The table predictably divided into those who didn't care what he did in the privacy of his own home, and those who thought he was a liar, a swindler and a cheat who should leave office immediately. Vanessa, unsurprisingly, was in the latter camp, shrieking in indignation about his behaviour.

Stephen stepped into the argument. 'What you have to remember, Vanessa,' he pontificated, claiming centre stage again, 'is that there's a strong European tradition of mistresses. Some of the finest parts of many cities, both here and on the continent, were built to house the second, third and even fourth illegitimate families of prominent men.'

Vanessa, taken aback, looked frustrated, and tried to intercept the flow of talk with the odd 'Yes, but . . .' and 'Surely if . . .' before Stephen swept over her again with detail about pediments and neo-classical porticos. She obviously hadn't yet said everything she wanted to say about men being unfaithful. The rest of us switched off as he relentlessly steered the conversation back to architecture, although Anne did an excellent imitation of being fascinated. She was looking wonderful, in stark black velvet with her thick white hair cascading loose. Her pale face, with its Roman nose, charcoal-definite brows and slash of red lipstick, was unforgettable. Looking at her, then round at the huge great hall with its carved buttresses, I was amazed that Max was prepared to leave all this for me.

At the end of the first course, everyone got up to help

Anne clear the plates, presumably to escape Stephen.

'We don't need everybody,' she waved us down. 'Clarissa can help me.'

Vanessa was beginning to look upset and bored, so Max stepped in. 'Tell us about this new programme, then, Stephen.'

He instantly abandoned the subject of adultery and architecture, and leaned forwards: 'Well, it's designed to combine the popularity of lifestyle programmes with the bite of the new, more vicious quiz shows. It's called *A Question of Taste*,' he explained. 'People are going to put their houses up against a panel of experts – I'm the architectural one – to find out if what they've done to improve them has actually been correct.'

'You mean like stone-cladding Victorian red-brick terraces or putting PVC windows into period homes?' Vanessa was clearly thrilled to hear that the programme was something she could really relate to. 'Pebble-dashing Georgian frontages, that sort of thing?'

Clarissa brought in several steaming plates of venison and two tureens, and everybody began to help themselves.

'Oh, all those things, of course,' said Stephen airily, 'but that's all pretty basic and audiences these days are getting so much more sophisticated. No, we're hoping to really catch people out. Like carriage lamps in front of a cottage. Or those French marble fireplaces.'

'French marble fireplaces?' I tried to catch his foot under the table. There were two at Merlins. 'But they're very pretty. Gorgeous, in fact.'

'Lovely,' he agreed. 'In their place. Which is France.'

He let out a shout of laughter. 'But people actually put them in English Victorian drawing rooms!' He gave the table a thump of appreciation at his own joke. 'I mean, any fool can see that the proportions are all wrong – they're much too low and come too far forward into the room – but you wouldn't believe the people who just don't notice.'

Vanessa paled, and began to pick at her venison. Merlins, a red-brick Victorian vicarage, had two very pretty white rococo French marble fireplaces in the drawing room, installed by Vanessa, who had torn their predecessors out. Presumably the point of the programme would be humiliating people like her, and no one would mind because she's rich and good-looking. I wondered if Stephen really was being thick, or whether he was using this programme, and his new-found success, to take revenge for years of feeling poor. I felt a mouthful of vomit rise up sharply in my throat and swallowed. I'd drunk too much, and looking round the table, I could see I wasn't the only one.

'Well,' I said firmly. 'As the programme title implies, it's all a question of taste, and if people think marble fireplaces look attractive, and virtually everyone does,' I raised my voice deliberately, 'then any programme saying otherwise is going to look pretty stupid.'

Stephen went very still and white, staring at me as if I'd said something sacrilegious. We hadn't argued since that terrible row the evening I'd left him.

Max stepped in again. 'And I gather that there are a couple of books in the pipeline, too, Stephen?' This was dangerous, as I'd told him about the books on one of our many long telephone conversations and Stephen might wonder how he knew, but I could see he was trying to draw Stephen's fire away from me or Vanessa.

Podge looked impressed. 'Books, eh? I've always wanted to write a book. Haven't got the contacts though.'

Stephen gave him a slightly too patient smile. 'It's a question of content, not contacts.'

I racked my brains to think of a topic of conversation that avoided affairs and architecture.

Eventually, seized with inspiration, I asked Vanessa if she was managing to fit in any skiing before her round-the-world trip.

'I'm going to Vermont just after the New Year,' she confided. 'To just the prettiest resort you could possibly imagine. It looks as if it was built in the days of Scarlett O'Hara . . .'

'That was in the South,' interrupted Stephen.

'The Federal style was in the North, and married classical influences with New World ingenuity,' snapped Vanessa, surprising me. 'I'm staying in a lovely old clapboard farmhouse, built in typical Federal neo-classical style, and fully restored with historical integrity.' It sounded suspiciously like a quote from the brochure, but at least Vanessa was fighting back.

'I very much doubt it, my dear Vanessa.' Stephen gave a superior laugh. 'Very, very few historical buildings, especially ones where tourists stay, are truly restored with historical integrity. It's the same here – the crassest mistakes hit you bang in the eye just driving past. I mean, only the other day, I saw this lovely Georgian terrace, and do you know what?' He glared belligerently round the table, and had another slurp of wine. 'All the front doors were a different colour. One was even lilac!' He slapped the table again, and guffawed.

Everyone looked puzzled. 'What's wrong with that?' ventured Clarissa.

'They should all be black, as originally intended,' he said, firmly.

Vanessa, who was determined to go down fighting, said that she was the first to appreciate architectural purity but surely that level of control was outrageous. 'In the US, they're rather more liberal about such things.'

'The US doesn't have our heritage,' pontificated Stephen, topping up both her glass and his.

Vanessa said that, in terms of heritage, Vermont was a damn sight better preserved than most of the towns and cities in England. 'And they manage it without ordering everyone to paint their front doors in identical colours. Living in a house in an identical row with everything the same colour is like . . . living in some kind of . . . factory.'

'Like council housing,' interjected Podge. 'Sounds like council housing!' And he laughed at his own joke, rather too loudly.

Stephen glared at him, and spent a long time explaining why individual choice shouldn't be allowed when people really didn't know what they were doing.

He turned back to Vanessa again. 'For example, did you ever do any research into what *ought* to have been done to any of your houses? Or did you just flick through a few magazines and follow the latest fashions?'

I could see that Stephen had gone over his alcoholic

limit. He was like Jekyll and Hyde. Absolutely charming sober, unbelievably rude drunk. Most of the time he knew enough not to get that drunk.

It was time to clear away the main course, and I jumped up. Podge followed with some more plates. Anne rootled around in the larder and brought out a cheeseboard and a chocolate mousse. 'Biscuits in the very top cupboard,' she informed me briskly, disappearing through to the Great Hall with the mousse and leaving me to bring the cheeseboard.

I fished a biscuit tin out of a high cupboard. As I left the kitchen I bumped into Max coming the other way.

'There must be something we can do,' I hissed. 'He's absolutely crucifying Vanessa. I'm so sorry.'

'It's not your fault.' Max looked worried. 'I'll think of something.' He looked round to check there was no one present, and dropped a quick kiss on my lips.

At that very moment, a side door opened, and Podge stood framed between us, still zipping up his flies. He looked from Max to me, with recognition slowly dawning in his face.

Max slapped him on the shoulder. 'I'd be grateful for your discretion.'

'Oh, of course.' Podge was seriously taken aback. 'Nothing to it, old boy.' But, as he lumbered back to the Great Hall ahead of us, jiggling his trousers back into position, I thought I could detect the eagerness of a man who is dying to impart gossip.

Well, with any luck, he couldn't tell Clarissa before getting home, and she probably wouldn't rush back in the middle of the night to pass it on to Anne. I was beginning to think that Anne had heard the rumours, and had invited Podge and Clarissa tonight specifically to see if Podge recognized me. The sooner everything was sorted the better. One reason why cabinet ministers ought to resign if they were having affairs is that adultery requires such intensive, full-time concentration to remain undetected that it scarcely leaves any unoccupied brain cells left over for things like running the country.

When I got back to my seat, trembling slightly, it was Vanessa who was now unstoppable, passionate in her belief that everyone should be able to choose, even if the choice was technically wrong. Max tried to catch her eye. Stephen wasn't really even listening to her, just telling her what he was going to do in our new house and why it was right.

Vanessa grew shrill with the determination to put her point across. Stephen merely repeated what he'd said earlier, but more loudly.

'Women,' said Stephen portentously at the end of the meal, taking the port from Max, who'd tried to interrupt several times, but had been shouted down by whoever was talking, 'have no idea about logic. You're absolutely typical, Vanessa, absolutely typical. You haven't listened to a word I've been saying.'

Vanessa stood up, threw the remains of her last glass of wine at him, and stormed out, sobbing.

There was a silence round the table and Podge, who'd actually dropped off, woke up. 'What was that about?'

'Stephen believes that if you live in a classical Georgian terrace you should only paint your front door black,' explained Anne. 'And Vanessa thinks you should paint your own front door any colour you like wherever you live.'

'Oh,' said Podge. 'I thought I'd missed a bit.'

'I'll see to her.' I got up.

'Well, I'm dreadfully sorry,' said Stephen. 'But how was I expected to know that she'd react like that?'

No one said anything.

32

'She can't drive in that condition,' said Max as I opened the door to go to Vanessa. 'Are there any extra beds made up?'

'She can stay in Lavender,' replied Anne, referring to one of the smaller bedrooms on the top floor.

I found Vanessa sobbing in the bathroom and steered her into Lavender, a sweet little blue-and-white painted room with a tiny iron fireplace and a comfortable blue armchair. Vanessa collapsed on this, and I sat on the arm.

'I'm so sorry, Vanessa. He's drunk, and he's tired. He doesn't mean to be so rude. He just doesn't know what he's doing.' As I said the words, I realized I'd made these excuses before – not often, admittedly, because Stephen was usually clever enough not to drink too much. But other friendships had come to a sudden end, to the sound of desperate apologies on my part and a sullen silence on his.

'He'd never have done it if Barry had been here,' she sniffed. 'That's what it's like, you know. Being single again. People you thought were friends can be just horrible.'

I was shocked. 'Really, it's nothing to do with that. Nothing!' I hugged her. 'Honestly. He thinks the world of you.'

She shook her head, and continued to cry, her beautiful face going blotched and ravaged. At one point, she raised her head to look at me and, for the first time, looked every one of her fifty years. I realized that Stephen, with the unerring instinct of the practised bully, had indeed picked a fight with the most vulnerable person in the room.

'I'm so sorry, Vanessa,' I said, again. 'So sorry.'

She sniffed and blew her nose. 'It's not your fault. You don't have to make the excuses.' She patted my hand.

I almost told her everything there and then, but she was in no state to receive confidences. After a while, she told me to go back downstairs.

'I'll be fine, now, I promise. I'll just have a bath, and go to bed. Tell Anne I'll probably slip away early in the morning because someone's coming about the garden at nine. I feel so embarrassed – Anne works so hard to make everything perfect, and then I spoil it by doing something like this.'

I told her that Anne would understand, and that we all did things 'like this' from time to time. As I shut the door softly, she called out. 'Suzy?'

I stopped, and turned around. 'Yes?'

'Thank you.'

In the kitchen Anne and Clarissa were doing the washing up, which surprised me. Clarissa was obviously a much closer friend than I'd realized if she was allowed in the kitchen after dinner. I offered to help, and Anne, in her usual tranquil, self-contained way, refused. 'Just go to bed.'

When you know you're in the wrong, you can get paranoid, but when Clarissa turned a face of pure hostility to me, I was sure that Podge had already told her what he'd seen. It was just a question of whether Clarissa had passed it on to Anne.

'Goodnight,' I said, into the air of tension.

Neither of them answered.

As I walked away, a rush of hot rage engulfed me. Anne had done absolutely nothing to help her oldest friend. Max had tried to divert the conversation several times. If Anne had done more than simply sit there, looking elegant and interested and providing delicious food, the two of them, as hosts, might have succeeded in stopping Stephen from monopolizing the conversation. But Anne was too busy 'being wonderful' to get her hands dirty psychologically.

It occurred to me that she was supremely selfish. Nobody was ever allowed to criticize Anne – even Max, when mapping out the problems in his marriage, justified her remoteness and coldness as being an understandable consequence of her chronic depressive condition. But her dark silences and inability to give him the love he deserved couldn't be wholly explained that way – even if she was depressive; I had known several others in my time who had hidden their pain behind a façade of gentle smiles, courage and an all-too-self-effacing desire to care for other people far better than they cared for themselves. It wouldn't surprise me, I thought, if Anne was as efficient about her depression as she was about everything else, using it ruthlessly for her own purposes.

*

I looked into the drawing room, and saw Podge, Max and Stephen.

'Another brandy?' asked Stephen. Obviously on a mission to be obnoxious, he was still explaining why he was right to have said what he did.

Max looked at his watch, and cocked an eye at me. I nodded. Frankly, once he was that drunk, he'd get belligerent if you tried to stop him having any more, and with any luck he'd just pass out.

He didn't. Max propelled him upstairs about fifteen minutes later, after I'd heard Podge and Clarissa drive away, calling their thank-yous into the night. As Stephen stopped in the loo, Max put his head into our room looking worried. 'Will you be all right?'

I nodded. 'I've seen it all before. He's difficult, not dangerous.'

'I hate leaving him with you like that.' He put his hand to my cheek, and I held it.

A loud rush of water announced Stephen's return, and he walked, almost in a straight line, into our bedroom with his arms open. 'Suzy. The love of my life. Come to me.'

Desperately wishing I didn't have to shut the door on Max, I ignored him, and began unzipping my dress. 'Why were you so beastly to Vanessa?'

'Dearest, you simply don't understand. And neither does she.'

'I don't care about historical integrity, I just don't think you should have made her cry.' I stepped out of the dress, disliking the way his eyes followed me. I picked up my pyjamas, and decided to finish undressing in the bathroom.

'Don't wear those.'

The past few months had been balanced on neither of us refusing the other anything that was asked for. And neither of us asking anything that might be refused.

I left the pyjamas on the bed, but came back wrapped in a towel, having spent as long as possible doing my teeth and removing my make-up, in the hope that he was drunk enough to have fallen asleep.

He wasn't. I slid into bed as modestly as possible.

Too late. 'You've got slimmer. Lost your pot belly.' He assessed me with what looked like unfocused lust.

I ignored this and picked up my book. A hand snaked out, and wriggled under the bedclothes to my thigh. It felt cold and slimy, like a dead fish against my flesh, as it moved upwards.

I pretended not to notice.

'It's been a long time.' The maudlin note in his voice gave me hope. He might still fall asleep before we got to the point where I had to say either 'No' or 'Yes'.

'Well, quite a lot's happened,' I said, in my best bright teacher voice, not taking my eyes off the book.

The hand snaked further up and started hopefully twiddling my nipples, as if looking for a particularly obscure radio frequency.

I couldn't bear to be scrabbled at. I knew I wasn't going to get away without either a massive, quite possibly violent, row, or just giving in.

It would be quicker and less messy to give in now. Feeling sick, I put down the book and turned to him.

With a sigh of satisfaction, he launched himself on top.

Even in his muddled state, he realized that this was a bit sudden. He looked down at me. 'Are you sure you're ready, darling?'

I felt like shrieking 'Just get on with it', but murmured something appropriate.

It went on for ages. I counted to a hundred in my head (twice), then tried to make the best of it by telling myself that this could, perhaps, offer me some pleasure if I tried. It couldn't – in fact, it grew increasingly painful, as he pushed me and pulled me around, desperately sawing up and down, completely shut off in his own world by the alcohol. He was like an automaton.

Eventually I decided to switch my mind off from the experience entirely, and got through the last bit by trying to think of recipes you could cook if you had a vegetarian, a diabetic, someone on a wheat-free diet and another with an allergy to peanuts all coming to dinner at once. After what seemed like forever, he let out a shout, twitched like a landed fish, and slumped on top of me with the weight of a bag of concrete. I lay there for as long as seemed polite and edged out from underneath him.

He lay snoring and I lay awake, staring at the spidery lines that criss-crossed Stonehill's magnificent ceilings.

When we got back to London, I made a decision to betray the people I love the most in the whole universe, hurting them in the deepest way possible. I decided to leave, knowing that I would take the girls' sense of home with me. If you think one can say that they are already

411

grown-up, that they don't care and that they have their own lives to lead, you are wrong. If you allow yourself to believe that it doesn't scar them deeply not to know where to call home, or to see their parents bewildered, torn apart and in pain, you are wrong again. You are deceiving yourself and them.

But in spite of all the pain I knew I'd inflict, I also knew, now, what had been missing in my life with Stephen. Love. Real grown-up love. Not passion in that feverish, trembling, can't-live-without-hearing-your-voice desperation, not the kind of love that sits by a telephone and waits, feeling sick, for a call, but the passion that comes with understanding. When I finally understood Stephen, all the passion went, and what was left just wasn't enough. I remembered Barry saying that: 'It's not enough, Suzy, it's just not enough.'

I didn't know how Max and I would manage, but at least we would be together. We would have love. And that is why I had to leave.

33

Deciding something is one thing. Doing it is quite another.

Firstly, how and when do you say that you are going? I refused the easy way out: the letter on the mantelpiece. I knew I couldn't avoid a confrontation, and Stephen would have to be the first to know. We would have to decide on how to tell Polly and Jess together.

I lined up two cases in the hall. After so many months of living out of a suitcase, this was the easiest part. Truffle, who knew what suitcases meant, wound herself around my legs, occasionally looking up and mewing, showing a pink mouth and indignant eyes. How could I leave her to a man who worked twelve hours a day? I felt invisible silk cords tighten around me as she wove in and out. Now I knew what it was like to be Gulliver, anchored to earth by thousands of tiny ties.

'I'm sorry, Truffle,' I said, meaning it. I bent down and tickled her gently under the chin. 'I promise I'll come to get you when I have somewhere to live.'

I was standing in the hall when he turned the key in the lock.

'What's the meaning of these?' He knew, instantly and exactly, what their meaning was. He just had to ask.

'I'm going. For good this time. I'm sorry.'

His face flushed a dark, angry red, mottled with distress.

'We've been through all this, for God's sake. You really are the most selfish bitch I've ever come across. What about the house? Don't tell me you're screwing that up again?'

I nodded. 'I never agreed to buy it.'

His face turned ugly. 'As good as. As good as. Now you've changed your mind again. You utter bitch,' he repeated. 'You total hundred-carat diamond-hard cunt.'

I flinched, just beginning to feel slightly frightened. He stood between me and the door, and both his fists were clenched.

'I've given you fucking everything,' he roared. 'Everything you ever fucking wanted. Children, a family, you're going to have your own business, a lovely house, what more can you want?'

'I'm glad you asked that. I want love. Or the chance of love. Whatever we had in that respect has gone long ago.' I hugged myself tightly, willing the scene to be over soon.

'Love!' He sneered at me. 'Who do you think is really going to want you? You're forty-six bloody years old! Wake up and smell the coffee! And speaking of love, motherly love, the kind of love you seem to have forgotten about entirely, do you think the girls will ever forgive you? Not while I have breath in my body! Because the one thing you do owe me is that you have to be absolutely bloody honest about this. *You* are leaving *me*. I haven't done anything to cause this. You choose to go. I haven't been unfaithful, I haven't become a drunk

414

or a gambler or committed a fraud, or been violent. I've tried, God knows I've tried, to make you happy. You are not a person who can be made happy. You are a spoilt, selfish bitch.'

Suddenly the air went out of him, like a punctured balloon, and he leant against the door, banging it with his fists and sobbing. 'I take it back, Suzy, I take it all back. I just don't want you to go.'

I closed my eyes. 'Please, Stephen, let me go.'

It took half an hour. He told me I was mad, and that he could get me sectioned. He told me he was seriously worried about me, and would do everything he could to support me while I was going through this manic depressive state. He blamed the menopause, the fact we now had more money, my sense of insecurity now that he was so successful, the burglary and the children leaving home.

He said everything he possibly could, but, finally, he said: 'You needn't think that you can live on my money – I'll fight you every bit of the way. It's going to take you a long, long time to get as little as possible. That I can promise you. I've got a reputation to maintain and I won't settle for living in some dingy bedsit while you swan about on my earnings.'

'I don't want you to live in a dingy bedsit, and I'm not going to swan,' I whispered. 'I only want what's fair. I've contributed to this marriage too, you know.'

'Fair! Fair! It's not fucking fair that you can take a single penny of my money.'

'It's our money. And there's plenty for both of us.'

'Plenty,' he sneered. 'Hardly. You and your small-town

ambitions. No wonder I had to keep things hidden from you. You couldn't have coped.'

'You only care about the money,' I said. 'If I thought you actually cared about me, it might have been different.'

'Dream on!' He punched the wall again with his fist. 'Fucking dream on.'

I flinched, revolted. And frightened.

I dragged the suitcases out of the door and down to the street to find a taxi. He didn't follow me into the lift. As I closed its old-fashioned wire gates, I heard our flat door slam.

Vanessa hadn't said anything about Stephen as she'd slipped quietly out of Stonehill on Sunday morning, but she'd pressed a key into my hand. 'Just in case.'

I phoned Max from Vanessa's house. He answered the phone.

'Suzy.' He sounded exhausted, and slightly distracted, as if he had to remind himself who I was.

'Max, I've done it.'

There was a complete silence, so I had to repeat myself.

'I've done it. I've left Stephen.'

There was still no response, so I added. 'For ever, Max. It's for ever, this time.'

I found myself counting the seconds as I waited for his reply. One, two, three, he can hardly believe it and is too delighted to speak. Four, five, six, he still hasn't heard me properly. Seven, eight, nine, there's someone in the room, and he can't talk.

Ten.

'Suzy. I'm sorry.' His voice was heavy. 'I can't leave. Not now. Not yet.'

It was my turn to be silent.

'I'm sorry, Suzy,' he repeated. 'It's Anne. She's been in hospital. I can't walk out on that.' Anne, it transpired, had made a suicide attempt on Sunday evening. Max had found her 'before any harm could be done, thank God', and had called an ambulance. 'I've been up all night, and at the hospital all day. She's home now, but the doctors say she's very fragile. Anything could push her over the edge again.

'I love you, Suzy, more than anything, but I can't leave now. Surely you see that.'

I didn't believe that Anne was fragile. 'Do you have proof, that what she suffers from is really depression and not terminal selfishness?' I asked. I should have been more sympathetic, I suppose.

'I've lived with this for a long time, Suzy.' Max's voice was tinged with frustration. 'It isn't easy for her. Or for me. Or for you. When you're looking at another person's pain, you can't slice it up and analyse it, and decide which bits you believe in.'

'I think,' my voice was shaking with fear, disappointment and anger, 'that Anne is rather more in control than you realize. She knew, on Saturday night, that you'd been seeing me. That's why she invited Podge and Clarissa. To confirm it. And she knew you'd find her if she faked a suicide attempt.' I couldn't believe how brutal I sounded.

Max sounded unutterably weary. 'We've no proof of that. And I can't take the risk. I just can't.'

'Well,' I clutched the telephone, feeling cold and frightened, 'you can't have me and her. There'll never be a right time to leave. Anne will see to that. A divorce would endanger her precious Stonehill, and she won't have it.' I felt like a child, behind a plate-glass window, desperately scrabbling to reach something I could see but not touch. 'It's time to choose, Max, it's time to choose.'

'I'm sorry, Suzy,' was all he said. 'Desperately, desperately sorry.'

I let the telephone fall back into its socket, and sat there, trembling.

Had I been stupid and thoughtless to make him choose now? Of course, I had. He couldn't leave a seriously ill woman, just because I asked him to. She might be really at risk. I almost picked up the phone, to call him back and to say that I'd have him on any terms, any terms at all. I would wait for years for him, for centuries even. All I wanted was to have his arms around me again.

But I couldn't unsay what I'd said. I knew Max very well and so did Anne, and we both knew that he would never leave anyone in trouble. This particular attack of 'depression' was just too convenient. I believed that what I'd told him about Anne and the divorce was true. I wondered what form the 'suicide attempt' had taken. Even if you know you're going to be found, that takes a lot of determination and courage. Anne was going to hang on until the end, and Max simply wasn't ruthless enough. He was a kind man, and Anne would exploit that as if it was a weakness.

I never, at any point, thought that Anne's suicide attempt had been genuine. It was too convenient.

And I couldn't go back to Stephen. I'd already discovered that going back doesn't work.

I thought of that fragment of song. 'You're the link in my daisy chain.' I used to make daisy chains when I was a child, but the fragile grassy stems often split under my eager fingernails. I would try to repair the damage by making a link in another place, or threading the flower through differently, but the more I tried to fix it, the more it would fall apart. In the end, I'd have to throw away the broken, bruised flowers and pick more, but the sight of the discarded daisies dying on the grass would seem like such cruel, wanton destruction, that I'd often stop, saddened, and go inside. You can't mend a daisy chain.

I sat alone in Vanessa's house, trying not to panic. I had no home, very little money, and a part-time, badly paid job. Nothing now stood between me and that parallel universe.

Fear is like a parasite. Once it has found a way into a host body, it spreads, colonizing parts it could never have reached from the outside. Fear of burglary becomes a fear of strangers, of crowded places, then of being alone, then of everything. Wide spaces, confined spaces, new places and old places. Fear works its way insidiously into them all. I think it even burrows its way into your genes, and is passed on. Perhaps that was why Max, the child of people who had been hounded out of their homes or murdered, had understood it, while Stephen had merely been impatient.

But without either of them – Stephen or Max – I had only fear, from the tips of my toes to the top of my head. It was time to reclaim some of the territory the parasite had taken.

Think. I walked up and down. The only way is forward. Start with the practical side. Begin with whatever is easiest.

That had to be the plans for my new business. They were already concrete, with tentative financing in place. I needed to find somewhere that could be a home, and a base for it.

My solicitor confirmed that, although we couldn't be divorced for two years – or five if Stephen dragged his feet over it – Stephen was obliged to pay me some maintenance immediately. 'And we've sold our house fairly recently,' I said down the phone, trying to suppress the trembling in my voice. 'As it was in our joint names, could I get my share out before everything else is finalized?'

Indeed, I could.

Still shaking, I rang the estate agents about the Eggleton property, to check that it was under offer.

'Yes,' chirped the girl. 'I'll consult my colleague, but we were talking about it on Friday, so I'm pretty sure it's gone.'

She came back. 'Well, actually it was under offer, but in fact the purchaser dropped out this morning.'

I took this to be a wonderful, brilliant, overwhelmingly

positive omen. I went to see it that very day, taking Vanessa with me.

She shrieked in horror. 'Darling! Absolutely not possible! Listen, dearest, it has a tree growing through one of the bedrooms. Trees are meant to grow in gardens, not bedrooms. Even my architect wouldn't suggest such a thing.' She thought for a minute. 'Although I must mention it to him.'

'It's incredibly cheap.'

'That's because,' she spoke as if to a small child, 'no one can live in it. It's falling down and needs very, very expensive, specialist repairs.'

'It would have five or six bedrooms. I could do bed and breakfast, which would improve my cash flow, and I could use the shop to sell my furniture.'

'Would anyone come all the way to Eggleton to buy stuff?'

'Probably not. But I could use it as a workshop as well and drive pieces into London or Ipswich to be sold.'

'Mm.' She was coming round to it. 'It's a pretty village. And you could stay at Merlins while you're doing it up. I'd feel happier about having someone in the house when I'm away.' I was warmed by Vanessa's generosity as she had a perfectly good burglar alarm.

It wasn't so much the prettiness of the village that drew me. It was the enclosed feeling, the way everyone's windows looked out over the village green. There were no high hedges or long drives, no walls or fences above shoulder height. What Stephen would have called 'overlooked' seemed like safety to me. If you're frightened – and I was, particularly at the prospect of living alone –

either you live behind locks and bars, with twenty-four-hour porters and CCTV cameras, or you live somewhere where people can see who comes and goes. I couldn't afford the former, and I liked the latter better. Because it had been a shop, it was right in the middle of things.

Cheap or not, my more immediate problem was getting the money from somewhere.

But I'd been restricted by common sense and hampered by worry for too long. If I was ever going to beat the gremlins I'd have to be brave, and it might as well start with being brave about money. I remembered Barry counting the years ahead, and dying before he could live them. I didn't want to waste any more of my own life. I put in an offer and it was accepted.

We stopped off at the square grey church to visit Barry's grave on the way back, because I wanted to thank him – not, of course, that I told Vanessa exactly that.

'It's funny,' said Vanessa in the churchyard. 'But I thought there'd be more sense of him here. In this lovely place.'

We looked at the wooden cross, awaiting its specially designed headstone. There was a posy of weeds in a jam jar: sea lavender, gorse, dune grass and the very last blackberries clinging on to the remains of autumn.

'It must be children. How sweet,' Vanessa blew her nose. 'Rather pretty in a naïve way. It makes me think of the sea. Barry loved the sea.'

I went to see Louise at her Camberwell art gallery.

She exuded enthusiasm: 'Look!' She immediately drew me into the back. 'I just love this new artist I'm representing. I haven't had time to hang this yet, but come and see.' I followed her into the back, past a bucket. 'Sorry about that,' she indicated it. 'Can't mend the roof, I'm afraid. Still, if this chap takes off, I might be able to. In this job, you're always chasing the next rainbow.'

The painting was a blaze of brilliant blue, a shoreline with a few tiny pastel houses at the tip of it.

'I've changed my life,' I told her.

She smiled. 'I thought you might have done. You look better. Less tired.'

'I feel as if I could climb a mountain and fly off the top. Sometimes. At others, I feel too tired to put one foot in front of another.'

'I know exactly what you mean. But you'll come out the other side. It goes like that. But be kind to yourself.'

I wasn't sure what she was getting at.

'Climbing all these mountains,' she explained. 'It's essential to do it, because when you get to the top of one you feel so much better about yourself and the rest of the world. But don't try to do everything in one go. Give yourself lots of treats along the way.' She lit a cigarette, and I saw how thin her slightly trembling wrist was. 'I'm probably not making much sense. But one of the things about . . . well, violence . . . is that it makes you feel worthless. And treats, not self-destructive ones like this, mind –' she indicated the newly lit cigarette and stubbed it out again '– are a way of telling yourself you're not. Heigh ho, I must give up.' She gave me a dazzling smile. 'Every day, I say that. I'll get there in the end. But hey, one mountain at a time.'

I showed her some photos of my work. She liked it.

'I might be able to sell the odd piece but I don't have a lot of space. But . . .' she brightened. 'I'd like to do an "affordable art" exhibition some time next summer. Show lots of fun things that people don't have to take too seriously. You'd be great in that.'

'I'm sorry I couldn't be more help,' she said, as she followed me to the door. 'All I'd say is believe in yourself and go for it. Just don't look down.'

As I left, I realized I'd made my first friend as a single person. Someone who knew me as Suzy, not as Stephen-and-Suzy.

Once I'd calculated what I'd need I worked out a business plan, adding two to three bed-and-breakfast rooms to the furniture-painting business, and I took it back to a bank, ultimately underpinned by my divorce settlement. If Stephen was seriously going to fight, though, we'd both be left with very little after the legal fees. I just hoped that he'd see that too, before it was too late. Vanessa had called him stingy, which might be the saving of it all.

My solicitor, George Black, reported back to say that our house – *our* house – had been in Stephen's name only, and that, as a result, there were no capital sums that I could extract from it until everything was settled. 'Did you actually check that it was in both your names?'

Feeling panicky, I tried to think. I'd left all that to Stephen. 'But some money I inherited from my parents paid off part of the mortgage.'

George sighed. 'It doesn't mean a thing without your name on it. It's a common mistake, I'm afraid. And, by the way, he won't agree to a divorce. You'll have to wait five years before you can get anything more than the most basic maintenance out of him. Unless, of course, you want to petition for adultery or unreasonable behaviour . . .' He left the question hanging in the air.

I couldn't do that to Stephen, and the girls would be even more hurt and angry. As he'd said, it was my choice to leave. Anyway, I wasn't sure I could make unreasonable behaviour stick. Everybody else seemed to think he was so wonderful.

'Speaking of maintenance,' he added. 'Your husband seems to be claiming that his salary is very low, considering how high-profile he is. Sometimes this happens when people want to minimize their assets for the divorce. They channel as much money as possible into their business.'

'He's been doing that for years,' I replied, wearily. 'Can't you check the business accounts?'

'He won't let us see them. We'll have to go to court to insist.'

And so it went on. I could see that Stephen was determined to make everything as difficult as possible.

'We'll get it in the end.' George tried to sound positive as he rang off, but we both knew we were in for a fight.

Vanessa, just emerging from probate, offered me a loan until the divorce. I promised to pay interest. I was going to be in debt – literally hundreds of thousands of pounds' worth to Vanessa and the bank – until I could get the divorce settlement.

I told Alice that I would be leaving, but offered to supply her with furniture. She looked offended.

'Really! It's very inconsiderate of you.' She switched tack in typical, illogical Alice manner. 'But as it happens I won't be able to take any furniture, because I'm selling up.'

It turned out that she'd been applying to get a change of use for the shop, and having finally got permission to have it turned into a restaurant, now had a buyer lined up. No wonder she'd never been particularly worried about profit.

'What will you do with the stock?'

She paused. 'Well. You might as well have it.'

I was astounded. Alice was not usually generous.

'I'm very aware,' she said stiffly, 'that the shop's made a bit of a profit since you started here, which it wouldn't have done otherwise, so I think you deserve to have the lot for nothing if you promise to take it away.'

I shocked us both by bursting into tears.

'Hang on.' She sounded alarmed.

'It's just so nice of you,' I sobbed. 'I wasn't expecting anyone to be nice.'

'Well, you probably need that crap more than I do,' she retorted, reverting to Alice mode, but she gave me her address and telephone number and asked me to stay in touch.

'Good luck,' she added. 'It's not really my thing, I prefer proper antiques really, but I'll try to buy something when you open up on your own.'

Within a month, The Old Bakery was mine, and I had enough money to convert it and start the business. Every penny of it borrowed.

'You used to be terrified of having an overdraft,'

Vanessa reminded me. 'You used to feel completely dominated by it.'

'Ah, but that was then,' I told her. I was beginning to learn that you can't go on being frightened for ever.

The worst part was telling Polly and Jess. Stephen insisted we do it together, one Sunday morning, at the flat. He didn't want me poisoning their minds against him, he said.

I promised that I had no intention of doing any such thing.

And he emphasized that I must make it clear that tearing the family apart was entirely my decision, and that he was not going to take any responsibility for it.

We all assembled in the sitting room, with an air of expectation, as if it was Christmas or someone's birthday.

Until I told them.

They couldn't understand it.

Polly, her pale blue eyes stunned with shock, literally locked her hands together in supplication. 'Please don't do this without thinking more carefully. You've been so funny since that burglary, you're probably still not right from that.'

That caught me unawares. Could she be right? I wavered, then tried to remember everything else. The secret bank account, the baby we hadn't been able to have, our arguments and the last few months of stilted concern shimmered in the past, difficult to grasp in the face of her ashen horror.

'I'm sorry, darling, I have thought. Very carefully indeed. I'm terribly, terribly sorry.'

'No, Mummy, no.' She hunched up, wrapping her arms around her shoulders defensively, as a tear slowly dripped down the side of her nose. 'Where will we live?'

'You'll have two homes, one with your father and one with me. He's going to stay in this flat until he finds somewhere he wants to buy, and I'm going to live in a little village called Eggleton. You'll be able to have your own bedrooms, when it's finished. I hope you'll come and choose the colours.'

Their eyes told me that they were no longer children, to be fobbed off with a pleasant little diversion.

'But why?' Jess was incredulous.

'Your father and I care for each other, still, but we just can't live with each other any more.' It's so useful to have a cliché when you really don't want to tell anyone the truth.

Stephen cleared his throat, and raised his eyebrows. 'I can live with you. I didn't want any of this.'

'It doesn't make sense.' Jess was always the uncompromising one. 'None of this makes any sense so far.'

Stephen spoke quietly, as if he was grieving. 'Mummy found a bank account I hadn't told her about. She felt I was lying to her.'

The girls looked disbelieving. 'You're leaving Daddy because of a *bank account*?' asked Jess. Her voice shook, as if she was trying not to cry. 'I don't understand.'

'And,' Stephen swallowed again, doing an excellent impersonation of a contrite man, 'I very stupidly tried to rush her into buying a house that she hadn't seen. It was wrong of me, I know that now . . .' He spread his arms in self-deprecation.

428

'Poor Daddy!' Polly jumped up and ran to him, and his arms folded around her. 'Daddy, I still love you.' She began to cry, hopelessly, like a child abandoned. 'I love you.'

'Everyone makes mistakes,' said Stephen hoarsely. 'I'm just so terribly sorry.'

Jess glared at me, her hands on her hips. 'And did you think about us amongst all these problems with bank accounts and houses? Did you care at all?'

'You've always been what I most care about in the world,' I told her, my face burning.

'I don't think so,' said Jess. 'I really don't think so. Don't come back unless you're coming back for good. We don't want to see you.'

I tried to tell them that I loved them desperately, and that I wasn't leaving them, only their father, but they both drew closer to Stephen. Their eyes told me that if I did love them, I would never have gone.

Stephen tightened each arm round them both – Polly was now making small snuffling noises into his jacket – and kissed the tops of their heads in turn. 'Sh, darlings. I'm here.' Jess had one hand on her hip, and stood defiantly. The three of them together, and apart from me. He looked up: 'I think you'd better go now. You've said your bit.'

'You're determined to make this as difficult as possible, Stephen. The girls didn't have to be put through a scene like this.'

'There isn't an easy way through what you're doing,' he replied. 'You need to see the pain you're causing, Suzy. You have to see the pain.'

I stumbled out of the flat and into Vanessa's car unable to see anything for tears. She'd been determined that someone should be around 'in case he hits you, or something frightful like that', and had offered to drive me over. 'I knew that bastard wasn't going to make it easy for you.'

'It wasn't him,' I sobbed. 'It was them. They hate me now. And they're suffering so much, and I did it. I always used to kiss them better when they got hurt. They never, never expected me to be the one who hurt them.'

When I rang him the following day to find out how they were, he told me that Polly had moved back into the flat temporarily, and had spent the rest of the day crying uncontrollably. 'I had to give her a sleeping pill in the end.' Jess had gone back to university, furiously angry with me. 'I really wouldn't try to contact her, Suzy, she doesn't want to hear from you.'

Nevertheless I wrote them letters, one to Polly's flat and the other to Jess's student lodgings, asking for their forgiveness, hoping that one day they would understand, and telling them they still had two parents who loved them very dearly. I wasn't leaving them, I told them, only separating from their father. They were returned, unopened, to Stephen, who took great pleasure in sending them on to me at Vanessa's. 'They don't even want to know your address.'

Vanessa, outraged on my behalf, thought the girls were adult enough to know how complicated love could be. 'I mean, darling, would they want to be married to somebody who was mean? Who told lies? And haven't they ever just come to the end of the road with a boyfriend?'

'They've lived with Stephen all their lives, Vanessa. They can't understand why I can't do it any longer. And if I've destroyed their faith in one parent, it certainly isn't going to make it any better destroying their faith in the other.'

I couldn't face telling her, and definitely not them, about how dead I'd felt when we last made love. Or the other little things, like his humiliation of Vanessa, his jealousy of Max, and, less trivially, the fact that I didn't believe he loved me either. I was now fairly sure that the only real reason, right deep down, that he didn't want a divorce was that he didn't want to split his assets in half. And, of course, he was furious and humiliated that I'd been the one to leave. It would have been quite a different matter, I thought, if Stephen Everett of the Crown Project, media pundit, style guru and author-to-be had found a high-profile and successful blonde as arm candy. Everyone would merely have commented that successful men often outgrow their dowdy first wives.

'I just hope he finds someone else soon.' I could hardly speak for crying, tasting the tears on the edge of my lips when I spoke. 'Someone nice and rich and successful who he can't bully.'

'Darling, no one would want that horrible man,' declared Vanessa, who, now that she had switched into loyalty mode, and especially since the dinner party at Stonehill, would not hear a good word about Stephen.

She liked her issues in black and white, and put an arm round me, rocking me gently, as if I was a child. 'Sh. There, there. Let's open an enormous bottle of champagne to cheer you up.'

34

I managed to exchange contracts and start work on The Old Bakery before Christmas. As no one was living there, the builders – John, Dave and Mervyn – were able to move in before we completed, which gave us three weeks' work before everything ground to a standstill until after New Year.

It was three weeks of pure destruction, of tearing down bricks, removing vegetation (as well as the tree, there was a jungle of ivy working its way through the walls) and propping up ceilings. Tarpaulins were stretched over the roof and whole sections of wall came down. I worked alongside the builders, bagging up smaller rubbish, clearing the wilderness garden, making sure that nothing was thrown away that could be used later. I found a beautiful claw-footed iron bath in the undergrowth, and a surprisingly intact white china Belfast sink in a side shed.

I made sure that I worked too hard to be able to speak at the end of the day, in order to ensure that my aching muscles and throbbing bones muffled the more powerful pain deeper down, where my memories of the girls tortured me as if I'd been cut open without an anaesthetic. However often Vanessa reassured me that they had their own lives, and that they'd left home, I knew that I had hurt them more than anyone else in their lives ever had. And there was nothing I could do to take that pain away.

'Where they live now isn't the point,' I told her. 'When your children need you, they need you, and you can't predict when that will be.'

'If they need you, they'll find you,' reassured Vanessa.

'Unless Stephen's turned them against me completely.'

Stephen and I had agreed that everything must be done to minimize the effect on them. 'But you can't eradicate what they feel,' he'd told me sharply. 'They're shattered. They say that if you hadn't chosen to leave, we'd still be a happy family. It was your decision, and your choice. The rest of us have just had to fit in with you. That's what they think.'

I was so determined not to antagonize him further that I didn't say that no one ever walks out on a completely happy family.

According to reports that trickled through from various people, the girls were being 'wonderful', going back to the flat regularly because they were 'worried about Stephen', making sure that he had food in the fridge and cooking him meals from time to time. Rumour had it, via the same grapevine, that Stephen was absolutely devastated by my desertion, that he'd lost about a stone in weight, and that he was working even longer, harder hours in order to 'deal with it'.

'It's not fair,' I screamed to Vanessa when she passed this on one evening, having decided to join me at Merlins for a few days' 'rest'.

'He's perfectly capable of going to a supermarket himself. He can fill a fridge, boil an egg, and order a takeaway. He can even cook quite well, for heaven's sake. Why is he making the girls feel responsible for his wellbeing?'

'He's a broken husk, Moira Etherington-Thomas said.' Vanessa looked mischievous. 'A broken husk of a man.'

'They need a father, not a broken husk of a man.'

'Well,' said Vanessa. 'It is quite difficult dealing with things on your own. They did have two parents, and now they only have one.'

'Actually,' I pointed out, 'they still have two parents, it's just that everyone refuses to acknowledge that. And you can bet your bottom dollar that Stephen is not trying to persuade them to see me or forgive me, or to let me comfort them. He is not, absolutely not, mentioning that there were a few little problems in our marriage that were not created by me alone.'

Vanessa shuddered. 'Just a few.'

I had hoped that Christmas might provide an opportunity to start mending bridges.

'I'm taking them skiing,' Stephen told me on the phone the next day, with satisfaction. 'We all feel that it would help us get through this first Christmas if we did something completely different.'

'Oh. Of course. Well, I hope you have a nice time. Could I send you their presents?'

'I hope you're not trying to buy them back with expensive gifts,' he said, sharply. 'They're too hurt to fall for that.'

I used every ounce of will power I had to remind him, apparently casually, that we had both agreed that the

435

girls' happiness must be paramount in everything we did.

'The girls' happiness *is* paramount in everything *I* do,' he asserted.

I ignored that. 'I do worry that they'd only feel worse if they felt honour-bound to send my presents back. So would you make sure they get them? I'm sure they'd take them from you.' I made myself sound as humble and grateful as I possibly could, fingers silently crossed.

There was a silence. 'I can't guarantee anything, of course,' he said in a huffy tone of voice, 'but obviously I'll do my best.'

'They're not expensive,' I reassured him. I couldn't, in fact, imagine what I could give them. They seemed so remote from me now. In the end, I settled for pretty, but rather anonymous, presents that Vanessa helped me buy, and which I really couldn't afford: delicious bath oils and a silky dressing gown for Polly, and a cashmere sweater for Jess because I worried that she might not realize how cold it would be in a ski resort. I had never spent so much money on them before, not ever, and simply trusted that Stephen wouldn't realize it.

Vanessa and I both wanted to ignore Christmas altogether. She decided not to give her annual Christmas Eve 'drinks for neighbours'.

'Just think, darling, it was only a year ago that Barry was standing there beside me.'

And I didn't want to be invited to Stonehill. Of all the holes that had appeared in my life, the absence of Max was the biggest, most gaping and the one that was most likely to trip me up when I least expected. Everything reminded me of him. Going past couples in restaurants hurt – even ones we hadn't been to together. Browsing in bookshops did too, because I suddenly realized that for the past year I'd mentally, secretly, been buying for both of us. I'd look at the jacket of a book and think: 'Would Max like it? Would he and I agree on it, or would we have one of our happy, teasing arguments about it?' But I had resolved, when I put the phone down the day I left Stephen, that I would not contact him. I would only get sucked in again, and I'd never be able to concentrate on making a new life for myself. I had no idea, therefore, whether he'd realized I'd meant it when I'd left Stephen. I assumed Stephen would have told him, but I begged Vanessa not to mention it, and she had reluctantly agreed. 'They'll find out from someone. Stephen will talk about it. Don't you want to put your side of the story first?'

'Really, Vanessa,' I told her wearily, 'I don't want anyone to take sides. Stephen is Max's oldest friend, and I don't want to put him and Anne in a difficult position.'

'But Max introduced you, didn't he?' she asked. 'I'm sure I remember you telling me that that's how you met Stephen.'

I remembered Stephen cutting into my halting conversation with Max at Hell's Basement all those years ago. 'I wouldn't call it an introduction. But, anyway, that makes it all even more awkward.' I was brisk. 'Honestly, I'd be happier not to have any contact at all with Stonehill.' I longed to confide in her, but I might as well take out an advertisement in all the major newspapers.

And a small voice inside told me that if Max cared, if

he really loved me, then he'd find out how I was. He must be wondering how I was surviving, surely? Perversely my pride was wounded at the thought that people might feel sorry for me, and tell him what a tough time I was having, but I felt equally furious at the thought that anyone might tell him that I was absolutely fine. I wanted him to worry.

Vanessa's voice broke my reverie. 'They do give very good parties, and a good time is what we both need at the moment.' She sounded wistful.

'You go, Vanessa. You go.' And I squeezed her lightly on the shoulder and set off for my last day on the site before everything came to a complete halt until after the New Year.

I didn't feel that I deserved parties, or presents, or a good time. I deserved to be utterly, thoroughly miserable, the way I'd made everyone else feel.

As it turned out, I wasn't. I actually enjoyed myself during the fortnight that spanned Christmas and the New Year, apart from the constant ache of missing Max and the gnawing anguish of the girls' rejection. The contents of The Past had been transported to Vanessa's disused barn, and I started painting and converting several of the pieces. It was an old brick tithe barn, dating from the fourteenth century: very pretty but bitterly cold, especially as I had to have the big barn door open in order to get the light. I could see my breath as I worked, but I could also see out of the barn every time I looked up, across the marshes, and the sense of space under the huge vaulted sky lifted my spirits.

Once Vanessa had packed up the London house and finished the London parties – about a week before Christmas – she stayed at Merlins and took an interest in what I was doing. Every morning, at about eleven o'clock, bundled up as if she was going skiing, she brought us two cups of steaming coffee, and sat down on a yet-to-be-converted chair to talk.

'Really, you ought to write about this for a magazine,' she said, one day. 'Lots of them publish DIY pages, but none of the things in them are as much fun as yours.'

I stopped. Not a bad idea. I spent two whole days taking photographs of the things I did, typing out step-by-step instructions and sending them off, with a letter suggesting a series to about ten magazines. I didn't expect to hear from any of them.

And after twenty-something years of sorting and clearing, storing and stacking, shopping, slicing, peeling and chopping, washing and ironing, wrapping and garnishing, and driving, collecting, meeting and reassuring, just looking after myself was utter, if slightly guilt-inducing, bliss. Vanessa's house, of course, was brilliantly comfortable, and we took turns to cook. Vanessa went out more than I did; several times to Stonehill. When she returned she didn't say anything about who'd been there, or how everyone had been and I didn't ask her. It became a little no-go zone between us.

Vanessa minded being something of a social outcast much more than I did: 'I'm more popular as a widow than a divorcee,' she mused, 'but still definitely seen as a destabilizing influence.' But she often chivvied me to accompany her out, and provided it was nowhere I knew well, or to anyone who might know Max, Anne or Stephen, I went.

I couldn't bear the quizzical 'But you always seemed so happy,' or the astonished, slightly defensive 'We always thought you were the perfect couple.' People wanted to know why, they wanted to make sense of it all, or to reassure themselves that it could never happen to them. I couldn't see any point in trying to blacken Stephen's name in order to defend myself. Lots of people have much worse partners but they love them enough to forgive them. I'd discovered that I didn't. That was my failure as much as his.

Even worse, I occasionally met other women who looked at me with cautious amazement, as if I was a heroine who'd been parachuted into enemy territory. These always took Vanessa's telephone number, looking nervously over their shoulders, and insisted that we must, absolutely must, have lunch, desperate to strip me of every ounce of wisdom or advice I might have. I knew that they'd link everything I said to a similar – or perhaps completely different – situation in their own marriages. It might be selfish of me, but I simply didn't have the energy to get involved in anyone else's problems yet.

Most of all, though, I found casual remarks about my daughters desperately hurtful. People would say: 'It must be such a relief to know that they're old enough to look after Stephen,' or 'I gather the girls are being absolutely wonderful to their father, which must make it so much easier for you,' as if I'd deliberately waited until I could pass the responsibility for my husband over to them.

So I met new people instead, and liked them. Merlins

was quite close to Eggleton, so I was putting down the first tentative roots of belonging. Everyone reassured me that Eggleton was a lovely village – 'very quiet and peaceful', they'd say, testing me, as if I might want to wear red dresses with low cleavages and dance on the tables every Friday night.

'Good,' I said, over and over again. 'I'm looking forward to quiet and peaceful.' The shape of my future in Eggleton still wasn't clear to me, but people were beginning to say 'Good morning' or 'Good afternoon' when they passed me on the street, and I received the odd nod of recognition in the pub. But I still felt very aware of lacking a home. Merlins, just twenty miles from Eggleton, was heaven, but of a temporary kind, and real life was waiting for me round the corner of the New Year.

On Boxing Day, Vanessa left on one of her mysterious visits to Stonehill. I thought I'd go to Barry's grave again.

I'd started talking to him in my head, maintaining a narrative between two people who'd both walked out on their families. I'd ask him questions, and listen to the answers that wove their way back and forth in my brain, but every so often, I'd want to know, really want to know, what he would actually have thought or said. Then it would be like facing a brick wall as I remembered that he was dead. Every time I thought this, his memory grew a little more fuzzy and two-dimensional and, however hard I tried to conjure up his face, it slipped away from me.

I walked across the bare fields from Merlins to the

church, but as I got halfway across, the sky turned the colour of dull zinc, and huge individual drops of rain began to thud down one by one, in a slow hand-clap. As I got to the church, lightning cracked across the countryside, menacingly close to the church tower. A large black dog raced home through the gravestones, out through the lychgate of the church and down the street. I ran to the porch to shelter from the rain.

I couldn't see the dog's owner, and Max's story about the Black Shuck, the legendary black dog forked with lightning that appears all over Suffolk, made me feel cold and shivery. Nothing else bad could happen now, surely. Barry was dead, my family was in shreds, and, having found Max again after twenty-five years, I'd lost him again and he was now trapped with a suicidal Anne . . . wasn't that enough for one year? I thought of Polly and Jess, and everything hurt again. Please don't let anything happen to them, I prayed.

The rain came down in sheets – you could hardly breathe for the density of water – so I waited in the porch, peering out towards Barry's grave. There was a second's let-up in the stream of water, while the clouds regrouped for a fresh attack, and I could see a slight figure, just standing there. I raced out, gasping with cold and wet.

'Kelly, for God's sake, come in out of this rain.' I seized her arm.

She shook her head, and hunched her shoulders more tightly. 'It makes me realize I'm alive,' she shouted over the water. 'I feel dead most of the time.'

I couldn't just leave her alone, so we stood there in

silence, by the wooden cross, as the rain hammered down the backs of our necks, slicked our hair to our scalps, poured down our legs, left our feet and shoes utterly sodden, soaked my jeans and worked its way damply through to the sweater under my coat. I could even feel water around my waistband, under several layers of clothing.

As the storm moved away, and the downpour eased to a drizzle, I started to shiver. 'It's freezing.'

We looked at each other and began to laugh. She was right. We were alive. 'Come on,' I grasped her by the arm again, 'brisk walk over the fields and I'll get you dried off.'

I only remembered that it was Vanessa's house, not mine, when we entered through the kitchen, and I could see Kelly looking round, taking in the distressed blue-painted pine dresser, the big scrubbed wooden table, the hanging pots and baskets, the wicker drawers full of vegetables and the Christmas cards strewn everywhere.

'Bit different from that slab of concrete in London,' she commented. 'I couldn't believe that house. It must be like sleeping in the Tate Modern.'

'Actually, it's very comfortable.' I hadn't brought her here to criticize Vanessa.

'Sorry. You get into the habit of being bitter.' She pulled off a wet sweatshirt and jeans and handed them to me. I shoved them both into the drier and pushed her into the downstairs shower with a handful of my clothes.

When she came out again, she looked better.

'Would it be all right if I looked round?'

I hesitated. 'Vanessa's been very kind to me,' I warned her. 'And she's been hurt as much as you have.'

I thought Kelly was going to protest, but all she said was: 'I know. It doesn't stop me hating her, but I know. And I won't do anything. I just want to see if there's anything of him here.'

I moved round the house after her, staying slightly back. I really shouldn't be showing Barry's mistress round Vanessa's house. Vanessa would feel utterly betrayed if she knew. But Kelly didn't touch anything, except occasionally to lift a photograph and peer into it, as if there might be some message there.

'No,' she said finally. 'No. He's gone. I can't find him anywhere. I thought –' she sat down at the kitchen table, and I handed her a mug of tea '– that there might be some trace of him here that I could cling on to. There was nothing in my life. You see, my flat was sold the week he died, and then we completed on the house he never lived in . . .'

'How did you manage? For the money?'

She shook her head. 'It was terrifying. But I sold it and I'm living at my mum's while I buy another flat.' She shrugged. 'So that's fine. And, in a way, I don't mind having to get somewhere new. It might be easier that way. But there isn't anywhere special where I can remember him, except on the yacht, of course.'

The yacht. Vanessa never mentioned the yacht. Kelly saw my face.

'Oh, I'll have to give it back once she remembers it's there, but until then I'm paying the mooring fees and keeping it in shape. I go out in it, sometimes, on Sunday mornings, like we always used to do. And then I visit his grave.' It was Kelly who was putting the wild flowers in the jam jar by the wooden cross.

I had wanted to talk to Barry so often, it was with a jolt of surprise I realized that I could talk to Kelly instead. They had both been through the same experience, and, although Kelly's face was turned permanently against Vanessa, she seemed kind, calm and loving. She would be on my side, but distant enough to see the realities of the situation.

So I confided the whole story of me and Max to someone else for the first time.

'And I told him he had to choose,' I concluded. 'I said that he couldn't have both of us. Do you think I did the right thing?'

Kelly wrinkled up her face. 'There isn't a right thing. I put my life on hold for Barry. I only thought about when I was going to see him, not about what my future would be if we didn't end up together. Now he's gone, and I'm still in the same old job, doing the same old things, but five years older.'

She thought for a while. 'So yes, I think you did do the right thing. I don't regret a moment that I spent with Barry, but I wish I'd got on with my life while I was doing it. At least this way, you can decide what's right for you without being pulled off balance by thinking about Max, and whether you're going to meet soon. It's awfully easy to measure life out in little doses. I used to think "Oh, good, only three days to Thursday and then we'll be together." And that was good enough for me.'

She looked up at me: 'Would you have left your husband if it wasn't for Max?'

I thought about it carefully. 'I think I would, yes. I should never have married him in the first place.'

I'd said it. At last. I'd admitted what I'd known as I walked up the aisle on my father's arm, which was that I was marrying Stephen because he was a friend, I liked him, I was pregnant and I was frightened, and I didn't think there were any other options. As Barry had said, it's just not enough. I should have fought, however hard they turned out to be, for the other options instead.

After Kelly had changed back into her own clothes, I gave her some Christmas cake and she walked back to the church.

'I'm glad I've seen it here, though,' she said. 'This house was his favourite – I used to feel quite jealous of it.'

'Well, you don't need to.' I thought of my last conversation with Barry. 'Once he moved in with you, he forgot all about it. But I'm glad you told me because it means Vanessa wasn't wholly wrong to have him buried up here.'

'I think she was.' Kelly zipped up her jacket. 'But she has. So there we are.' She looked up at the sky. 'Sunnyish. I might just make it back to the car if I walk quickly. Thanks a lot.' And she kissed me on the cheek. 'Good luck with your life. Barry was very fond of you, you know.'

'And good luck with yours,' I shouted after her. She waved her hand in the air, once, without turning back.

35

After the New Year came the dark days.

I kissed Vanessa goodbye at Heathrow. She looked nervous under the tan of her recent skiing trip.

'I've never travelled alone before.' She checked her tickets and passport for the tenth time. 'Not this far, anyway.' Then she laughed. 'Who'd have thought it? Me, a backpacker at fifty?'

'Hardly a backpacker, Vanessa.' I smiled at her.

She picked up her neat little tote bag, and hugged me. 'Look after yourself. You've got some tough times ahead, but it does get better. Eventually.'

'I'll miss you,' I said, hugging her back.

As I watched her petite blonde form disappear through customs, I realized that I really was on my own now. Living with Vanessa had been fun, but it had partially masked the reality of what I'd done.

Every morning I drove through the twisty roads, past bare, muddy fields and frosty hedges to Eggleton, arriving just as a low-level glow of sunlight began to turn the darkness into a pale grey day. The trees were stripped, the ground was brown and lumpy, and there seemed to be no way of keeping the weather out of The Old Bakery.

We began the long, depressing second stage of the

renovations. The excitement of fresh air blowing through the house had gone, and all the fascinating discoveries – scraps of ancient wallpaper, oak floorboards in reasonable condition and gas lamps that might possibly be usable – had already been found. There'd been a magic about the house, when its past had seemed immediate, almost tangible, and its future welcoming me to a new world ahead.

But, now that we'd gutted everything, the magic had evaporated. 'Fresh air' became 'living outside', and even the lightest shower of rain turned everything to mud. There was nothing more to discover except problems: beams eaten away by wasps, floorboards that turned out to be rotten after all, foundations that needed underpinning, drains that needed rerouting and roof struts that needed replacing. As the work got heavier, there was less I could do to help, so I eventually retired to Merlins to work on the furniture.

Unfortunately, as it took me a couple of weeks to discover, everything promptly ground to a halt in my absence. Mervyn got flu (although someone in the village muttered about 'a quick job down Ipswich way'), John's daughter had a baby, which meant that he and his wife had to drive to Northumberland for five days to look after her toddler, and Dave, on his own, was more or less hopeless. He'd appear at about eight in the morning, go off for his 'breakfast', get back at nine, stop for a break at eleven, go off for lunch at twelve and return at three, only to clock off at four because it got so dark. I could see the precious months I'd budgeted for slipping away.

Just as I was beginning to feel that I might never achieve anything, I took my first load of furniture to London, and got two small orders. It was like being injected with rocket fuel. I should have been ticketed for speeding driving back, as I sang along to the radio at the top of my voice. I even risked my luck dropping off at Eggleton to see if there'd been any progress that day.

My luck held. Dave, John and Mervyn were all present, together for the first time for weeks, nodding their heads dolefully over a hole in the ground that had sprouted some water when the drains were rerouted. I practically kissed them, just for being there. John told me that someone was coming to sort out the plumbing tomorrow, and within a week we'd have the piping for the central heating. 'We can even rig up that sink if you like.' I felt as if I was about to move in at last.

Alas, all this merely signalled that we'd reached the third stage of renovation. That's when everything takes three times as long as promised, and nothing and nobody arrives when they're meant to. The plumber was delayed by three days. When he did run the waste pipe through the newly dug and damp-proofed floor, someone else came along and told us the fall of the pipe wasn't steep enough to comply with regulations. The bath I'd found in the garden, due back from the restorers, was sent to Egham rather than Eggleton and took a week to be re-routed, going via Staffordshire for some reason. The new bath, for the other bathroom, got trapped in some warehouse dispute. The floorboards, chosen to match up with those that remained, were delivered on time but turned out to be the wrong width and a different kind of wood. The central-heating piping was supplied without some tiny essential bit (I offered to drive to the factory and get it, but was told it was in Inverness, so post would be quicker – it wasn't). But the roof went on and the windows were in, and it began to feel like a house.

By the end of February, I was able to go back to working alongside Dave, John and Mervyn again, finding odd jobs that I could do, like painting the windows, grouting the tiles, and, once the plaster was dry, even painting the walls.

The weather was icy, freezing the tips of my fingers as I sealed the wood on the front bedroom window, ready for painting. I thought I might make this room, the first one to look almost habitable, mine. The ceiling and walls were criss-crossed with oak beams taken from local ships in the seventeenth century, and the room had two big square-paned Georgian windows overlooking the village green. The pain in my fingers slowly iced the rest of my body, in spite of several layers of old T-shirts and jumpers.

John, Dave and Mervyn usually went to the pub for lunch, or into their Portakabin. I liked to eat a sandwich in solitary silence, visualizing the walls of the rooms painted in glorious shades of blue, grey or terracotta and imagining the bookcases full of books. It was all still a long way away.

One day I heard a heavy tread, about five minutes after they'd gone to the pub.

'John?' I tried to make my voice sound confident, rather than squeaky.

I heard an indistinct male voice, not John's.

'Yes?' I stood up and grabbed a plasterer's shovel, casually, as if it was the sort of thing I always carried around with me.

'Suzy?' A head appeared in the doorway, a very familiar head that I'd promised myself I wouldn't see again. He looked just the same: his now-charcoal grey hair still too long, and his dark eyes locking instantly on to mine.

Trembling slightly, I sat down and put the shovel on the floor.

'I had to see if you were all right. I was worried about you.'

'Max.' I remembered what Kelly had said. I could easily measure out my life by our meetings, filling the spaces in between with waiting. I'd never ever move on. 'I meant it, Max,' I said, as if we'd only spoken an hour or so earlier. 'We can't have an affair.'

He settled himself on one of the builder's boxes. 'No. I promise. I've only come to help you. If you need it.'

I remembered Vanessa's stories of 'helpful' men, and looked at him suspiciously.

'Listen. Your builders seem to be doing quite a good job, although I saw one or two things you should be keeping an eye on downstairs.'

I sighed. 'I just don't know how to keep an eye. That's the trouble.'

'I could pop down once or twice a week if you like. Give everything a once-over. I've done five cottages on the estate, plus Stonehill. Just as a friend. I really do mean that.'

I tensed. Stephen's 'you'll never last five minutes on your own, you never have' had echoed in my brain over the past three months. I had to prove to myself that I could. And I didn't, definitely didn't, want this to be the beginning of a shoddy little affair. Max had made his choice between Anne and me and that was that.

On the other hand, I desperately needed someone I could trust. John, Mervyn and Dave were good builders, but they would much rather do things the easy way than the way I wanted them to. I never knew how far to insist, or what I should be checking.

'Thank you. Help gratefully accepted.'

His face creased into a smile.

'As long as,' I added, 'that's all it is. Okay?'

'A deal.'

I explained what I was planning, and we walked round the house. He picked up a few details that weren't quite right, but was pleasantly impressed by everything.

'Well, I'd better go. By the way,' I could tell, from the way he tried to sound casual, that he was about to say something important. 'I rang my goddaughter to see if she'd like to go to the theatre as a birthday present.'

Polly. Her birthday. I had been thinking about that.

'They're not talking to me,' I told him. 'Either of them.'

'So I gather. Is there anything I can say or do?'

'Whatever I say to defend myself would only seem like an attack on Stephen, and that turns them into piggies in the middle who have to decide who's right and who's wrong. They're angry and sad at the moment, but at least they've got one clear person to blame, and one person who they can turn to for comfort. I don't want them to feel let down by both their parents.'

'Mm.' Max looked thoughtful. 'If I take the line that sometimes people grow apart, and no one's to blame?'

'You can try. The image of Saint Stephen as the devoted husband and father kicked in the teeth by a demanding and ungrateful wife is being painted pretty strongly at the moment. Have you seen him at all?'

Max shook his head. 'Stephen always lies low when things go wrong. He tends to get back in touch again when he's on a winning streak.'

It was a very accurate assessment. Max had known him so long.

'We're fighting over money.'

'Surprise, surprise.' Max looked sympathetic. 'Have you got good lawyers?'

'I suppose so. I don't know how you tell.' Stephen had made it clear that he intended to delay the divorce as long as possible by suggesting pitifully small settlements. The latest suggestion had been a monthly allowance that would stop if I married again. I thought of the times he would pay it late or not at all. He had already deducted the cost of things he'd bought the girls from the maintenance that we'd agreed through the solicitor. And I knew that he would also use it as a way of trying to control my life. He would question what I'd spent, and criticize everything I did. I wanted to be free of him, not be demoralized by his constant carping. 'I only want what's fair,' I'd told him. 'A sum of money that reflects what I put into the marriage, and that I can use to make a new life. It'll be better for both of us.' He'd told me, in return, that I was useless with money, and that if I had a lump sum I'd simply run through it, and be left with nothing for my old age. 'I'm thinking of you, you know,' he'd insisted.

'How's Anne?' I changed the subject. I only asked to be polite. Because one does.

'Anne.' He sounded wary. 'I think she's stabilizing. It's always hard to tell. It's not like a visible, physical illness. People can look cheerful and be dying inside.'

I reminded myself that it was none of my business any more.

'And you?' he asked. 'How are you finding it on your own?'

I knew that Max understood. The nightmares, the inexplicable noises and the ever-encroaching fingers of fear that could reach into my life at any time and freeze me into paralysis.

'It's okay,' I told him, truthfully. It wasn't, yet, better than just okay, but at least Merlins was cosy and solid, and completely armed with state-of-the-art security systems. Living in my own house, alone, would be quite another matter. I was beginning to worry about it, and once again to wonder whether I'd done the right thing. In my dreams, there were still shadowy forms that hovered around corners and clouds of menace shimmering across the horizon. Perhaps I ought to move in sooner rather than later. Face my demons.

'You don't need to do everything all in a rush, you know,' said Max, apparently reading my thoughts. 'Take it all a step at a time.'

'I know.' I had a thought. 'Just a minute.' I rifled through my bag to find some snapshots I'd just collected from the chemist, and dug out some blank paper that I

454

kept to sketch ideas on. 'Can you hang on a second while I write a quick letter to Polly?'

I didn't have time to think about it, which was probably a good thing.

Dearest Poll,

Here is a photograph of your bedroom with a tree growing through the middle of it. I've taken away the tree and added a roof and some windows, but I won't do anything else until you tell me what you want. You could have a different room, if you liked, but I thought you'd want this one because it overlooks the fields at the back. They're real Suffolk meadows, gently rolling in towards each other then disappearing into a haze on the horizon, where you just know there's a wonderful stretch of sea even if it's too far away to see. There's a little grey stone church, and a few cottages, but they're too far away to disturb the sound of birds calling to each other. In the summer the fields will be fringed by wild poppies, and I'll start to work on the garden.

Come and see it all soon, Polly, because you'll always have a home here when you want it (and even when you don't). I love you very much, and am sorry for everything.

Mum.

I didn't have an envelope, so I just folded it up and handed it to Max.

'I'll make sure she reads it,' he promised. 'Whatever she thinks about it, she can at least read it.'

He set off down the stairs: 'I'll call you after I've taken Polly out. I'll try to get her to see sense.'

'Without blaming Stephen,' I added in warning,

scrambling down the tiny, twisted staircase after him. 'Whatever you do, don't say anything bad about Stephen.' The last thing I wanted was an avalanche of accusations that I was using Max to try to turn the girls against him.

'Without blaming Stephen,' he agreed, unlocking the car door, and taking a last look at The Old Bakery. 'You've done miracles here so far. I can't believe you've managed all this in only three months.'

We didn't kiss goodbye.

'Come again soon,' I shouted. 'Come and check up on the building work.'

With a wave he was gone, just as Dave, John and Mervyn reappeared with the news that the base units for the kitchen had gone to the wrong warehouse.

'Well, I'll just have to drive off and get them then,' I said. I felt absurdly and stupidly happy again.

36

I knew, of course, that Max coming over, 'as a friend', wasn't exactly the fastest way to heal a broken heart, but, in spite of the excitement of my new life, I was lonely. And it's not as if we could have got up to anything on a building site – you can't have affairs, or even erotic thoughts, against a background of churning concrete mixers and men in overalls stamping all over the place with buckets of wet plaster. There wasn't even anywhere to sit down – let alone lie – apart from whatever box had been delivered most recently.

As the world gradually woke up to spring, Max came over two or three times a week, and strolled round the building, acknowledging good pieces of work and pointing out potential problems. He knew a great deal about local building techniques: 'You'll need crinkle-crankle here,' he'd indicate, 'that's what it'd have had originally.' Reluctantly, I conceded that John, Dave and Mervyn reacted much better to his comments than to mine. 'They just won't accept a woman in charge.'

Max laughed. 'I'd never thought of you as a feminist.'

'It's not feminism, it's just basic respect. Why should they take more notice of you than me?'

'Because I've done up six houses already and this is your first.'

'Hmph.' We never dared risk going to the pub, as it

was one of Podge's six or seven regular haunts, but I used to buy a couple of pints, take them back to the house, and return the glasses later. We'd talk through the next stage of the renovations over a lump of bread and cheese, watching the bare bones of the house appear as the work progressed, and I'd feel a sense of tranquillity creep over me.

Until I thought about the girls. I now wrote to them every week, telling them my news and saying, each time, that I loved them and was sorry. I had never received any acknowledgement for the letters, or for Christmas or birthday presents. The silence was absolute. Sometimes I felt as I used to do when they were toddlers and I lost sight of them in the park – a sensation of overwhelming panic that I would never, ever see them again. After five months of silence, this terror was turning into the chronic nerve-nagging pain of acceptance.

Polly had refused to discuss my split with Stephen when Max took her out, and had simply gazed at her plate while he'd trotted out his bit about people growing apart and life being too complicated to assign blame. 'She read your letter, though, and put it in her bag. I'm sure it's just a question of time.'

I hoped so. I knew that Polly would be the first to forgive. She always had been. Occasionally I saw something that reminded me of them – a little white car like Polly's or the back of Jess's tall, slim figure with frayed, long hair. My heart would turn over, then cramp up in the bitter grip of disappointment.

Outside, crocuses and daffodils proved their resilience by poking their heads up through weeds and builder's rubble. I began to look at the garden. There was a broken-down wall all round it, which I planned to re-build at the sides. The back would be open to the fields. Staggered around the garden in unlikely places were rose bushes just beginning to send out little green shoots. There was too much ivy, of course, and scrub, but underneath I could see traces of something that had been a cottage garden almost a hundred years ago. There was even grass in the middle, hardly grand enough to be called a lawn, but at least it was a break in the jungle.

'The veg patch would've been here,' said Dave, of an overgrown space behind the shed that faced south. 'Good sun. Good soil.'

We cleared it of gorse and I had it double-dug. Visions of serving the bed-and-breakfast customers with my own organic vegetables fuelled my determination to get it all planted this year, so that it would be fully operational next year.

'Start with the easy things,' said Max. 'Potatoes, onions, everlasting spinach.' And he brought me cuttings and seedlings from Stonehill.

One day, I spent all day planting everything out, and missed writing my letters to Polly and Jess. Later, in bed, when I remembered, I wondered what that meant.

I couldn't let this estrangement go on much longer. Every day we were apart loosened the links between us for ever. Suppose I had a car crash, or got ill and died. The girls would think that I had meant to leave them completely. And even without a tragedy, an argument can become a rift, and a rift can become a habit. The years would slip past, taking with them the last points of contact between me and my daughters. They would become, at best, polite visitors to my life.

But I'd done everything I could, and none of it had worked. I decided that next week, when I went down to London to take a consignment of furniture to the shops, I'd go and find Polly and camp on her doorstep until she talked to me.

When my mobile phone rang the following morning, I thought, for one heady moment, that it was her, ringing to talk to me at last.

But no. It was Marzipan, the magazine stylist who'd arranged my house for the magazine pictures almost two years ago.

'Marzipan!' I was amazed.

'It is you, isn't it?' she queried. 'The one with the bathroom covered in shells, and all the necklaces dangling from light fittings?'

Well, that was one way of defining me.

'You wrote to us,' she added. 'And I thought I recognized your name. We're interested. I thought your house was great, and I really like your style.'

I booked in an appointment with Marzipan's editor for next week. 'We want a regular DIY page, but it's got to have a bit of oomph, for God's sake,' she said. 'It seems very difficult to get people to move on from painting everything in primary colours and changing the handles.'

I did a little dance round the room when I clicked the phone off, and Mervyn looked alarmed.

*

460

As April moved into May without getting noticeably any warmer, I started to be invited, gradually, to people's houses. Barbara and Tim Brand, for example – she was an artist and he was a doctor – had big pot-luck kitchen suppers around a huge scrubbed table. Occasionally I'd hear snatches of conversation that reminded me that perhaps it hadn't been such a good thing to buy a place so close to Stonehill.

'I saw the Galliards the other day,' someone said, one evening. 'They seem to be through their bad patch.'

'What's he done now?' asked a voice. 'Not another affair, surely? I thought he'd stopped all that years ago.'

'Some old girlfriend, according to Clarissa. Still, he 'fessed all and promised not to do it again. Honestly, Anne's an absolute saint the way she keeps having him back. God knows what he'd do if she finally put her foot down.'

My cheeks burned in the candlelight. I touched my forehead and felt traces of sweat damp against my fingers. Barbara's sharp eyes missed little and she looked worried. 'Are you all right, Suzy? Shall I open a window?'

Everyone looked at me. I felt like jumping up and saying, 'No, I'm not having a menopausal hot flush, I'm really not old enough yet.' Instead I mumbled something about working outside in the fresh air all day. Everyone looked knowing and faintly amused, and the conversation switched to how cold it was for the time of year, and what a terrible summer we were clearly going to have.

But Barbara's delicious chili con carne tasted like bits of ground-up India-rubber in my mouth. He'd talked to

Anne about me. That was a real betrayal. I had to stop pretending about Max. It was time to move on.

Moving on meant moving into the house. Living at Vanessa's, even without her, wasn't real life.

Until I made The Old Bakery my home, I was still a traveller. I had walls, floors, ceilings, electricity, and the beginnings of plumbing. There was a sink fitted to a tiny downstairs washroom, and a downstairs loo. Everything ready to camp in one of the bedrooms.

John, Dave and Mervyn were deeply disapproving, sucking their back teeth and shaking their heads.

'We don't want a break-in, or squatters.' I justified myself.

'Ooh, I wouldn't like to be a lone woman facing a break-in,' tutted John. 'Not round these parts.'

That got me. 'But this is a very quiet village, everyone says so,' I squeaked.

'Well, *quiet*, yes.' John made quietness sound deeply sinister. 'But things go on.' He tapped his nose, which always infuriates me. 'I wouldn't like to be a woman on her own here at night without a burglar alarm.'

We seemed to be going round in circles, and nobody was coming up with any concrete reasons why I shouldn't move in. I suspected that they just didn't want me knowing what time they clocked on in the mornings. I had to learn to survive alone, I absolutely had to. Otherwise I didn't think I'd be able to have a relationship without getting too dependent, as I had so long ago in my original relationship with Max, or trapped because I was afraid to leave, as had happened with Stephen.

Unless I could actually live on my own, the last six months, and all the pain I'd inflicted on the girls, would have been pointless.

I asked my friendly neighbour if there was much trouble locally. 'Oh, bless you no,' she said. 'You get the odd hooligan here and there if they know a property's empty, but I don't usually hear a thing.'

When I passed this on to John, he said: ''Course Janet Blake don't hear a thing, she's as deaf as a post. Well, it's your funeral.'

I hoped not. 'Well, if hooligans go for empty properties we'd better make sure this one isn't. Anyway the burglar alarm's going in next week.'

'If it *arrives*,' Dave reminded me. 'The floor varnish was delivered this morning and it's not what we ordered.'

I got a bed installed at record speed before I lost my nerve. It was my house, and I had to learn not to be frightened of it. I thought of Louise telling me to have lots of treats, and bought the best white linen I could find.

The first night, with its echoing silences, ghostly stepladders and smell of paint, was terrifying. When I switched on the lights – just one or two lightbulbs that had been run in by Dave to provide temporary light fittings – it seemed even more shadowy and sinister. It was cold, unbelievably cold for early summer, dark, and, as I woke up at two o'clock, at four-fifteen, and at five-thirty, I could hear rustling – followed by the occasional curdled howl or high-pitched scream – outside the window. Country sounds, I told myself, pulling on another jumper under the bedclothes and telling myself that it would all look better in the morning. It didn't, and neither did I. Could you function entirely without sleep? It seemed as if, once again, I would have to.

Max appeared on Thursday of that week, stepping through the back door and into the workshop in his usual familiar way.

My heart turned at the sound of his voice. I was working on a chest of drawers, and couldn't bear to look up.

'John says you've moved in.' He was surprised. 'That was sudden.'

I painted a line, extra carefully, still refusing to look at him. 'Not really.'

He put a hand on my shoulder. 'What's up, Suze?'

I shook it off. 'Two nights ago I heard that you'd made it up with Anne. Confessed about me, and promised never to do it again. Like a naughty boy. And she's forgiven you.'

'Look at me, Suzy.' Max sounded furious. As well he might. He hates people talking about him, presumably because it means people find out what he's up to.

I looked at him, hoping I wasn't going to cry. There'd been far too much crying in the past year.

'You heard this, did you?'

I nodded.

'From a reliable source?'

'It came from Anne telling Clarissa.'

'Well, that seems reliable enough.' He turned round, took his keys out of his pocket, and headed for the door.

'Max?' I hadn't meant him to react that quickly.

He stopped. 'This is never going to work out, is it, Suze?' His voice sounded so horribly final.

I shook my head. 'I'm sorry.' I wiped my nose with my sleeve, because I really couldn't stop crying now.

'We're just never pulling in the same direction at the same time.'

'No,' I whispered.

For one moment he moved towards me, and I thought he might be about to comfort me. But he turned round again, and left the room, stopping at the door to say, 'Goodbye, Suzy. It's not because I don't love you . . .' And looking much older, suddenly, he was gone.

'It's just that love isn't enough.' I completed his sentence into the bright, cool May morning, as I heard the roar of his car disappear down the road.

I went back to Merlins that day because I didn't want John, Dave or Mervyn to see my face. The sky seemed to go dark as I drove away from The Old Bakery.

But even as I lay under Vanessa's floral duvet covers, unaccountably shaking with cold, I got two phone calls on my mobile from the shops that had taken my furniture, asking for some more.

And a third call from someone who I'd never expected to hear back from, saying that they'd give me a try. My order book, as I liked to call the silk-covered A4 notebook that Vanessa had given me as a good-luck present, was full.

The telephone rang again. 'Your husband has let us know that he's ready to settle for a quickie divorce,' said George. 'He says that if you want *him* to sue *you* for adultery or unreasonable behaviour, he's prepared to do it.' I heard a note of irony creep into his voice. 'As a special concession.'

'Well,' I thought about being free of the permanent worry over the settlement, 'he's absolutely determined to maintain his complete innocence in the breakdown of this marriage. But, honestly, I just want out. He can say I'm as unreasonable as he likes.' For one mad moment, I considered telling Stephen he could sue for adultery, and owning up to Max, properly, now that Anne seemed to know. Fortunately, I stopped myself in time. I remembered the links between Stephen and Max and me. This might have been a strategy to confirm his suspicions.

As I put down the phone, feeling that it would probably be best if I simply forgot about this latest development until it became more of a reality, a postcard from Vanessa plopped through the door. She was on the Plain of Jars, apparently in Xieng Khuang. '*Stunning scenery. Plain littered with 2000-year-old jars – no one quite knows why. Have met a university professor called Mike, just getting over his wife's death so lots in common. Nothing serious!!* (this was underlined twice) *But having loads of fun, hope you are too, xxxx.*'

You have to keep going. You just have to keep going.

37

I filled the hole Max's absence left in my heart and mind with an order book, my new magazine column – they had taken me on almost instantly – and several appointments with the local tourist board, the council and the rest of officialdom to get The Old Bakery listed as a bed and breakfast as soon as possible. Now I really didn't have anyone to joke with about Mervyn, Dave and John, or someone who'd buy me a lunch-time pint of cider to celebrate a new order. Even my plans to find Polly had come to nothing – her flatmate told me that she spent most of the time at Paul's now, and only returned once or twice a week to collect her post. No, she didn't have the address.

Away from everything and everybody who'd made up my life for the last twenty-five years, living at The Old Bakery was like camping on a mountain top in distant Peru. I felt sealed off from the real world, living with a plug-in kettle and microwave, a sink of cold water, a bed and a loo. The physical work made me stronger and harder than I'd ever been: I pushed furniture and packing cases around, scraping, preparing and painting – either the furniture or the house, depending on what seemed most urgent. I'd managed to transfer all my stock from Vanessa's barn to what had been the main room of the shop, because, as this was going to be my workshop, it was more or less as decorated as it ever would be. I slowly got too tired to be frightened at night – or at least all night – but when the darkness fell and the builders went, the fear was always there, on the edge of it all. I knew it hadn't gone. It was just biding its time.

It was a busy life, but it seemed a long time since I'd seen or spoken to anyone I loved. I couldn't help wondering if it wouldn't have been better to stay in a marriage that had lost its fire and still be surrounded by other kinds of love rather than be so totally isolated in this way.

I regularly received postcards from Vanessa:

'*Angkor Hindu temple complex in Cambodia a mesmerizing spiritual experience,*' she'd scribbled. '*Making me think differently about everything. Travelling on own makes it easier to meet people* (what had happened to Mike, the university professor? It didn't seem to worry her), *and have come across several women doing the same. One of them, Angela, comes from near Stonehill and knows the Galliards! Small world! Am longing for a hot bath, but otherwise fantastic time.*' I smiled, after the inevitable jolt of pain of seeing Max's name. Even mesmerizing spiritual experiences couldn't quite destroy Vanessa's desire to name-drop.

Two weeks after Max left for good, I saw the little white car that I'd occasionally mistaken for Polly's, parked outside the pub. It was a Saturday morning, and Eggleton was beginning to come to life at weekends, as second-home owners and holidaymakers unpacked their huge cars and opened up the houses that had stood shuttered all winter. The sky was an aquamarine blue and the roses were budding in the village gardens. There wouldn't be time to get The Old Bakery garden straight this summer, I thought, but perhaps I could plant a few climbing roses and wisteria up the front, now that the porch and windows had been painted.

Two people got out of the car, and, out of the corner of my eye, I caught a flash of blonde hair. I thought of Polly, but couldn't bear the disappointment. I closed the door of The Old Bakery behind me, and began to get out my paints in the workshop.

When I heard bare knuckles rap on the side door, I didn't even bother to hope, but when I opened the door, there, as neat and blonde and pretty as she had always been, stood Polly, holding a box. Beside her stood a nervous-looking young man.

'Oh, Poll!' I hugged her and, reluctantly, she allowed herself to relax into it. 'Come in, come in.'

'I just wanted you to meet Paul,' she mumbled, going pink. 'We're getting married.'

'That's wonderful,' I burbled. At that point, anything would have been wonderful. 'I've got some champagne somewhere, oh look, it's even cold, how incredibly unlikely, it just shows it was all meant, it's been sitting here waiting for you, just like me, I suppose . . .' I ran out of breath, pumping Paul's arm up and down and grinning like a maniac. He beamed, nervously, back.

'It's only half-past ten in the morning,' said Polly. 'It's a bit early for champagne.' She looked worried. Stephen had obviously suggested that, on my own, I would completely fall apart and start drinking at breakfast.

She must have seen my face fall, because she put an arm on my sleeve. 'Show us your house, first, and all the furniture you've told us about, and then we'll celebrate.' She had grown up, I realized, to have such poise. She'd learned these lessons without me.

Well, that's what growing up is. I couldn't teach her anything any more.

'And I've got something for you.' She indicated the box. There was an indignant mew.

'Truffle!' I prised open the top of the cardboard travel case and a pink nose emerged, followed by an outraged feline shape. Glaring at me, she began to wash.

I tried to extract a purr, but she wasn't having any of it. 'Thank you, Poll. I've really missed her.' I stood up and closed the side door so that Truffle couldn't get out. 'I've really missed you all.'

'Well, it didn't seem fair on Truffle with Dad working so much, and now . . .' Polly didn't finish her sentence.

I showed them round the house, filling in all the spaces between us with breathless chatter interspersed with anxious motherly questions such as: 'So what do you do, Paul?'

While he told me that he was an accountant, had just finished the endless years of exams at last, and that he'd met Polly because one of his company's clients was the restaurant where she worked, I tried to make him out.

He was medium height, pale face, chestnut-brown hair, nice friendly eyes, deferential, kept looking at Polly as if she was a rare, mysterious jewel . . . but none of this was any clue to the essential Paul-ness of him. Would he be having affairs and keeping secrets from her in twenty years' time? Would Polly-and-Paul, now an indivisible unit from the way they kept unconsciously touching each other at any opportunity, grow slowly apart, like the branches of a tree, until one of them was in the sun and the other, bent and twisted, in the shade?

I came to the room at the back. 'And this will be your room, Polly.' I threw the door open and sunlight streamed in.

She looked anxious. 'But I don't think married women have bedrooms in their parents' house. Do they?' She looked from Paul to me, obviously torn.

'You can,' I declared. 'It'll belong to both of you. It can be Paul and Polly's room, so that you can come any time you like. I'll give you keys, and this can be your home in the country.'

'That's very kind of you, Mrs Everett.' Paul looked pleased.

'Suzy,' I corrected. 'I'm not Mrs Everett any longer.' When the magazine had asked me what name I wanted to write under, I'd suddenly decided to run everything under the name of Suzy Sheridan, my maiden name. It folded the comforting mantle of childhood around me, but seemed new and exciting at the same time. 'I think we'd better talk about all that later. Now, can you stay the night?'

'Here?' They looked at the empty room.

'I've got to buy a good double bed some time. You could help me choose it. We'll get it delivered today. Somehow.'

They exchanged glances. 'Well, if you're sure . . .' said Paul.

I was sure.

*

After that, it was wonderful. I made one-pot curry in the microwave – perfectly possible if a little messy – and served it on the plasterer's table, balancing unevenly on packing cases, while we all drank far too much wine and laughed until my cheeks ached. As well as the bed, I bought glasses and plates, pots and pans, and even two tea towels.

'What on earth having you been living on, Mum?' asked Polly. 'Not to even have tea towels?' I had the odd sensation of our roles having reversed.

The following morning Paul went out to find some newspapers.

'Polly?' I washed up the last breakfast plate and handed it to her to dry.

'Yes?' She knew something important was coming.

'Paul is lovely. I really, really like him.'

'So do I.' She smiled, a secret, warm smile.

'But I want you to be absolutely sure. Really, really liking isn't enough, you know. Not to get married on.'

'Is that what happened with you and Dad?'

I was careful. If you tell your daughter that you should never have married her father, that's like saying that you wished she didn't exist.

'I don't regret marrying Dad because if I hadn't I wouldn't have had you and Jess,' I told her, and realized it was true. 'But all the things that made us break up were there, at the beginning, if only I'd chosen to see them.'

'Like what?'

I thought about Stephen's sulky silences, his need to

be in control and his obsession with money, the way he put work first, all the time, not just during the day, even the fact that he wanted me because Max did, rather than for myself. I couldn't talk to Polly about any of them, because she loved her father. Turning her against him was no way forward – not just because it would upset her but because adding to the acrimony would only make things worse between me and Stephen.

'Look,' I said. 'We did have some wonderful times in your childhood, and we made a good family, I think. But when it was just your father and me, well I just couldn't live with him.'

'No. I can imagine that.' Polly smiled, two little dimples appearing on either cheek. I hadn't seen those dimples for far too long.

I realized that she'd been quietly working things out for herself during our long silence, and was glad I hadn't forced her to break it. Seeing my face, she almost corrected herself. 'Not that I think you should blame him. He has been very hurt.'

'I know. How is he now?'

'Dad? Oh, he's fine now.' There was an odd intonation in her voice. There was something she wasn't telling me, but I could tell from the look on her face, that that was that.

Polly waited for a moment. 'Mum, is there someone else? You know, in your life?'

I didn't want to lie to her, because she would feel so betrayed if she found out from another source.

'Polly, there was, for a bit. But there isn't now, and he didn't break anything that wasn't already broken.'

She seemed to accept that, and Paul appeared at the window, waving the Sunday papers victoriously. 'You have to drive for miles to find an open shop,' he said. 'But I think it's great round here. Where I grew up has been covered in roundabouts and housing estates. I didn't know there was still real countryside left.'

38

They drove off after a pub lunch on Sunday, promising to come back soon with Jess.

'You know what she's like, Mum,' Polly said. 'Everything's black and white to her. All she can see is what you did to Dad.' She threw her suitcase on to the back seat and got into the car. 'But I think that might be changing,' she added, with that slightly odd note in her voice again.

Just as they were driving off, I had a thought. I tapped the car window. She rolled it down.

'Dad hasn't got a new girlfriend, has he?' I asked.

She went pink. 'I think you'd better ask him.'

Well, well. The house seemed even emptier without their laughter and the sound of their footsteps. It was Sunday afternoon, and I wouldn't be speaking to anyone else until the builders came on Monday morning. Truffle strolled in and mewed at me, obviously disconcerted by the lack of soft, warm places to curl up. I stroked her silky fur, and felt less lonely.

On an impulse I dialled Stephen. I'd never done that before, always preferring to communicate through solicitors, as I spent quite enough time avoiding his hectoring phone calls not to want to instigate any of my own.

A woman answered. She had a poised, confident voice, which was even slightly familiar. Briefly, I entertained the possibility that he might be shagging one of our friends.

'Who's that?' I was surprised into rudeness.

'This is Karen Coombe speaking.' She sounded very calm and collected, as if she was used to being in charge of his telephone.

'Oh, I'm sorry. I must have the wrong number. I wanted to speak to Stephen Everett.'

'This is Stephen Everett's flat. Can I give him a message?' It was like talking to the speaking clock.

'Could you ask him to call his wife?' I couldn't help phrasing it deliberately. A bit wicked, but there you are. Until he got on with the divorce, I was his wife.

Karen Coombe. As I put down the phone, I remembered who she was. Stephen had mentioned her a few times when he'd been an adviser for a documentary called *Architectural Vandalism*. She'd been the presenter. I'd read a piece about her in Dave's paper last week because she'd just collared a plum job presenting a day-time TV quiz show. She'd been labelled 'up and coming'. There'd been a profile of her in new, glittering outfits. Apparently she was creating a stir because she'd got the job, at forty-three, against two traditional twenty-something blonde airhead presenters. 'Is this a sign that TV is finally dumbing up, instead of dumbing down?' the paper had asked, cruelly.

Stephen had really hit the big time if Karen Coombe

was cosying up in his flat answering his phone. I wondered if I could find the paper again.

Rootling round in the bins, I found it, and spread the interview out, tea-stained and sticky. Yes, there was 'someone special' in her life. 'I can't say who he is,' she simpered, 'but we're very, very close. Watch this space.' I noted, later on in the article, in a boxed-out section titled 'My Health', that she was allergic to cats, wheat and dairy products.

Aha. 'Well done, Truffle. You sprang yourself out of there.' I knew there was nothing Truffle enjoyed more than the challenge of getting really, really close to an allergic person.

All in all, this definitely seemed related to the sudden change of tack from his solicitors.

Well, well, I thought crossly, again, as I sanded down an Indian bedhead I'd bought in a second-hand shop in Southall. If she can put up with him, good luck to her. She's welcome to him. It was only slightly galling that here I was, the one who'd left in the first place, sitting on my own in an empty house with no one to talk to on a Sunday afternoon, while he was reclining on a sofa, probably toasting crumpets by now, with a hot TV star.

I sanded extra hard to get rid of my bad temper. No churlishness, I told myself. No dogs in the manger. I should be happy that he was happy. It would get him off my back. I told myself, very firmly, that this was what I had wanted, and that I couldn't complain about getting it.

*

'Suzy?' The phone rang only half an hour later. Stephen sounded anxious. 'Did you want something?'

'Oh, er . . .' I couldn't admit to having phoned out of sheer nosiness. 'Oh, I just wanted to say that I'm pleased about your agreeing to a quickie divorce. Do say that I've been as unreasonable as you like.'

'Well, I was just thinking of you, you know.' He sounded relieved. 'Bit much for you to start a business and have all this hanging over your head. Basically, you know that I only have your best interests at heart. If that really means a lump sum . . .' He trailed off, obviously trying to make 'a lump sum' sound as appealing as congealed custard.

I suppressed amusement at the thought that anyone would find 'a lump sum' distasteful. 'Thank you. That will be a relief.' I suspected that suing me for 'unreasonable behaviour' might well rebound on him as far as the girls were concerned, so I wasn't being too noble.

'I'll have to move out of the flat, of course, and find something smaller,' he added, in a self-sacrificing voice. 'I gather you spoke to our friend, Karen Coombe.' I was surprised he was so anxious to bring her name up.

'Our?'

'She's been very kind to the girls. She's just popped round to talk to Jess about a career in the media.'

'Oh, is Jess there?'

'Well, er, not absolutely at this moment, just nipped back to uni, you know . . . Karen was just on her way out.' He seemed so desperate to justify Karen's presence that I couldn't help teasing him.

'So she's not a girlfriend, then?'

'Heavens! No! Of course not, absolutely just . . . er . . . you know, a friend . . . acquaintance, really,'

I hoped Karen was listening to this. He'd obviously raised the subject to prevent my getting any ideas after she answered the phone.

'Look,' he sounded nervous. 'I just happen to be in your area on Tuesday to look at a new site, so I could pop in for a cup of tea. Just to show no hard feelings. I'd like to see this place of yours, ha, ha.'

Now what? It was awful to be so cynical, but I think he wanted to keep Karen a secret until we were properly divorced, just in case his being linked with a high-profile, high-earning woman could, in any way, affect my financial settlement. He would maintain, stringently and to the last, that paying me money – anything – would significantly damage his lifestyle.

She was welcome to him, after all. I put the phone down, sadly. I didn't know why he wanted a cup of tea on Tuesday, but I had the distinct feeling that he didn't just 'happen' to be in my area.

Apart from the odd occasions when Dave or John left their tabloid newspapers behind, I was virtually cut off. Although I listened to the radio as I worked, I felt immune from the world outside. There's something pleasantly remote about the radio; without the pictures and personalized sob stories of TV and newspapers, I was informed, rather than engaged, by the news.

And warnings you hear on the radio are never so scary. There's something impressive about headlines in black and white that makes you believe them, and television always has an air of panic about it. Radio is so calm.

So when I heard crackled, lengthy, detailed warnings about storms on Tuesday, I didn't listen to the mention of East Anglia. I just carried on painting. I wished Stephen wasn't coming. It was an intrusion.

And I was completely engrossed. I'd chosen rich, dark colours for some rooms: a wonderful Prussian blue for the main bedroom (which would be for the bed and breakfasters), a royal red for the dining room, and a daring emerald green for the small sitting room. Other rooms, the lighter ones, were to be in delicate shades: soft, grassy greens, petal pinks and aquatic, crystal-clear blues. I wanted to reflect the colours of the fields outside the windows at the back, and echo the clear, innocent shades of wild flowers.

'Nearly ran over that bloody dog,' muttered Mervyn as he returned from a lengthy lunch break, ostensibly combined with picking up some more building materials. 'People ought not to allow their dogs to roam on the roads.'

'Perhaps it's Janet's and it's got out,' I worried. 'Was it a Pekinese?'

'Nah, one of them black Labrador thingies. Nice dogs, usually. Didn't like the look of that one.'

'Oh, I expect that's the Black Shuck,' I joked. 'Appears all over Suffolk as a harbinger of shipwrecks and disasters. They say he's dragged children out to sea, and even got into a church once and tore the throats out of the worshippers.'

John, Dave and Mervyn all stopped what they were

doing, and stared at me, stony in their silence. They had the same expression on their faces that they'd had when I'd told them to paint the sitting room in what they regarded as an outrageous shade of green.

'It's all just a legend. A smugglers' tale to stop people going out on dark nights.' I added, 'I've seen or heard of the Black Shuck twice and absolutely nothing's happened to me. It's all in the mind.'

John raised his eyebrows and I could tell that he didn't believe me. I mean, what was I doing here, without a husband or family, trying to rebuild a ruined house, if nothing had happened to me? And I suppressed the thought that Barry had died after I'd first heard of a sighting of the Black Shuck.

None of them said anything. I turned the radio up. It was a jingle about tampons.

And, of course, anything for an excuse to knock off early. They started packing up around three, because it was getting dark enough for November. I could hear the wind beginning to whip through the trees, and John gave the roof a worried look.

'Come on, boys, let's get everything tied down good and proper.' Before he went, he stopped me. 'You need to go back to your friend's house. It's going to be a bad'un.'

'It's pretty secure here, isn't it? I mean, the roof's not going to come off or the walls cave in?' I swallowed at the thought that John was worried about me. Until now, they'd treated me as the boss, a well-known volatile substance without even a dash of humanity.

'Mm. Good as any in the village.' He studied the

house with concern. 'But you'll be frightened here alone.'

'I'll think about it,' I promised him. 'I'd just like to finish today's painting first.' What I really thought is that if I could survive a storm here, I'd never be frightened again. I could defeat the gargoyles and gremlins that stalked the parallel universe in my mind. I was beginning to think that I couldn't run away. The fear only follows.

They had just driven off when Stephen arrived, looking groomed and shiny.

'New car?' I asked, studying the sporty little Mercedes with its spanking-new number plates.

'Er, this old thing? Not mine, I'm afraid. Had to sell mine.' He gave me a hard look to make it quite clear why.

'Karen's?'

'No, for God's sake. She's just a friend. I told you. No, if you must know it's . . . on temporary loan to the company.'

Salting away his dosh, I thought, newly wised up since my telephone conversations with George Black.

'That's my new car.' I pointed to the battered white van I'd bought for a pittance from Dave, the builder. He'd assured me that it wouldn't let me down, and so far, it hadn't.

'Good Lord.' He frowned at it in disapproval, and started studying the house.

My insides began to cramp up. Criticism, almost definitely, was on its way. Reasons why something was bound to go terribly wrong or why something else had been done badly.

He was silent for a few moments. 'Well,' he conceded. 'It often takes several years before the real problems in a building project become obvious.'

I tripped on the step as I led him through the shop and into the tiny sitting room, newly painted in its invigorating shamrock shade. It even had one piece of furniture in it – a battered sofa I'd recently found in an auction room. It was the kind of sofa whose springs did not permit you to get out again in a hurry. Once down, you stayed down.

'Mm.' He was obviously reluctant to commit himself to any comment, and wisely walked past the sofa.

In the kitchen the white units had just been installed. He ran his finger along them. 'Very basic, of course, but frankly the mass market's so good these days, there's no point in buying anything expensive.' As I offered him tea, dropping one of the new mugs and breaking it, then clattering the dustpan and brush too loudly as I cleared it up, he asked me what kind of kitchen range I was buying. He spent about fifteen minutes telling me why another brand would have been better, after which he knocked his head on the old beams in the dining room.

'You'll never sell this place again with beams this low.'

'I don't want to sell it. Anyway, it's only this room and not everyone's as tall as you.' You don't have to justify yourself, I thought, too late. All the confidence I'd tentatively gained in the last few months had drained away as he'd walked in the door. My nerves were screaming. What was he doing here?

He nodded seriously at all the bedrooms and tapped the plumbing in the bathrooms, turning on the taps as if he was checking work in his own house. I told myself that this was just habit, and tensed up, waiting for him to discover problems.

'Well,' he said, downstairs again. 'I'm glad I've had the opportunity to give it all the once-over. I couldn't have lived with myself if I hadn't checked that you were managing to get by. Builders can take advantage of a woman on her own.'

'Mine haven't.' I wasn't going to offer him any more tea, as I couldn't trust myself not to drop something again. Had I always been this apologetic, grinning appeaser?

'I wouldn't mind a top-up.' He indicated the pot.

I hastily poured some more tea, and folded my arms, glad that there still wasn't anywhere to sit in the kitchen.

He cleared his throat. 'Er, there's something I've been meaning to say for a while.'

My knees felt weak. I'd hoped that there was nothing more he could do to undermine me, but it sounded horribly as if he had some kind of bad news.

'I mean, I really should have said something before, I realize that . . .'

Get on with it. Every fibre of my being screamed in tension.

'But I was worried about you. I didn't feel you were ready to take on the responsibility . . .'

'Stephen.' I unfolded my arms and folded them again. Shouting at him would only delay it all. 'I really am quite ready to take any responsibility now.' I hoped he hadn't noticed that my voice was shaking.

He took something out of his pocket and handed it

to me. 'I've found this. I thought it was only fair to bring it myself.'

As I looked at the chain of diamond daisies in my hand, he added a typical rider: 'Of course, it will have to be taken into account when we divide everything up. I've had it valued and told my solicitor.'

Don't shout at him, I thought. You'll never get the truth. I struggled with the possibility that it had been Stephen who had taken the necklace all along.

But even I couldn't believe that. It's just that once trust goes, there are no boundaries to judge by any more. 'How long have you had it?'

He shifted uncomfortably. 'Well, er,' he swallowed. 'I found it when we moved out of the house. Underneath a chest of drawers. It must have got kicked under there in the . . .'

He saw the look in my eye. 'I was so worried about you at that point. You weren't thinking straight. I thought you might sell the necklace and do anything, if I gave it back then. Anything. Really. I couldn't just hand you the weapons of your own destruction.'

'The what?' I suppressed a manic giggle.

'You know.' He sounded sulky. 'If you'd had a lot of money in your state at that time, you might have done anything.'

There was no point in trying to argue with him. He would simply leap through further hoops of self-justification.

'Fine.' Why had I ever allowed myself to be dominated by him? He was impossible. I'd seen that at last. After twenty-five years, I just wanted to be rid of him. 'Well,

I'm absolutely capable of dealing with it all now, and I'm very busy, so I'd be grateful if you could let me get on with it.'

'Of course.' He couldn't get to the car quickly enough. 'I was only thinking of you, you know. There's a very bad storm forecast tonight, by the way. You will be careful, won't you?'

As he got in, I said one more thing.

'Stephen?'

He turned, looking guilty.

'I'm sorry. I was never the right wife for you.'

He coloured. 'Er. Well, I wouldn't say that, well . . . erm, good luck.' He shrugged, looking embarrassed, and I knew that this was the closest I'd get to an acknowledgement that he, too, had made some mistakes.

It wasn't until his car had disappeared from sight that I finally understood. I had my necklace back.

I realized that even he couldn't have justified selling it and keeping the money, and, anyway, he would never do anything that was actually illegal. He couldn't have given it to the girls without my finding out, and if he'd returned it to me after the divorce he couldn't have claimed a share in it. Presumably, he hadn't given it to me when he found it, because he knew that I'd use the money to leave him.

I clipped it on round my neck, over my polo-neck sweater, and looked at myself in the dusty wedge of cracked mirror that I'd propped up over the sink. The freedom it offered glittered back at me.

Giving it back, now, meant that he was serious about

settling the divorce as soon as possible. The links were finally breaking for ever.

I was all right until about six, when I finished, somewhat mechanically, painting the Prussian-blue room. It would need one more going-over in the light, I thought, in case I'd missed bits, but it looked pretty good. I was planning on creamy-white curtains and bedspread, as a contrast, and just one or two pieces of furniture: a nice old cherrywood chest of drawers I'd bought quite reasonably at an auction and a marble washstand. The bed-and-breakfasters would want real furniture, not fake-fur headboards and zebra-striped chairs.

The rain was drumming down hard by now, rattling the windows and roof, echoing in the empty house. There was something very aggressive about the sound, and I had to suppress the thought that Vanessa's house would feel safer.

But just as lonely. I realized, shivering slightly, that I was much more frightened now that the necklace was back, in spite of being overjoyed to see it again. After months of owning nothing worth taking, I now had something that someone might want to steal. And it was no good telling myself that no one knew I had it, because all I could hear was the sound of the wind howling round the corners of the house, whining, roaring, then dropping into a sudden, menacing silence before starting up again.

I told myself that this storm would be a good test of how watertight everything was, as I took my book to the pub to spin out a bowl of beef stew as long as I could manage. People knew me there now, and nodded, leaving me in peace, while I calculated what the return of the necklace meant. It didn't change my position in a big way – it wouldn't pay off the mortgage, for example, but, if necessary, it offered a few months' more breathing space to get established, and a fall-back fund in case of any disasters. As I was doing better than expected at the moment, I would wear it once more, I thought, to Polly's wedding.

'Storm's going to be bad,' called out one of the regulars, who were all discussing the extraordinary changes in the weather patterns worldwide. 'Very bad for this time of year.'

I nodded. 'Luckily, we've almost finished the house. It's pretty watertight.'

Everybody looked at me, as if they knew something I didn't. 'You're not there on your own tonight?'

I hesitated. I didn't like the idea of admitting that I would be alone. 'It'll be fine,' I waved. 'I need an early night.'

'Tie everything down or lock it up, won't you?' said Bill, the publican. 'And if you do get scared, for goodness' sake don't drive anywhere if the storm is really bad. You're more likely to get crowned by a flying branch on the open road.'

'Really,' I wasn't used to all this concern. 'It's only weather.'

The wind was slapping against the trees, and I could see even the biggest branches swaying and rustling as I walked the few short yards home, bracing my body against the force of each gust. I wasn't sure whether to feel warmed or threatened by everyone's concern. They all knew I was on my own that night.

The back door was whipped out of my hand by the wind and banged shut behind me. Once I'd felt around for the switch, the bare bulbs cast shadows over the boxes. We had all the electrics fitted now, but I'd had no time for shades or lamps.

It was going to be a long night. I switched the burglar alarm on, but doubted that, if it did go off, anyone would hear it over the sound of the storm.

I didn't even dare get undressed. I wanted to face whatever it was with my clothes on, and lay there in bed, curled up in a ball, listening to the crash and roar of the storm outside. It rattled and groaned, moaned and whistled, shaking the windows and doors like a drunk determined to get in. Truffle slid in under the duvet and I pulled her little body close to mine. She purred, forgave me finally – it had taken two days – and curled up in a ball.

I told myself that the weather couldn't hurt me. I thought about the summer, and about the faces of the girls.

Eventually I drifted off into a semi-dream world with Stephen telling me that I was someone who could never be made happy. That wasn't true, I thought; except for the hollow ache about Polly and Jess, and the sharper, more piercing pain when I finally split from Max, I'd been happy for the past seven months. I floated in half-consciousness, thinking that I would do anything, literally anything, to get Jess back.

And then what? I drifted off. No Stephen, now, at last. And no Max. The chain, finally, had been completely broken, but I'd lived with it for so long that I wasn't sure what to do next. The hole in my life left by Max's departure would always be huge, but I had the sensation that I had walked all the way round it and had measured its size. It was a chasm in the centre of everything now, but as I moved on, I could, I believed, leave it behind me. People can live with pain. They have to.

Work, I suppose. Make friends. Even love again. Like Vanessa, I'd already had other people's husbands pressing me against walls and, with beery breath, telling me how much they'd always liked me. Even Podge had made a lewd suggestion when I bumped into him in the pub one day. I'd smiled, and declined politely. I didn't want to make local enemies. But I'd also seen a spark of interest in the pain-filled eyes of a man who'd lost his wife to cancer, and a glimmer of fellow-feeling in another who'd left his desirable executive residence and socialite wife to become a potter in a tiny cottage. I hadn't been able to respond, then, but now I thought I could. Genuinely free. I slept, and dreamt of Max walking away from me, into a fog.

I was woken by the sound of the world collapsing around me. A roar deeper than thunder, a rolling boom, shook the house from its foundations, followed by the unmistakable sound of breaking glass. It echoed, seeming to come from somewhere deep underground. A cannon? You think such daft things on your own in the middle of the night. Hardly. A bomb, perhaps? But who would want to bomb me? An earthquake? This little house couldn't possibly withstand the kind of force that seemed to be pitched against it. I felt around for the bedside lamp. It didn't work. Everything was totally, utterly dark. My breath caught in my throat. My mobile phone. Where was it? I always kept it by the bed. I felt around, but cowered back at the sound of another crack. That was lightning that time. I'd seen the whole room in it, and my mobile was across the other side on the floor. But who would I call? Stephen? Hardly. He was in London and would only say, 'I told you so.' I didn't think that the Plain of Jars, or wherever Vanessa was now, would be in mobile contact, and, as for Max, he was no longer a part of my life.

It occurred to me that whatever had happened – possibly the roof collapsing or the house beginning to slip into the foundations – might have only just begun, and I could be trapped under an onslaught of falling masonry.

But I was too frightened even to get out of bed, anyway, and propped myself up, knees drawn into my chest, staring desperately at the darkness, waiting for the walls of the house to slip away, or for whatever had crashed down to move again. Eventually my eyes tuned into the darkness, and my heart rate slowed, slightly.

There was another crash, this time obviously in the village, and a car alarm went off. I jumped so violently I thought I might have a heart attack.

In spite of the darkness, I knew I had to find out whether it was safer to get out of the house, and ask someone in the village for shelter, or whether the house was intact enough to withstand the rest of the storm. I needed to know whether whatever had happened had meant that I should be calling the emergency services, or if it was merely a question of waiting until morning to inspect superficial damage. Daylight seemed so impossibly far away.

I needed a torch. I couldn't remember where to find one, but there were matches in the kitchen. We'd bought them for our candle-lit dinner on the plasterer's table on Saturday night. I swallowed and stood up, edging my way across the room, flinching at the occasional stab of lightning. My knees were shaking, and my mouth was dry. Suppose the crash had been someone using a battering ram on the door? No one would hear in the storm.

I told myself that, in that case, the burglar alarm would have gone off, but couldn't remember whether the loss of electricity would also cut that out. I remembered the faceless man. I could never look at him again, I knew that. My heart would simply collapse.

But I opened the door, as quietly as I could. Over the rain, I could hear a faint, intermittent scraping at one of the back windows, and an occasional low creaking groan. I thought of all the people in the pub who knew I was alone, and wondered if any of them would rob, kill or steal.

If I died now, I thought, what would I regret? All the obvious things. The baby. Accepting everything Stephen said, and not questioning him from the start. Not fighting for what I believed in. Not changing my job earlier. Almost all 'not's.

Not marrying Max. I knew, back in the basement flat

when he'd asked me to marry him, that I'd always told myself that it was a joke because I'd been afraid to think about the alternative. In fact, I'd been so determined not to be a victim that I became a coward. So frightened of being betrayed that I placed pride above love.

I heard the back door bang with a sense of finality. It banged twice. My security, my precious locks and keys that kept the fear out, had gone. The burglar alarm screamed over the wind, adding to the deafening chaos. Whether the house was collapsing in the storm, or someone was taking advantage of the weather to break in, I would have to face it. I had been running away for too long.

I felt my way down the tiny, twisted staircase and into the kitchen, expecting to feel a hand at my throat at any moment. My necklace was still around my neck, under the jumper now. I would give it to anyone who wanted it. Anything to make them go away.

But I got downstairs. I don't know how long it took. It seemed like ages. The matches were on the windowsill, where I'd left them. I lit the candles again and the kitchen flickered into light. It looked exactly as it had when I'd left it, but the light made it even harder to see outside. I used the candle to find the torch in the workshop, along with a stout hammer. I would defend myself. The parallel universe had no right to invade my life like this.

The back door swung on its hinges, and I thought of Truffle. She'd only been here for two days, and she'd be terrified of the thunder. If she'd shot outside, she would have no idea where she was. She'd be lost for good.

I fought my way back upstairs again to see if she was

still in bed. The torch made it quicker, but I was eerily reminded of the flickering lights I'd seen in the downstairs rooms in London when I discovered the burglary. If you've got the light, you can be seen. You're a target.

I'd left the bedroom door open, and Truffle wasn't there. Now I really did have to get outside to find her. 'Truffle,' I called, my voice sounding feeble against the storm. 'Truffle.'

I told myself that if anyone was in the house, they would have found me by now. There is no one here, I told myself. There is no danger, except to Truffle, and possibly from the weather. But fear never listens. It only strains its ears to pick up imaginary dangers.

Still sliding flat against the walls, because it felt safer rather than for any sensible reason, I went down to the kitchen again. 'Please, Truffle. Puss, Puss.'

As soon as I stepped outside I was hit by a sheet of rain, which made it hard to keep my eyes open. The ground slithered beneath me, and the rain whipped down the back of my neck. I saw a branch fly by. So stupid, I said wearily, and almost out loud, so very stupid to worry about non-existent thieves rather than terribly real, solid objects flying through the air.

Peering through the torrent with the light of the torch, I could see what had happened. A tree had collapsed against the scaffolding at the back. There might be some superficial damage to the roof and brickwork, I thought, and there were two broken windows.

But it was the storm, and not human malevolence. And even I could see that the house was standing as solidly as it had for the last two centuries. I leant against the wall of the house, soaked by a steady stream of rain, elated. I had survived. Without Max or Stephen.

I heard a mew, and shone my torch back at the house. It was Truffle, who clearly had no intention of going out in this. She had a sense of survival, even if I didn't.

As I pushed the door closed and managed to wedge it shut – one of the branches of the tree had hit it particularly hard and split the lock off – a sense of calm crept over me. I realized that fear is as much a part of life as love is, and that it will always be there. But it doesn't have to be in control. I could go out into a storm, alone and in the dark, if I needed to. It was just the beginning of what I could do.

I went back to the workshop, with a candle and a torch, and began to paint a small side table. I was completely awake, at home, in the middle of the night in a particularly noisy storm, and I was perfectly happy about it.

Even when I heard a knock at the door, I was surprised rather than threatened. I looked at my watch. Quarter to six. A bit early for the milkman. Perhaps there was to be flooding after all, or maybe someone in the village had a problem and wanted to borrow something like jump leads. Exhaustion began to filter through the exhilaration of survival. Once I'd got rid of whoever it was, I'd go upstairs for a couple of hours' sleep.

There was another, louder knock, and I put away my tools, removing the wedge from the door.

It swung open, and my heart crashed against my chest. 'Max!'

He was soaking. Five seconds outside in that rain was enough to drench you to the skin.

'I've come to see if you were all right.'

I waved him in. 'I'm fine. As you can see. It was hard to sleep in the storm so I did some work instead.'

He looked at me, carefully, and I realized that he'd been the only person who'd really understood what the burglary had done to me. To everyone else, it had been an irritation that I would 'get over' sooner or later.

'I'm fine,' I repeated.

He stroked a finger down the line of my jaw. 'I've missed you desperately.'

I was strong enough to be honest. 'I've missed you too. More than I'd believed possible. But, Max. No more Max and Anne and Stephen and me. Or me and Max and Anne. I have to get on with the rest of my life.'

He stood there, dripping wet, his hair plastered to the side of his face. 'If you'll still have me,' he spoke slowly, 'I've come for good.'

Could I bear to start all this again? I felt like a piece of fabric that had been torn and mended over and over again. One more tear and that would be it.

'I've driven here,' he told me, his jacket soaked with rain, 'through flying branches and falling roof tiles. I came because I knew you'd be frightened. I came because I knew you were so sodding stubborn that you wouldn't go back to Vanessa's. I came because I thought you weren't quite ready to be alone on a night like this. Most of all, I came because I love you.'

'Why?' I'd often asked myself, over the months, why

Max, with all his choice of women, had never really let me go. Was it that he simply couldn't bear to lose?

He looked surprised. 'Why what?'

'Why do you love me?'

He looked puzzled for a moment and then smiled. 'Love doesn't have a why. I just know you, that's all. That's how it is.'

'What did Anne say? And what about Stonehill?' It suddenly became very important to know whether he had really left his life, the way I had. Whether he, too, had broken all the links.

He understood. 'I've given Stonehill and Anne everything I could. It was never enough. There's no going back. I promise you that.'

'What would you say if I told you it was too late?'

'I'd go away. Find somewhere to call home. And come back every day until I convinced you that it wasn't.'

I took a risk. Confidence, like fear, starts with the little things and spreads into other parts of your life.

'You can call this home, if you like. While you carry on convincing me, every day.'

I felt the rainwater running down his face as he kissed me. 'You might have to start by convincing me every hour, in fact,' I mumbled.

'It's stopped raining.' We looked out of the windows. The crystal clarity that only comes after a storm had turned the dawn the palest blue of forget-me-nots.

'There's one problem, Suzy.'

We wedged ourselves comfortably down in the battered old sofa, unable to believe that we were both here, at last, for ever.

He told me about his last conversation with Anne: 'I had known, of course, what you suspected, which was that sometimes the depression was real, sometimes it wasn't, and sometimes it was a kind of anger against me just for being me and being there. But I couldn't risk leaving her if she was really in danger from herself.

'Until the storm. There was something about all that terrible force flying about in the air that made me realize that you can't give someone else something that isn't yours to give. Anne's happiness, ultimately, has to be Anne's responsibility.'

He'd stood there, in the stone-flagged hall at five in the morning, and Anne had opened her bedroom door and come down the stairs. She'd remained, white-faced, on the bottom step of the broad, curving staircase, rather like Boadicea defending her kingdom, I thought.

'If you go,' Anne had said, 'I can't manage Stonehill without you. It'll have to be sold. You'll be robbing your own children of their home and their heritage.'

'I've had to create my own home,' Max had told her. 'If they have to, too, it will be the making of them.'

'You haven't made a home. You've borrowed mine and made it yours. That's not the same.'

'No.' Max had turned away, to look at his favourite picture one last time. 'It's not. That's why I've got to go before it's too late.'

'You needn't think you'll get a penny out of the estate. I shan't sell, in fact. I shall keep it all.'

'I've given you everything I have, Anne.' Max had

turned back to face her. 'I'm not asking for it back. But I do need something.'

'There is nothing,' she'd said, spitefully. 'Nothing that you can take.'

I thought that when he finally realized that he wasn't going to get anything, then that would be the point at which he'd understand that in real life, as opposed to the privileged existence he'd lived so far, you have to make compromises. That you can't be a forty-seven-year-old man without a job, a home or money, and expect to start again. But he'd told her the truth instead.

'I'm going to Suzy. I thought you ought to know.'

Anne had nearly spat at him. 'She's got nothing either.'

'No,' he'd said. 'But I love her. We're going to make something together. If she'll have me.'

'Go, then,' she'd turned away. She was too proud to beg, both Max and I knew that. She was the sort who walked away with her head held high. You had to respect her for that.

But she'd turned round one more time to hurt him. 'I've had everything I need from you. I only married you to save Stonehill, you know.'

'I know that,' he'd said. 'Now.'

'So what's the problem?' I was relieved that it had all been so definite.

'She means it, Suzy.' He turned my hand over to kiss my palm. 'She really does mean it. All my money has gone on repairing roofs and fences and all the rest of it. The estate is in her name. It always has been. I've got three suitcases in the car. That's all I possess in the world.'

'And all I've got in the world – all that isn't mortgaged to the hilt,' I rummaged around under my sweater, and produced the diamond necklace, 'is this.'

'Stephen?'

I told him.

'Oh, dear,' murmured Max, kissing my fingers as he handed back the necklace. 'He really is one of those people who knows the price of everything and the value of nothing.'

I kissed him. 'But we can't go on being friends, can we?' I felt anxious. This friendship between Stephen and Max had been too corrosive.

He shook his head. 'We've all betrayed each other too much for that. No, it's just you and me, and your diamond necklace and my three suitcases . . .'

'And the car!' we both shouted in unison. Even second-hand, the price of Max's car could buy us a few months of time, plus a run-around to replace it.

Max laughed as he put his arm round me. 'I'd like to have another chance at painting before it's too late. I might have to paint houses and walls first, of course, for a bit, just for cash, but otherwise I want to start again. I'm afraid I'm not going to do the decent thing and get a proper job to keep you in the style you've been accustomed to.'

'Good,' I said, meaning it.

We walked to the edge of the garden and looked over the fields. The storm had left them green and clean. The roses bushes stood limply, with some of the arms broken off, and all the delicate petals blown on to the damp ground. The destruction of the fallen tree and collapsed scaffolding was behind us, but the little patch of grass was studded with daisies, just opening up to the sun. They looked fresh and new, as if there had never been any wind or rain.

'"The rose has but a summer's reign",' quoted Max. '"The daisy never dies." That was written by James Montgomery. I didn't really know what he meant until now.' He drew me to him, tighter this time. 'We can manage. We can be like the daisies and survive on very little.'

'There's my magazine column,' I reminded him. 'And the bed-and-breakfasters and the furniture.'

'And I'll work on people's houses all winter and paint all summer. We'll earn a fortune between us. We'll be rich, Suzy,' he joked. 'We'll be rich.'

I leant into the warmth of his coat. 'Better than that. We'll have enough.'

Acknowledgements

I'd like to thank Louise Moore and Harrie Evans at Penguin for extraordinary levels of inspiration and patience, Hilary, Richard and Hannah Talbot for lending me a base in Suffolk, the Suffolk 999 services for rescuing me off the dunes nearby, Mary Allen and Sarah Stacey for taking me round some glorious houses and gardens while I was still on crutches, Nish Joshi for making the crutches redundant, Chris Galinski, whom I have never met, but who has kindly lent his surname to a book he knows nothing about, invaluable names and background from Stephen, Magda and Tony Peto, Brett and Peter Moore and Lucy de Grey for providing some good architectural arguments and Jackie Jones-Parry for postcards. Inspiration came from houses and gardens all over Suffolk, including Annabel Baker's, James and Tizy Wellesley-Wesley's, John and Diana Huntingford's and the moated houses in Suffolk's Invitation to View programme, especially Leslie Geddes-Brown and Hew Stevenson's and the Innes'. Thank you, too, to Amanda Fitzalan Howard for many happy hours in Walberswick and Fay Sweet and Susan Marling for inviting us all to The Old Post Office, Middleton.

I'd also like to thank Graham and Jane Campbell for reading all my books for libel, although as all the characters are completely fictional any resemblance to anyone living is a coincidence. The legal team has now been joined by Edward Campbell, who has made his own unique contribution. I couldn't write without my mother, Margaret Campbell, keeping everything going at home, and the support of David, Freddie and Rosalind.